M. A. MADDOCK

The Sixth Amulet

To Mary & Maurice
warm wishes
Miriam

Cover Design by
Diana TC – Triumph Book Covers

Interior Design & Formatting by © Platform House
www.platformhousepublishing.com

M. A. MADDOCK

The Sixth Amulet

(Revised Edition)

Book One

Dedicated to all struggling writers. Don't give up!

For Sherlock

Forever by my side. Forever grateful to you.

Had Shez not bounced into my life, when he did,
I may have never written this novel.

ShAW

FORWARD
By
Graeme Johncock
Writer and Storyteller - Scotland's Stories
Instagram: scotlands_stories

Everybody loves a good story, and I'm no exception. I truly believe that stories are one of the few pieces of true magic we have left. In seconds, they can transport us across the world or into another time or universe, altogether.

The medium of storytelling has changed in the modern age; instead of sitting around a campfire, people are more likely to cram themselves in front of a TV. But there is something much more satisfying about picking up a good book and losing yourself in its pages.

I met M. A. Maddock through my work, as the writer behind Scotland's Stories, so we have had countless discussions around myths and legends. Much of my time has been taken up reading and writing hundreds of short tales, so I'd like to think I know a good story when I see it.

Well, I definitely see it here.

It's no easy task to write the first volume of a fantasy series. Introducing the reader to this new world you've created, while encouraging them to form connections with characters they've just met. *The Sixth Amulet - Book One -* succeeds by weaving together strands of traditional folklore, real Scottish locations and an exciting new story.

I found myself catapulted into a story I didn't want to leave again. It's no surprise I now have an overwhelming urge to visit Balloch and imagine the book's events taking place around me. Fortunately, out of all the twists and turns, the most exciting three words come at the very end of this epic read – To Be Continued …

Chapter One

Scotland: 1564 — Balloch, Lac Lomond.

"'Leave this place … or you will be next!'"
Those words—her mother's last—had never stopped haunting her.
I should have listened.

The ill-fated young woman stood in the same place as her mother had—three months earlier—trembling with fear. The small, makeshift courtroom—once a slaughterhouse—was crammed with eager spectators. She could still smell its lingering, foul stench of death; the irony of it sickened her. Her eyes darted about as if looking for an escape. But it was a hopeless situation. She knew there was no way out; all the doors and windows were blocked.

Her heart pounded, as the sinking feeling in her stomach signalled what she had been dreading.

I'm going to die! She winced, as the rope prickled and burned against the skin of her bound wrists. *Oh, God! I'm going to—*

Her train of thought was severed by an imperious voice rising above the maddened crowd, along with the pounding of wood on wood, demanding silence. The crowd hushed, now straining to listen, as he prepared to make his delivery.

He paused and raised his hand, desiring to seize their full attention. He could sense, almost smell, their impatience. A faint smirk appeared on the corner of his mouth. He relished in their anticipation, knowing their hungry eyes were scrutinising him. Waiting ...

They can wait, he thought.

More was yet to come …

His black, judgemental eyes slid towards her, devoid of emotion. She looked away, repelled by his lecherous stare—the same look he had given her when he came to her cell, on more than one occasion, to "discuss" her situation. She felt nauseated, recalling the musty odour of his ageing body, and the feel of his clammy hands still lingering on her skin.

'I will see to it that you get your reprieve,' he had mumbled in her ear while stroking her face.

But she knew he had lied. There was never going to be a reprieve.

And, with no jury, he had appointed the service of a *Witch-Pricker*: a man, who, by the positioning of a pin or needle over a naked body, was said to be capable of finding the *Witch-mark*. The mark—a claw-like scar—was believed to be permanent, and created by the Devil himself, to seal the loyalty of his initiates—and, also, a known way to expose a follower of Satan.

She was fully aware of the Witch-Pricker's presence; he was the quiet one, standing beside the magistrate's pew, tapping the instrument, in question, on his thigh, while staring at her.

Following the magistrate's prompt, the Witch-Pricker—his preference, to remain nameless—stepped out into full view. He was an unassuming-looking man with a kind, round face and soft features—unusual for someone with such a sinister occupation. Well-dressed, clean, and unshaven, his whole poise exuded youth. His hair was thick and lengthy and neatly tied back. His eyes were piercing blue and seemed to have a "sympathetic" look about them.

As he moved across the stone floor, his stride long and defined, he discreetly surveyed the impatient crowd as their voices dropped into complete silence, watching him. Some, he'd been told, had never witnessed this event before. He smirked; he would give them a performance they would never forget.

2

He turned his attention to the accused, aware of her eyes boring into him, her face pale and stiff with fear.

As he approached her, she imagined she saw the twitch of a smile. But when he looked her straight in the eye, his true demeanour came to light, his dead-pan stare casting its shadow of doom; it was written all over his face. Gone were the soft features, now replaced by ugliness and dishonesty.

He looked her up and down, regarding her pathetic state, then shook his head, sneering at her, making her feel utterly worthless.

Aware of all eyes watching him, he leaned towards her … then leaned closer. He sighed in her ear, releasing a subtle moan, before muttering, 'I'm simply doing God's work.'

The feathery touch of his lips against the skin, just below her ear, sickened her.

The crowd shuffled, though maintained their silence, as the Witch-Pricker circled her like a predator. She swallowed as her eyes tried to follow his movements. When he paused, behind her, she tensed and swallowed.

Looking to the bench, where the magistrate sat, the Witch-Pricker waited calmly for the order to commence. With a flick of his hand, the magistrate gave it.

The Witch-Pricker tugged at the stained, putrid gown she had been forced to wear, frowning as he fumbled to remove it, her bound hands making it difficult. She jolted at the room's cold air, trying to recoil, in a desperate bid to keep her dignity. Frustrated, his face hardened, throwing her a warning look. Realising her struggle was useless against the strength of his determination, she yielded, averting her eyes.

With one final tug, he removed what was left of her self-esteem.

Gasps echoed through the crowd, stunned by her nakedness. Feeling violated, she promptly lowered her tied hands, to cover her modesty, while eyeing the torn garment that had been flung to the ground. An uncomfortable silence followed as she stood isolated and exposed. Feeling the assault of her spectators' eyes, as they leered at her vulnerability, she kept a fixed stare on the stone floor and shivered, aware of its coldness as it crept up to her bare feet.

With a subtle, disdainful nod from her condemner, the Witch-Pricker circled her again—this time, more closely and methodically; it was obvious what he was searching for.

When he stopped abruptly, subtle gasps could be heard from some of the crowd; they anticipated his next move, hungry for it. His eyes travelled up and down, narrowing, as he examined her torso. Gripping her arm, he swung her round; she almost stumbled at the sudden movement.

Dramatically, he raised his other hand as high as he could, brandishing the dagger-like implement for all to see, its silver, highly polished and gleaming—scrupulously cleaned, from his last victim.

'Behold!' he cried out.

The crowd gasped—the sound of their voices a cacophony of fear and excitement. One thing was clear: he was the "performer" and *she* was their "entertainment." Then, in the same melodramatic way, he pointed the needle to her lower back.

She arched forward, feeling the cold pinch of its fine point against her skin.

Voices mumbled as the crowd pushed forward, straining to see the small crescent-shaped mole.

A sneering curl appeared on the corner of the Witch-Pricker's mouth; he would now be paid more for discovering it—for discovering *any* mark, for that matter.

Struggling under his grip, the girl shook her head, frantic with fear.

'But—'tis only a birth—'

'Proceed!'

On the magistrate's second command, the Witch-Pricker went to work. Holding her firmly, he stabbed her with the needle.

She screamed out in agony.

The audience shuffled, almost feeling her discomfort, then stopped, when the magistrate rose from his seat. 'Well?!' he bellowed, leaning forward, waiting.

The Witch-Pricker, running his fingers over the wound turned and, with a sleight of hand, pressed his thumb hard, covering it, to stem the blood flow. Holding the girl's arm up, for all to witness, he replied, 'No blood has been drawn, my lord.'

More shouts of disbelief rang out across the "courtroom" at the revelation.

The young woman struggled against the Witch-Pricker's grip, her wrists burning and raw from the constant friction of the ropes.

'No!' she screamed. 'He's lying!'

'Quiet!' roared the magistrate, still unable to resist letting his eyes travel over her naked body.

She drew back, humiliated, her quivering breath visible like puffs of mist.

He coughed, clearing his throat. 'Continue!' he called out, lowering himself back into the comfort of his velvet-cushioned chair.

Having subtly, and successfully, stemmed the blood flow from the puncture wound, the process was repeated, followed by her constant, whimpering cries for mercy. But no one cared. The humiliation of being stripped before an audience of familiar faces, and prodded like an animal, had made no difference to her appeal, despite her cries with each incision; she was, after all, just the daughter of another, accused.

'Once more, my lord … no blood!'

As the spectators made their deliberations, the With-Pricker and magistrate shared a look. The young woman noticed it; it had been a mutual one of understanding …

She drew a sharp breath: *They're plotting against me!*

The magistrate smirked. It had been a tidy arrangement between him and the Witch-Pricker. The girl *had* to go; she had threatened to reveal his sordid, secret little visits to her cell. And, with a few years left to retirement, he was not about to risk his position of authority—not to mention the privileges that went with it.

No, he thought. *Not over that little whore!*

With a dismissive gesture of the magistrate's hand, the Witch-Pricker knew his job was done. As he turned to walk away, he stopped and looked down, seeing the tattered piece of clothing on the ground. He snatched it up and turned back around, staring at the young woman he'd just condemned, with contempt. Then, with a flick of his wrist, he threw her garment of "death" at her frail body, and walked away. She clung to it, welcoming its return.

A fresh silence spilt out over the "courtroom" for several moments. The crowd watched the young woman, her hands shaking as she held the garment against her front, in a vain effort to cover herself. Seeing her quiet and with her head lowered in submission, the crowd grew increasingly restless; it seemed she had given up the fight. It then turned its attention back to the magistrate …

Despite the crowd's frustration, the judge maintained his derisive gaze on her, prolonging the inevitable, waiting for his moment. He raised his head slowly, biding his time; he wanted her to look at him, wanted to see the fear of death in her eyes … and he *would* see it.

The seconds passed.

Finally, the young woman lifted her head, eyes wide with terror.

Behind her, the whispers had now turned to murmurs, gradually growing louder with expectation.

The wait was over.

'In the name of our good Queen, Mary,' the magistrate began, loud and clear, 'and, by the *Saóirse Act* of 1563, you have, hereby, been accused of consorting with the Devil, and indulging in all forms of sorcery associated with him. 'Tis the law of the land—one, may I add, punishable by death … yet to be determined.'

The court erupted, whipping its audience into a frenzy of approval.

'I'm innocent!' she cried out, exasperated, trying desperately to be heard over the rapturous crowd.

The magistrate looked down at her, his expression cold and heartless as the two willing volunteers stepped up and gripped her with their hardened, grubby hands. She struggled against them, in vain.

'What a waste!' the younger of them mumbled in her ear, his breath stale from the remnants of strong, peated whisky still lingering in his mouth.

She flinched, feeling the tip of his wet tongue slide against her cheek.

'I see myself as a reasonable man,' her condemner said, drawing her attention to him.

'Therefore, I have taken it upon myself to give you a choice—' He stopped, a smirk now in place.

'Or, perhaps you would like to follow in your mother's path?'

'Aye, let her burn!' a voice cried out.

Her eyes darted to the crowd, thinking she had recognised it and caught a middle-aged woman cowering away from her gaze.

The judge raised a brow. 'Well, it appears *they* have decided for you.'

The young woman, reminded of her mother's harrowing death, shook her head wildly, recalling her mother's agonising cries; the memory of the flames; the stench of burning flesh. They would be forever ingrained in her mind.

'No!' she screamed, lifting her voice above the crowd. 'You'll not do to me, what you did to *her*.'

The magistrate recoiled in his seat of authority, taken aback by her sudden backlash. 'So, you wish to avoid the *stake*, then?'

'You *know* I am—'

'So be it!' he promptly interrupted, fearing she would "talk."

The crowd suddenly hushed, exchanging looks of confusion. Had the magistrate gone mad? Was he going to let her go, denying them more "entertainment?"

The young woman took a sharp breath and stared at him, with a flicker of hope in her eyes. *Am I to have my reprieve?* she thought. But then she saw it: the contemptuous smirk, appearing on his face.

Slowly he shook his head, as though he knew what she had been thinking. He had been toying with her all along.

I should have said something. I should have—

Again, the crowd cheered, severing her thoughts. Some even laughed, amused by his attempt to humour them.

The outcome was now inevitable.

'You're going to—' She stopped. 'Oh, my—'

'Bring the prisoner closer!'

'I have done nothing wrong!' she yelled, fuelled by her rising, inner strength. 'My only "crime" is one of mercy—for helping the sick of this'—she stopped, gritting her teeth— 'deceitful village. Yet, in return, I am rewarded with lies and treachery. I'm innocent! Do you hear me, sir?! Innocent! I won't let you—'

'Enough!' the magistrate interrupted, slamming the gavel down on the sound block. 'Remove the *Witch*!'

She gasped, horrified. *Witch!* The demonic word echoed in her mind, making her blood run cold. She had been *branded*; her new title to be etched in their memory. And, should she be worthy of a headstone, it would be carved for future generations to presume:

Witch. Guilty! Damned for eternity.

Despite her continuous appeals, they went unheard. Who would listen to the supplications of a condemned Witch?

No one.

With her sentence finally handed down, her spectators turned their eager faces away, now interested in the fate of the next unfortunate victim: ongoing accusations of alleged sorcery meant that they, too, stood no chance against the irrational mindset and ignorance of their neighbours—especially when death waited in the wings.

As she was hauled away to her tiny, dank cell, screaming her innocence, the younger of the two gaolers whispered taunts of salacious acts in her ear.

Repulsed by the thought of his intimation, she stopped and turned her head to look at him, her eyes stabbing him with hate and disgust.

'I will remember *you,* in death,' she quietly vowed, through gritted teeth.

He backed off. 'Stay away from me, Witch!'

His accomplice threw his head back and laughed, displaying his stained, rotting teeth—half of them missing.

'She's put a curse upon me!' he retorted, glaring at his senior for mocking him.

'Do ye not know, laddie?' his colleague jeered, throwing open the cell door. 'Ye should never scorn the condemned.' He leaned towards him, lowering his voice in a foreboding tone. 'For they'll come back to haunt ye.' He laughed out loud, then his face suddenly dropped, as he turned to the girl.

She winced as he removed the rope from her burning wrists.

'Away with ye, lass!' he said, shoving her into her tiny prison.

Stunned, she stood with her back to the door, jolting when it was slammed behind her. She closed her eyes tightly on hearing the key being turned, its grinding sound marking the moment her fate had been sealed, without any reprieve.

'Ye called her *lass*!' she heard the younger say, over the echo of their departing footsteps.

Their voices continued to reverberate throughout the gaol as they made their way to the next hearing, their tone brightening.

'Auch! Sure, 'tis all the same to me, lad, "Lass," "Lassie," "Witch," as long as I get paid me *Testoon*. Aye, 'tis all the same.'

'Aye, too true,' said the other.

'Anyway, lad, just a couple more, then I'm off to have me a wee dram, or two. Will ye join me?'

'Aye? I will, ta. Auch! What say we …'

Their voices soon faded, leaving her behind, still clinging to the remnants of her garment. Carefully, she drew it around her, then slumped to the freezing, stone floor. Hands grasping her legs, she stared at the cold stone, shivering and in pain, until a stream of sunlight, filtering through the bars of the small window, high above, distracted her. She looked up, its pale, yellow light enticing. Slowly rising, she groaned, aching. She reached up—the tips of her long, thin fingers touching it, feeling its warmth, giving her some solace.

She looked sharp—the distant faint sounds of the "courtroom" finding their way to her cell: the hammering of the magistrate's gavel calling for "order" as the hungry crowd cried out for the next poor unfortunate souls' judgement. She pitied them.

9

When the noise ceased, she returned her attention to the window; the sun had dipped, taking with it its comforting light, plunging her into a grey, depressing mood as the tiny cell began to close in on her.

With nothing but time and her thoughts to keep her company, she took herself to the coarse, woollen blanket—the pathetic excuse for a bed—and lay down, its rough fabric irritating her sensitive skin. She tried to avoid scratching, but it persisted. As she attempted to ease the itch, she looked down, noticing the new, dark stains on her tattered garment; the blood from the incisions had finally seeped through. *What does it matter?* she thought. Nothing mattered now.

She curled up, nestling her head on her hands, clasping them together as a makeshift pillow. She glanced over at the water bucket, too tired to contemplate dragging herself to it, to quench her thirst; besides, it was likely they had not changed it. Next to it, a dish had been left with food—no doubt, unfit to eat. The mice were welcome to it.

The tears began to flow when her mother's cries returned to plague her. She recalled being forced to watch the excruciating pain being inflicted on the innocent woman. And her "crime?"

Her occupation: Herb-wife.

Their natural remedies—*trade secrets*—had been passed down through their family and used to help the sick; simple yet effective formulas to cure common ailments.

Life had been good to them, until a sudden misadventure. Through no fault of her own, her mother had become embroiled in an incident: accused of the death of a young child—eventually leading to her wrongful incarceration. Before that, they had relied on one another, since her father's death, when she was a child. The guilt had never left her after he had given his life, to save her from the Loch; but now, it seemed its waters would finally have their way with her. The irony of it.

If only you had survived, she thought, imagining her father could hear her. *Then, perhaps, we would still…*

They had survived on her mother's skill of making ointments and healing lotions, extracted from the forest's wild plants and herbs. Her mother taught her all she knew, and it was clear from a young age, she, too, had inherited the "gift."

Many from the Burgh came seeking their help, and those who were treated welcomed a swift recovery. But rumours had begun to spread of the "gifted woman," leading to false accusations of sorcery—some, even made by the "Godly folk" whom she had treated successfully.

From then on, the mere sight of her mother gradually sent fear into the local community; to be associated with a "Witch" would render them her accomplices. They soon learned quickly; by denying all association, their betrayal would assure their evasion of death.

The young woman now knew what awaited her. It was becoming a "popular method," according to her condemner: tied to a wooden seat—at the end of a large, plank of wood—she would be taunted at, while left suspended above the Loch's icy waters. And should she survive? It would mean that the waters associated with Baptism would have rejected the *Tool of Satan.*

A Monarch had once claimed: "Water is so pure an element, it repels the guilty."

It was almost laughable. Even if she did survive, there was the possibility they would *still* burn her. Regardless of it, both methods of torture were used for one thing—and one thing only: to elicit a hopeless confession.

"The proof of innocence is survival!" *they* had also proclaimed.

'Then I must try,' she whispered to herself. 'I must survive!'

In her mind, she then repeated her words, to the point of near madness.

I must survive! I must survive! I must…

Soon, tiredness and hunger took their toll, taking her into a deep and troubled sleep.

Two long weeks of endurance dragged her to her day of reckoning.

When her gaolers returned, she cowered into a corner, hearing the approach of their eager footsteps. One of them was whistling a sprightly, old Gaelic tune—the older one, no doubt.

The door flew open. A momentary silence passed between them, as they regarded her pitiful state.

'Not so appealing now,' the younger remarked, running his hand under his nose before wiping it on his mud-stained breeches.

Her hazel eyes, once brimming with life, glared at him through their deadness.

He stepped back, disturbed by her vacant stare.

The older one, rolling his eyes, shuffled towards her. He had something in his hand and was smiling.

'Right ye are, lass!' he said, beckoning her with his deformed finger— the thick stump visible where its tip used to be.

He held out the item to her, ignoring her stare; he'd seen it all before—that deadpan look on their corpse-like features before the execution. 'Put that on!' he said, still smiling. 'His Lordship wants ye looking bonnie.'

For one sweet moment, fooled by his light-hearted tone, she eagerly snatched the clean, white smock, daring to believe in her absolution, and put it on—covering the stained, tattered piece of cloth she had worn since her trial. Perhaps the magistrate had changed his mind …

Her hopes were quickly dashed when the younger one stepped out from behind his senior, toying with an object in his hand. She stared at the thick rope, then slowly looked up at him, crushed and resentful.

He hesitated. His eyes flashed towards his senior, unsure.

'Step lively, lad! She won't bite!'

But he was reluctant to touch her, recalling her sinister words as she glared at him:

'I will remember you, in death!'

'Give it here!' the other insisted, growing frustrated. His rough hands wrenched her forward as he tied the rope around her tiny wrists, aggravating the circular red marks, where the wounds had almost healed, since her trial.

She winced and looked down at them. It was only then she noticed how thin and pale she had become. Her long, dark hair fell limp about her face, its lustrous sheen long gone. She swallowed hard, fighting back tears. *I must be strong,* she told herself. *I must!*

Her gaoler paused and looked at her, his face emotionless, it marking her imminent fate.

'Time to die, Witch!'

Chapter Two

With no reprieve, she faced her demise.

Hauled out into the dark of night, her short journey to hell was one of endless humiliation—the villagers taunting her along the rugged path from her prison, to her point of death. Forced to walk, she struggled to keep up with the two gaolers, stumbling on the rocky surface beneath her bare feet, as she was dragged past her spectators.

She winced when the rope burned into her delicate skin, re-opening her wounds as she was tied to the wooden seat. Not once did her gaoler look at her as he secured her place in death. Behind him, the younger one watched yet kept his distance, still wary of her threat.

Satisfied with his handy work, and that his job was done, her gaoler nodded once, turned, and left.

Her anxious spectators watched and waited in the damp night, growing restless in her presence. Many she knew, their faces betrayed by their torchlight. They looked away when her gaze met theirs.

'Cowards!' she shouted at them, as the large beam of wood was slowly forced out, over the lingering depths.

'May God forgive you!' replied one brave soul, out of pity.

'*God*, you say?' she retorted, spitting the word back at them. 'What kind of world do I leave behind, that a "God" could instil such evil, inflicting it on an innocent soul such as I? If this is the way of it … then you may *take* it!'

At their silence, she glared at them, scrutinising their faces—one, in particular, standing out: the face of the man who had wrenched her from her father's arms to safety, before he had drowned. He had been hailed as a "hero" for saving her life. For a brief moment, their eyes met; now she saw nothing but shame in his cowardice. Guilt-ridden, and fearing association, he lowered his head and discreetly walked away.

The night was biting cold; it mattered no more to her. She looked into the murky deep, its blackness waiting like an old enemy—waiting to take her. Through the dim light, she caught a glimpse of her distorted reflection, on the quivering surface. And when the waters momentarily calmed, an image of her mother appeared, smiling up at her.

'If this is madness,' she whispered, 'then I gladly welcome it.' She smiled, feeling comforted by the thought of their reunion, and braced herself.

A sudden jolt forced her back as the beam was pushed forward by three strong men, selected to perform the deed. She felt its unsteadiness as it hovered above the Loch. As the night's freezing breath clung to her, she shuddered, waiting for the hands of fate to cast her to her death.

The onlookers hung on, anticipating the drop.

She looked out at the night spread wide before her, feeling the weight of their stares. No. She would not leave them in silence.

'Before you send me to my death,' she began, gasping when the cold air hit her lungs, 'know that I am innocent, as was my mother. *You* are the guilty ones. *You* own the blame for my condemnation. And for that, I say to you all; I have committed no sorcery—nor am I a *Witch*. But as you have already sealed my fate, by wrongfully declaring me so, I shall *not* disappoint you, then.'

The villagers exchanged nervous looks and words, confused by her meaning. She smirked to herself, relishing in their uneasiness. Satisfied, she prepared her final farewell: 'I curse those of you who betrayed me,' she warned, 'and vow to return to you in your dreams, where I will haunt them for the rest of your days.'

Gasps of horror were thrown out into the night, shocked by her words; some, sobbed uncontrollably, convinced by them.

'*Fear* me!' she persisted. 'For I fear you no more.'

'Drown her … drown the Witch!' one woman desperately cried, throwing salt, to ward off her *evil*.

15

'May you have a long and painful death, Witch!' her condemner—the magistrate—retorted, before finally sending her to her watery grave.

She took one long final breath.

As she entered the dark waters, its freezing impact stabbed her like sharp blades, forcing the air from her lungs. She gulped at it, desperately trying to prolong her life.

Eager to watch, the villagers dared to push forward. Raising their torches, they strained to see, hoping to witness a magic spectacle, of sorts; no evidence of a Witch rising from the waters had yet been documented. They hoped to be the first to see it.

'Look!' a boy shouted, pointing to the Loch. 'I see her! The Witch has saved herself!'

The crowd pushed dangerously close to the edge—some almost losing their footing. They gasped, when tiny bubbles rose frantically to the surface, anticipating her return.

But no sooner had the bubbles appeared, than they subsided.

Beneath the inky surface, the young woman struggled to free herself—the rope now tearing into her flesh with each pull and twist. Her mind raced; time was running out. She tried not to panic as her body's natural defences fought for survival.

Looking up through the murky waters, she saw the faint lights from their torches; they were dancing above the surface, searching for her.

She fought hard, clinging to her diminishing breath—the stabbing cold, hampering her efforts. As the remnants of life slowly began to leave her weakening body, she watched as it rose through the water.

"They say, drowning is a peaceful death."

Her mother's words—after her father died—came back to reassure her. But there was nothing "peaceful" about her barbaric death sentence; it was all too real as she felt the pressure through her agonising pain mount with each struggle. Distraught, she prayed for death to take her quickly.

Suddenly she was thrust forward; they had forced the great beam down into the Loch, to make certain her demise. Panic now took over as she slid from its perch into her slow descent. She thrashed out. Her white tunic swirled in unison with her long hair, impairing her sight. And as her failing body began to spasm, her breath shortened. It was a hopeless struggle.

Numb with cold, she no longer felt the pain of her mutilated wrists; nor the ropes which had bound her. She looked down, watching the ghostly beam disappear into the blackness below, her body now floating, giving her a sense of freedom. Convinced it a trick of the mind, she embraced the elation that unexpectedly came over her.

But the moment was short-lived, as she felt the pull of death slowly drag her down.

She looked up again—the water now stinging her eyes—watching the torchlights fade into tiny speckles, knowing her diminishing strength would not take her to the surface, even if she tried.

Finally, she accepted her end; the Loch could have her now. But in the moments before unconsciousness took hold, a sudden, swift movement caught her eye, in the form of a dense, black shadow. At first, she struggled to see it, through the murkiness. It rushed by her again, this time growing closer with each flowing movement, its size increasing as it drew nearer. Her eyes flickered when its ghostly shape came into view.

It suddenly stopped, floating freely before her.

Staring into its large, black eyes, she felt an overwhelming sense of peace, and smiled.

No longer frightened, she closed her eyes, and reached out …

Chapter Three

For days, she drifted in and out of consciousness, tortured and restless. He watched her, moving closer when she stirred, as she inwardly battled her demons, mumbling words that made no sense … except for *one*. Then she would stop, settling into another deep slumber. But he knew the demons would return.

'It *will* pass,' he kept whispering to her, urging her to fight the nightmare that had brought them together … again.

The smell of smoke filled the small, candle-lit room, touching her senses. Gradually it roused her from her deep-rooted nightmare. Every muscle of her fragile body ached, with the slightest movement. Her wrists throbbed beneath the gauze that had been tenderly wrapped around them.

It will pass…

It will pass…

The young woman's eyes flew open, to the soft, welcoming glow of flickering light. *Am I dead?* she thought, her mind muddled in confusion.

The crackling sound of a log fire and the enticing smell of hot food renewed her senses, telling her she was very much alive. Well … almost. She drew in the wafting smells, wincing from the pain that shot through her lungs. Her bloodshot eyes widened when an image of the creature jumped into her mind. Had she imagined it?

She struggled to recall her last moments before …

She gasped.

It saved me!

Opening her mouth, she desperately tried to speak, but her throat burned. Anxious, she struggled through the pain.

'Be still, lass!' came the soft voice by her side. 'You have been through quite an ordeal. Now rest.'

Heavy with tiredness, her eyes searched until she found the voice's face. His features were strong but kind. She noticed his hazel eyes; similar to hers and displayed warmth. It was clear he had years on her, but she could not distinguish his age.

'You're safe now,' he assured her. 'And your audience have returned to their homes, safe in the knowledge they have rid their world of yet another "Witch."'

The scathing tone in his voice was followed by a smirk. There was something in his manner that made her trust him. A weary, faint smile crossed her face.

'Ah! A sense of humour, perhaps?'

She lowered her eyes, embarrassed.

'We will have you back on your feet, soon enough,' he said, 'casting more *evil spells* on your neighbours.'

Her eyes shot up, glaring at him, reminded of her plight.

'Forgive me,' he said, seeing the terror in her expression. 'In my miserable attempt to make light of your ordeal, it seems I've offended you, instead.' His voice was now soothing, and apologetic.

She forced a broad smile, flinching with pain.

'I promise you,' he continued, with a sudden spark of anger in his tone. 'They shall *never* harm you again. You have my word.'

Before she could react, he rose from her bedside. Her eyes followed him as he moved about.

He was tall and broad and had the look of a labourer. His clothing was loose and casual: a pale shirt beneath a waistcoat, and breeches tucked into boots. She lifted her head slightly when he reached for something: an iron rod.

She stiffened as he paused, holding it in his hand like a weapon while he stared into the fireplace, watching the burning embers. He seemed distracted, as though momentarily lost in thought.

"Damn them!" she then heard him mutter, as he plunged the poker into the embers, dispersing them, before adding more firewood.

She had many questions to ask him, but in her attempt to speak the rawness in her throat prevented it. *There'll be time enough*, she thought, eager to discover how, and why, she was still alive.

While he tended the fire, she looked around the small room. *Where am I?* she wondered, though realised it no longer mattered. *It's not like I'm going anywhere!* She had no home to return to—not now. Her weary mind suddenly raced, with thoughts of an uncertain future.

What Will I do?

Where will I go?

I have nothing … absolutely nothing!

It was then, that the awful reality of her dilemma struck her, hard. Her head throbbed at the mere notion of it all. And as she struggled to accept it, exhaustion took its hold again, giving her temporary relief.

Her strength gradually returned with each passing day, along with her voice.

She noted her rescuer's comings and goings—leaving at the same time, each morning, and returning in the late afternoon. In time, she found the strength to leave her bed and, sometimes, after he left, would take interest in his abode—inspecting the cosy lounge, taking care not to disturb a thing. His means were simple, and yet her impression of him was that of something else—something … *finer!*

Something is amiss, here! she mused as she explored, becoming embroiled in her curiosity. She was searching for clues to his identity. *Most def—*

'Up and about I see!'

She spun at the unexpected sound of his voice. Standing in the doorway, his frame seemed to fill its space. As his eyes rested on her, she looked down, quickly grasping the front of her clean tunic in a vain attempt to hide her embarrassment, failing to conceal her blushes.

Sensing her awkwardness, he gave her a reassuring look. 'I'm a respectful man,' he stated, shutting out the cold, fading light of day.

She gnawed on her lip without answering but looked up to meet his gaze.

'And … I am trustworthy … in *every* way,' he added, carefully removing the damask cloak from his broad shoulders. The luxurious fabric flowed gracefully from him at the bare touch of his hand. Its deep, rich shade of noir was weaved beautifully with a subtle silk garnet thread, hinting at quality. She observed how he consciously placed it on a single hook, behind the closed door. Then, with great tenderness, he slowly ran his hand down the soft fabric, pausing, before turning to face her again.

They lingered in a moment of awkward silence.

'Why did you save me?' she blurted.

He raised his brows, taken aback by the sound of her voice.

'I did not expect such strength to come from—'

'A woman as weak as myself?' she snapped, interrupting him.

'You are by no means weak …' He paused, waiting, hoping she would say her name.

Maintaining her silence, she lifted her chin in a display of strength and frowned.

It was when he noticed the familiar faint line of determination, between her brows, he was reminded of a woman he had once known—Sarah—the one name she had repeated over and over in her disturbed sleep. He *had* to be sure, though; it had been a long time, since …

''Tis strange,' he continued. 'Having tended to your needs that I do not know your name.'

She closed her eyes tightly, blocking out an image of him tending to her, before realising he did save her life. And, for that, she would be indebted to him. She then opened them, trying to overcome any

21

embarrassing thoughts of his attentiveness; however, still reminded of it, she frowned, pressing her lips together. He had, at least, the right to know her name.

'Kristene.'

When her name glided from her mouth, he sighed. 'Of course, you are!' he uttered beneath his breath, relieved.

She tilted her head. 'What did you say?'

'I like it!' he swiftly replied before she could question him again.

'It was my grandmother's.'

'You must be like her—for your parents to name you after her.'

'It seems I inherited some of her qualities, according to my ...' Her voice trailed when fatigue suddenly hit. Feeling light-headed, she reached out to hold on to a small wooden table—standing alone by the fireplace—but missed.

In an instant he was by her side, catching her as she fell into his hold. 'You're still weak, Kristene,' he stated, carrying her back to his bed.

She allowed him, without argument, letting him cover her with blankets, making her comfortable again. Making her feel ... *safe*.

'Thank you,' she whispered, smiling, her eyes red and heavy with tiredness.

'We need to build up your strength and appetite,' he insisted, turning from her.

She watched as he moved about his small domain, busying himself. Her nose twitched as the smell of food found its way to her senses, a few minutes later, its pleasant aroma comforting. She slowly propped herself up, feeling a pang of hunger—the sudden need to eat, marking her improvement.

As if reading her mind, he returned to her bedside and handed her a bowl of hot broth and some fresh bread. She took both, willingly.

While she fed herself, he sat in the seat from where he had watched over her, during her fever, and nodded, satisfied. 'The broth, I take credit for,' he said, grinning with pride, 'the loaf—I must confess—was purchased from the market, in Balloch.'

Taking another bite, she looked up at him and smiled.

When he smiled back, his face lit up; it was infectious.

She pondered his age again; it was difficult to tell. He had seen years but was not *old*. His skin was sallow, showing few lines of age on his strong, but calm features. Yet he had a determined look about him; a look that had experienced life. His thick, dark hair fell loosely on his shoulders and, when he ran his fingers through it, she noticed the subtle, strands of silver, highlighting it.

'Good?'

She nodded, smiling, relishing in the broth's warmth before taking the last bite of bread.

When she'd eaten her fill, he took the empty bowl from her, then handed her a plain, pewter goblet.

'What is it?' she asked, staring at its pale-amber watery contents.

'Just a natural remedy,' he said. 'Trust in its curative qualities, and it will restore you to health, in no time.'

She raised it to her nose; it had a familiar pungent aroma. She took a mouthful, her brows knitting in thought. 'You know the forest and its herbs,' she commented, regarding its taste.

'Somewhat,' he replied.

'I recognise it,' she said. 'But it has an unusual bitterness I'm not acquainted with,' she added. She tasted it again, her brow still furrowed. She lifted her eyes to his then shrugged. 'I'm just … curious.'

'Indeed, you are!' he grinned.

'What?' she asked, tilting her head, a little confused.

'Intriguingly *curious*.'

She now sat up, smiling. 'Is it a secret?'

He lowered his head, frowning. 'If I told you, it would mean certain death,' he joked.

The smile slipped from her face. 'Please—don't—'

'Forgive me, Kristene,' he begged, pulling an apologetic smile. 'That was in poor taste.'

Silence divided their awkwardness again as she quietly drank the rest of the warm liquid, savouring its restorative allure until it was almost gone; already she was feeling the better for it.

'My mother used to make medicines like this for—' Her voice broke off as she stared into the goblet, lost in thought.

He regarded her, contemplating her words before replying, 'I know.'

Her eyes shot up. 'What did you say?!' His remorseful look answered her question. 'Did you … *know* my mother?'

Slowly he nodded then took a deep breath.

'Aye. I knew her well. We had a deep friendship.'

Her eyes widened, mouth gaping, in astonishment.

Alert to her likely conclusions he drew back, lifting his hands as if in self-defence. 'Nothing more! I assure you. She simply provided me with great strength at a time when I needed … guidance.'

Her face gradually softened, relieved. 'How did you meet?'

'Oh, by mere coincidence.'

She leaned towards him, showing interest, beckoning him to continue. For an instant, he saw the face of the little girl he had met all those years ago—the one who had now grown into a beautiful, strong-willed young woman.

He recalled their first meeting: he had come to her mother's aid when a sinister threat had presented itself. She had just been a child, and he presumed she had been too young, then, to remember him *now*. He was thankful for it.

'I had spent my years travelling, as a merchant,' he lied. 'Our paths crossed when'—he stopped to correct himself— 'when she fell into a minor difficulty. It was that chance meeting which led to our friendship.'

'What difficulty?'

'Your mother never interfered in the business of others, Kristene,' he began. 'She only wanted to care for those who were sick. Her heart was larger than her spirit of inquiry. We met when I intervened in a heated exchange of words between herself and some villagers; they were quite suggestive, concerning her "practice", making immoral accusations which, to her misfortune, drew on the ignorance of those she helped.' He hesitated, then sighed, slipping back into his thoughts and regrets. 'Little did I know it would be the beginning of her downfall.'

She recoiled, gasping in disbelief, clasping her hand over her mouth. 'You mean—you *knew*?!'

He stared back at her, aware of his error: for subconsciously voicing his inner thoughts. Her silent, desperate plea for answers was evident in her hazel eyes as she looked at him, lost for words. But his temporary silence only heightened his guilt … and her suspicion. However, there were certain things he simply could *not* share with her; at least, not yet.

Finding her voice, her hand slipped from her mouth. 'I—I'm at a loss, sir. I … don't understand. You *say* you knew my mother yet—' She stopped and stared at him, aware she had called him, "sir." She shook her head. 'Who *are* you?'

'A friend,' he blurted.

She grunted. 'A *true* friend would have saved her.'

'I—I know.'

'Then why?! Why didn't you?!'

'Kristene, believe me when I tell you, I would have tried but—' He hesitated and looked away— 'I was …'

She glared at him, growing impatient. 'Well?!'

He sighed. '… too late.'

Hearing his admission made him cringe with shame. He closed his eyes, feeling hers boring into him with resentment. But he knew he would have to face her, and explain. Taking a deep breath, he released it, then opened his eyes, meeting hers.

'Let me explain!' he pleaded, his voice urgent yet calm, reflecting on her anger.

Silence.

He waited—and would continue to do so, for as long as it would take for her to listen.

The moments quietly passed, locked in their stubbornness, until a sense of calm returned. She remained still, holding her stare, her eyes now filled with enquiry. He knew she was ready—ready to *listen*.

'If only she had been as curious as you, Kristene,' he began. 'It may have then—'

'Saved her life?'

He shrugged. 'Perhaps—then again—there is no way of knowing.'

'I tried to warn her,' she blurted.

'You did?'

She nodded, her eyes fixed on his.

As she held his gaze, he could not help but compare her likeness to that of her mother's—the strangeness in her beauty, making him feel a little vulnerable in her company. He cleared his throat. 'There was no mistaking the look of accusation on their faces,' he continued. 'The villagers were narrow-minded. But your mother dismissed their ignorance … or, at least, *chose* to. It led to some disagreements between us. Another regret, I'm ashamed to admit. My stubbornness has, at times, been *my* downfall—and at a great cost, too.'

Kristene drew her brows and tilted her head; something was niggling at her; there was something about him. A vague expression crossed her face as she struggled to recall a memory. She promptly glanced back at him when it suddenly entered her mind. 'You argued!' she blurted.

He sat up, alert; he did not expect that.

'I remember!' She nodded. 'And what's more … I remember *you!*'

Chapter Four

'Your name is Oran!'

He lifted his head, taken aback by the accuracy of her memory. It was strange, hearing her speak it again—and, more so, in the voice of the woman she had become.

'I can tell by the look on your face that I'm right … *Oran!*' she said, emphasising his name with an underlying tone of sarcasm. 'That *is* your name. Isn't it?'

He held her determined stare, then nodded.

'I *knew* it! And *she* defended the villagers against *your* accusations. 'Tis vague, but I recall it.' She lingered on the memory, for a moment, then scowled. 'That was when you *left* us!'

He stood up, turning his back on her as the memory of that day returned to haunt him. He snatched the poker in his hand, again—as a distraction—ready to stoke the fire.

'Why?!' she pressed.

Such was the desolation in her voice, he was unable to face her. He stared into the flames, trying to block it out.

'Why would you leave, when you knew she was being taunted?'

'I had no choice. I *had* to.'

'No choice?!' she hit back. 'You *could* have stayed! You could have at least *tried!*'

He spun, glaring at her, his face hardening, reliving the rage it still provoked in him.

'I had threatened to *kill* them, Kristene!' he blurted, his hold on the iron rod strengthening.

She jolted, seeing the storm of anger in his eyes, then lowered hers, and stared at the item in his tightening grip.

'And, given the chance—' He stopped, realising what he had done. He glanced down at the poker and, shamed by his behaviour, stepped back and calmed himself, his breath steadying. Returning the rod to the hearth, he moved towards her. 'I'm sorry Kristene, but try to see it from my perspective. They treated Sarah like a—' His voice broke off. He sighed, shaking his head. 'Your mother was no "Witch."'

Her eyes shot up when he said her mother's name. But it was the *way* he had spoken it: with passion and respect.

Again, he sighed, shaking his head.

'And yet, she *still* defended them. Nonetheless, it invited more unwanted attention, leading to further disputes between us. Therefore, she *suggested* I leave … for her sake. I refused, at first, but she insisted, convinced they would never harm her.' He turned to face her. 'She *sent* me away, Kristene. That's the truth of it. You must understand; it was a difficult situation.'

The tears streamed down her flushed cheeks. 'I'm trying to,' she cried, wiping them away. 'I only wish she *had* listened.'

'I stayed away for far too long,' he admitted, slumping back into his chair. 'I was torn between concern and anger. I tried to go back. But as each day passed, it became increasingly difficult to return. The more distance I put between us'—he shrugged— 'the easier it was to keep going. My pride eventually won—a grave error I will always regret—and one I hope never to repeat.'

'Then why *did* you come back?'

He shrugged, shaking his head.

'I'm not sure. Something inside—call it a gut feeling—brought me back. So, I swallowed that pride and followed my instincts.'

'Then it is a great pity, Oran, that your *instincts* did not bring you back, sooner,' she retorted.

He remained silent in acknowledgement of his misconception. And as he sighed, staring into his past, she could now see and feel his deep regret.

In a moment of pity, she let her defences drop. 'She did not deserve to die,' she said, her voice lowering to a whimper. He looked up, seeing the tears build in her eyes. 'And the way they—it was barbaric. I can still hear her screams for mercy as the flames took hold'—she glanced towards the fireplace— 'and the smell of her burning flesh and—'

'Do not torture yourself, Kristene,' he broke in.

'But it's so hard not to think of it.'

As he reached out to console her, she drew back, and then diverted her eyes.

Divided by silence, again, Oran leaned back in his chair, his guilt now getting the better of him; it was eating him up inside, making it harder for him to find the right words to comfort her, knowing she was still raw with grief.

'She didn't do it, you know,' she then stated, her voice quiet and solemn.

He lifted his head. 'Do what?'

'Kill him.'

Eyes widening, Oran slowly leaned forward—the startled look on his face telling her he was oblivious to her meaning. 'Kill *who*?'

'The child.'

His face dropped, in disbelief.

'It was *not* her fault,' she persisted. 'The child was too ill—gone beyond help. I begged her not to interfere—because of the accusations.' She paused, swallowing. 'You see, they had started again. But, despite my pleas, she insisted. She did her best to save him and … *still* they…' She slumped, closing her eyes.

'Tell me!' he urged, pulling his chair closer.

'She warned me—you know—to leave. But I didn't listen. How foolish is that?'

'Do not dwell on it, Kristene,' he said, clasping her hand. 'You're safe now.'

Reassured, she smiled faintly, feeling the warmth of his hand on hers, then slowly relayed the events which had led to her mother's incarceration and untimely execution.

29

He sat back and folded his arms, listening intently. He was fully aware that Sarah could not have harmed a living soul, let alone a child.

I should have come back, sooner, he thought, blaming his stubbornness for keeping him away. *Should have, could have, would have—what difference does it make, now?* Sarah was dead—because of a simple act of kindness, seen through the eyes of ignorance as "Witchcraft".

But he was here now, considering the face of her daughter as she stared back at him, broken by the same hurt and betrayal. He would make it right … for *her.*

'And what are your intentions now?' Kristene demanded, tearing him from his thoughts. 'Do you plan to leave again, now that I am almost recovered?'

I owe it to her, he told himself. It was the least he could do, having failed her mother.

He leaned towards her. 'I may have been too late to save her, Kristene, but it is not too late for you. I vowed, after her callous death, to watch over you. And I did … from a distance. But I needed to stay hidden in the shadows, away from those same judgemental eyes. I could not take the risk of being seen by anyone who might have recognised me. Do you understand?'

'I'm trying but …' Her words trailed.

''Tis a lot for you to take in.'

She slowly nodded.

He could see the redness in her eyes and the dark circles beneath them, telling him she needed more rest, and yet …

'If I may …' He stalled; he was eager to know more of what had followed, after his untimely departure, then thought better of it; his questions could wait.

'Ask what you will,' she replied, maintaining her enthusiasm.

'There is time enough,' he said. 'It can wait 'til—'

'Please, Oran,' she said, lowering her head. 'I insist.'

How can I refuse her? he thought, looking into her persuasive eyes. He then nodded. 'What happened after I left?'

'I believe a sense of normality returned to our lives. If there *had* been trouble, it never showed on her face.'

'Because she was protecting you—from the accusations,' he stated.

'And yet, she continued to help those who needed it. She *had* to … if we were to survive. There was no other income since my father died. I was only a child, then.'

'Do you remember him?'

'I have few memories.' She paused. 'Though, there are times I'm haunted by his face. I still see that look of death staring up at me before the Loch's waters wrenched him from us.

He gave his life because of *my* stupidity. Had I listened to him, I never would have slipped on the rocks and …' Her words trailed on the memory before shaking it away. 'My mother spoke little of him after that.'

'It was her way of surviving,' he said, trying to reassure her. 'She told me how he died; it was not your fault. It was the most natural thing any parent would do for their child—for any child. Your mother was reluctant to dwell on "what was". *You* became her priority. She felt it her duty to shield you from harm.'

'I wish I could have protected her,' she returned with remorse.

'You were too young, Kristene. She expected nothing from you.'

She subconsciously raised the goblet to her mouth, taking the last sip of its contents. He smiled when she made a face at its now cold, bitter taste.

Putting it aside, she continued; 'It was when I grew older, that I began to observe subtle changes in her personality.'

He tilted his chin, with added interest. 'In what way?'

'She developed a *need* to look over her shoulder as if someone was watching or following her. Perhaps I'm mistaken, but I am sure it started after the encounter with'—she stopped, recalling the face from her past— 'with that odd-looking man.'

He lowered his head in a sideward glance. 'Odd?'

She noticed the intensity in his interest. 'Aye, he looked … *different*, in that, he was not a villager; nor was he from this land.'

'What did he look like?'

She lifted her eyes, calling to mind their features: 'Not very tall. His hair was dark—black—or perhaps—deep brown. It was difficult to say in the light of dusk.'

'Dusk?' he said, impressed. 'Your memory *is* good.'

'Sometimes, it is the little things about my mother I remember, vividly.' She smiled sadly. 'The moon was unusually bright that evening. She loved the beauty of the night sky and all its wonders, always making a point of sharing it with me.'

'What else do you remember about him?'

'His clothing was dark,' she continued. 'I could not distinguish any colour. His skin was sallow—no—pale and … his eyes stood out; they were dark, like ours, only deeper and intense. He looked almost … *ghostly!*'

Oran's eyes narrowed. 'Where did this *encounter* take place?'

'We were returning from a neighbour's house. She had been treating him for an ailment … of sorts.' She paused on the memory, smiling to herself: she would always accompany her mother on her visits. And, when whispers had spread, regarding William Crane's ailment, she could not contain her growing curiosity. Told to "wait outside" she had broken her mother's rule by stealing a glance through his window. Her mother had seen her out of the corner of her eye. She recalled the long walk home in silence, expecting a scolding, on their return. But it was never discussed.

'Kristene?' The sound of his voice roused her from her nostalgia.

'It was near our home when he came upon us,' she continued. 'I can still see the agitated look on my mother's face.'

'Do you think she knew him?'

Kristene looked at him, suspicious of his enquiry of the *unusual* stranger. 'Am I to believe that *you* know this man?'

Oran raised a brow, startled by her perception. 'Did he return?' he asked, avoiding her question.

'No. You see, while they spoke, he kept looking at *me*. It made her uncomfortable—nervous. And when he drew down to the level of my eye and smiled—that's how I remembered his eyes—she pulled me away, threatening him. I remember how tightly she squeezed my arm as she drew me behind her. It was like she was protecting me.'

'Do you recall any of their conversation?'

'Not much. He said I was'—she shrugged— 'I can't remember the strange word he used, but it sounded nice.'

'What did he do, then?'

'When he tried to touch my face, she screamed at him. It was frightening. I imagined her voice must have carried through the village and beyond. It was the last we saw of him. He simply … disappeared, into the night.'

The room fell silent, save for the crackling and hissing of wood coming from the roaring fire—the flames making its shadows dance and quiver.

Oran sank back in his seat, musing over their conversation, then rose abruptly. 'We must leave this place!' He moved towards the little window beside the door and partially drew back the small curtain, glancing out as if expecting someone.

Her voice lifted with excitement. '*We?*' she echoed.

'As soon as you are fully recovered,' he said, peering out into the darkness.

'Where are we going?'

He returned to her side and looked down into her eyes; they were alive with hope. But he also knew she would soon quiz him further about his past; this he would avoid—for the time being. However, if they were to embark on a journey together, he would, eventually, have to share some of his secrets. But first, he had to be sure of her trust.

'You *are* right in your assumption, Kristene,' he admitted.

'I *knew* it!' she said, moving closer. 'You *do* know him!'

He could feel her energy when she drew near; it was exhilarating. 'Perhaps,' he returned, pulling back slightly. 'Which is why we cannot risk staying here.'

'Do you think he'll come back?' she said, her eyes darting towards the door.

'I have my suspicions.' He surveyed her carefully, before inquiring. 'How old are you now, Kristene? Sixteen? Seventeen?'

'Almost Eighteen!' she returned with an air of maturity. 'Why do you ask?'

All the more reason to take you with me, he thought. 'Do you trust me?'

She hesitated before replying, trying to read his thoughts. Inside, her instincts screamed, *Yes!* Outwardly, she answered, 'I have nothing left in this world to keep me here. I have no choice *but* to place my trust in you.'

'I will only take you with me if I have your *absolute* trust,' he insisted. 'And … I shall only accept your honest reply. It is, for this reason, I will ask you, one last time. Do you trust me, Kristene?'

She nodded with certainty.

It was enough to convince him. 'Then, know this,' he said. 'I will never let another soul harm you in any way. You have my word. I will take you far from here, where no one will know us.'

'And I shall gladly go,' she replied. 'But, if I am to spend time in your company, however long it shall be, you must answer *my* questions.'

He prepared himself for the onslaught of her enquiries.

'What *did* I see in the Loch?'

He did not expect it; when the creature brought her to him, she was unconscious, barely alive. *How could she have known?* he thought.

'You *know* what it was,' she stated.

He opened his mouth, prepared to lie.

'I saw it!' she blurted. 'For a brief moment, before I—'

'Kristene, what you saw was perhaps … an illusion, most likely caused by your—'

'It was no illusion,' she persisted. 'I *know* what I saw'—she hesitated, now glaring at him— 'because it looked at me before I lost consciousness. My instinct told me to reach out to it. It was the last thing I remembered …'

He diverted his eyes from her intense stare.

'Do not play me for a fool, Oran!' she hit out. 'I see it in your face.'

He shook his head slowly, in the defeat of her perseverance.

'You *are* no fool, Kristene Blane,' he said, fascinated by her awareness. 'How clever you are.'

'So, it *does* exist—the Kelpie!'

'Indeed,' he replied.

She frowned, tilting her head as she recalled the myth. 'But—does it not lure its victim to their … *death*?'

He nodded.

'Aye. The Kelpie is a solitary creature. It lives wild and free and can never be tamed. It has always shared this land alongside "man" who, unfortunately, has not always respected its privacy, leading many to drown under its influence. I, however, have always shown it the greatest respect and care. And, in return, I receive its trust and loyalty.'

'But why did it save *me*?'

He hesitated. 'Because *I* asked it to.'

She stared back at him, amazed. 'You are no ordinary *man*, Oran.' The words drifted slowly from her mouth—filled with the suggestion. She moved towards him, to inspect him further.

'So, tell me, truthfully!'—she leaned closer— '*Who* are you?'

Chapter five

Triora – Italy: 1571

The girl ran with a sense her life depended on it, her heart pounding with every step as her youth carried her swiftly through the dark, narrow cobbled streets. The moon dipped in and out between the heavy clouds, occasionally lighting her way. But she knew the route well and was glad of it as she quickened her pace.

Distant voices suddenly disturbed the silence. She stopped abruptly, listening for their approach while taking a moment to catch her breath. Glancing behind, from whence she came, she watched for any sign of movement. The badly-lit street was devoid of life; everyone else seemed to be hiding behind their doors. Even its familiar night prowlers were nowhere to be seen; it was usual to hear the whining of the street cats in conflict with one another, and yet not one had ventured out on this particular evening. Perhaps they, too, had sensed it.

The eeriness hovered over the small cittadina as if waiting to pounce on its unsuspecting victims. She held her breath a moment, thinking she had imagined its unnatural air.

She had not.

Rumours had escalated of a sinister attachment to the city, casting suspicions on the restless townspeople, hinting they might be true. Trusting her instincts, she glanced around, making sure no one had followed her.

Gripped by a sudden chill, she turned on her heel, taking a shortcut through a quiet laneway—one she frequently used. It had become her saving grace when she found herself delayed; the Mistress hated it when she was late.

I can't be late! she thought, reminding herself of the radical changes in her Mistress's persona of late, displaying bouts of anger for her slightest error. Even the boy did not escape her wrath.

The thought of another scolding spurred her on. She hoped the Master would be there. But he was seldom at the house these days, looking for excuses to stay away while leaving them to suffer the consequences of *her* ever-changing moods.

'Please, be there! Please, be there!' she repeated, through her tiring breath.

The end of her secret little laneway drew near, urging her to stop again. Once more, she listened.

Nothing.

It was as though the whole cittadina had abandoned her, leaving her alone to face the unknown entity lurking in the shadows. On that thought she quickened her step, knowing the great house was not far.

At last, through the darkness, she could make out the shape of the old building. She ran towards it. But when the moon reappeared, illuminating the façade, she slowed to a stop as its ghostly hue crept over the exterior; its ominous front seemed to crawl up from the depths and stare down at her, its presence suddenly disturbing. She shuddered at the notion of having to pass through its doors again—then thought, *Better in there than out here.*

She suddenly jolted, hearing the return of distant voices from the streets. She looked back sharply, listening. *They're coming this way!* she realised, forcing herself towards the entrance. But when she reached it, the doors were locked.

She knocked hard and quickly on the wood, continuously glancing over her shoulder—the constant rapping echoing above and beyond the rooftops.

When the door swung wide, she was relieved to see the face of Petrio, gaping at her. The young boy stared, confused by her frightened expression.

'*Dov'è?*' she blurted, trying to catch her breath. 'Where is he?'

He could sense the urgency in her voice. 'Who?' he replied, his curious, dark eyes looking up at her.

'The Master, *idiota!*'

The boy continued to stare at her, bewildered.

Frustrated, she took hold of his small frame, and shook him hard. 'Where is he, Petrio?!'

'In his study,' he growled, 'with orders not to—'

She disappeared before he could warn her of the argument which had ensued earlier, between their Master and the Mistress. Over what, he did not know but was aware of how frequent the quarrels had become. This was, perhaps, the reason why the Master went out so often—too often, for *her* liking—which would then lead to her unpredictable moods.

The girl knocked once, before barging into his study, unannounced. Wrenched from his thoughts, the Master threw himself back in his chair, in disbelief, at her unexpected entrance, and looked up at her, wide-eyed.

She hovered at the open door, holding on for support, her head spinning as she paused to catch her breath.

'My … *Mio Signore!*'—she swallowed hard— 'they are searching the streets and buildings!'

Any notion of scolding her now melted away as he realised her meaning. 'Close the door, Lucia!' he said, his tone steady as he beckoned her in.

She edged towards him, her long, black locks clinging to the beads of sweat on her forehead; her round face was pale with fright. She paused when he moved, slowly resting his elbows on the elaborate walnut table. Then, clasping his hands together, he held her gaze.

'Where were you?' he inquired, his tone now low yet demanding. It then dawned on him; he knew *exactly* where she'd been.

She opened her mouth to answer—almost letting it slip—then hesitated. He sensed her awkwardness as her eyes lowered in shame.

He sighed. 'Never mind, as much as I am aware of it,' he said. 'Now, what have you seen?'

Her eyes flickered in response to his remark. *How did he know?* she thought. But she no longer cared. She would defend his disapproval; after all, she was of age and intended to marry Aldo … when the time was right. She loved him and wanted to be with him.

'Lucia!' he snapped, snatching her from her thoughts of love. He rose from his comfortable, cushioned armchair. 'Forget it! Forget *him!*'

She jumped at his demand, taking a step back as he approached her.

'It—it seems the whole cittadina has gone mad, my lord,' she replied, lifting her eyes to meet his. She raised a brow, regarding him; he looked tired, worn out—the dark, heavy shadows beneath his eyes, displaying his lack of sleep—no doubt the result of his flamboyant lifestyle, his constant entertaining keeping him up most nights. It was evident it was all catching up on him. She glanced down at his clothes; they looked unusually dishevelled for someone who took pride in his appearance, especially when mixing with influential people of society.

Nor had he changed; she'd seen him in the same attire the previous night, before he went out.

Even the fine study lacked its Master's attention. Regarded as his pride and joy, if he was not out fraternising until the early hours of dawn, he would lock himself away in his world of literature, surrounded by his precious books. His study was adorned with them: works by authors and scholars she'd never heard of. Often, she would sneak in while he was out, letting her fingers caress their exquisite leather-bound covers, envious she had not been well-educated enough, to appreciate their well-written pages.

He had always kept his library orderly and well documented … until tonight. His books were now strewn everywhere—some open—as if he'd been looking for something. Aware of this, she was now convinced something *was* wrong—desperately wrong—for as he approached her, not once did he look at his books, ignoring the works as though they no longer mattered; unlike before, where he would look upon them like lovers, deciding which one to re-visit. He had something on his mind—

something disturbing—and she knew it; it was there in his brooding eyes, no matter how hard he tried to hide it from her.

'The *whole* town has gone mad?!' he mocked, trying to make light of the looming situation. 'Surely not!'

'I fear they'll come here, *Mio Signore*. They are searching certain properties and—'

'Lucia, there is nothing to fear,' he interrupted, placing a reassuring hand on her shoulder, seeing the mounting concern in her deep, amber eyes. '*They* have no reason to come to this place. There is nothing of interest here, and besides … is this not a respectable house?'

Surely, he must have sensed it, she thought, looking at him with a vague expression, trying to ignore the smell of stale brandy and smoke on his breath. She knew he was no fool. Then again, perhaps he had been preoccupied with the Mistress's peculiar behaviour, to notice what was going on beyond his domain.

'But … have you not heard the talk among the people? There are rumours—'

'Idle gossip,' he interrupted again, dismissing it with the flick of his hand. 'That's all it is, Lucia: rumours, spread by foolish, superstitious people, with nothing worthwhile in their lives.'

As he turned away from her, she stared after him, speechless, thrown by his casual dismissal of her deep concern; while the streets of Triora were growing restless, *he* appeared unruffled by it all.

Inside, she felt her anger rising. 'I *know* you feel it, too,' she retorted, daring to challenge him.

He suddenly turned on her. 'Go about your business, child!' he yelled. 'See to your Mistress!'

The sudden outburst almost threw her off balance. Never, in all her time in their service, had he displayed his temper towards her or the boy. She then heard his sympathetic, long-winded sigh of regret.

'Forgive me, Lucia. I beg of you. It has been a trying time, and I am tired.' He yawned. 'I do not expect someone of your youth to understand.'

Offended by his remark, she felt compelled to remind him she was no longer a "child." Had he paid more attention to those around him, in the last year, he would have seen how much had changed. She blamed it on the elite company he had been keeping, it luring him from his responsibilities.

It had started quite harmlessly, with the Mistress regularly accompanying him to events and parties. But as time passed, something distracted her, and she soon grew bored, leaving the Master to his amusement, despite his protests.

"They are my friends and noble acquaintances!" she had heard him argue.

"Friends?!" the Mistress had hurdled back at him. "They are nothing of the sort; they will bleed you dry until there is nothing left. Where is your nobility among them? You seem to have lost all sense of it."

That was how it began: their road to destruction.

The Mistress continued to taunt him, pushing him away from their home. It forced him to stay away longer, sometimes until the early hours of daylight. Her presence about the great house became less as she kept to her quarters. At times, a day would pass—from dawn to dusk—in total silence, without their company. Lucia had her suspicions the Mistress ventured out alone, and that the Master neglected to notice, or, perhaps, *chose* not to. But that was *their* business, and she tried to avoid being dragged into it.

Meanwhile, she and the boy usually kept to themselves, enjoying the peace when the house fell empty. She felt protective of him in his innocence, and he looked up to her as a big sister. But things were changing, heightening her concern for their safety.

'What if they come here?' she then asked, suddenly fearing for their lives.

The dread in her voice disturbed him, and when she looked at him, it was evident by her pleading eyes she was seeking his reassurance. And should things, *get out of hand*, he knew she would then rely on *his* protection. Though he matched her concerns, he had to keep up the pretence for her sake.

41

Forcing a smile, he moved to embrace her concern. 'There is no one coming here, Lucia. I am sure of it.'

She stepped back from his unexpected touch.

Conscious of her unease, he moved away, looking around for his cloak. 'I'm going out,' he announced, then retrieved it from where he had left it, in the early hours: thrown in a ball, behind the door.

'Onto the streets?!' she cried. 'But—it's not safe, my—'

'I *will* return, Lucia, shortly,' he cut in, reassuring her again. 'And, if it makes you feel secure, lock all the doors when I leave, and answer to no one. Do you hear me?'

'Unless it is you?'

He nodded.

'Take charge of your usual duties, and do not worry yourself, where I am concerned. I'll not be long.'

Her eyes widened as panic gripped her, and when she drew her hands over her mouth, they shook. It was clear his attempt to regain her composure had failed; he knew she was frightened and aware of the worrying threat towards her as a young, impressionable woman. Innocent souls from other towns had already succumbed to the vile accusations being made against them. He had hoped to shield her from it, but the rumours *had*, without doubt, escalated. They were on the cusp of dangerous times.

He hesitated before leaving. 'If the Mistress should enquire as to my whereabouts ...'

'I will think of something to say,' she said, rolling her eyes.

He winked at her. '*Grazie!*'

She forced a smile, hating the fact she was, at times, the go-between in *their* disputes. Still and all, she liked the Master and knew she would cover for him.

'Now go!' he urged. 'I won't be long.'

Lucia closed the great door behind him as he stepped out into the night. She drew her hand, making the sign of a cross, praying for his safety, before searching for Petrio. She hoped the boy was not playing hide and seek. Like all children, he was obsessed with adventurous games. The great house was riddled with hidden nooks and crannies, not to mention the old, secret passageways. Normally, she would indulge him for hours while the house was empty. But instinct urged her to find him—to protect him from what might come.

The boy's start in life had been difficult. She had been told how his poverty-stricken parents could not support him, let alone themselves. They had begged the Master to take the baby—to give him a better life. The Mistress was reluctant, at first, but after much persuasion, she surrendered to their pleas. That was all Lucia knew. And yet, an air of secrecy still clung to the child. However, in time, she dismissed her curiosity, accepting him for who he was.

She moved swiftly through the open hallway, towards the servants' quarters, at the rear of the house. If he was not already in the kitchen, interrogating Sofia on her cooking skills, then she would begin the dreaded task of searching the hidden passages. All staff, save for the cook, had long gone home. Sofia was a perfectionist in what she proudly called her *"Cucina"*, sometimes staying late in her kitchen, to take orders of stock—should she need to go to the *Mercato* the following morning.

But of course! Lucia thought. No doubt Petrio would be there, playing with the dogs near the larder, and throwing them scraps behind Sofia's back.

The dogs! It had only come to her attention, their notable absence. It was usual to see them, pottering about or following Petrio around. However, she had failed to notice them all day, or hear the patter of their paws on the hardwood floors, with the Mistress's voice in the background complaining how their nails were destroying the highly polished surface.

As she made her way towards the kitchen she slowed, distracted by a voice. Pausing at the base of the winding staircase, she listened, thinking the Mistress had called her.

Tempted to ignore her, she thought better of it; her demands had become intolerable, and it was difficult to predict her moods, from day to day. Lucia imagined she was possessed by two personalities.

She then heard the voice again and sighed. *I'll look for him later*, she decided, throwing her eyes to heaven. Aware of the potential scolding she would receive—should she ignore the summons—Lucia reluctantly began her ascent up the elaborate staircase, towards her Mistress's quarters.

He lingered, listening for the sound of the bolt being pulled across the door. Satisfied she had secured it, he moved a few paces away from the house. A sudden feeling of unease came over him, forcing him to stop. He looked back, surveying its subdued facing as though its hidden history reached out to lure him into its secrets. But he had no interest in its past, only those that held its present. Pulling his cloak over his shoulders, he then drew his hood over his head, and moved on, keeping to the shadows.

Lucia was right. There was no denying it; something sinister *was* afoot, and there was a familiarity about it. The girl was perceptive. He had sensed it the first moment they met, doubting she was even aware of it, herself.

Lucia, on the death of her previous employer, more or less came with the house. He was uncertain of her age … eighteen … nineteen, or thereabouts. As he ventured further into the dark streets, the memory of their first meeting came back to him:

The Mistress had taken an instant dislike to the girl, voicing her demands;

"Get rid of her!"

"Lucia has no one," he had hit back. "She stays!"

And so, it had been settled.

However, as time wore on, the Mistress eventually warmed to Lucia. Only a few years stood between them—the Mistress being her senior. Both were beautiful, in their unique way. But lately, there had been a fit of underlying jealousy over Lucia's youth, prompting the Mistress to obsess with maintaining her own.

He had noticed the way she watched the girl—monitoring her every move. He found it menacing, at times, and hoped Lucia was oblivious to the curious eye of her surveyor.

He shuddered with the passing of a sharp breeze and cast an eye towards the night sky. The clouds had thickened, blocking out the moon in its entirety. The world now seemed to enclose itself around him in ominous silence. The quietness heightened his senses. He tilted his head, listening.

Still no sound.

Perhaps she imagined it, he thought. Or perhaps it had been the fear of being caught with her young lover. He smiled. Most likely the ramblings of a young woman in love. And yet, something else troubled him about the girl: her perception; it never failed her.

'Let us hope it does, this night, Lucia,' he muttered aloud.

The sudden awareness of his echoing footsteps on the narrow streets made him stop. Again, he listened. Shrouded in silence, he felt strangely relieved by the eerie absence of noise. But the quietude abruptly ended.

Distant voices now grew in volume, in pursuit of the evil *they* believed to reside in their little town. He glanced over the rooftops, catching the flickering light from the torches they wielded. He concealed himself in the darkness of a deep doorway. The thunderous sounds of banging on doors, followed by demanding voices, echoed through the streets and alleys.

'Aprire!' they shouted. 'Open up!'

Hidden behind their locked doors, the residents lived in fear, refusing to let the determined crowd cross their thresholds—should they find what they were seeking.

There's still time! He knew how thorough they would search each household … but there was no doubting what they were looking for; he had sensed it the moment he left the great house.

Just then, something terrible occurred to him: Triora's local gossip had just become his living nightmare.

Chapter Six

'Forgive me, Lucia.'

He spoke the words—out loud—in his desperation to get back.

I should have seen it! he told himself, angered by his negligence and selfishness. Too long had he indulged himself in the company of arrogance and hypocrisy; *they* were only interested in his heavy pockets. And all the while, under their influence, he had failed to see what passed beneath his own eyes.

He then stalled, remembering Lucia's secret shortcut. She would never forgive him if she learned he had followed her, on several occasions. He had been concerned by her "nightly strolls", at first, eventually discovering her reasons for them. Secretly, he had hoped she would find happiness with her lover … far from Triora's ignorance.

A sense of urgency spurred him on through her little laneway until he emerged from its dark passage to see the great house waiting for him. But as he approached it, something compelled him to stop, making him stare up at its façade. It was then, at that moment, he sensed it: the evil seeping from behind its walls, its chilling effect creeping out onto the street.

Wanting to avoid the main entrance, he hurried round to the side of the great house. He hesitated, to listen; the voices had faded into the distance. For now. A glance, then, told him he was alone. He then slipped into the overgrown gardens where throngs of shrubbery had been allowed to grow wild and neglected—on his orders.

He drew back a thick, large thorn bush, taking heed of its lethal needles. Concealed behind the growth, an old, ironbound door showed itself to him. Despite its size—inadequate and uncomfortable for a man, especially one of his stature—it was sufficient to pass through.

Only two possessed a key—the Mistress keeping the second. As to where she hid it, he did not know, nor did he care. He had been aware, of late, she, too, used it for a purpose. Had it been to spy on him, he would have known it. *Perhaps she has a lover,* he thought, removing the key from his belt. If so, he *would* find out.

The brass key was old and tarnished, and the lock stiff with age. Nonetheless, it had never failed him. The door hinges creaked, too; however, he had made a point of checking them regularly, stealing some of Sofia's olive oil as an unguent. It had been his usual routine, during his comings and goings, to pass through the doorway slowly and quietly—while making sure it was always kept locked.

Leaving the night behind, he quickly closed it behind him. Shrouded in darkness, he reached into a small crevice in the wall, removing the little lantern he had left there for his use. He was certain the Mistress was unaware of its presence; it had never been moved upon each return.

With a small gesture of his hand, the lantern's flame sprung to life, on his silent command. Then, raising it to the level of his eye, he waited for his eyes to adjust.

The familiar passageway stretched out before him. It was centuries old, created long before the house was built—and, thereafter, had been concealed from man's curious eyes forever, until *he* came upon it, by chance.

It was while on one of his indulging visits to Sofia's "*Cucina*" he had noticed a small army of ants going about their business, in perfect formation. Weighed down with morsels of food, scavenged along their way, they marched in regimental order behind their leader. He had marvelled at their discipline, before watching them disappear beneath the dusty, stained floorboards.

"What is down there?" he had inquired of the cook. Judging from the perplexed look on her face, he had perceived she knew nothing of its existence.

Both Master and servant's curiosity enticed them to investigate. With the use of a poker, he ripped back the floorboards, revealing a small space. The ants scattered at the unexpected disturbance.

"Just a storage space, *il Padrone*," she surmised, shrugging her rounded shoulders, before returning to her duties.

Disappointed, he moved to replace the boards, then stopped, when he noticed the ants reforming, to resume their journey. He lingered, watching their movements. When the little army disappeared, through a small yet obvious gap below the foundations of the house, he realised there could be more to discover, it feeding his interest.

And so … he had waited until the house fell into its nightly slumber, to see what other secrets the old building might give up.

He recalled his first venture down the passageway: the knocks to his head; the cuts and bruises; and the countless times he had lost his footing. And yet, no one seemed to notice his minor injuries; if they had, they kept it to themselves.

With frequent visits, he soon mastered its route, taking him beyond the walls of the house. At times, he speculated on how the Mistress came and went, before casting the thought aside; he would know it if she came this way.

He now moved with rapid ease until he saw the familiar shape of the second door—made from solid beech and crossed with iron strips, for added strength. He inserted the same key. On the other side, the ascending steps—which would guide him back to Sofia's kitchen—waited for him.

As he opened the door, he stopped dead. The smell of dampness—he had been accustomed to—was now replaced by an unwelcome stench. Lifting his head, he searched for its source and paused, drawing in its pungency; it seemed familiar to him.

As it toyed with his senses the sound of a faint voice followed it, whispering words he did not recognise:

Night ... trustiest Keeper of my secrets and stars,
who, together with the moon—follows on from the
fires of the daylight. And you, Hecate, of the Three
Heads—who know all of my designs—who
comes to help my incantations and the Craft
Of the Witches ...

The voice in his head grew louder, deafening his thoughts. Desperation drove him up the steps. The hidden trapdoor—he had secretly made after his discovery—remained closed, beneath the floorboards. The stench grew stronger, dulling his senses, while sinister, conjuring words of immoral implication attempted to corrupt his reason.

The *voice* now screamed in his ear:

... and of the Earth who furnish us with power over
mountains, and seas ...

He reached up to open the little door; it refused to budge. He pressed against it; it was bolted from the other side.

Someone had locked him in.

'Who could have—' He stopped, unable to think for the *voice* in his head, its persistence troubling him. 'The voice ... the voice ... the—' His eyes widened. '*That* voice!'

He looked back from where he came from. *It will take too long*, he realised, growing anxious. He cast his lantern aside—the light extinguished the moment it left his hand—and placed both hands on the door, manipulating it with his fingers.

'Open!' he commanded.

Instantly—and of its own accord—the door flew open, to the bewildered faces of Sofia and Petrio.

'Where is Lucia?' he demanded, taking hold of the boy's arm.

Petrio stared at him, his dark eyes filled with tears. 'You're hurting me!' he cried.

49

Frustrated, he turned to the cook. '*Per favore!* Please, Sofia, where is she?'

'I do not know, *Mio Signore!*' she replied, raising her hands in confusion. 'I ... I have not seen her in a while. Is she not with—'

'No, she is not with *him*,' he snapped, aware his cook had been privy to the girl's rendezvous with her lover. 'But I wish she was.' He cast a quick eye about the *Cucina*, noticing another absence. 'Where are the dogs?'

The cook glanced around her small domain before it dawned on her; she had not seen them, either. They were always with Petrio, sniffing at his heel. It had irritated the Mistress, so much so, that she regularly threatened to "rid the house of them."

Sofia's silence was enough to arouse his dread. Sensing the boy trembling beneath his grip, he then released him. As he moved to question them further, he winced—the throbbing *voice* in his head growing louder by the second. If it didn't stop, he imagined it would drive him to insanity. He clasped his hands over his ears, trying to block it out; he *had* to stop it.

Disturbed by their Master's unsettling behaviour, Sofia and Petrio shared worrying glances.

Then suddenly it ceased, giving him time to think. In his moment of clarity, he felt drawn to the upper chambers of the house, and as he looked up, the disturbing *voice* returned:

> *... and may the Gods of the groves, and all the Gods*
> *of the night, be present to help and serve me.*
> *Renew my soul*
> *Renew my life*
> *Renew my beauty ...*

The incantations continued, clouding his thoughts again.

'Wait here!' he insisted, his voice urgent as he turned on his heel.

'*Signore?*' Sofia called after him.

He stopped in the doorway of her little *Cucina* and turned to see the look of bewilderment on her face, her eyes wide, mouth gaping—and the boy staring, his innocent eyes darting from one to the other, equally confused.

'Stay with him,' he urged, eyeing Petrio. 'And do not follow me, Sofia,' he added, his warning made clear by his sideward glance. 'No matter what!' He then hesitated, now seeing a different look in her eyes—one of fear. 'Remember what I told you—should anything …'

Sofia's face dropped; she knew what he meant. Taking hold of Petrio's little hand, she nodded her silent assurance.

'*Grazie!*' he returned, through a forced smile, then left.

Quickly he ran past the pantry and on through the little corridor, leading to the servants' quarters. As he stormed up the steps, which lead to the main hallway, a deathly chill crept its way through the great house, engulfing it with its menace. He felt its omen as he approached the hall, but as he began to quicken his pace he was forced to stop. There, slumped at the base of the staircase, lay the lifeless bodies of the boy's much-loved pets.

He checked the dogs over; they were dead—but not by natural causes. He stared down at them—the saliva still dripping from their gaping mouths, and their vacant eyes open, staring into the abyss of death. He then noticed something strange. He looked closely; their teeth were stained black and reeked. It was clear something else—something malevolent—was to blame.

How am I going to tell Petrio? he thought, shaking his head. *This will break his—*

He looked sharp, his attention now directed up the grand staircase. *It's coming from up there.*

Reaching for the baluster, he attacked each step, in earnest—the *voice* still in his head:

> … *night wandering Queen, look kindly upon this*
> *Undertaking.*
> *I command you!*
> *Serve me well*
> *Serve me always …*

51

When he reached the top of the staircase, he stalled; it was unusually dark and bitterly cold. Not a single lantern was lit, adding to the grim atmosphere. As he stepped onto the landing, an eerie silence gripped him.

The *voice* had stopped, again.

He glanced up and down the landing, unsure, then shuddered, feeling its over-bearing ice-cold presence. Suddenly he drew back, seeing *it*— the sight of it almost causing him to stumble from the top step. There, out of the darkness, a pale, misty hue appeared from the far end of the landing. He watched as it floated over him, swirling, as it crept back and forth down the hallway as if searching for something … or someone.

It then stopped—outside a door.

He surveyed its ghostly hue for several moments as it hovered, before deciding to follow it. But as he crept closer, it seemed to take the shape of a woman.

Then it was gone.

Fearing for the Mistress's safety, despite their differences, he rushed forward, reaching for the elaborate gold-plated handle—now tarnished black, like coal. But even before his hand touched it, he knew he would be unable to gain entry—the unfamiliar power preventing it, its menace pushing him back.

His eyes darted up, hearing a noise coming from behind the door— the sound of someone gasping for breath. Panic struck him. He *had* to open it—and there was only one way to do that now.

'You will not keep me out!' he snarled at the unknown force.

Reciting ancient words from his inner greatness, the door flung open on his command.

Inside, the room was filled with blinding light, stopping him in his path. However, as he raised his hand, to shield his eyes from its intensity, it quickly faded at his intrusion.

As the light diminished, the blurred image of a figure came into view. He focused on it, waiting for his eyes to adjust. Slowly, the silhouette of a woman emerged. He drew back, stunned.

'Kristene!'

Her eyes flickered at the sound of another presence in her chamber. She lowered her head, scowling, in acknowledgement of their unwanted company.

'Kristene! What have—'

As the aura around her gradually dwindled, it exposed her new persona.

He reached out his hand. 'Come to me, Kristene!' he urged. She appeared dazed. He dared to move closer.

She stepped away.

'Please!' His hand remained extended, waiting for her to take it.

She did not waiver.

'I won't harm you,' he said, keeping his eyes focused on her, taken aback by her appearance; she was barely recognisable from the woman he knew. Her features now radiated—enhancing the beauty of her oval face. Her flawless, ivory skin glowed with the renewal of youth. Her long, thick hair—once a deep shade of brown—now gleamed with vibrant copper, and flowed loosely over her shoulders.

He moved to encourage her further, then stalled, when she suddenly looked down; she was holding something. Curious, he followed her gaze.

Clenched in her small hand, he saw a dagger. It looked unusually substantial in her tiny grip, and as she clutched it firmly her knuckles almost protruded her soft skin. The long blade bore symbols, deeply engraved in its steel. He struggled to recognise their origin until the image of an unorthodox cross resurfaced from his subconscious. Beneath the unlikely symbol, he noted a mythical creature: a dragon, with its tail touching the cross, uniting them. But still, he could not determine where he had seen it before. He desperately scoured through his turbulent past, when his concentration was abruptly broken by horror.

The shock of it struck him hard as he stared at the stained dagger; it was covered in fresh blood.

'What have you done?!' he cried, in outrage, grabbing hold of her wrist.

Her eyes, devoid of all sense of reality, stared back at him. He regarded them with caution, before seeing it: their colour had changed. They were no longer hazel, like his, but deeper, intense yet disturbingly familiar.

A sly, smirk crawled across her mouth, its menace disturbing him. Her new amber eyes slid towards the bed, encouraging him to pursue her. An instant feeling of dread rushed through him. Reluctant to follow her emotionless gaze, he *knew* he could not ignore his inner voice. *I have to know. I have to—*

His mouth fell open in dismay as he let go of her wrist. At first, he was speechless, struggling to grasp the reality of what he was forced to see until her name poured from his mouth:

'Lucia!'

Draped over the large, four-poster bed—he and her Mistress had once shared—the body of their young, loyal servant lay motionless.

'No! No!' he yelled, in disbelief, racing to her side.

'Please—Lucia—be alive!' he begged, staring in horror at her garments as the blood continued to seep through, where the dagger had been driven into the centre of her innocent heart. Frantic, he pressed his hands firmly on the fatal wound, to stem the blood flow. But as he looked into her pale, dead eyes, locked in death, something struck him: *Her eyes! Impossible!*

Denial began to set in, clouding his judgement. He shook her lifeless body, in his hopeless attempt to rouse her, while repeating her name; 'Lucia. Lucia! Lu—'

'The girl is dead.'

He stopped, hearing the familiar, deep voice from behind. He drew back sharply, his doleful eyes still fixed on Lucia's corpse. Staring down at the stain of her death on his hands, he was sure his ears had deceived him.

But the sinister voice spoke again; 'She is of no more use to you … Lord Oran.'

Chapter Seven

Magia Nera: The name itself was the epitome of corruption, fused with dark depravity.

The slender figure watched and waited in silence while surveying his rival; Oran felt his searing eyes scrutinise him from behind, all the while imagining the smirk on his mouth. He contemplated his dagger, concealed beneath his cloak, deciding it would be ineffective against the individual he was about to face … again.

It was time to confront his past.

Oran slowly turned, stealing another glance at Kristene, who remained in a transient state of detachment.

'What have you done with her?!' he demanded.

'Is that how you greet your old friends, Lord Oran?' his rival mocked, in his thick accent.

'Do not call me *that!*'

'Denying your true identity?' Magia persisted. He slowly shook his head, tutting. 'Such a betrayal! What would *they* say if they heard you, now?'

Outraged by this ridicule, Oran subconsciously reached for his dagger.

Magia Nera threw his head back in laughter. 'Oh, *Amico Mio!* You were always the humorous one, my *friend!*'

Seething inside, Oran reluctantly returned his weapon to its sheath, feeling somewhat the fool.

'I had no more use for mine,' Magia sneered, acknowledging the dagger still clutched in Kristene's hand.

Oran stared at him, now calling to mind the symbols on the blade; his face dropped when it finally registered.

'Ah! I see you remember!' Magia observed. 'I began to wonder if time had endured itself on your memory, Oran. Clearly not! Although … I *do* see traces of it etched on your face and—' He gasped, drawing back, feigning horror, as he placed his hand on his chest. 'Are they silver hairs I see, Lord—'

'Be warned, Magia!'

'How long has it been? One? Two, perhaps? The centuries seem to slip from one to the next—far too quickly.'

Oran tilted his head, scrutinising the dark Warlock, then drew closer. As he did so, he watched with amusement as Magia stretched his height in a bid to meet his rival's, while lifting his head, inviting his nemesis to admire him.

It had been more than two centuries since their last encounter. Though similar in age, Oran noticed little change in his adversary. His sable hair was as he remembered it: long, full, and drawn back from his narrow face; and his skin—the colour of ivory, and flawless. Oran recalled the scars that had once marked it—now long vanished. The finest clothing hung gracefully on his frame, as though created by the *Gods* themselves. The perfectly tailored silk shirt, matching that of his skin, exuded excellence. But it was the full-length, sleeveless damask cloak that stood out, its charcoal colour—Oran surmised—almost matching that of its owner's black heart. Oran glanced down at his rival's soft, leather boots and smirked—the long coat failing to hide the thick heels, fooling the eye into a false impression of height and stature.

However, despite his deficiency, Magia Nera's intimidating presence dominated the chamber; Oran subconsciously stepped back, tilting his head to the other side. 'You should be … *dead!*'

'*Should* be,' Magia replied, spreading his arms wide. 'Yet here I stand, Warlock!'

Oran threw him a disgruntled look, only to have it returned with a smug grin.

'I see it has been quite some time since someone called you *that*,' said Magia.

Ignoring the remark, Oran paced back and forth in front of his rival. He paused, frowning, as the memory flooded back.

'But I watched you die … on the battlefield of Wallachia,' he recalled, staring into his foe's warm, amber eyes, certain they had once been blue. 'You fought with us.'

'And what a great battle it was!' Magia replied. 'And *you* fought well, Warlock … but of course … you were much *younger*, then.'

'Whereas, *you* have not aged,' said Oran, observing him. His eyes narrowed with suspicion, contemplating it. 'Why would that be?'

Magia Nera maintained his grin, antagonising him further.

'Answer me, or I shall—'

'Kill me?' said Magia, unable to contain his amusement.

'I *saw* you die!'

'Why, Oran,' he teased, 'surely, someone of your worldliness knows, you cannot kill that which is already *dead!*'

Oran's eyes widened as the truth began to unravel, incredible as it seemed.

'*Si!* You saw me fall,' Magia began, 'but in your haste to win the battle, you failed to notice the figure standing over my dying body, toying with my life, deciding whether I should live or … *die!*'

'Tepés?!' cried Oran, disturbed by what he was hearing. 'The Impaler?!'

'You should not have turned your back on me, Oran,' he replied. 'It was my last memory of you—fleeing in the moments before I took my final breath. You see … Tepés restored me to *life!*'

Oran stared at him, horrified.

'*Life!*' Magia laughed. 'The irony of it!'

Oran shook his head.

'Impossible! Did *they* not—'

'You are surprised? You wonder, how it is possible? But here I am.' He pulled a solemn face. 'Do not look so … disappointed.'

'How could Tepés have possibly …?' Oran's words trailed off as he tried to make sense of it. *'They* destroyed him! Decades before.'

'Sciocchi!' He grunted. 'The fools! They failed to *finish* the task.'

'I don't understand.'

Magia approached him with menace, casting a quick eye towards Kristene who remained in a dream-like state, oblivious to their conversation.

'They neglected to cut off his head!' he said, holding Oran's gaze. 'And, in failing to do so, he was not quite … *dead!* His band of loyal followers retrieved his body from beneath the altar, where he had been secretly buried, and took him back to his homeland.'

'In Wallachia?'

'Where else! It was his haven, where he could be renewed. He told me so. And so, there he stayed, in his immortal world, continuing to fight his battles. His army was sworn to secrecy—no one else, except his daughter, knew he still *existed.* And when *we* fought him, on *his* soil, he saw his opportunity—*I* being the chosen victim for his revenge.' Magia paused, musing on the memory of it. '"I will take you as one of my own, Warlock",' he then said, quoting Tepés. 'Those were his last words to me, before he—'

Oran glanced at Kristene. 'Please tell me you did not—'

'No!' Magia snapped. 'I would not inflict this curse on *her,*' he stated, pointing at Kristene. 'Although … it has its advantages.'

Oran cast him a sideward glance, his suspicions quickly mounting.

'Tepés lured me into his hidden, fatalistic world, where he nurtured me in the ways of his dark arts, entrusting me into his covertness. He thought it was impenetrable. How arrogant of him.' He stopped and looked directly at Oran. 'He believed his concept of power is—*was*—comparable to ours. Ours! The insolence of it!' Magia's eyes flared with rage at the notion. He then stopped himself, pausing to contain his annoyance. It did not go unnoticed.

'Was?' said Oran, raising a brow.

The question roused Magia's attention towards his rival. 'Tepés should not have placed his trust in me, so much.'

58

'Do you mean to say'—Oran hesitated, raising his brows— 'Vlad Tepés *is* dead?'

'Unlike our peers, *I* made certain the task was carried out—by *my* hand. Tepés was careless—not realising with whom he was acquainted. I still see his face as his immortality ceased to exist. I gained much knowledge from him yet took little—only that which I required.'

'His dagger,' Oran surmised, diverting his eyes.

'Amongst other things,' said Magia, catching him steal a glance at Kristene. 'Is she not ... *bellisimo?!*'

Oran dared to move towards her.

'I have watched her movements since she was a child—as with *yours.*'

'So, it *was* you!' Oran sneered, glaring at the smugness on Magia's face.

'Why—did you think it was *them?* That your past had caught up with you?'

'I wasn't sure,' Oran admitted. 'At times I sensed their presence ...'

'Which is why you fled—taking the girl with you.'

Oran felt uncomfortable, having discovered he had been followed, not by his superiors, but by the lone adversary they thought dead.

'Naturally, you *would* sense it,' said Magia. 'Are we not of the same essence?'

Oran glared back at him, insulted by the mere suggestion. 'Do not cast aspersions on me, Magia,' he retorted. 'I had my reasons for leaving; they were justified.'

'To yourself, perhaps. But I can imagine what *they* would say if they knew of your whereabouts.'

'And what of *yours?*'

'You forget'—the corner of Magia's mouth curled— 'Warlock!'

Oran gritted his teeth.

'I am dead to them. They have no cause to search for *me*. After all, they accepted your word, thinking I was "no more." And so, I was ... *dispersed* into the universe—to be nothing more than a distant memory.' He pondered on that thought. 'I wonder if my absence is still felt among them?' he added, unable to resist mocking their peers. 'Oh, how touching that would be.'

'Hardly,' muttered Oran.

At that moment, their eyes locked on one another, briefly forgetting their surroundings, as though they were the only two present.

'I have no interest in you, Oran of Urquille,' said Magia, breaking the silence.

The words flowed, without thought; Oran's heart sank at the mention of his Realm—the one he had abandoned.

Magia turned and pointed towards Kristene. '*She* was my only interest from the moment I laid eyes on her. The chance meeting with her mother was brief, but enough to convince me; I was in no doubt as to the child's "gift" when I first looked into those eyes.'

'A look that haunted her,' Oran muttered.

'And such a beautiful child,' he said, ignoring the remark, his eyes resting on Kristene. Slowly he began circling her like a predator, hesitating, to admire her flawless beauty. For an instant, he imagined he saw her flinch. 'The potential was not to be ignored,' he added, turning to Oran. 'I know you saw it, too, whereas *I* saw so much more.'

'I was certain it was—'

'What the eye of a child sees,' said Magia, 'is quite different to that of their elders. But she was too young, and her mother … a little too protective. So, I let the years dictate when the time was right—when she came into her own.' His eyes slid back to Kristene. 'I watched as they condemned her mother. A pity you were not there to witness it.'

'And witness an innocent woman burn?!' Oran lashed out. 'How can you even suggest that *I* would condone such a barbaric act?'

'I am not completely heartless!' Magia hit back. 'I mused over her liberation, but *she* was not the "gifted" one. As quaint as her archaic remedies were, the woman was of no benefit to me. Had she lived, it would have been a great inconvenience; she would have stood in my way, or at least … *tried* to.'

'Then why did you not simply discard her?'

Magia glared at his rival, infuriated. 'I have *never* taken the life of a woman!' he snapped. 'But … I will confess—to my shame—her execution was rather convenient. However, I did not expect the same fate of the mother to fall on the daughter. Now *that* was an inconvenience.'

'She would have drowned had *I* not been at hand,' Oran informed him.

'It seems that time has also affected your memory, Oran. You forget—I was also watching *you*. Quite the bold move—sending the *creature*. What can I say? *Impressionante!* Quite impressive!'

'Again, you let another do your bidding, Magia. Or were you afraid to get your boots wet?'

'Where is the harm in that?' he swiftly replied, failing to see the sarcasm in Oran's wit. 'I knew she was in safe hands. But her talents were raw. I was content to let her stay with you, so you could encourage her, teach her … *prepare* her.'

Oran regarded him with a sideward look. 'Prepare her for *what*, precisely? You have not squandered these last years, keeping her in your sights for nothing. Your motives have always been for self-gain.'

'I was simply … protecting my interests,' Magia said. 'And I commend you, Oran. She is … *almost* perfect.'

'Almost?' Oran's eyes darted towards Kristene, apprehensive.

'Questions, questions!' said Magia, rolling his eyes. 'You do realise, time is against us, *here*, in this place?'

Oran watched as his rival moved with swift precision towards the bedchamber's large window. The long, drapes were drawn; Magia's hand glided across them gracefully until they parted, giving him a sufficient view of the street below.

'They are still searching,' he stated, looking down. 'They *sense* it, and will soon arrive at your door with their pathetic threats. Was it your intention to take her away, Oran?'

'It *is* my intention!'

Hearing the determination in his tone, Magia turned and stared at him before filling the room with laughter, mocking his rival, again.

'In your disregard of her, Lord Oran,' he said, '*she*, found me! A vulnerable soul is easily influenced. It was no difficult task in luring her into my confidence. When we came upon one another, again—here—I thought she would remember our first meeting—when she was a child.'

Oran glared at him. '*Here*, you say? In Triora?'

Magia lowered his head, eyes transfixed. 'Right under your nose, Warlock,' he gloated. 'And why not? Is this place—this country—not part of Meddian—the Realm *I* once presided over?'

Oran swiftly turned his attention to Kristene. The true nightmare had yet to unfold. 'I should have seen it!' he whispered to her as if pleading for her forgiveness.

Her eyes flickered erratically. He stepped back.

'She hears me!'

'I admire your optimism, Oran,' Magia teased. 'You see what you wish to believe. But why would she listen to *you*, now? You averted your attention from her, for far too long, indulging yourself in the finer things in life, while neglecting the most precious item you possessed. It was only a matter of time before she would succumb to the attentions of another. And while you amused yourself in the company of those you would call "friends", I was willing to bide my time.'

Oran tried to obliterate Magia's increasingly irritating voice while concentrating on Kristene.

'Take a good look, Oran,' he urged. 'Look closely at her!'

'Kristene!' Oran whispered, observing her perfect features.

Her eyes flickered again.

'Listen to my voice, Krist—'

'She no longer recognises that name.'

Desperate to lure her from her spellbound state, Oran reached out to touch her but was compelled to withdraw his hand. 'Kristene!'

Detecting the growing anguish in his voice, Magia simply could not help himself. 'She has accepted her new soul,' he revealed.

Oran tried, once more, to gain her attention. 'Kristene!'

'She will have powers you cannot imagine,' Magia boasted. 'This "Sorceress" will be indestructible!'

Oran turned sharply. 'Sorceress?!' he roared in disgust. 'She covets the soul of a Witch?!' His nightmare was now unravelling into a disturbing reality.

'She is no Witch!' Magia retorted, offended. 'She is—'

'What possessed you?!'

Their voices continued to rise as they now faced one another in verbal combat—one rival striving against the other for the precious stakes.

'Everything!' said Magia. 'Everything about her possessed me!'

'Do you have any concept of what you have done?'

'It was my intention from the start. She is the perfect *host*.'

Oran stepped back, aware of the sound of his angry breath, torn between hate and jealousy. Turning his back on Magia, he tried to compose himself.

'I can hear your heart racing, Warlock.'

'Who is it?' asked Oran, his voice reposed as he stared into Kristene's face, searching for the woman he knew.

Magia lingered, goading him with his silence.

'Do not taunt me!' warned Oran. 'Or have you forgotten, who *you* once were? Whose wicked soul does she host?'

'Someone great!' Magia replied. 'From centuries past. *They* condemned her to the fires. But I was asked to *steal* her soul—by her lover, no less, until such time they could reunite.'

For a price, no doubt, Oran thought. 'Who asked you?'

'Does it matter?'

'Another Warlock?' Oran surmised.

'The pleasure of doing it—and right from under them—amused me. I vowed to restore the soul, but ...' Magia tilted his head from side to side.

Oran turned to face him. 'You broke your vow!' he stated, 'despite knowing the penalty for betraying another Warlock.'

'True,' said Magia. 'But they failed to notice, hence there was no betrayal on my part.

'The one I stole it for was in no position to speak out against me, as the "affair" was forbidden. He knew the consequences—had he been found out. Desperation makes the "foolish" do desperate things.'

Oran shook his head at Magia's casual display of arrogance.

'You just couldn't resist.'

'Such a tragedy that I was unable to … *help* him.'

'Yet you led him to believe you could, by giving him hope!'

'The temptation was too great,' Magia declared. 'And so, I lied. I knew it was only a matter of time before I found the necessary incantations. However, I did not bargain on the lengthy wait.' He sighed. 'Time *can* be cruel. Nonetheless, I shall always be indebted to the one who thought himself greater than I.'

'Tepés!'

'But of course!'

At this point, Oran had heard enough of his counterpart's self-indulging arrogance and egotism; it was more than he could endure. With no warning, he threw himself forward, forcing his rival towards the window.

'Your heart is as black as the garb you wear,' Oran sneered, taking hold of Magia's throat. 'Remove *it* from her!' he warned. 'Give her back to me, or I shall—' He stopped, suddenly aware of Magia's red eyes and his distinct menacing grin.

'I cannot!' he stated, maintaining his irritating smirk.

'Cannot or *will* not?' Oran maintained his hold. 'Undo what you have done!'

'Even if I could, Oran of Urquille, I have no desire to do so.'

Oran tightened his grip. 'Then I shall make—'

The unexpected sound of an object, falling to the floor, silenced the two rivals. Oran released his hold on Magia. The Warlocks turned their heads at the timely interruption, unprepared for what stood before them.

Chapter Eight

L'Ordana's new eyes sprung to life as she inhaled her surroundings. 'How can this be?' Magia whispered, breaking away from Oran. He approached her with authority. 'I have not released you!'

She held his enraged gaze as he drew near.

Oran looked on, confused, though slightly amused when she summoned the dagger into her hand before holding it to Magia Nera's heart—the blade's point forcing him to stop.

'What is this?' he cried, feeling its sharpness against his cold skin as it pierced through the fine silk of his long waistcoat.

'Fools!'

Oran's mouth gaped when he heard the power in her new voice; he no longer recognised it, nor the stranger who now clearly dominated the chamber.

'You fight each other like two pathetic lovestruck mortals,' she began, scolding them, 'craving for something you cannot—and *will* not—have, all the while thinking you can control me?'

'Remove this blade!' Magia insisted, wary of the implications—should she thrust it deep. Unlike his antagonist, *he* was aware of her capabilities ... or so he thought.

'Kristene!' called Oran, as he pushed Magia by the wayside, his voice distracting her to him. ''Tis I, Oran, your—'

'Keep your distance,' she warned, now turning the blade on him.

The threat was real; it was there in her eyes. 'Your eyes!' he whispered.

'The eyes are the *portal* to the soul,' Magia remarked, his tone smug and teasing.

Ignoring him, Oran looked down at the dagger—stained with Lucia's blood—then towards the large bed where her body still lay. He had forgotten the dead girl with all that had occurred and felt shameful for it.

Then something struck him. He cast a quick look back at L'Ordana, seeing it now: her eyes matched that of Lucia's. Now he knew what Magia meant. Gone were the sultry, hazel eyes that once smiled at him, through Kristene. He was now looking into the deep, dark amber eyes that were once his servant's—the one difference: they were devoid of life.

'Why her? Why Lucia?' he cried, pointing at the dead girl. 'Why take her life?'

L'Ordana looked down her nose at him, unwilling to justify her actions.

'It was necessary,' Magia answered, on her behalf.

Oran's face hardened. 'To deny a young woman the right to live?! Lucia was kind, beautiful and—'

'*There* is your answer,' said Magia.

Oran drew his head back, his brow knitting tightly.

'See how young and beautiful my Sorceress is? For her to remain so, she requires the spirit of a young woman.'

'But why choose *this* one? Surely, there are enough maidens in Triora who would satisfy *her* vile needs.'

'Nonesuch as she,' Magia replied, glancing at Lucia's corpse. 'The girl was perfect and *pure*.'

'She had a lover!' Oran blurted, hoping to disrupt his plans.

Magia grinned. 'One she had given her heart to—but nothing more.'

'Do not presume to know this, Magia. It is possible Lucia was no longer a—'

'Ah, but you see,' Magia responded, smirking, 'you were not the only one who followed her. You should have been more thorough in the investigations of your servant girl. She was carefully chosen.'

Oran closed his eyes and sighed as a wave of guilt consumed him. 'Forgive me, Lucia,' he whispered.

'It appears you have also failed *her*,' sneered Magia.

Fuelled by hate and remorse, Oran turned on his rival, preparing to strike.

'What will *that* achieve?' Magia cried, bracing himself. 'It will not bring your servant back. Do not waste time on something that is—'

'Shall I tell you *how*?' L'Ordana interrupted, stealing their attention.

'I don't wish to know,' said Oran, turning to face her, seething and outraged by their calmness.

'See *this*?' she continued, displaying the dagger.

He was sickened by the sight of it. The grim reminder of hearing Lucia's last breath would haunt him forever. Oran looked at the symbols engraved on the red steel—their representation of evil.

'I drove it deep into the core of her heart—right through—until her final breath, then waited … until all the youth she possessed was passed to me.' She held up the dagger, making sure he could see it. 'What once was hers—is now mine.'

'The girl was her first!' revealed Magia.

'Her *first*?' Oran was appalled as it registered with him; more innocent victims would succumb to the depraved wants of his rival's so-called "Sorceress."

'Indeed!' said Magia. 'And if she is to retain her youth, then I shall be there to make certain of it.'

L'Ordana slowly turned her attention to Magia, intent on wiping the smirk from his long face. 'You?!' Her eyes burned with anger as a deep rage simmered from the depths of her past.

With every passing moment, she felt revived with youth and vigour. A new feeling of power engulfed her, surpassing anything she could envisage. It was enduring. Then the words the two Warlocks had spoken began to form sentences in her mind; they had had no inkling of her awareness while they discussed her freely. Her thoughts raced.

'Have you forgotten your place, L'Ordana? Or do you need reminding of—'

'You could have *saved* her!' she said, letting the words escape from her mouth.

Oran's eyes widened, hearing the echo of his words. 'She's remembered!' he stated, amazed.

Everything fell silent. The absence of noise within the chamber brought with it a sense of dread. Magia looked from one to the other with unease.

Images gradually came to her as their words continued to swirl in her mind. She looked directly at Magia. 'It was *you*!' she cried out. 'You *let* her die! You stood by and watched as she burned. Why would you do that?'

'I fear your mind is playing tricks on you, L'Ordana,' Magia swiftly returned.

She spat her rage at him, through gritted teeth. 'Do not insult me! I heard you speak of it—both of you!' she revealed, toying with the dagger, her mind now thrown into a frenzy of lies and conspiracy. 'If I had known this truth, Magia Nera, should *I* have been content to die, also?'

'Your thoughts are not your own,' he persisted. 'You have not yet come into your own.'

'But you—'

'*Could* not save her!' Magia blurted, watching her as she searched through the wreckage of her past.

Oran cast him a resentful look; it was clear to him his antagonist had no desire to be found out.

L'Ordana lingered in silence, eyeing her rivals.

Oran regarded her; she looked lost and lonely in her pale-silver night garments. For a precious moment, he was taken back to when they first met—after he had saved her. *There still could be time*, he thought. *It's now or never!* He needed to make one final attempt to rouse Kristene from her vexation—to break the curse or spell she was under, and rid her body of the spirit that had been placed inside her.

But as he moved towards her, her body suddenly stiffened, as though frozen by a nameless source. She slowly lowered her head and then jolted back, her breathing erratic, launching her body into spasms. As she desperately fought for air, Oran rushed to her aid but was thrust back by the invisible barrier protecting her.

'If she dies …' he threatened, turning to face Magia, 'I will find the means to destroy you!'

The sinister smugness displayed on Magia's face now alerted Oran to something new and unsettling, as an eerie silence gripped him, commanding his attention. The Warlock reluctantly turned his head, his mouth slowly gaping; the woman—he had once known and loved—had been completely transformed, her persona now emanating power and authority. It simply radiated from her, and he felt its overbearing influence.

'*Alla fine!*' cried Magia, lifting his hands. 'Finally! She has come into her own!' He approached her with a feeling of possession, sensing it was his right. '*Magnifico!*' he exclaimed, clasping his hands together, pleased with himself.

'Back!' she commanded, in a domineering and threatening manner.

Oran's eyes darted towards Magia. 'I would do as she asks,' he stated, with a sense of foreboding.

L'Ordana scrutinised their every move with intent, her determined eyes boring into them.

'I created you!' Magia reminded her. 'Did I not teach you all that you—'

'Enough!' she snapped, beginning to pace back and forth as new thoughts churned in her reawakened mind. Her movements were like that of a lioness, contemplating her prey.

The Warlocks regarded her, in anticipation; they could sense something was about to happen—see it in the waking of her hostility.

She then paused, surveying them with her intense, arcane eyes, holding them in her gaze for several moments. And when the malevolent curl appeared on the side of her mouth, it was enough to warn them …

As the flames burst forward, it spurred the Warlocks into action. With no time to spare, they desperately called on their defences, shrouding themselves in their invisible shields, diverting their eyes from the intense heat.

The flames obliterated everything inside the chamber. It was then the Warlocks realised: a moment wasted—would have meant their demise.

Now, cocooned beneath their protection, Oran and Magia were forced to reunite, momentarily, as L'Ordana continued to conjure up words of destruction towards them—unaware of their self-defence.

Oran, feeling the magnitude of her attack pressing down on him, forced himself to look up, his eyes widening when a feast of flames shot out above them. Even beneath his protection, he could feel their effect and struggled to maintain his guard as they spread across the chamber.

He looked over at Magia; the dark Warlock was huddled next to him, covering his sensitive eyes, knowing the consequence—should he open them. In those moments, Oran recalled how they had once fought together as allies, protecting their world, their Realms, against sinister forces—forces that proved an even greater threat to mortals. And now, here they were, locked briefly in time, trying to save themselves from the individual who had forced their paths to cross, again: the woman they both loved—the one they were about to lose.

He closed his eyes, and waited; it was all he could do.

Time seemed to pause as the intense heat began to subside. She gaped at the destruction caused by her hand, sparing no thought for the memories she had obliterated. Shaking herself from her stupor, she approached the two huddled figures, smirking to herself, as they cowered like children, fearing the unknown.

She stopped and looked down at them; they were oblivious to her movements. Her eyes then slid across to Magia, widening when she saw it: the item she desired. Tilting her head, she hesitated, eyes transfixed, fingers flexing, itching to have it. She leaned over their crouched forms. Then, slowly extending her hand through their defence, she smiled.

'Come to me.'

Chapter Nine

What seemed like minutes, passed in seconds for the Warlocks. They began to feel a gradual, cooling sensation as the burden of her deathly attack lifted.

Quickly casting away his invisible defence, Oran rose, preparing to battle against the undesired enemy. But his eyes stung, temporarily impairing his vision; and yet, he was reluctant to open them. As he listened to the empty silence, something brushed against his face. He flicked it away, then felt it again ... and again. Compelled to satisfy his curiosity, he gradually opened his eyelids, blinking uncontrollably.

The vibrant bedchamber—they had once shared—was now shrouded in a cloud of colourless gloom. As the last speckles of ash fell about him, like deathly snow, it blurred his vision. He rubbed his irritated eyes, trying to focus again on his surroundings.

Gradually, the devastation unfolded.

Horrified, he cast a hesitant, sideward glance towards what had once been their bed; Lucia's charred remains, her outline softened by the black dust, were now unrecognisable—the young woman whose only crime had been her beauty and innocence.

She did not deserve this, he told himself.

Aware of the grim atmosphere still lingering in the chamber, Oran spun, drawing up his invisible guard once more, searching through the veil of settling dust, ready to fight.

'Come forward!' he growled, through gritted teeth.

All remained still.

Oran strained his eyes, expecting another assault. But there was nothing—only the chill of death that clung to the air. He dropped his defence with a stark realisation: L'Ordana was gone.

Dejected, he looked down, in disgust, at the figure still crouched beside him. 'Look what your *creation* has done!' he snapped.

Magia, dismissing him, rose, his eyelids burning like fire. Too long had he existed below the streets of Triora in darkness, that light had become a distant memory—and a constant threat to him.

'Look at it!' cried Oran, pointing.

Magia forced his eyes open: the chamber lay silent as he surveyed the decimation.

'Where is she?' Oran demanded.

'*Scampers!*' Magia whispered, in awe of her disappearance.

'She cannot have simply … *vanished!*' said Oran. 'For all the powers our kind possesses, even *we* cannot just … *disappear.* 'Tis impossible!' Confused, Oran paced about the chamber, leaving footprints in the ash beneath his feet. 'There is no secret door, no passageway to—or from—this room.'

'That *you* are aware of,' said Magia, rubbing his eyes.

Detecting the hint of sarcasm in the dark Warlock's reply, Oran advanced towards him, frustrated, brushing away the remnants of ash on his clothing. 'What do you know?' he pressed, noting Magia's crimson eyes mocking him.

'I did only what she asked of me,' he began, raising his hands in a display of innocence. 'She became obsessed with her "gift," craving it … begging for more. How *could* I resist? She was desperate to learn the secrets of the *Stregonaria.*'

Oran's mouth fell. 'You taught her the dark arts?!' he yelled. 'Have you lost your mind?!'

'Her appetite for knowledge was insatiable!' Magia returned, then stalled, detecting his nemesis' underlying jealousy. He smirked. 'I could not refuse her, Oran. She became increasingly … *persuasive!*'

Oran ground his teeth, incensed at the idea of them together—Magia's capable hands touching her, caressing her, and ... He shook the image from his mind, refusing to give in to his adversary's claims.

'You took your eyes off her, Oran,' said Magia. 'And while they were diverted, she was secretly educating herself, elsewhere.'

Oran ignored the taunts; he had nothing to gain by their purpose—save for the disturbing element of truth lurking behind them.

'There still may be time,' he thought out loud. 'She could not have gone far.'

Magia sneered at him. 'Is that your presumption, Oran of Urquille? That you *presume* you can find her? How *mortal* of you.'

'Aye, perhaps it is. But do not underestimate me. I'll find her. And I *know* where to begin.' He moved towards the blackened window. Nothing now remained of the thick, long lavish drapes that once concealed her privacy. 'If I'm not mistaken, Kristene has returned to the place where you crawled from—beneath the foundations of these streets.'

'You are more the romantic fool than what I recall from our earlier years, Oran. Your *Kristene* is long gone; L'Ordana now prevails, and will grow stronger with each passing day—should she accomplish her dreams.'

Oran turned to question him further, then stopped. He stared at the dark Warlock, slowly narrowing his eyes, scrutinising him. Then, with a sense of urgency, he marched towards his rival; Magia drew back as he reached for the collar of his shirt, unravelling it—the dark Warlock staggering, bemused by the abrupt and bold move.

'Where is it?' Oran inquired, staring at Magia's throat, failing to notice the two small, circular scars at the base of his neck.

Confused by his meaning, Magia looked down.

'Your amulet?' Oran persisted. 'Where is it? I saw it about your neck the moment I set eyes on you, this night.'

Magia's stunned silence confirmed Oran's inkling.

He shook his head.

'It seems you have underestimated your *creation's* powers. Does she know?'

'No—*Niente!*' Magia snapped, in defence. 'Nothing of its purpose.'

'Then why would she take it?' said Oran. 'Or, perhaps … you talk in your sleep, Magia.'

'I confess, I do not—'

'You heard her speak!' Oran reminded him. 'You saw the look in those eyes. If what you say is true, we will not be able to stop her. The knowledge contained in our amulets can only be known to *our* kind. Need I remind you of the repercussions should she …' He paused, surveying the devastation she had inflicted on them. 'She is hell-bent on revenge for the ruin placed upon her, and for the loss of those she loved. If *this* is an indication of what is yet to come—bearing in mind, her powers have not yet come to fruition—' He stopped dead, and stared into Magia's attentive eyes. 'Then what hope do we have? What hope? She will destroy us all!'

Magia's thoughts were drawn to the possibility of it. There was truth in it yet he was torn between the magnificence of that which he had created—a Sorceress with enviable powers he could master, or the pleasure he would gain in destroying her. He hesitated. No, the latter was out of the question.

'She must be stopped,' said Oran, pacing the chamber again. 'There is no question of it!'

'And where is *your* amulet …Warlock?' Magia retorted.

Detesting the continuous sarcasm in his tone, Oran returned it with vehemence. 'Unlike *you*, mine is hidden from the very prey that has taken yours. I, too, love her—but trust her?' He shook his head. 'Who is the "fool" now, Nera?'

Magia's face hardened. *She has made a mockery of me*, he realised.

'There is no way of knowing how long we have,' Oran determined. 'It may be months … years!' He pondered a moment, suddenly aware of the uncertainty of time. Regardless of it, he knew they could not be complacent. He would have to act quick. 'It has been two years since the Great One's passing. We have been fortunate, in that, the peace he brought to our world has remained stable. But now I fear it is threatened by her aspirations—no thanks to *you*—and should the Elliyan discover what has happened here …'

'Who is it you fear most, Oran?' Magia's sinister curiosity forced his attention. 'L'Ordana? Or the Elliyan?'

'I fear nothing—and no one.'

'Oh, I have my misgivings; I sense it. You fear losing the privileged life you have known, since our Great Lord's demise—and the inevitability of being summoned by the Elliyan once more. After all, you are a Warlock—still bound by duty.'

'And is that *your* presumption, Magia, or have you forgotten who *you* are?'

'I have not!' Magia hit back. 'I am reminded of it every day. I feel its burden about my neck.'

'A burden she has relieved you of without your knowledge.'

'She is welcome to it.'

Oran stared back at him, sceptical of his statement.

'What use is it to me?' said Magia, lifting his shoulders. 'After all, what interest would *they* have in a Warlock who had been tainted by darkness, in his defeat of death?' He smirked. 'Unlike you, my *friend*.' Oran cringed at the unlikely reference to their acquaintance. 'I had nothing to lose, whereas now … I have so much to gain.'

Oran grew suspicious of his contender's meaning; Magia could not be trusted. It was time to play pretence. 'Does she—L'Ordana—know *when*?' He was repelled by her new name and what it stood for; to speak it confirmed her existence in his world, raising his concerns for the unsuspecting mortals they walked among.

'No—*that* I am certain,' came the blunt reply.

Oran doubted it. 'Then I will ask you again. Where is she?'

'Who can say?' said Magia. 'But there is one thing I do not doubt.'

Oran clenched his fists, waiting, as he tried to hide his vexation.

'She intends to travel the Realms of our—this world—to …' Magia paused, amused.

'To?'

'Shall we say ... broaden her horizons?'

Aware of Magia's reluctance to reveal the extent of L'Ordana's intentions, Oran now read between the lines: his rival was—beyond a doubt—protecting his interests.

'If she's not found,' said Oran, 'she will search for the sinister side of each Realm. And when she finds it, she will master it—marking the end of our kind.'

'Then you had better search for her,' said Magia.

'You can be sure of it,' Oran replied with determination. 'And ... when I do ...'

'You will what?' asked Magia, sensing his uncertainty. 'Destroy her?' He threw back his head in laughter, then stopped abruptly. He glanced towards the window, hearing the heightened voices of the townspeople, their anger spurring them on—and towards the great house.

Oran watched the smirk slowly creeping across Magia's face.

'Such a pity they are too late. *Sciocchi!* I would have liked to have seen their faces—had she stayed; she would have annihilated every one of them. Naive *fools!*'

Oran ran to the window, pushing Magia aside. Wiping the ash away, he could see their torchlights dancing feverishly in the wind. As desperate thoughts raced through his mind, they were then severed, by the sound of a young, terrified voice, crying out for his attention.

Petrio! He had forgotten about the boy and Sofia.

'They are coming! They are coming!' The boy's voice grew louder with fear as he stomped up the stairs.

Oran looked back towards the bed. *I can't let him see her!* he thought, realising he had to spare the boy from Lucia's horrific death. Hearing his eager steps grow nearer, anxious to find him, Oran glanced at the door; it was still ajar.

'No, Petrio!' he cried, rushing to stop him.

He was too late.

The boy stopped dead on its threshold, his chest heaving.

Oran's heart sank as shock gripped the child's innocent face. Petrio's eyes slowly widened, his mouth gaping as he tried to comprehend the horrendous sight before him.

'Don't look, child!' Oran pleaded, taking him in his arms, duty-bound to protect him.

Petrio shook with fear as he stared at the bed. At first, he could not distinguish what remained of it, but when intuition took over ...

'Lucia!' he cried out.

The boy's scream was heard beyond the walls of the house—and Oran knew it; the voices outside heightened, having heard him. He promptly knelt before Petrio, diverting his gaze from the bed.

'Listen to me, boy,' he begged, shaking his small frame. 'This is not my doing. I swear it! Evil lives in this house. The man who stands behind me is responsible for it. Trust me, he will pay for—' He stopped, seeing the look of doubt in the child's watering eyes.

'What man?' he whimpered.

He stared at Petrio. The boy was grief-stricken. Doubting his words, the Warlock looked around, to discover they were the only two left in the desolate chamber.

Magia Nera had disappeared.

Chapter Ten

Turning to face the child again, Oran was now met by the look of blame. He felt condemned, reading the accusations in Petrio's innocent eyes.

Gripped by panic, Petrio struggled to break free from his hold.

'Petrio,' Oran begged, trying to maintain calm, for the boy's sake. 'I would *never* harm you. You must believe me.' Never before, in his long life, had Oran pleaded his innocence. 'Lucia died at the hands of …' His voice trailed, unable to tell the child *who* had committed the hideous crime on the girl he had fondly called "sister." 'Please—please, I beg that you trust my word, Petrio. Lucia's death shall be avenged. If I must travel to the ends of each Realm to find her killer, I shall do so.'

The boy looked at him, confused. 'Realm?'

Oran had forgotten himself. How could he even begin to explain? The boy was too young to understand; therefore, he chose to ignore it.

'That's why I must leave this place,' he said, relaxing his hold on him.

The reality of being left alone now terrified the boy. 'No!' he sobbed. 'You cannot leave me here,' he then pleaded—the tears now streaming down his flushed cheeks.

'I must go, Petrio. But I need you to—' Oran's words were interrupted by the sound of banging, coming from the street below; they were now pounding at *his* door.

'Are they coming for you—and the Mistress?' The boy had failed to notice her absence; he had grown accustomed to it. For once, Oran was thankful for her lack of presence.

The banging grew louder with every wasted second. Fearful, the Warlock swept the boy off his feet and then ran to his chamber. Locking the door behind them, he carefully placed Petrio down.

The room, brightly lit with small lanterns, was surprisingly simple in its means, so as not to attract unwanted attention to its hidden secrets. One prominent piece stood out in its simplicity: the gilded, hand-carved *Arezzo* mirror. Standing long and majestic, it commanded the attention of its admirer. Oran stood before it in a moment of vain weakness then sighed, seeing the truth behind the familiar reflection staring back at him; it looked worn—*he* looked worn. But there was no time to reflect on the damaging lifestyle that had led him to it.

From the corner of his eye, he then caught the boy staring up at him, waiting in anticipation, while occasionally looking over his shoulder, watching the door, expecting the intruders to barge their way in at any given moment.

Oran touched the mirror with his fingertips; it appeared to come to life.

Petrio's eyes widened in amazement as its glass quivered before parting, revealing a hidden chamber. But the boy's astonishment was briefly interrupted, by the deafening echoes of continuous banging below, and raised voices, yelling;

"Stregonaria!"

'As large and strong as they are, the doors will not protect us much longer, Petrio.'

'Sofia!'—the boy jolted, fearing for the safety of his friend— 'and the dogs!'

Oran drew back.

The dogs! he realised. *How could he have not seen them?* He wondered what had happened to their bodies, then felt the lump in his throat tighten; he could not bring himself to tell the child his beloved pets were dead. 'Do not underestimate Sofia,' he said. 'She's clever and knows what to do. She will look after them,' he added, feeling the guilt of his lie— knowing the necessity of it. 'Now, come with me.'

The instant they stepped through the mirror—away from view—the threatening mob crashed through the entrance of the great house.

Oran and Petrio were met by peaceful silence. The boy looked behind him, staring back into the chamber, its light penetrating through the glass, illuminating the space in which they now stood.

'Don't worry,' Oran assured him. 'We are quite safe.'

Petrio gazed around the small yet spacious annexe; it was filled with unusual items that looked valuable. He was in awe of their beauty and curious as to their origins. Oran watched the child's astonished face, his eyes preoccupied with wonder.

'This is all yours now,' he told him. 'A little premature, I must admit but … all yours, Petrio.'

The boy's mouth fell. He then looked up at him, speechless.

'I cannot begin to explain it all to you, Petrio; there's no time. But you must listen to what I *can* tell you. Do you hear?'

The child nodded with such enthusiasm, Oran smiled, imagining his head would fall from his little shoulders. The Warlock turned his attention to a small, walnut casket, sitting alone in a corner. The boy marvelled at its beauty: its deep grain was distinguished, and its hinged top highly polished, emphasising its exceptional quality, while the front was divided into three ebony panels—each one applied with pure gold rosettes—the centre panel containing a simple, brass lock.

The Warlock leaned over it, for a moment. Its lid then slowly lifted before them. Petrio moved closer to see. When Oran moved aside, its contents lit up the child's stunned face.

In his short life, the boy had never seen the bulk of so much gold. He quietly observed Oran hastily fill some tanned, leather satchels, with as much as he could, before closing the casket.

The Warlock promptly rose and turned away from the corner, to face a blank wall. He then placed the palm of his hand gently against it. From behind, a light ignited, taking the shape of a great sword. The wall seemed to melt away, to reveal an array of fine battle swords—one behind the other, in perfect order.

Oran tenderly removed two, gazing upon them like old friends. He turned to show them to the boy, but Petrio was stood frozen, staring back into the mayhem now taking place inside his Master's bedchamber. The intruders had demolished the door with axes, before ransacking the room. Petrio stepped back when one of them approached the mirror, pointing and peering at it; he was terrified they would break the glass and discover their hiding place. The man appeared to be saying something to his comrades, but Petrio could not hear them. However, it was evident from their actions the mirror would not succumb to harm.

'They take too much pride in exceptional things,' Oran remarked, watching them. 'Besides, they could not break it—even if they tried.'

Petrio looked sharp, holding his breath—the fear still evident in his innocent eyes.

'Don't worry,' said Oran. 'They cannot see or hear us.'

Relieved, the boy released his breath, letting go of his concern.

With nothing to find, the trespassers left as swiftly as they entered. However, Oran knew where they would go next. He turned away to study the wall again and placed his palm against it. This time, the light took the shape of his hand before revealing the one precious item he would not leave without.

Left suspended and alone in time, it had waited for its Master to retrieve it.

Oran reached out and held the item first, reacquainting himself with it; despite it being years, his amulet still sat perfectly within his hold— where it belonged. Carved by ancient craftsmen, to represent his Realm, each Warlock possessed his own; engraved with distinct—and unique— inscriptions, it identified its owner. Carefully, he lifted it.

Its thick, gold chain draped over his hand as he stared at the centrepiece. The captivating drop diamond remained as black as its origins. Oran looked deep into its core as if expecting the long-awaited "light of life" to show itself to him, announcing to each Warlock, that the new ruler—the Magus—had entered their world.

'What is that?' the boy asked, stretching his neck to see.

'Nothing that concerns you,' said Oran, quickly placing the chain around his neck. He felt revitalised by the amulet's touch as it came into contact with his skin. And yet, it lacked the strength and power he had hoped to feel from it. No, it was not yet time.

Kneeling before Petrio, he held his gaze. He noticed how his thick, dark locks were dishevelled. The boy hated having them combed. "It hurts!" he would always moan to Sofia, who strived, without success, to straighten them.

The child's eyes stayed fixed on his. Looking into them, Oran had always mused over their strange colour—sometimes grey, tinged with dark hazel or green. But at that moment, they appeared ashen grey and filled with doom.

'Whatever became of your parents?' he muttered.

The boy looked at him, puzzled.

'Forgive me, child. Just the ramblings of an ageing man.'

'You are not old,' Petrio replied, frowning.

Oran smiled at his innocence. 'I shall treasure the compliment.' The Warlock embraced him before returning to serious matters. 'Take this satchel to Sofia. There is enough gold to give you a comfortable life.'

'I don't want to stay here, Master. They might kill us. Please, take me with—'

'No—Petrio,' he snapped. 'They will not touch you.'

The boy jumped. He had barely noticed the Master's short temper— only when he was serious. This occasion now called for him to listen.

Sofia and her husband had been left childless and had accepted their fate. Oran had watched the bond between his cook and Petrio grow over time. Not once had he seen her scold him. He recalled the conversation he had had with her, concerning the boy's welfare, and the guilty look of joy on her face, despite her attempt to conceal it.

"Should anything happen to myself, or the Mistress, can I rely on you to take him into your care?"

Together, they agreed: should the circumstances arise, he would provide for their needs, while she and her husband would raise the child.

"You have my solemn word, *Signore.*"

He trusted her, implicitly.

'Sofia and Gino will take care of you—with this,' he added, pointing to one of the satchels. 'She can give up work, to look after you. Do what she says—educate yourself well, and—'

'Will you come back for me?' the child begged.

Oran was struck by the sadness and desperation in the boy's plea. Forced to lie again, he nodded. For an instant, he noted a hint of green in the child's eyes as they sparkled with hope.

'Are we agreed, Petrio?'

The boy reluctantly nodded.

'Good. Now—there is something I want to give *you*.' He turned and removed one of the swords.

The great weapon gleamed in Oran's hand, as though it had been newly forged. The boy admired the strange engravings on the blade, as it was held out to him.

'What do they mean?' he asked, his eyes widening.

'That it belongs to me,' said Oran, with an air of pride.

Petrio stroked the weapon with his small hands, its steel cold and smooth, its weight too much for his slight frame as he attempted to lift it.

'It is for you,' said Oran, trying to hide his amusement. 'For when you are older.'

Petrio gasped and looked up. 'Why are you giving it to *me*?'

'So that it will protect you. This sword cannot be taken from its owner. It must be *given*.'

'What will happen if someone tries to steal it from me?'

Oran grinned. 'Trust me, they won't!'

Petrio stared down at the oversized weapon in his hand, imagining himself using it in future battles.

Seeing the glint in his eyes, Oran reached out and took it from him. 'But it will remain here, for the time being,' he insisted. 'However, it is important I give it to you now, so it will know you when you return to claim it. Then learn to use it well—for the right purpose. Promise?'

Petrio nodded, gaping at the other weapons.

'Will you take them all?' he asked.

'This is all I require,' he stated, removing another, matching that of the one he had bestowed on the boy. 'I shall leave the rest behind, along with the life I had here.' He looked through the mirror, into the chamber. 'When they have finished their pointless search of this house, they will eventually give up, and leave.'

Petrio's bottom lip trembled as he fought back the tears. 'But what of Lucia?' The image of her smouldered body returned to haunt him.

Oran sighed. 'She is dead, child, and *they* will blame the one they are searching for—who is long gone.' He slowly nodded. 'Aye, they'll know, soon enough, there is nothing more for them, here.'

'But what of the Mistress?'

Oran hesitated, then frowned, another lump forming in his throat.

'Is—is she not going with you?'

'No,' said Oran. His reply was firm and final. 'You will never see her again.'

The boy gasped, then thought of the cook. 'Sofia! Will they take Sofia?'

Oran shook his head.

'I assure you, Petrio. They have no interest in a middle-aged servant.' He leaned towards him. 'But do *not* tell her I said that,' he added, winking. 'No, I promise you, Sofia is safe.'

Petrio sighed, relieved there would be someone to look after him until the Master returned.

'If, in the future, you need more gold,' Oran continued, showing him the casket, 'it is here for you.'

'But—how will I open it?' the boy asked, tilting his head.

Oran smiled at him with genuine affection. 'Your inquisitiveness will carry you through life, Petrio. Always ask questions yet be prepared for lies. Do not judge people, until you are certain of their character. And never presume. If something can be opened and closed … then surely it can be opened again. True?'

'But where is the key?' He frowned, lifting his shoulders. 'I saw none.'

Oran raised a brow, surprised. 'How clever of you,' he stated, then leaned forward, lowering his voice. 'There is none—because the key is my *name*.'

'Your name?' he gasped, captivated by the mystery of it.

'Watch, and listen,' said Oran beckoning him closer. The Warlock knelt before the lock and then whispered his name into the small hole. It was the first time Petrio had heard it. The lid slowly opened to the name of its overseer.

He turned to the boy. 'Did you hear it?'

Petrio nodded, still in awe of the new wonders being introduced to him.

'What is it, then?'

'Oran,' the boy whispered, for fear of someone listening.

'Remember it, for you can only speak it *here,* in this place. Do you understand?'

Petrio nodded again.

'Good,' said Oran. 'It will also take you through the mirror.'

'Does Sofia know your name?'

'No—nor will she. Do I have your word on that?'

'I promise, Or—' Petrio stopped himself quickly, by placing his small hand over his mouth, frightened the name should escape it.

Oran smiled, nodding in approval, then turned and stared back into his chamber. The door had been destroyed, giving him a glimpse into the dark hallway beyond. There was no sign of light or movement. *Perhaps they have gone*, he thought. He hesitated before making his decision, his concern now for the boy.

Taking the child's hand, they stepped through the mirror. As they moved to leave the secret room, something caught Oran's eye: the flickering of a tiny flame; it was making its way towards them, from outside the chamber. He promptly turned, intent on entering the mirror again.

'*Aspettare!*' The familiar voice was welcoming. 'Wait!' it called out, again.

Oran and Petrio stopped, after hearing Sofia's voice. The cook entered the room, heeding caution.

'Sofia, Sofia!' Petrio cried, throwing himself at her, then clinging to her for dear life.

She embraced him, still clutching the candle, its quivering flame creating dancing shadows on the walls and ceiling, as it shook in her trembling hand.

'Did they touch you?' asked Oran, rushing to her side, placing his hand on her shoulder.

'Me?'—she shook her head— 'they would not dare!'

Oran sighed with relief; if anything had happened to her … He refused to think of it.

They looked at one another. Without uttering a word, he could tell by the anguish on her face that she had been to the Mistress's chamber and seen the devastation. They nodded in understanding, mindful of the boy's feelings. Then, quietly indicating to one of the leather satchels, he placed it discreetly on the floor.

Sofia then knew it was time.

Oran looked down at Petrio as the boy clung to her thick waist. The lump formed again in his throat at the idea of parting from him—from them both; also, leaving behind the remains of Lucia, without giving her a decent burial. He knew Sofia would see to that.

'Look at your gowns, *bambino*!' she started, attempting to scold him. 'Your doublet is filthy!'

'Where are the dogs?' Petrio then asked, ignoring her, his innocent eyes looking up, waiting for her reply.

Sofia chewed on her lip, then glanced at Oran, her mind racing, thinking of something to say; she had seen them, too— *dead!* —at the bottom of the staircase when she rushed to lock the main doors against the approaching mob. And so, to spare the child the grisly horror, she had promptly removed them.

She cleared her throat. 'They ran from those men, Petrio,' she lied. 'I am certain they will return, in a day or so. But if they are too frightened to come back …' She paused, stealing another glance. 'I promise, we will get you two new puppies. Would you like that?'

His face lit up. 'Can I have three?'

'As many as you wish,' she promised, taking his hand, and leading him away. 'But, for now, it is important we go. *Si?*'

'*Si!*' he replied, nodding with enthusiasm.

He quickly turned, his excited eyes searching the room for his Master. Oran was gone.

Chapter Eleven

England: 1587

Captain Reece Molyneaux rode away from his young wife of two years, fighting the urge to look back; he was more than aware of her tearful blue eyes watching him leave. It pained him to know she would remain standing in the little doorway of their modest home, until he disappeared from view, even though he had insisted she stay inside. But no, she was determined to see him off.

He had hoped to have more time with her, and there was still much to be done. *When I get back*, he promised himself. At least he had repaired the leaking roof and secured the draughty windows, earlier in the year. Though the winter had been unusually mild, a hint of snow now hung in the cold, biting air; he could smell its icy breath bearing down on him.

He had dreaded telling her—but that was the way of it; the Kingdom had called him to duty. There had been much unrest since the execution of Queen Mary, and rumours were rife as to her demise. It seemed she had been implicated in plotting against Queen Elizabeth—her sister, no less. How much truth there was to it, he could not say, and yet somehow it did not surprise him. Therefore, once summoned, there was no question of it; he simply *had* to leave. No, there was no escaping the orders of his superiors.

His thoughts kept slipping back to his wife: their nights together, locked in each other's arms; the feel of her soft skin against his; her scent; and the heat of their passion, wanting it to last beyond the bounds of ecstasy. He would remember it all—those precious moments no one could steal from him—and would take them to the grave, should he never see her again.

She had desperately wanted him to stay, her agonising pleas still clear in his mind, and yet this time, there was something more to them; as harrowing as they were, he sensed an underlying tone of foreboding.

"Please, don't go!" she had begged, holding on to him. "We can go away, head north."

As tempting as it was—him considering it in a moment of madness—he knew he had no choice. They both did.

He closed his eyes, trying to *feel* her one more time, his growing ache weakening his determination, so much so, it compelled him to turn his head.

She waved slowly when he looked back. He watched as she drew the warm, green shawl over her head, concealing her long, fair hair from him. She wore the item—which had belonged to her late mother—as a reminder of her, giving her a sense of comfort each time he was called away. And if there was one thing, he was glad of, it was knowing he was now too far, to see the tears he knew she would shed for some time yet.

Still, his heart ached for her.

Their precious moments together crept back into his thoughts; he quickly shook them away. It was pointless torturing himself; he could not go back. Also, desertion was not an option. No, he would rather face the hounds of hell on the battlefield, knowing, as long as he survived, he'd be returning to her—the thought of her mere existence, urging him to stay alive. He would endure that, rather than face execution, for discarding his duties to the *Crown*.

Besides, he was no coward.

With those thoughts, along with her voice in his mind, his ache now turned to fear and dread. It disturbed him. He stopped, feeling the sudden need to turn his horse—to go back—to take her in his arms once more—to protect her. But the consequences—should he abandon his command—stuck with him like a disease; he would suffer the same penalty as the Scottish Queen. If not—worse.

Defeated by requirement, he pushed forward—the fading sound of his horse galloping further away from her, taking him to a fate unknown.

Reece eventually slowed his horse to a canter—confident his wife could no longer see him. Still, he tried not to think of her. But she had been his weakness since their first encounter. Surrendering to his thoughts, again, he recalled their simple wedding day:

It was winter, and the snow had fallen thick and heavy. They had met at the wedding of her close cousin, Lieutenant Rae Mackinnon, who still served under him. The unlikely invitation had come as a surprise. Tempted to turn it down, he had then felt obliged to attend. It seemed his whole life had been bound by duty … until that day.

She had taken him with a single glance, and after a determined introduction, he had made it his priority to pursue her. It was *she* who had given him the reason to face each dawn, to return safely, knowing she was there to love and welcome him. At times he tortured himself, wondering what fate would have delivered him, had he not attended that wedding. He was thankful he had.

Two opposites in every sense, their differences failed to keep them apart … Except one: her father. He had been reluctant to part from his only daughter—because of their difference in age and background— she, fifteen years his junior and from the Northern Kingdom, while he hailed from the South. However, had it not been for her mother's influence on her father, he imagined they would have eloped. He smiled, recalling her words of persuasion, as they waited for the approval after he had asked for her *hand*:

"What are a few years, husband? Can you not see when something is meant to be?"

Tragically, she did not live long after that—the consumption finally taking its toll on the poor woman. But, despite her illness, she lived long enough to see them wed before the *Grim Reaper* called—one month after.

"Why is it the good and the blessed die young?" her inconsolable husband had cried out at her funeral.

However, in the months that followed, he gradually lost the will to live, without his beloved wife. By simply wasting away, he waited for death to reunite them. Reece never forgot the words he spoke to him in his dying moments, before welcoming death.

"I could not have wished for a better husband for my daughter."

Until then, Reece had never imagined it could be possible to die from a broken heart.

Their parting, as always, was heart-wrenching, but he was content in the knowledge she was not alone, despite being strong-willed and stubborn.

While away, their Landlord, Thomas Drew and his wife, Marian, looked in on her from time to time and, in return, she tended their house and occasionally cooked for them—the couple insisting on paying her a small wage. Reece always noted, on his return, how much weight his Landlord had gained in his absence. Still, it was a means to her living, and Landlord and tenant got on well, allowing him peace of mind when the *Crown* beckoned.

His Captain's wage paid little, and when home, he was more than happy to provide basic lessons in sword-fencing to Thomas Drew. Though never discussed, he knew their Landlord and his wife feared for their safety, their religious beliefs being different to those they were acquainted with. Therefore, they chose to conceal them—an unfortunate necessity of the times.

Their neighbours, although sparse, were also kind, but old. Reece could not rely on *their* visits being frequent enough, making him anxious—should anything happen to the Drews.

"If something happens to me," he had warned her before leaving. "If I never come back, you must return home to your uncle's people, in the North."

At first, she had been reluctant, refusing to listen, but his insistence eventually won her over, forcing her to agree.

Reece had no desire to reach his destination too eagerly, regardless of the journey; it was long enough. Living short of two leagues outside Nottingham, it had been the perfect compromise: she loved to embrace the spirit of the forest, and it provided him with a temporary haven from the trials of war.

"Our little sanctuary," she had called it.

A sudden, sharp cross-wind made him shiver. Pulling up his collar, he cursed the lengthy winter and longed for spring. His hands brushed against his unshaven face, reminding him to remove the unsightly bristles when he reached his destination; it was expected of him, to promote a good example to those under his command.

He was glad of his knee-length coat. It was thick-quilted and partially covered with black leather, keeping him relatively warm. The quilt's vibrant shade of crimson stood out in the drabness of a winter that still clung to the bare branches of depressed trees. He glanced down at his boots; he would have to request a new pair, on his return—the leather so worn, they let the dampness seep through. He then checked his leather gloves, before putting them on. *They'll do*, he thought. There was only so much the *Crown* would replace, depending on your rank.

From the corner of his eye, he noticed tiny, white flowers growing sporadically, reaching out to hold on to the fading light of day. She had told him their name once. Again, he diverted his thoughts, doing his utmost to recall it. *Anything to break this quietness.*

'Can you remember their name, Altan?'

His mare jolted slightly, at the sound of his voice. It was only then he noticed it: the ghostly silence. He looked up, now aware of his surroundings. It was unusually still, and the evening twilight loomed fast. The night forest would soon bring with it its crossover of life. He imagined a stranger passing through in its re-awakening—them thinking it might be cursed, such were the haunting sounds that came from its depths. However, *he* was familiar with the wildlife that scurried through the foliage.

Usually comforted by their presence, they were, now, nowhere to be seen or heard. He looked into the woods, expecting to glimpse the eyes of night peering back at him; but with no moonlight, they would be difficult to see.

Nothing. Not even the sound of an owl, hooting down from above, could be heard. All of a sudden, he felt deserted on his journey—left alone in the universe with only his loyal mare for company.

Conscious of it, Reece felt an uncomfortable change in the forest, as though it were watching him. He checked the broadsword, fastened to the side of his saddle. *Just in case*, he thought. And should he be parted from it, he knew the item, concealed inside his right boot—his basilard dagger—the lethal, two-edged, long blade—was there for added protection. But somehow, despite their presence, they gave him little comfort, now.

Altan suddenly grew restless. Unable to calm his horse—much to his annoyance—Reece dismounted, to lead her on foot. But the mare, refusing to budge, continuously thumped the hard ground with her hoof, pointing towards something. She froze, her ears flicking back and forth, detecting a sound coming from deep within the forest.

Reece looked towards it, listening, while remaining vigilant. With each passing second, it grew louder and more familiar.

'It's only a fox, my beauty,' he said, recognising its distinguished call. Persistent in its human-like cry, he surmised the mammal was in pain. He inclined to leave it—to let nature take its course—but the sound of his wife's voice inside his head pleaded:

"You cannot abandon it, Reece! If it is gone beyond help, you must put it out of its misery, and bury it before the other wild animals have their way."

He sighed. 'She would never forgive me, Altan,' he said, stroking the mare's flank. She neighed in response to his touch, though, was still anxious. Perhaps she felt the fox's pain; after all, animals had a sixth sense. Rolling his eyes, he reluctantly turned on his heel, leaving his horse alone on the rugged path.

As darkness hovered above, waiting to descend on what remained of the dusk, Reece left the path, passing over the threshold and into the forest's domain.

The mammal's pain heightened as Reece made his way through the trees, in search of it. It seemed to call out to him, luring him closer.

He paused, checking his location. A few paces to his left, standing alone in the gloom, he identified the ghostly, dead branches of a large, silver birch, which had ceased to live, three winters before. Some locals claimed it to be the sinister work of witchcraft. He dismissed all notions. In truth, the tree's mysterious demise had been the fault of a poisonous fungus that had latched itself to the roots, bringing its life to an end. It had simply *died*, leaving the bare branches white—emanating an unearthly presence within the forest.

Hearing the fox's agonising cries grow louder, he knew he was close. As he passed the silver birch, heightening his pace, he glanced at its base—able to distinguish the outline of its killer, still clinging to its roots.

Reece looked above him. Despite the dark, his vision was good, and he could see the night sky; it was covered with heavy, white clouds, promising snow. He shivered, feeling the biting cold, tempted to go back to Altan, and continue on his journey. But when the fox cried out, again—now just a few yards away—he chose not to abandon it.

The fox fell silent, hearing the sound of advancing footsteps. Alerted to another presence, it looked up, its eyes wild with fear when Reece came into view.

Reece slowed on his approach until he came to the place where the helpless creature lay—mangled to the point of death—and felt pity for it in its ill-fated struggle, to hold on to life.

Removing the dagger from his boot, he looked down at the fox and then sighed, reluctant to kill it. At that very moment, Reece felt more compassion for it than for the lives he had taken on the battlefield. But that was war. The innocent creature, now staring up at him, deserved to die with dignity.

As though aware of its fate, the fox looked into his eyes, with a sense of peace.

'Forgive me,' he appealed, leaning over it. 'But, I do you a great favour.' Raising the basilard, Reece knew it would take one clean sweep, to bring it peace.

It never came.

Chapter Twelve

'*H*e wakes!'

Reece woke with a sudden jolt on hearing the foreign voice in his head. Dazed and confused, he groaned, feeling a stinging pain. Raising his hand, he discovered the wound where the blood had dried around it—at the base of his neck.

He winced. 'How did …?'

He struggled to recall what had taken place. *Think!* he told himself, searching through the mass of cloudy images in his mind. But nothing surfaced. Slowly he moved, aware of the freezing ground beneath him. His body felt leaden and ached, hampering the need to drag himself to his feet. Stiff and sore, he eventually forced himself to rise, but as he found his footing he jolted back, grasping his throat.

Choking, unable to breathe, Reece felt the air being cut off from his lungs. And when the stabbing pain took over, throbbing as it pulsated through his body, he imagined his end was near.

'*Do not fight it.*'

Hearing a voice, he struggled to reach out to it, silently pleading for help; but none came. Suddenly his chest contracted, throwing his body into spasm, in its final bid to cling to life. It was not how he had visualised his death.

'*It will pass.*'

As though the voice had released him from the clutches of death, Reece drew back and inhaled deeply, gulping the precious air, until he could speak.

'Who—who's there?' he croaked, cradling his aching body.

No reply.

Narrowing his eyes, he searched through the void yet still saw nothing. He hesitated, listening, then dismissed it, convinced his mind was playing tricks on him through his ordeal. It was nothing new to him; he had seen it so often in a soldier's final moments—how they rambled on, thinking they could see and hear their loved ones.

Trying to clear the bleariness from his head, Reece breathed in, deeply; however, the intake of breath made him dizzy. Losing his balance, he fell hard against a jagged wall, its sharpness grazing his hands, causing them to bleed. He stared at the dark-red liquid oozing from the wounds, its sweet smell surprisingly enticing.

Bemused, he took a few moments to compose himself, before looking down at his sorry state. His coat was torn and dirty, and the collar was stained with dry blood. He groaned, knowing he'd be severely reprimanded, for reporting for duty grubby and dishevelled looking. Next, he checked the inside of his boot for his dagger, relieved it was still there.

'Where—' He stopped when it occurred to him. 'My sword—my horse—my—' He was at a total loss as to where they could be—and as to where he was …

Stepping away from the wall, he let his eyes take in his strange circumstances, through the soft glow emanating from small lamps— one hanging on each wall. *Where the Hell am I?!* he asked himself, baffled. He looked around, trying to retrace his last steps: he had been in the forest …

Now, he found himself in an old, stone chamber—one that looked like a crypt, and yet there were no sarcophagi. It was empty, save for a few broken pieces of stone scattered on the floor. The low, arched roof was supported by elaborate stone pillars—each decorated with faded paintings and carvings, representing the beliefs of a bygone age. Its old, musty smell was overpowering to his senses, and he perceived no one had tread its vault for a long time … until now.

He turned and noticed a stone staircase, and made for it, scrambling up each step, halting when he reached the top. A set of heavily-chained iron gates were blocking his path—and behind them, a sealed wall.

There was no way out.

A spark of anger ignited inside him. 'Who keeps me here?!' he demanded, flinching at his echo. 'Show yourself!'

But the echo of words faded into the void, throwing back a bleak silence. He cursed it, stepping back before it dawned on him: 'I'm a prisoner!'

Disturbed by his predicament, Reece returned to the crypt's interior to think. But his throat was parched with an unquenchable thirst he could not apprehend. He hesitated, suddenly aware of the sound of trickling water coming from an underground stream. He thought it unusual—a well inside a stone chamber—though, not impossible. Panting, he moved swiftly—the sound of his footsteps carrying throughout, as he searched for it.

With each heavy step, Reece perceived he was being watched. He paused a moment, listening, drawing on his intuition. Instinctively he breathed deeply, inhaling a presence. Confused by his heightened senses, he surmised the emptiness of the crypt emphasised its recesses, leading him to envisage it was the ghosts from its past, keeping his company—and nothing more.

Distracted, and enticed by the constant trickle of water, he quickly found the little well, drawing on its contents; it tasted strange and unappealing. Despite it, no matter how much he consumed, he could not satisfy his dryness.

'Try as you may, it will not quench your thirst … Not yet.'

Reece spun round, water still dripping from his mouth.

The young-looking woman stood before him—small and slight in build. Her mane of chestnut hair fell perfectly down the length of her spine. Her skin was pale—tinged with the hue of youth. He sought to determine her age—no more than twenty years—a few younger than his wife, perhaps. She stared at him, her deep-set, brown eyes surveying him with curiosity.

'Who are you?' he asked, slowly rising.

She remained silent and poised as she followed his height, watching him subconsciously rub his aching neck.

With no more than three paces dividing them, Reece almost towered above her. And as he looked down, taking in her features, he noted a softness in her round face that hinted kindness—but her eyes told a different story; he detected a sadness behind their glower. He ventured to ask another question, to break her silence.

'What is your name?' he asked, daring to move towards her. She remained still, unthreatened by him. He paused, noting her attire, thinking it more suited to a man. The dark, rufous buckskin, gracing her body, was tailored to perfection, exhibiting the leanness of her frame. On her feet, she wore thick, black leather boots, up to her knees. She had a warrior look about her—ready for battle—yet held no weapon.

Intrigued by her casual nerve, Reece moved to question her further, then stalled, sensing they were not alone. His eyes glanced down as he considered the dagger concealed inside his boot.

'Her name is, Wareeshta,' declared another voice—clear and precise. 'And I believe you so bold as to *use* it.'

Reece looked about him, trying to locate the source, his hand open, ready to draw his weapon.

His wait was brief.

From the far end of the crypt, a figure came into view, their stride long and graceful. At first, it was difficult to distinguish their features, as they moved with confidence between the dim light and the shadows of the crypt. Whoever they were, their presence was strong; it exuded charge and influence.

Reece measured her height as she drew closer, noting she was taller than that of the silent one, who had now stepped aside to let her pass. Her thick, titian hair was lustrous and vibrant, its locks nestled high on her crown. A long, fine, ivory-silk gown—embellished with embroidered gold and silver—fell loose to the ground, covering her footwear. It flowed in perfect harmony with her every move, as though she commanded it—its paleness blending with that of her skin. A thick chain of the finest gold, hung gracefully around her long neck, disappearing beneath the bodice of the gown. Her lips were neither full, nor thin, and wore their natural colour.

She stopped, within feet of him, maintaining her distance.

For a moment, his eyes dropped slightly, noting the inclination of a silver scar, below her left ear. It was the one solitary flaw that stood out among her beauty. She noticed his observation of it.

'The one time I foolishly let down my guard,' she began. 'A mistake, I will never repeat. But you will meet the one who gave it to me, soon enough. I contemplated having him destroyed, for his insolence, but he was … *is* exceptional—as are you, Reece Molyneaux.'

He stared at her, speechless. *How does she know my name?*

'It is rare to see someone like you,' she stated, admiring his striking features. He wore his hair unusually short, its blackness contrasting with his pale, clammy skin. His cheekbones were high and his lips full.

'They are exquisite!' she added, observing the uniqueness of his stunning, green eyes. Lowering her gaze, she studied him further.

Reece stepped back, perturbed by her remark; he felt vulnerable and exposed in her company. Inside, he was shaking, uncontrollably. *What's happening to me?* he asked himself. *I don't under*—He looked sharp, his thoughts severed by her staring down at something. *What is she doing?*

As the smirk crawled across her face, it suddenly occurred to him: *She's challenging me!*

Battling against his instincts, Reece shook his head, desperately trying to resist. However, the soldier inside him was urging him on—*telling* him to fight.

He reached down …

The sound of steel, colliding with the hard ground, reverberated throughout the crypt.

Reece grasped his scalding hand, feeling the excruciating pain that had been inflicted on him by his dagger's searing handle. He flinched when the smell of burning flesh rose, attacking his heightening senses. With anger rising from deep inside him, he looked up, his hostile eyes now glaring at her.

'You *knew* it was there!'

She grinned, mocking him with her intimidation. 'Lesson learned!' she remarked, drawing closer. When she did so, Wareeshta moved with her, keeping near. 'Look at your hand, Reece!' she then stated, pointing with her chin.

He stared down, in disbelief, watching the skin repair itself until all that remained was a faded scar. 'Impossible! How is this …?' He shook his head.

'It is a reminder, each time you look at it, *never* to threaten me again,' she warned. 'Let us hope it will be your first … and last.'

'What have you done to me?' he said, holding out a fisted hand at her. 'Who are—'

'What you are feeling is none of *my* doing, Reece,' she continued. 'The blame falls on Wareeshta. She merely follows my orders.'

'I—I don't understand. What do you want from—' Reece stopped dead as her eyes rested on his. His mouth fell open, seeing the likeness; it was uncanny.

She smirked, then inched towards him, allowing him a closer look—intent on playing with his emotions. 'What do you *see*, Reece?' she teased, lifting her head. 'Do you see … *her?*'

He slowly drew back, his mouth gaping in horror. 'My wife!' he cried out, wanting to lunge at her, but was unable to. 'If you harmed her, in any way, I will—'

'What would you do, Reece?' she replied with a disparaging smile. 'Kill me? How tremendously ambitious of you!'

Inside, a newfound strength began to surge through his body yet, somehow, he knew he was incapable of using it against her.

'I will tell you what I want from you; all in good time, though. As for your wife …?'

He held his breath, prepared for the worst.

'She is unharmed, and shall remain so …'

'Unless?' he snapped.

'You *are* quite the arrogant one,' she returned.

'I take it, you wish to make a bargain,' he stated.

She hummed. 'Somewhat,' she said, turning away from him.

He quickly marked Wareeshta's close attention to her every movement, rarely taking her eyes from her. It was evident the silent one was her protector or guardian.

She stopped and, turning her head slightly, hesitated as though distracted. 'Do you have any children, Reece?'

The question was intrusive and unexpected. He declined to answer.

She turned to face him again.

'I thought not,' she taunted, playing on his silence. 'That is unfortunate,' she added, tilting her head.

'Then, why ask?' he retorted, gritting his teeth.

From the shadows of the crypt, he heard the distinct, low sound of someone laughing, like they were mocking him. He moved his gaze from the two women, searching for it until the slow, menacing movement of a large figure caught his eye. He felt uneasy, knowing he was being scrutinised.

Show yourself! he wanted to yell, sensing the threat.

'Where have you been, Kara?' she demanded.

He quickly glanced back at her. She appeared unperturbed by the hidden presence, her authoritative tone telling him *who* was in command. And when she spoke, Wareeshta discreetly stepped back, suggesting *she*, however, was intimidated by the hidden figure, as they lingered in the shadows contemplating their entrance.

After much deliberation, they decided to come forth.

'Searching for more,' they finally replied, coming into view, their raspy voice deep and contemptuous in tone.

Reece threw a second glance as the figure revealed herself in her true glory, scrutinising her appearance on her approach. Her stride matched that of her tone—bold and impertinent. She stood, he surmised, a few inches above his height while towering over her Mistress, by a good foot, and dwarfing the silent one.

Dressed in an elaborate bodice of silver armour, her strong physique startled him. The baroque, grey tunic she wore beneath it barely covered her muscular thighs. Silver guards, matching her armour, protected her lower legs and arms. She wore it like a second skin. Her long, golden hair was set in several plaits—neatly tied back—and held in place by a thick, band of gold on her forehead. Set in its centre—in the line above her crooked nose—a large, black-onyx stone took pride of place.

He might have thought her impressive, had it not been for her icy, grey eyes, their coldness betraying what truly lay beneath her exterior. Above her shoulder, he noted the hilt of a large sword, its markings foreign to him. He could not, however, deny his admiration for the weapon in her hand. The deep, emerald-green lance stood taller than its owner, its long, silvertip, extending its length. The make he could not distinguish, and yet its likeness was similar to glass.

'Were you successful?' her Mistress enquired.

Pausing in front of him, Kara surveyed his features with subdued interest, forcing him to raise his eyes slightly. He sensed the malice in her scrutiny.

'I was not … my lady,' she answered, in a flat, distinct tone.

'Then we shall not pro-long our stay,' she replied. 'Besides, we have begun to attract unwanted attention.'

She turned to Wareeshta. 'We will leave as soon as he is ready—finish it!'

Wareeshta now turned to Reece—the bleak expression on her face, alerting him.

'Finish what?!' he blurted.

Kara sneered at him.

'Are *you* also immune against my dagger?' he retorted, reaching for the weapon still lying on the ground. As his hand hovered over the blade, his fingers twitched, wanting to snatch it up—to draw it across her throat … He changed his mind.

Kara looked at him with contempt; he ignored her.

'What *is* your intention?' he demanded, addressing the nameless one as she turned to leave. 'To kill me in cold blood? For what?'

Kara and Wareeshta stood back as she approached him. 'As you are so insistent,' she said, 'then I shall tell you, Reece. Your world is plagued by war. There are too many Kingdoms, ruled by leaders who thrive on greed and destruction. I have seen young, valiant men perish on your battlefields … and for what? To see who should claim who's land? To satisfy their vanity? Such a useless waste of life—not to mention time—when their courage can be used elsewhere … with added benefits.'

Reece looked at her, confused. '*My* world, you say? Is it not also yours?'

She paused, her eyes drifting in a moment of recollection.

'It was—once. But I was cast out. *You,* like so many, share your world with *another*—one you are not yet aware of.'

'Impossible!' he replied. 'There is *only* one world.'

'Shared with a greater power,' she informed him. 'However, it is concealed by your ignorance. *This* is your first taste of it. Take a look at them, Reece!' she said, acknowledging Kara and Wareeshta. 'I saw the expression on your face when you saw them. Do you know who—*what*—they are?'

Reece threw them a sideward glance, keeping his silence.

'They, too, were discarded from their kind. It was by chance we came upon each other. Three outcasts seeking—'

'Revenge?' he scorned, interrupting her. 'Or perhaps—absolution?'

She held his gaze a moment. 'We three are beyond *that.*'

'Then I assume it's revenge.'

'And I *will* have it!' Her reply was calm and definitive.

The sense of dread that had consumed him on his journey now finally revealed itself, in the three forms standing before him. But he had yet to discover his purpose in all of it.

'Only *one* ruler hails over "Five Realms" as they are referred to by some,' she continued. 'You will soon discover that power, Reece. It is universal; there is none like it. But their Ruler has been dead for many years, and some wait, in reserved silence, for the coming of his replacement. We all wait … for our own reasons. The *child*, however, has not been born yet. But when he takes his first breath, I shall know it, and will seek him out.'

Reece saw her intentions unfold, between every sinister word she spoke.

'You would *murder* a child?' he said, unable to comprehend the deed.

'I wish to gain all power over both worlds,' she revealed. 'I intend to unite them—as their one Ruler.' Her eyes blazed with the thrilling notion of possessing it, in its entirety.

'You?!' he responded, trying to grasp her full meaning.

'But I cannot do it alone,' she said, her eyes resting on his, with purpose. 'With the aid of my loyal servants, I can and *will* achieve it. Therefore, in answer to your question, Reece … I expect to destroy the "One" we all wait for, however long it takes.'

Her words resounded in his head, compelling him to ask in desperation; 'What, precisely, *are* your plans for me?'

Chapter Thirteen

'I have created a multitude of fine warriors from every corner of this world,' she began. 'Unique in their making, they are virtually impossible to destroy by your—by mortal man. I have Wareeshta to thank for it.'

His eyes darted towards the young, silent woman. However, knowing his fate, Wareeshta diverted her gaze from him, aware of what she would be asked to do, again.

'Her inherited "gift" is to be commended.'

Gift? he thought, baffled by her meaning.

'Our numbers are increasing ...' She paused, casting a perturbed glance at Kara. 'But they are younger and need proper guidance. The one who did *this*,' she said, pointing to her scar, as a reminder to him, 'has been their tutor for more than a decade—but seeks more help. I discovered him in the Far East. Strange in his ways, but a Master of swords, no less. As with him, I seek the great skills and knowledge of another—one who, also, has experience of the battlefield.'

Reece, narrowing his eyes, slowly lowered his head with suspicion.

'Which leads me to *you*,' she added.

Sensing the life, he had always known, about to be cruelly snatched from him, Reece shook his head.

'No!' he cried, in dismay, as its reality began to sink in.

'I will not be part of this ... whatever *this* is. I'll—'

'Oh, but, Reece,' she interrupted, 'You have no say in the matter. You see, what I want from you is your commitment to me.'

'My commitment is to *my* kingdom and my wife,' he snapped, his panic betrayed by the nervous fear in his voice. 'I serve no one else.'

'I admire your passion and loyalty, Reece,' she said. 'But, should I return you to her, the seasons will pass swiftly. You will watch as time steals her youth until you witness the inevitability of her passing.'

'And I *will*,' he returned.

Again, he heard Kara's snide laugh.

'No, Reece,' she said. 'You see—*you* will continue to live ... for centuries to come, serving *me* in *my* kingdom.'

He glared at her, sickened by what she was saying, and yet it made no sense to him. Shaking his head in denial, he felt the stab of pain return as it shot through him.

'Tell me, Reece, does it hurt?'

He threw his hand on his throat, feeling the puncture wounds, then pressed hard on the area, as if trying to prevent the pain from inflicting itself on him further.

Kara grunted, revelling in his inner torture.

'What *have* you done to me?' he implored.

'You have been given the gift of *immortality*,' she replied, casually, 'until time dictates your demise. You see, Wareeshta is not all that she seems. Her conception was far from *normal*; her mother was a *mortal* and, while she maintains many of her human qualities—which cannot be helped—it is the "gift" she inherited from her father that surpasses her mother's weakness.'

She paused, studying him. 'You see, Reece, Wareeshta can easily ... take or give life. For one so small and slight, do not underestimate her abilities.'

His face contorted in agony as he dropped to the floor. 'This can't be happening!'

'Say farewell to the life you once knew, Reece Molyneaux,' she informed him. 'From this moment on, you are bound and committed to another. Your loyalties now lie with me. However, I am not so cruel as to deny you everything from your world. You shall have your horse, and when her time comes, I will replace her with another, then another ... then an—'

'You will *not* decide my fate!' he yelled, launching at her.

106

She flinched at his unsuccessful attack. Despite it, the attempt impressed her greatly.

'He is not like the *others*, my lady,' said Wareeshta, in a soft voice. 'The first time was not enough. We will need to keep a watchful eye on him.'

Reece looked from one to the other, his pain gradually increasing, spreading through his body while they casually discussed his fate.

'My—my wife!' he pleaded, struggling to come to terms with his new reality. If he could not live his life accordingly—be it to a ripe old age—to die, still in his youth, on the battlefield—or to lead a quiet one, with the woman he loved—it would be too much to bear.

'You shall not steal my life!' he vowed, retrieving his dagger. 'No—it is *mine* to take!'

The basilard seared into his flesh as he turned it on himself. But his efforts to drive the dagger into his heart were in vain; no strength of his own would allow it. Overpowered by the unknown force, he let the blade fall to the ground.

'*Now* do you understand?!' she exclaimed, glaring at him, her triumph tainted with anger. 'You *cannot* destroy yourself! Only *I* possess the power to do so. Accept your chosen fate, Reece Molyneaux.' She grinned. 'You belong to me now!'

Silence reigned over the gloomy crypt for what seemed like an eternity.

Reece hung his head, overcome with despair. He sought to recall his wife's face, but it seemed to fade from his memory. Distraught, he fought to hold on to her. 'I—I can't see her,' he stammered. 'I—I'm losing her.'

Repelled by the malevolence exuding from her, Reece stared at his captor—no longer seeing the beauty in her outward appearance.

'Do not torture yourself,' she said. 'You will forget her in time—the one thing you will have plenty of.'

'If this is my fate,' he replied, 'I want assurance she will come to no harm.'

'You are in no position to ask favours,' Kara sneered, tempted to strike him.

'I think it a fair bargain,' he persisted, to the nameless one, desperate.

She held him in suspense, contemplating his plea. 'Agreed,' she then replied, holding his gaze. 'A life for a life!'

Though he felt some solace in her agreement, his heart sank, leaving him in deathly silence.

Suddenly she reached out, placing her cold, slender hand on his forehead. He tried to recoil but fell to his knees as she grounded him with her touch.

'What are you doing?' he said, 'I—I thought we agreed!'

Tilting her head, she smiled. 'Merely a precaution,' she said. 'I need to make certain you do not remember all I have just told you. I cannot abide traitors.'

He frowned before a sharp intake of breath took hold of him. Feeling the pressure from her cold fingertips, the details of her plans slowly dissolved from his mind. Satisfied, she drew back, removing her hand. His head spun in a drunken stupor as he struggled to stand.

'Do what you must, Wareeshta,' she instructed, finally taking her leave. 'When he is ready, bring him to the castle.'

Looking at her, through a daze, he attempted to call out. 'What … what is your—' But his words were slurred, making little sense. He tried to focus, staring into the shadows as she disappeared from view, her silence leaving its mark.

Staggering to his feet, Reece faced her two loyal servants, completely defenceless against them—and unaware of their intentions.

'He is all yours,' said Kara, stepping away, with a smirk on her face. 'For now.'

'Where are you going?' asked Wareeshta.

'It is none of your concern,' she replied, in disdain. Then, turning her attention back to Reece, she deliberately leaned towards him.

He lifted his nose to the sickly, scent of lemon oil wafting from her hair; it was overpowering, and yet strangely appealing.

'Mourn her now,' she whispered to him. 'For she will die, soon enough.'

Kara's words had little time to resonate as Wareeshta descended on him, her swiftness taking him unawares. Inside, he felt the power of her gift at work, it gradually taking control. But before it took its final hold, he caught a shocking glimpse of Kara, as she turned on her heel.

Chapter Fourteen

Balloch: Scotland - 1627

'They wish to see you!'

The boy stood, determined and patient, waiting for a reply. He refused to repeat his words; once was sufficient.

Sparks continued to spit from the constant spin of the grinding stone as its Master held the blunt axe in his strong hands with firm precision. He had been wise to the boy's discreet presence, for some time, speculating when he would finally present himself. He stopped what he was doing and waited for the stone wheel to grind to a halt, irritating his uninvited visitor.

'"Demand" is the more appropriate term I should imagine they used,' came his sharp reply.

Oran looked down at the boy's arrogant expression as he stared up at him, devoid of emotion. Barefoot, and dressed in a grubby shirt—hanging loosely over a pair of breeches—Oran surmised the child could easily pass as a village local.

'Did you think *they* would not find you?'

'I had hoped,' said Oran, toying with the axe in his hand, before placing it on his workbench.

The boy's lifeless, grey eyes surveyed it. 'Not quite the weapon of a Warlock,' he sneered.

'No—but that of a hunter,' Oran returned.

'A hunter, no less?' replied the child, observing the swords and daggers waiting their turn for the grinding stone. 'It seems you have traded your sword for—'

110

'If I have … what of it?'

'It would *displease* them.'

Oran leaned down towards the boy in a threatening manner. 'Now that you have *found* me,' he hissed in his ear, 'I *insist* you tell me what they want.'

The boy, unperturbed, held his gaze a moment, then replied; 'You covered your tracks with extreme care, Lord Oran—making it difficult to locate you.'

'And here you are—years later. What took you so long?'

Ignoring his comment, the child stepped away into the warm sunlight, its intense rays highlighting the red strands in his dark locks. But the overbearing heat forced him back into the shade of the small workshop.

'What do they want of me?' Oran growled, frustrated by his mere presence.

'I think you know,' the boy replied, scratching his skin.

'I think not,' Oran retorted.

'It would not be wise to deny them *council*,' he reminded the Warlock.

Oran pondered over the statement, then sighed. 'Why now?'

'Unsettling signs are coming from the Southern Realm of Ockram.'

Oran shrugged.

'I have sensed nothing.'

'Naturally … since you chose to sever yourself from your duties,' the boy hit back. 'And, because of *that*, you have failed to notice the goings-on in our world.'

'I have made a life here—a normal one for myself. It occupies my time.'

'A wife *and* siblings, I see,' the boy remarked.

Oran bent his eyes with suspicion.

'You *have* done well. However, if you ignore their summons—'

Enraged, Oran reached out towards the child, snatching him in his grasp, then, raising him above his head, kept him suspended.

'If you dare threaten my family …' he started, glaring up into the boy's cold eyes.

The boy smirked down at him. 'Not I, Oran of Urquille. The—'

'Oran! Stop!'

Oran turned, meeting the glare of anger on his wife's face, and groaned.

Rosalyn Shaw stood shocked at what she had witnessed, almost dropping the basket she held in her hands. She gasped when her husband released the boy, who dropped to the ground, gently finding his feet again.

Unharmed, the child smiled at her, his wry grin making her feel uncomfortable. It was then she noted something disturbing in his eyes: the lack of warmth and innocence usually associated with a normal child.

'They expect you,' he stated, turning to address Oran. 'You know how to find it?'

Again, the boy waited for his reply. Oran quickly glanced at his inquisitive wife, before returning his answer with a slight nod, fearing he had just signed away his quiet life.

'Then it is agreed,' the boy concluded. As he walked away, he stopped and looked back at the Warlock, adding, 'Do *not* keep them waiting.'

Rosalyn felt a chill as he casually strolled by her, maintaining his sinister smile. She watched after him until he faded from view, then turned to her husband, catching him breathe a heavy sigh of relief.

'Ah!' he said, reaching for the basket of food draped on her arm. 'I'm starved!'

'No, you don't, Oran Shaw!' she argued, snatching it away from his opened hand. 'Not until you tell me …'

'To come between a man and his food is taking a great risk, *Wife*!' he replied, mocking her, hoping she would succumb to his witty charm. But he sighed when she slowly tilted her head, and lifted a brow, fully aware of her expectations of him.

Her unusual eyes—one, deep blue, the other, green—examined him with an inkling. Beads of sweat clung to her dark brow after walking the distance from their home, to the village. Her face was brown, where the summer sun had kissed it, as were her bare arms. Quite often she would alter her clothing to suit the seasons. The long, pale-green dress she wore had no sleeves, displaying her shapely arms. Her long, golden-brown hair was tied neatly in a single plait, away from her kind, round face.

But at that moment, he could only see anger displayed across her features—the crease on her forehead fixed, like her stare, as she waited. He moved to embrace her; she stepped back, tilting her head to the other side. This, he knew, was one battle he could not win.

'I must go!' His admission was defined, and solemn.

Rosalyn drew back her head, her eyes widening. 'Where? When?' she asked, surprised by his prompt reply. 'And that boy! Who is he?'

Oran opened his mouth to answer, then hesitated. 'It doesn't matter, who or …' He paused again, unable to explain. 'Soon. I must leave, soon.'

She moved to protest.

Sensing her agitation, he quickly stepped closer. 'We spoke of this, Rosalyn—when we made our commitment to one another—when I told you *who* I was. It was possible—probable—this day would come.'

'And what of our children, Oran?' she reminded him, her voice breaking as she felt the swell of tears in her eyes.

He reached out to wipe them away.

'You cannot leave us!' she blurted, recoiling from his touch. 'What would I tell them?'

'What we agreed,' he said. 'Do you remember?'

'I have *never* forgotten,' she replied, slightly vexed. 'I am reminded each time I look at him, all the while hoping *they* would leave us be.'

'Something is afoot,' he informed her, looking out into the openness of the busy village, expecting "it" to materialise. People they had befriended, since their arrival in Balloch—almost thirteen years prior—passed his workshop, daily, engaging in conversation or merely exchanging a friendly wave, as they went about their business.

'What is it?' she asked, lowering her voice, with mounting concern.

'Oh, something or—'

'Is that wee axe of mine sharpened yet?'

Oran and Rosalyn jumped at the sound of Heckie Grant's bellowing voice, his great head peering at them, somewhat amused at the reaction he had received. His large frame blocked the sunlight from their view. Rosalyn turned away, diverting her eyes from the kilt he so proudly wore—in the name of his family tartan—unable to bring herself to look at his thick, hairy legs.

'Would that be some of your fine baking, lass?' he asked, eyeing the basket. His cheeks roared flaming red from the heat, while the fine strands of hair, still left on his crown, clung to his face. He lifted his head, inhaling. 'Auch! I can smell your cooking for miles.'

'Aye, it is,' she retorted, turning to face him, mindful of staying focused on his face. 'And you know where you can purchase it, too.'

Oran threw his head back in laughter. 'I fear she has you, Heckie.'

'Aye, indeed,' he responded, casting him a wink. 'Auch! And 'tis worth every penny, at that.'

'The axe will be done by the end of the day,' Oran promised.

'Grand. Sure, I'll send the wee lad to fetch it, later.'

'It will be waiting.'

Heckie beamed and nodded his large head, before stomping away.

'You see the life we have here, Oran,' Rosalyn began. 'These people have been good to us. I have no desire to leave it, or them, for that matter.'

'Nor shall you,' he assured her, staring into the space his neighbour had left behind.

She eyed her husband, unsure of his thoughts; regardless of them, now was the time to speak out. 'He is not going with you, Oran!' she stated, folding her arms in defiance.

He promptly returned to her side, determined to please her.

'Once I've left here, I believe you will all be safe, despite what—' He stopped himself. 'Look, *I* am the one they summoned, therefore, it is *my* duty to go. Gill stays here, with you.'

'Do you think they will—'

'No!' he snapped. 'They *can't* take him from us. It is I who must give him up.' He sighed. 'No, Rosalyn, we are not ready to let him go—not

114

yet. *I* will decide that, by making it my business to protect him—to protect you all.'

She shook her head, doubting him.

'I fear time may have run out for us, Oran. The past always finds its way back. Perhaps we *should* have given him up—when he was—'

'And deny him the normal life we have given him?' he said. 'No! Gill is *our* son, which is why I kept him hidden from them. He needed to experience a normal life, so he could understand what it's like to live as a—'

'But it might have been easier, in the long run,' she cut in, disputing the issue, 'had we done so.'

'It was never going to be easy,' he said, softening his voice. 'I *know* you, Rosalyn Shaw. You could not have parted with him, then. You would not have allowed it.'

Rosalyn sighed. 'When?' How long?' she asked, her eyes fixed on his.

'A week … perhaps two …' he lied, shrugging, then glanced at Heckie's axe—anything to avoid her persistent stare.

'In other words,' she said, 'you don't know.'

He smiled in admiration of her perception and turned to her again. 'You know me better than anyone, Rosalyn,' he professed.

'And you know better than to lie to me,' she retorted.

'Forgive me?' he begged, pulling a solemn face.

She rolled her eyes. 'As always.'

For several moments, they held each other's gaze, contemplating one another's thoughts, until she nodded, decisively.

'Then I will ensure everything continues as normal,' she said, 'until you return.'

'I *will* come home, Rosalyn,' he promised. 'Whatever their intentions, I will find a way to prevent this. Who knows, perhaps there is another who could take his place. But I will do everything I can … even if I have to deny my son. You *have* my word,' he added, placing a tender kiss on her forehead, before moving down to her lips. She leaned closer, encouraging him more, when he pulled away, playfully. 'Now, where is that food?'

Once more, Oran found himself alone in his small workshop, weighed down with the dread of having to say goodbye to his wife and two children. But there were things to tend to before his departure.

Removing the leather apron, protecting his shirt and waistcoat, he cast it aside. Although, not his usual garb, he proudly wore a kilt—the green, blue and red plaid associated with the Shaw clan—to fit in, to belong. Stroking the beard—he had purposely grown to make him feel part of the working male community—he decided he would remove it before leaving, having never bonded with its presence. Rosalyn, however, had admired it, taunting him on occasion, over the playful looks he had regularly attracted from the local women.

Concealed beneath a worn, thick red-woollen blanket, a plain oak coffer sat unnoticed. Simple in style, he had carried it with him throughout his travels, protecting the few items he held precious. Kept in the privacy of their home, for many years, he was eventually forced to remove it from the inquisitive eyes of his son and step-daughter.

Oran ran his hands over the smooth surface of the chest, before removing the little brass key from the pocket, inside his waistcoat. He carefully inserted it, turning it to the right, four times, until he heard the familiar sound of it letting him in. He drew back the lid. It made no sound, considering the length of time he last looked upon it. But there had been no reason to … until now.

Strewn across the surface, lay an assortment of daggers and swords—weapons he had used in the past—which were of no significance to him now. Beneath the old weapons lay the attire he had not worn in decades. He looked down at the kilt he wore and sighed. 'This will not do,' he mumbled to himself. 'Not where I'm going.' His other clothing—black buckskin trousers, matched with a long, dark-tanned leather waistcoat—would be more suitable; and folded neatly inside, was a wide, leather sword belt. But these were the decoy—the alibi to what truly lay beneath the covering of fine, black silk, concealing its invaluable contents.

116

Oran drew back the luxurious fabric, where the Albrecht sword waited for its Master's hand, to retrieve it once more.

Inlaid in fine, yellow gold, on the pommel, was his *nomen*—his name—engraved in sunken reliefs, displaying ownership. The black, shagreen-covered grip, still bore the indentation of his right hand from centuries of battles they had fought together. He raised it high, still in admiration of the impeccable workmanship created especially for him. Each Warlock held their own, forged to their uniqueness.

Oran slowly removed the scabbard, protecting the blade; it drew smoothly, and silently. The steel blade was still sharp, as though he had forged it himself the day before. And yet, he knew, no matter how advanced his experience, he could never create something as magnificent as the weapon he held in his hand.

In the history of his ownership of it, it had never required sharpening—nor would it. Its steel hailed from an unknown source, stemming back to the reign of the first known Magus. The blade gleamed, reflecting his image on the polished metal. Tiny, gold inlays of hieroglyphics adorned the surface, marking their long and glorious history.

For an instant, Oran thought of its other, wondering where it lay, or in what battles it may have participated; he hoped it had not been the latter. Musing over his own, he had hoped to never use the Albrecht again. But those hopes, he knew, were slowly diminishing.

Oran returned to the coffer, his mind preoccupied as he subconsciously continued to rummage through his past. He then winced, feeling the stab of something sharp. He drew his hand out, and seeing beads of blood trickling from his finger, quickly licked it clean. Hesitating, his furrowed brow curious, he reached back in, carefully removing the cause of his "injury."

'Now how could I have forgotten you?' he muttered, turning the item over before replacing the pin in its clasp. A little tarnished, he rubbed it gently on his shirt, before looking it over.

It weighed heavily in his hand—the piece made of solid silver, derived from the Romans whose hacksilver was once used to bribe troublesome Clans and Tribes, centuries before. The pieces were then reused to make pins, chains and finger rings; and, because of its value, many of the Clans had broaches made to symbolise their status and pride. Therefore, he had one fashioned, to mark his lineage, to give him that sense of "belonging."

The Clan crest, he held in his hand, was a representation of who he was, who his family were—the name *Shaw* allegedly connecting them to the ancient Picts of the Highlands.

'Fide et Fortitudine,' he whispered, reciting the motto engraved on its front: though worn with age, and barely legible now, he knew it by heart: *By Fidelity and Fortitude*. It was everything he, like his forebears, had stood for. And seeing the dagger—clenched in a fist, in its centre— reminded him of the strength and pride he, too, held in his ancestry.

'You belong to Gill now,' he told it, his intention, to give it to his son before his departure. But he quickly changed his mind; the last thing he wanted was to worry Gill; the boy would think he was never coming back. 'No. *When* I get back,' he said. Determination set in stone, he vowed to return to his family, before his son's coming of age … before Gill …

He sighed; there was a possibility, however, that his son may never be a father himself. Regardless of it, he would make sure Gill would never forget his family name.

Returning the broach to the coffer, he glimpsed the corner where he had last left it—the small, long ebony box, inlaid with mother-of-pearl. He reached out to touch it, letting his fingers and thoughts linger over the sentiment of the item. Although the temptation to look into his past was enticing, his willpower was stronger.

'No time to dwell on you,' he told it. *What's past … is past!*

It was the most prized object, resting alone in a small, black-leather pouch, tied with a simple burgundy cord, that he required. He had sensed its energy when the key was inserted, unsure what to expect.

As with the Albrecht, the item had remained hidden from view. Detached from his world—and the world of mortals, for decades—he had remained disinterested and uninformed as to any of its happenings, choosing to forget his past in exchange for a normal, though, secret life.

For years, the amulet's centred diamond had stayed dormant and black—in mourning for its lost Magus. And so, it remained in its lifeless state … until his son took his first breath, fourteen years before.

Oran hesitated before opening it, recalling that fateful night.

From the moment his wife announced she was expecting their first child, Oran welcomed the news, feeling his life would finally be complete, after leaving his turbulent past behind.

Dead and buried, he had told himself that night, letting it go. *My family are now my priority.*

But in the weeks, leading up to the birth, something—deep in his subconscious—troubled him. However, he dismissed it, blaming it on the natural apprehension experienced by an expectant father. He had, after all, felt it before—once—then quickly cast the memory from his mind. But, as the day drew closer, the feeling persisted. He became restless—unable to sleep—persecuted by dreams of his past.

The night Gillis Shaw was born, the child had caused them grave concern, when he failed to breathe, at first. But after a few moments—in the capable hands of a physician—he finally let his family *and* the world know he was very much alive—the first sound of his voice reverberating into the night.

As he looked into the radiant face of his exhausted wife, cradling their new son, Oran felt immense pride—beside them, his wife's mother and stepdaughter, who doted over her baby brother. Although not his, he had adopted the girl as his own, vowing to love both children equally.

But his happiness was short-lived as the disturbing feeling crept back, stronger than before.

As he watched over his family, something was luring him away. He tried to ignore it, but it persisted, commanding his attention. Finally, he gave in to its calling, compelling him to react.

And so, he waited until the house fell silent.

Oran found himself staring at the place where he had left it: hidden in an old coffer—concealed from prying eyes. For decades, it had remained there, untouched, and almost forgotten.

Rejecting any notions creeping into his mind, he could not help but sense a mounting dread—one determined to make itself known to him. As if guided by its energy, he hastily inserted the key, then lifted the lid from the coffer, where he knew the item would be hidden: among the personal effects from his past.

Oran reached in and retrieved the pouch from its resting place, and as he stared at it, contemplating the item inside, panic struck.

No! he told himself, refusing to think it. *It can't be!*

In a matter of seconds, the precious item—his amulet—was swaying before him like a pendulum, counting the uncertainty of time, its priceless, black stone reflecting his image in its lustre. He leaned forward as it gradually came to a stand-still—the item now demanding and craving its Master's attention.

He held his breath.

When the precious jewel fell from his hand, he stepped away, staring down at it—wide-eyed in disbelief; its centred stone had reawakened— ignited by a spark of light, announcing to every Great, and High, Warlock, the birth of a new reign—their Magus—*his* son.

Horrified by the truth of what he was seeing, Oran felt the life he had made begin to slip away.

An image of his newborn son entered his mind. Shaking his head, in denial, he quickly returned his amulet to its place of hiding. *Out of sight, out of mind.*

But, in the weeks after, he grew anxious, constantly looking over his shoulder, imagining the eyes of the world were watching him— following his every move.

He soon became over-protective of his family, causing his wife to question his unusual behaviour. Unable to hide it no longer, Oran was forced to tell her the fate awaiting their son.

She refused to believe him.

With the help of an unlikely source—her mother—she finally realised the dreadful truth. Seeing the look of devastation on his wife's face, as she clung to their son, fearing the worst, Oran knew she could not part with him—nor would he make her.

He was not ready or willing to give up his son.

Oran was suddenly jolted back to his present life, feeling the intensity of the item's energy.

Despite his reluctance to remove it, he *had* to know—had to *see* for himself.

Drawing back the cord, he opened the pouch and reached in, feeling the coldness of the thick, gold chain still attached to it. He hesitated, then took a deep breath. Slowly and surely, he finally lifted his amulet into the humbleness of his workshop, letting it back into his life.

Oran stared at it in utter silence, then dropped to his knees, shaking his head—reliving the same reaction it had given him, all those years ago.

Gone was the darkness of the pear-shaped stone, now replaced by the paleness of emerging sunlight. The diamond had finally come into its own, during his son's growing years, fully aware of the presence of its Overlord. Oran's face fell as he tried to comprehend its truth.

The small, priceless piece of engraved gold, clutching the stone, swayed on its thick chain, again, just as it had done before. When it stopped, he narrowed his eyes, noticing something deep inside its core yet could not distinguish the source.

Oran looked sharp, convinced someone was watching him.

Observing the normality of life, outside his place of work, he became aware of how quiet it had become—the lateness of the day, having unexpectedly crept up on him—by the lowering of the sun. Quickly, he calculated his thoughts, as to how much time he had. His mind raced as he considered his options. *The boy's age!* He sought to remember it.

Thirteen? Fourteen? he wondered. *His coming of age? How long before…?* Each question struggled to provide answers.

He then realised there *were* no options.

Oran felt the peaceful life he had come to love, fall into the clutches of his old one. It seemed the Elliyan might have their way, after all.

Not if I can help it! he told himself. *Whatever their intentions, I'll find a way.* That had been his promise to Rosalyn: to deny their son to the Elliyan— if it meant saving the child from the monumental burden awaiting him. *I'll do it!* he determined. *And damn the consequences!* He would graciously accept them, in exchange for his son's safety.

His mind was made up.

Taking the Albrecht sword, and the amulet, Oran locked the chest. He paused, considering the key. It would stay with Rosalyn. Only once, had she inquired about its contents.

"Oh, nothing of great importance, my love," he had told her. "Just some old tools, knives and a couple of blunt swords. I'll keep it locked away from the children's busy hands."

As to whether she had believed him, he could not say, and yet she respected the privacy of his lengthy past—never asking again. He trusted her implicitly; besides, he would have known had she attempted to open it—and was thankful she never had.

Placing the amulet about his neck, he regarded it, sparing a thought for the others who also possessed one. Staring at the stone, *one*, in particular, came to mind, when it suddenly occurred to him, prompting his subconscious to ask:

Where are you?

Chapter Fifteen

Oran's two-day journey on horseback took him west, across the great loch. He then travelled north along the Tayflu river, before heading east, his route taking him through the Aber hills, and on to Ellan Moy forest—the place he had had no desire to visit again. But things had changed now; there was no avoiding it.

A few tears had been shed on his departure with the assurance to both children, he would return from serving his "duty to the Kingdom." The image of his son's heartbroken face would stay with him, convincing him that the boy was, indeed, still too young to be taken from his home and family. Whatever the outcome, he would never regret his decision.

Oran knew the amulet would guide him, luring him to the portal which would take him to the Elliyan.

Each of the Five Realms had its secret doorway. Hidden from the eyes of mortals, they were known to those who wore the amulet, allowing them—and *only* them—to pass through swiftly, sparing them the long and laborious journey, by land.

Oran owned the title of *Overseer* of the Southern Realm of Urquille. Tired from centuries of battles, he had craved a normal life. After much persistence, he eventually came to an agreement with the Elliyan, after the Magus's death: as long as peace continued to house itself within each Realm, he would be allowed to pursue his dream. However, should it be disrupted, he was—bound by duty—to return to them.

But Oran had had other plans …

The moment life had diminished from their sacred amulets, it was his intention to simply disappear from their sights—even though he knew, one day, they would catch up with him. But until that day …

He sighed. *Time will always prevail.*

The sound of his black, steed's hoofs coming to a sudden halt, roused him from his thoughts. He looked up at the vast canopy of woodland spread wide before him, its great dule and beech trees towering above, marking the domain of Ellan Moy's great forest. Nature had certainly taken its course, by the strength of its overgrowth, since he had last crossed the Aber hills.

Signs of the summer blossomed all around him; the trees bulged with the weight of their healthy leaves, along with the scent of their foliage, it carrying on the gentle breeze. He lifted his head languishing in it, inhaling the freshness of the air, after a recent downpour.

Oran led his horse along the edge of the forest, searching for a gap wide enough for them to pass through. When he found it, he paused before looking back at the openness he was about to leave behind. He sighed—reluctant to do so. But, bound by duty, he had to venture on— the growing energy from the amulet, telling him to do so.

He pressed forward, taking in his surroundings as he guided his horse further into the wood's wild terrain; it had remained undisturbed for years, except for its residential wildlife, skulking about, disturbed by their presence.

Eventually, he located the path that had long succumbed to its natural surroundings. Though its outline was barely noticeable, he knew its route and where it would take him. As they continued along the trail, the trees above and beyond closed in on them, forming a natural arch along the way; they bowed and swayed in the warm breeze, slicing rays of sunshine between their thick branches, while spitting droplets of water at the intruders from the tips of their sodden leaves.

Trudging on, Oran could hear the dull rush of the river ahead, its sound increasing, almost thunderous, on their approach. Swollen and brimming with life, it flowed heavily along the left side of the path, beside them, threatening to surge up and over its banks.

The trail then took them on to a small incline, swerving left. Together, Master and horse continued to follow the "invisible" path— Oran still inhaling the pleasant surroundings, while taking in the busy sounds of nature going about its routine. It momentarily lifted his mood.

Following the path's natural curve, the sight of a small ruin— standing alone on a large mound of boulders—came into view, on his right.

The stone canopy, its roof held up by ancient pillars, looked down onto the river. How long it had reigned there, he could not say. He had a sense of it watching him as he passed the lonely structure. Looking up onto its balcony, he imagined two secret lovers clinched in a desperate embrace, while standing on its ancient ground, locked in time. Its ambience was enchanting, and yet a taint of sadness haunted the air; he sensed the heartbreak of a forbidden love.

Suddenly his horse jolted, stirring him from his daydream. He looked sharp, leaving behind the ghosts from his thoughts, then sighed, slumping back in the saddle.

'Well, Farrow,' he began, following the steed's gaze, 'there it is.'

He looked across, seeing the entrance to a large hollow gap, beneath a rising mound of earth. A row of large stones—placed by ancient hands—shaped its arch. Thick, dark-green moss clung to the joins while poison ivy hung in a threatening manner over the entrance. A place to shelter from the elements, or perhaps to hide from the enemy? Who could say? Although small in size, and deceiving, Oran knew its true purpose.

The sight of it stole away his mood as apprehension seeped in, dominating his senses. He could now feel the warmth of the amulet against his skin, telling him he had almost reached his destination.

A small, rocky footbridge—his only access to the entrance—peeped above the surface of the river before its waters parted, to continue on their separate journeys.

With a sense of defeat, Oran dismounted, leaving Farrow to drink from the freshwater. He left the Albrecht strapped to his saddle, knowing it would be of no use where he was going.

125

'I don't intend to stay long,' he told his horse, making for the bridge, his amulet weighing a little heavier as he drew closer.

Stepping onto the ancient structure—the link between the mortal's world and his own—he stopped when he was suddenly thrown into utter silence, as though all living things had ceased. The domain he had just entered had shut out the chimes of nature.

Oran looked back over his shoulder: through the silence, he saw Farrow continuing to quench his thirst; birds fluttering in and out of the trees, curious about the steed's presence; he saw a rat scramble from one hiding place to another—the bushes twitching as it scurried from sight. Oran lingered, unsure about having to face the world he would have willingly chosen to forget. But face it—he had to.

Taking a deep breath, he clenched his fists, his adrenaline rising as he moved closer to the entrance. Another step heightened it more. His heart beat faster, forcing him to stop again. Images of the life he had left behind, in Balloch, consumed him with guilt as the pressure of duty seized him.

'No—I can't!' he blurted, in retaliation, shaking his head.

He stepped back, ready to retreat, then felt an unexpected pressure from behind, pressing him forward. Oran called on his great strength to fight against it, but with each effort came failure, it feeding the powerful force. He had to act—and quickly—before it would take its final hold on him.

Unwilling, Oran glanced down at his amulet, aware of its rising heat as the seconds raced away. He reached to remove it, then let it go—the stone burning like a red-hot coal. He grasped the gold chain, its weight now an unbearable strain around his neck. But as he tried to relieve himself of its burden, his ears began to fill with the sound of humming, caused by the surging energy taking over. He cupped his hands over them, attempting to block it out, its power now dragging him, pulling him closer to the entrance. It was a losing battle; he felt his resistance waver as it finally lured him, to the point of surrender.

Just beyond the bridge, Farrow looked up from the water's edge, looking for his Master. He was nowhere to be seen.

Chapter Sixteen

The impact the Warlock's body endured, passing through the portal, almost crushed him; the pain, having caused him so much weakness, forced him to his knees. Feeling light-headed, he breathed slowly, waiting for it to subside, while trying to regain his senses. Eventually, the amulet lifted its weight, allowing him to rise. Slowly he steadied himself, until a feeling of normality returned, then released a long and retiring moan, knowing his past was about to catch up with him.

Oran looked around. The impression of a vast open space came to him. Shadowed lines of glowing torches, mounted on walls, threw out soft light towards its interior. At first, he struggled to focus on their setting, letting his eyes adjust. Gradually his surroundings came into view: stretched out, and encircling him from every angle of its far reaches, the Great Hall of Eminence manifested its overwhelming glory, dwarfing him in size against its grandiose scale.

Looking up towards its imposing arched roof, it seemed to soar into the heavens and the darkness beyond, such was its height. Below it, huge, lengthy iron bars crossed from one side to the other, supported by great, white marble columns. Hanging between the vast gaps of each sturdy rod, enormous lanterns looked down on him. Handmade in brass, each was lavishly decorated in different glorious shades of coloured glass. Emanated by their flickering flames inside, their array of colours threw some light above, distorting the hall's true height.

His gaze then fell back on the huge columns. Side by side, they extended down the length of the Great Hall—the black space between each disappearing like a void, into the abyss.

Where is this place? he thought, then paused, noticing the pylons had something in common: an elaborate cartouche carved deeply into the marble. Drawn to one, he approached it with caution, his footsteps echoing through the vastness then slowing, as he became aware of its meaning.

Embossed with onyx, the *nomen* of a Great Warlock, he had once known, stared back at him, their ashes having been interred deep inside the column. Oran drew his breath, feeling the sadness and guilt wash over him as he recognised the name.

'Tekkian,' he whispered aloud, guiding his fingers over his friend's name. 'If only I had known ...' he said. 'How long has it been, my friend?'

'Ten years have passed, since ...'

Oran spun round on hearing the deep, well-spoken voice he still remembered—despite the passing of time—to find himself looking into the wry smile of the Great Warlock, Tuan.

'Welcome, Oran of Urquille,' he said, his black, deep-set brooding eyes staring back at him.

Oran tilted his head, in forced acknowledgement.

Tuan scowled with disgust as his eyes lowered, scrutinising Oran's choice of clothing, already judging him. '*That* can be remedied,' he mumbled, under his breath.

Oran held the older Warlock's gaze, having heard his criticism, surmising he had not changed since their last encounter—nor had he any wish to recall it.

Tuan's thick, straight, grey hair rested on his shoulders, its colour in stark contrast with the long, burnished silver tunic he wore. Made of fine, Muga silk, the luxuriously pleated, long-sleeved garment fell to the floor, covering his feet. And beside him, two other figures stood, regarding Oran with apprehension, sensing his inner resistance.

All three wore the same fine clothing, save for the elaborate silk black belts about their waist, on which their *nomen* was embroidered, in gold thread, displaying their place within their *council*. And on their person— in full view—hung the same precious item Oran concealed beneath his shirt. Seeing them now, he could not help but notice the pale, yellow stone glowing within their centres.

Five Warlocks made up the Elliyan—each a ruler of their given Realm. Oran observed them in turn. As with Tuan, Lothian—the ruler of the Southern Realm of Ockram—shared his title of Great Warlock. Both were of similar age, give or take a century. Tuan, who had served alongside the Magus, presided over the Realm of Saó, declaring himself the role of *Advocate*.

Slight in frame, Lothian was quiet—paling in comparison to his collaborator. His lined, oval face still held its warmth and colour. His eyes sparkled like amethyst. Where Oran had always seen kindness in them, some considered it a "Warlocks' weakness." Unlike Tuan, Lothian's fine, white hair was kept tight, preparing for the day when it would finally lose its battle against time.

Tuan, however, lacked Lothian's gentleness; it was obvious in his features—his long, pale face displaying a hardness, devoid of compassion. Despite his seniority, he matched Oran's height, and though lacking in physique, Tuan's powers were far superior to that of the younger, High Warlock.

Standing alongside the Great Warlocks, the small features of Greer—High Warlock of the Western Realm of Kah-luan—kept his eyes firmly on Oran. Lacking in height, his broad, but compact, frame showed strength and prowess. Dark-brown facial hair crowded his great round face, making up for the lack of it on his crown. A distinct, gold band—inlaid with sapphires, matching his intense blue eyes—rested on his head. The display of personal vanity always irked Tuan and, despite several disputes, Greer simply chose to ignore his superior's distaste for it.

Quiet and secretive in his demeanour, Greer excelled in the knowledge of things unknown to the Elliyan, refusing to share his power of insight, unless the circumstances were exceptional. Although his capabilities did not match that of his two elders, it was, however, the one advantage he held over them—and none more so than Tuan, who realised its importance, especially during challenging times.

Oran had rarely held many conversations with Greer in the past, his fellow High Warlock choosing only to speak when there was something worthy to discuss, and, at times, keeping to himself—for reasons unknown. Yet, when in his company, Oran noticed Greer's intake of all that occurred around him. It showed in his eyes; they danced with excitement, absorbing all he needed to know, keeping it locked inside his learned mind.

Knowing he was under deep scrutiny, Oran kept his wits about him; after all, he had been detached from the Elliyan for far too long, choosing to lock away—in the vaults of his mind—the thoughts and memories of their history. But now he would have to turn the key and unleash them, to answer to his *council*. His mind raced in desperation.

'We have spent some time waiting for you,' said Tuan, maintaining his poise.

'I lost my way,' Oran replied sharply.

A faint curl appeared on the corner of Greer's mouth.

'Where is this place?' said Oran, letting his eyes wander about the Great Hall.

Tuan frowned. 'I *am* disappointed in you, Lord Oran.'

'In what way, Lord Tuan?'

'That you should not recognise a vital part of the very Realm that is *yours*.'

Oran glanced round once more. Nothing came to mind; he had never been to such a place before, making him suspect the Great Warlock was playing with his thoughts.

'This,' Oran stated with certainty, 'is not Urquille.'

'See it as you may,' Tuan persisted, acknowledging the Hall with his hands. 'But I assure you of its place in *our* world; each Realm has its own "Elboru," secretly waiting, hoping theirs will be the chosen one to house its Magus. Surely you *knew* that.' Tuan hesitated, eyeing him suspiciously. 'Or perhaps … you chose *not* to.'

The one thing Oran had dreaded—and hoped to avoid—now stared him in the face. Inside, he was panicking—*Deny everything!* —while on the outside, he casually shook his head, his cool exterior feigning any knowledge.

'This,' Tuan sighed, rolling his eyes, 'is *your* "Elboru," Lord Oran.'

Oran grunted, sneering at his elder. 'Mine?'

'Or perhaps you failed to notice its existence, while otherwise … *pre- occupied.*'

'Impossible!'

'And why would you think that?'

Tuan's smug approach began to grate on Oran's mood. 'Why do you taunt me?'

'The time we live in has become unsettling, to say the least,' Tuan replied, his jeering tone gradually altering to one of seriousness. 'Do you think, for one moment, I would waste any of it *mocking* you? Do you not know the reason why we have come to this place? The reason why we have resided here for years … *waiting*? When *we* speak of "time," Lord Oran, we refer to the day *your* son was born. Or have you forgotten?'

All eyes stayed fixed on Oran's vacant face as Tuan regarded the High Warlock's lack of response, through his cold, rigid calmness.

Deny everything! With shame in his heart, Oran kept his stance before replying; 'I have no son,' he lied, instantly feeling the stab of regret in his own words.

Lothian and Greer shared a worrying glance between them.

'Lord Oran, to deny your son—knowing his fate—is enough to ban you from the Five Realms.' Tuan's words spewed hate and disgust at Oran's renouncement of his son. Closing his eyes, he raised his hands, hell-bent on teaching the reluctant Warlock a lesson.

'No—wait!' cried Oran, in defence, feeling the swell of immense heat being inflicted on him, deep inside.

Tuan hesitated, opening his eyes.

'How did you—'

'Know he was yours?' Tuan retorted, taking a menacing step towards him. His penetrating eyes glared at the High Warlock with intensity, forcing him to recoil. 'We have known for some time.'

Oran shook his head, in denial.

Tuan raised himself to full height, standing tall, as a reminder to all present of his reigning authority. 'Your son is a fine young man,' he stated. 'You *have* taught him well. The girl, too … considering she is not yours.'

Oran glared at Tuan as the Great Warlock proceeded to give a detailed description of the life he had led, including that of his family. He had always been thorough, regarding their safety, especially his son's. It was the reason he had moved them to the quiet—and well-hidden— village of Balloch, after discovering the child's fate. If suspicion had been aroused among the locals, he would have known it.

But as more unfolded, Oran was left speechless, hearing the detailed descriptions of the life he had been leading, away from the Elliyan— some too much to bear.

A gaunt silence took hold of the Great Hall as Oran struggled to absorb what was being relayed. Feeling violated by their deceit, his face turned dusky-red, his eyes flaring as anger soared inside him.

'You had no right!'

'We had *every* right!' Tuan retorted. 'And will maintain it! Our future now depends on *him*.'

The weight of defeat began taking its toll on Oran; he felt his peaceful life slipping through his fingers and into the clutches of the Elliyan, knowing his powers and strength did not match theirs. It was no secret, that his skill in weaponry far surpassed his superiors—but against the force of their might, he felt small and incapable, unable to protect his own. Now, in his mind, he saw the face of a young, innocent boy—not yet a man—and wondered how he would cope, how he would survive the immense task facing him, in the coming years.

It was inevitable.

Suddenly Oran felt the huge debt of responsibility fall on his shoulders.

Sensing his pain, Lothian stepped forward. 'We have been watching you from a safe and protective distance,' he began, his soft, assuring voice inviting Oran's attention. The elderly, Great Warlock smiled kindly at him. 'He makes fine progress. It is clear to see where his gift of swordsmanship transpired.'

Greer nodded in silent agreement.

Oran managed a smile, silently accepting the rare compliment.

'Forgive me, Lord Tuan,' he implored, bowing his head. 'You must understand … he is my only son. I don't wish this burden to be placed on him. True—I confess to knowing his fate when he was born into *their* world. Therefore, I chose to conceal him, as best I could, from *ours*. It was my duty to protect my child. I could not abandon him'—he hesitated, maintaining his stare— 'nor *will* I.'

Tuan looked at Oran, bemused by his honourable plea. 'Quite noble, Lord Oran,' he replied, with a contemptuous smile. 'Quite noble of you, indeed, but have you not already abandoned him? And your … daughter? As for your beautiful wife, Rosalyn—'

'How dare you!' cried Oran, feeling his blood rise again. Tuan's words had reeked of menace. 'You should be mindful of your false accusations.'

'Or you shall do what?' said Tuan.

'I would *never* abandon my family!'

'Your memory is short, Lord Oran. History has a way of repeating itself, or has *that* also slipped your mind?'

Oran opened his mouth to protest, only to be cast down by his elder.

'Apart from your wife, do your children know where you are, or how long you will be away from them?'

His eyes narrowed at the looming threat in Tuan's latter question. Fear slowly gripped him as he surmised the truth behind it.

'If they do not feel abandoned by you now,' Tuan persisted, 'I should imagine, in time, they will, and perhaps even think you … *dead!* They will simply move on with their lives—for the short time they have left.'

Oran lost all sense of decorum as rage took its form, his face hardening as he clenched his fists. No one, not even the Elliyan, would threaten his family. Without thought, he lunged at the Great Warlock. Pre-empting the attack, Tuan raised his shield, sneering at the High Warlock's weak attempt.

Feeling the force of his elder's powers, Oran dropped to the stone floor—the shattering impact forcing him to cry out.

'What is the purpose of punishing one of our own?' said Lothian, turning to his peer. 'It achieves nothing but contempt. Surely, Lord Tuan, *you* should know that.'

'We cannot dwell on what is done,' added Greer. 'It is time we proceed.'

Tuan remained staunch as he watched Lothian guide Oran to his feet. It was evident he held no pity for the High Warlock. 'You have no choice but to face reality, and your fears, Lord Oran. It is because of your selfishness that too much time has been wasted. Had you accepted the boy's fate from the beginning, by offering him to us—'

'Like a lamb to the slaughter?' Oran returned, through gritted teeth.

Tuan breathed deeply, composing himself. He despised being cut short. 'If you had brought the child to us, in the first place, he would be prepared, and more accepting of his vital role. But most importantly, he would be mindful, and in more control of the Shenn.'

The Great Warlock's words resonated with Oran; there was truth in them. Despite his reluctance to accept it, he knew his elder was right. He *had* failed his son. Oran now realised the enormity of his grave mistake. *I've sentenced the boy*, he secretly admitted, *before he even begins to truly imagine the normal life he will never experience.*

A sudden thought entered his mind. Oran raised his head, still contemplating Tuan's words. No—he was not ready to give up his son … not without a fight.

Intent on returning the blame, Oran's confidence gradually crept back. He paced back and forth before the three Warlocks, aware of their eyes watching him, then stopped abruptly, returning his attention to Tuan. *Time to call your bluff, my friend.*

'If this is so … my Lord,' he said, with an air of arrogance, 'why then, did *you* not come for the boy? Have you not failed in *your* duty?'

Tuan's eyes slid from the High Warlock's taunt. Choosing to remain silent, he felt the penetrating stare of Lothian and Greer, as they waited with interest to see what he would say. Lothian caught his eye.

'It was agreed we would not interfere,' Tuan falsely admitted.

Though Oran felt compelled to mock him further, he changed his mind. The distaste for Tuan's inability to admit the truth was visible on his hardened face: they simply could not *take* the child. He knew it … and so did *they*. No—the boy had to be *given* up by his parents.

'Had those words come from another,' Oran replied, 'I may have believed them, and yet I have difficulty in understanding your conviction.'

'Then I shall explain.'

Oran casually folded his arms and dropped his head to the side, irritating the Great Warlock further.

Tuan's stale features glared at his smug display of self-satisfaction. 'After the death of our previous Overlord,' he commenced, 'peace prevailed and continued to do so. And, as you are aware, it was for this reason, we granted your leave of us, until such time you would be called upon. Was that not the agreement, Lord Oran?' Faced with the High Warlock's wall of silence, he continued. 'I, however, had my suspicions. Therefore, I had one of the Servitors keep a close eye on your … antics.'

Oran's mouth fell as he straightened. 'You let one of those traitors *spy* on me?'

'They are willing and loyal to us,' said Tuan, defending them.

'They are nothing but traitors to their kind!' Oran retorted, waving a clenched fist at his peer. 'And as for the one you sent—'

'Far from it, Lord Oran. I simply had someone watch over you. And I must admit,' Tuan added, smirking, 'you certainly took great advantage of the spoils of mortality.'

Images of his hedonistic lifestyle, linking him to several promiscuous rendezvous, came back to humiliate him in his present company. Oran diverted his eyes, momentarily embarrassed.

'Oh, do not be ashamed, Lord Oran; after all, you were not committed to another. Why deny you those pleasures?'

'Those times had long passed when I married,' said Oran, reminding them of the other life he had led.

'Indeed,' said Lothian, feeling sympathy for the High Warlock. 'But then we knew nothing of your whereabouts, after Sahraya and Raya's deaths.'

The pain of hearing their names stabbed his heart, bringing with it a moment of grief; he had not heard them spoken in more than a century and a half.

Oran closed his eyes, recalling the young, warm-hearted, beautiful woman from the Southern Realm of Ockram. With eyes, the colour of onyx, and hair as black as ebony, his wife's sienna skin had reminded him of the desert home he had taken her from. Sahraya would have travelled to the end of time for him.

Four years were all they had shared as husband and wife. Both she and Raya—their two-year-old daughter—were cruelly taken from him by the ocean when they travelled to be with him, rather than be parted, during his lengthy campaigns. An air of suspicion had risen, revolving around the unexpected deaths. However, as time passed, any notion of foul play was dismissed, due to lack of evidence, and, therefore, the incident was regarded as a "misadventure."

Oran's despair, after their loss—he had never accepted the outcome—sent him to the deepest, unimaginable desolation, making him forget all sense of reality.

'Grief has its way of taking hold if one should let it,' he muttered.

'As you *chose* to,' Tuan remarked, lacking sympathy.

Oran cast a glowering look at his elder. 'And, in my *choosing*, I was more than happy to reject my amulet,' he confessed, with satisfaction, observing the glare of dishonour shadowing Tuan's face. 'I detached it from all I knew, blocking its connection to me. But its persistence in refusing to separate from its Master was daunting. And so, I placed it where no light of day could find it, until all memory of it melted away with time.'

Oran looked from one Warlock to the next, imagining their dissatisfaction. While Tuan continued to stare down his nose at him, with disgust, he detected signs of understanding and sympathy from

Lothian, while Greer's piercing blue eyes were distracted, appearing to show a lack of interest in his peers' admission.

'I was glad to be rid of it,' Oran continued, grinding on Tuan's aggravation. 'I *wanted* to forget its existence.'

Tuan's face twisted in rage, as pulsating veins of anger rose on his forehead. 'How could you reject it, forget the bond it shares with you?!' he roared, giving in to his fury, his eyes burning with hate.

Oran's eyes glided towards the Great Warlock. 'Do not underestimate the ill effects of one consumed by anger and grief, Lord Tuan,' he said. 'It is enduring.'

Tuan grunted. 'I have no care for—'

'Do you not see?!' yelled Oran. He dared to move closer, letting his voice carry throughout the great space surrounding them. 'Am I not wearing it now?! See how it hangs from my neck! The constant reminder of the day my son was born, preys on my soul. Aye, I did forget it—until that day. It was *then* I chose to reveal its purpose to my wife, Rosalyn. Together, *we* decided it would remain hidden. Aye, it was a great risk—but one worth taking. I feared, during his first years, we would be sought out, and *forced* to give him up. Every day of his life was spent looking over our shoulders.'

'You thought you had outsmarted it,' Lothian stated.

Oran groaned. *Clearly not!* 'How *did* you find us, in the end?' he then asked.

'Look at them!' said Tuan, indicating their amulets. 'The stone's inner light grows in harmony with the boys' progression. If he is not aware of his place in our world … he will be, soon enough. The item you grotesquely describe as "hanging from your neck" was your betrayer.'

'It *guided* us to him,' Lothian said, feeling the need to maintain decorum. 'The precious stone will become more vibrant—more intense—until it has reached the peak of its power.'

'How long?' asked Oran, growing increasingly agitated.

'When he comes of age,' prompted Greer. 'But you already know that.'

Ignoring the remark, Oran rubbed his hand over his jaw, unable to recall his son's age.

'We have three years,' his peer stated, in his silence.

Oran turned quickly, smiling at Greer. 'Then this will give us sufficient time to prepare,' he assumed, feeling his mood lift. He nodded to himself. 'Aye, and it will please my wife to know she'll have her son for a while yet. And by then, we'll be ready to—' He stopped, catching the Warlocks as they eyed one another in awkward silence.

Oran narrowed his hazel eyes. 'Something you wish to share, my lords?'

'Unfortunately, a difficult situation has presented itself,' Lothian informed him, exchanging another look with the others. Oran gave them a sidelong glance, one brow raised. 'Even if your son was here, in Elboru, at this very moment, we could not prepare him.'

Oran drew his head back, frowning. 'And why?'

'As you know, the Elliyan is made up of *Five*,' Tuan reminded him. 'Each of which possesses an amulet. However, one is missing; we need it to complete the transformation if he is to become our new Magus. It is as simple as this, Lord Oran: without *it*, your son will not wear the Shenn. It is imperative that we have all five.'

Chapter Seventeen

'All five?!' Oran echoed, taken aback by the unexpected revelation.

More was to come.

'Since the demise of its owner,' continued Tuan, 'the fifth amulet has … gone astray. We believe it to be in the hands of another.'

'Another? Who?' Oran enquired—the feeling of unease creeping into his consciousness. It did not go unnoticed, his sudden eagerness arousing Greer's suspicions.

'We do not know,' added Lothian. 'We suspect it is still somewhere within the Realm of Ockram.'

'The birthplace of the late Magus?' said Oran.

Lothian nodded.

'Where he continued to rule, during his life, supported by the Elliyan.'

'Until his death,' Oran stated.

'Precisely. We suspect, whoever possesses the amulet now, knew these facts. They may assume the new Overlord will reawaken from the ashes of his predecessor—in the same place. There have been unsettling signs in Ockram … according to our sources.'

'The Servitor, no doubt,' Oran muttered.

'Do not underestimate them, Lord Oran!' Tuan snapped. 'They are discreet and trustworthy—more than you know.'

Lothian—the constant mediator between the two—stepped in again, encouraging calm. 'There is no time for pettiness, my lords. Whatever your differences, they must be put aside—better still—laid to rest. The fifth *must* be located. We have the advantage over its present bearer in that they are not aware of the process involved, nor the whereabouts of the boy.'

'Yet,' Greer stated, in his gruff voice.

Oran turned and scowled at him.

'The amulet's power is gradually increasing,' Greer went on. 'It will take momentum nearer the time, eventually guiding the "thief" to Urquille.'

'*Here*, you say?!'

Oran's outburst of shock came as no surprise to Greer; he perceived there was something his fellow Warlock was keeping from them. He pressed on. 'This is where your son was born, Lord Oran. And *here* is where he will rule, with the Elliyan by his side. It is where the Shenn— the *Sixth*—waits for him.'

Oran turned his back on the three, his mind racing as segments of his past plagued his thoughts. *Is it possible?* he asked himself, staring down the length of the Great Hall. In the distance, he thought he saw a small figure pass discreetly through its wide passage. He listened for their footsteps; hearing nothing, he dismissed it and turned to address his peers.

'What will happen if we don't find the missing amulet?'

'Its present owner will eventually discover the true value of its power—linking it to Shenn,' said Greer. 'Should time pass, and the amulet is not reunited with its rightful owner—your son—then it is there for the taking, be they man … or immortal.'

'However,' said Tuan, feeling the need to take charge of the conversation again, 'Magia Nera has been long dead, which makes our task difficult. And, as you are aware, our amulets cannot be easily taken from us.'

'Therefore,' added Greer, 'we are to assume he may have *given* it to another, before his demise … unless …'

Hearing his old rival's name, Oran's look sharpened, meeting Greer's discerning look. The High Warlock's gift of insight was at work—clearly visible in the flickering movement of his piercing, blue eyes.

'I believe there is something you wish to share with us, Lord Oran?' Greer remarked, peering at him.

Tuan and Lothian observed the tension between the younger, High Warlocks, their intense regard of one other concerning Lothian.

'Well, Lord Oran?' Greer prompted.

Oran inhaled deeply, as the mounting pressure emanating from Greer's intense stare finally forced his hand. Worn down by it, he sighed heavily before making his confession: 'Magia Nera'—he paused, closing his eyes— 'is not dead.'

The unexpected admission altered the atmosphere in the Great Hall, to that of astonishment.

As Oran lowered his head, a strange sense of relief fell from his shoulders.

Lothian moved to his side. 'Not *dead?!*' he said, his eyes wild with amazement.

'That is impossible!' cried Tuan, refusing to accept the revelation. 'We saw him—'

'As did I—Lord Tuan,' said Oran, cutting in. 'But I assure you, Magia Nera lives and, what is more … he has been cursed—damned to eternal life.'

'Is this true?' Lothian persisted.

'As true as you are standing beside me. I saw him—spoke to him.'

'When?'

Oran paused, reliving the regretful moment. 'Eighty years ago, perhaps,' he surmised.

'There was no mistaking his new identity. We have Tepés to thank for his survival.'

'The Vamp—'

'Yes,' came the firm, short reply.

'But—Vlad Tepés is *dead!*' Tuan stated, before turning to confront Greer. 'Did *you* not see to it?'

'Of course, my lord,' Greer replied, a little irked, sensing a hint of underlying doubt. 'His corpse lies where we left it—in Snagov—with a stake through his heart.'

Tuan moved closer to the High Warlock, taking him in. But when Greer subconsciously diverted his eyes, for an instant, it was enough for the Great Warlock to doubt him, forcing him to question him further: 'But did you *finish* the task?' he persisted.

Greer remained silent, his eyes dancing as he recalled the events, in his mind: he had struck down the tyrant himself, with the aid of their skilled mercenaries—the Bullwark—then threw his corpse into a crypt—beneath the altar of a small chapel, before driving a stake through his heart ...

When Greer's eyes stopped, his face then altered, to that of realisation.

'You did not remove his head!' Tuan yelled suddenly. 'How could you be so—'

'Where Lord Greer failed,' interrupted Oran, 'another reigned victory over Tepés.'

Tuan spun round, outraged by what he had just heard. He approached Oran with indignation. 'How is this possible?' he voiced. '*Who* was the victor?'

As Oran held his superior's gaze, the answer was clear from his ominous expression.

'No!' said Tuan, recoiling, with a look of genuine astonishment.

The three Warlocks stared in disbelief. Oran then proceeded, by divulging the events that brought about the demise of Vlad Tepés—by the hand of Magia Nera—explaining how their paths had crossed, and how he came to be.

'I perceive Tepés knew his end would eventually come,' added Oran. 'Therefore, not wanting his legacy to die with him, he needed to secure its longevity—by extending his band of loyal followers, including Magia Nera, and initiating them into his dark world of immortality.'

'Then Magia Nera's powers will be greater,' Lothian remarked, staring into the darkness of the Hall of Eminence, as though expecting the absent Warlock to appear from the shadows, brandishing the much-needed amulet around his neck.

'Indeed,' Oran responded. 'And I have seen their influence. Yet, as great as they are, his only solace is the night—with daylight being his enemy.'

'Then it is possible he may not be working alone,' said Tuan.

'But why Ockram?' Lothian mused over the unthinkable. 'Why go there? He is aware of our protocol. If Magia Nera wears his amulet, surely it would lead him here. Is that not so?'

Oran grit his teeth, still feeling the weight of Greer's persistent and annoying stare.

'Magia Nera is not present'—Greer stated, approaching Oran— 'for another wears his amulet. And it is my understanding … our absent friend knows *who*. Would you agree, Lord Oran?'

Oran kept his eyes diverted, choosing to retain his silence from Greer's suggestion.

'It appears you have aroused further suspicion, Lord Oran,' said Tuan. 'I suggest you should—' He stopped and tilted his head, listening. Exchanging glances with Lothian, the Great Warlocks promptly turned their backs on Greer and Oran, their attention now drawn and focused on the centre of the Great Hall. Tuan slowly raised his hand in a welcoming gesture, extending it towards a dimly lit space.

Oran breathed a subtle sigh of relief, thankful for the distraction. He looked at Greer, who followed the elders as they approached the central point.

The Hall took on an unfamiliar ambience, its aura displayed in a haze of azure, now capturing the inquisitiveness of the younger Warlocks.

They moved closer.

'Stay where you are!' called Tuan, his command precise and insistent. '*He* is coming!'

Oran opened his mouth to question the order when a tiny flicker of light came into view, hovering quietly in its palatial surroundings. Gradually, the tiny light began to grow, expanding and manifesting itself into shape. The Hall jumped to life as its intense energy took precedence.

Lothian and Tuan stepped back from its dominance, while the light replicated the shape of the precious stones within their amulets. Tuan drew his hand down, placing it across the *nomen* on his belt, promptly followed by Lothian, who did the same.

From within its centre a shadow appeared, slowly taking form. Increasing in size, with every moment, it moved forward, preparing to reveal itself. Fascinated, Oran and Greer looked on—having never witnessed the event—feeling the surge of energy from its core rush through their bodies.

Gradually the form ceased to grow. Standing tall and poised, within its protective light, it lingered before materialising into the figure of a man, through a veil of golden light.

In a welcoming gesture, Lothian and Tuan bowed in his presence, as Greer and Oran gaped. The figure seemed to glide towards them in his approach, before acknowledging their welcome.

Tall in stature, he towered majestically above them; his appearance was captivating. His hairless crown drew attention to his perfectly round features. His age, they could not determine. Devoid of blemish and flaw, his skin glowed like burnt copper. But most noteworthy were his piercing, almond-shaped eyes—matching the colour of lapiz lazuli; Oran detected tiny flecks of gold each time they blinked.

The figure wore a lavish, sleeveless, full-length linen robe—its colour in contrast with his eyes. Two pure gold rings adorned each index finger, containing the cartouche of the ruling Magus—each one bearing the *nomen*, "Lumeri"—the name he would take upon gaining his title.

The figure, Oran believed, epitomised perfection—save for his curiously bare feet.

'Their nakedness is a symbol of my servitude to the Shenn, and its Master,' he remarked. 'Yet I am a willing acolyte.' The words flowed like silk in its purest form from his mouth. His voice, alluring and soft to the ear, was precise and careful in its delivery. Turning to Oran, his full, dark lips curved into a smile.

'I am the Ushabti,' he began formally. 'And you are the boy's father.'

Oran bowed low, in respect and awe of his presence yet was unable to look away.

'We welcome you at this troubling time,' Lothian interrupted, breaking Oran's transfixed gaze. Both addressed each other with a welcoming nod. 'The Ushabti has guarded the Shenn amulet for thousands of years,' Lothian then informed Oran and Greer.

'He remains in long hibernation, guarding over it until the stone is re-awakened—on the birth of the chosen Magus,' added Tuan. 'He continues to protect the Shenn until it is bestowed on its new Master. It is his duty to make certain the task is carried out, in the time given to him.'

'And should he fail?' Oran enquired, finding his voice again.

Tuan glared at him. 'To fail is not an option,' he retorted.

Oran grunted. 'It is always an option, and one of possibility.'

'In the event of failure,' Lothian jumped in, 'it will be out of the Ushabti's control, rendering the Shenn dangerous. Should it fall into the lap of another, who is not born of a Warlock, the consequences will be catastrophic. However, it is not too late. We must find the missing amulet, if the boy is to be ready in time, to take on his role.'

A sense of dread filled Oran, at the emphasis on "time." He *had* been detached from the Elliyan for far too long.

Slowly and gradually, his past began to unravel the more sinister side of the Shenn, as the truth behind the rumours—he had once heard—became increasingly real. All the repose and decorum he had maintained, in the presence of the Ushabti, now fell by the wayside as he dared to challenge him.

'How did he die?' Oran asked, bluntly.

'Lord Oran!' Tuan snapped, raising his voice. 'Do not address—'

'And the others?' he demanded, ignoring his elder. 'The Overlords—the Magus—gone before my son. Is it true—the Shenn destroyed them?'

The Ushabti remained calm and unruffled by Oran's outpouring of demands, infuriating the High Warlock further.

'Did *you* fail in your duty to them? Is this the same fate that awaits my son?'

The Ushabti's eyes blinked once, causing the particles of gold to glint from the glowing light surrounding them. For a brief moment, Oran saw a faint hint of pity in them.

'The Shenn did not destroy them, Oran of Urquille,' he replied, his beautiful voice commanding the four Warlock's undivided attention. They waited as he gathered his thoughts, while thousands of years of evil conflict swam through his overcrowded mind, as he recalled each outcome.

'From the moment of its fashioning, the Shenn's creator was overwhelmed by its potency. The universe had provided it with a power so great, it had to be mastered and respected. But through greed and obsession, he lost all control—as did those who inherited it.' There was a brief pause. 'No, Lord Oran … the Shenn amulet did not destroy them. They destroyed themselves. Their ignorance of the greatest item they possessed, became their downfall. Your son is next in line. If he does not listen and respect its influence, he risks the same fate as his predecessors.'

Oran's heart sank to depths of fear for his son. He lowered his head with a sense of hopelessness, overwhelmed by the enormity of the burden placed on a child, who was in complete ignorance of his future.

His child.

Conscious of his inner torment, Lothian felt the need to assure his fellow Warlock. 'All is not lost, Lord Oran,' he said with compassion. 'Your son has the ability to prove his worth as our supreme Magus; he has an added strength of priority and pride. These special qualities, married with the Ushabti's guidance, will benefit him greatly on his journey.'

'Is this your belief or imagining?' said Oran.

Lothian looked deep into Oran's tortured eyes. 'In the Realm of my soul, Lord Oran, I believe him to be a great Ruler.'

'As long as he does not lose his way, or is influenced by the wrong sources,' the Ushabti reminded them.

'Then what am I to do?' asked Oran, feeling helpless.

'The Shenn is linked to all five amulets,' Tuan began. 'In the wrong hands, it is a weapon against all that we know. Without it … we can only surmise. However, according to Lord Greer, it appears you may be familiar with the bearer of the missing item and, for reasons unknown, wish to conceal, or dare I say… *protect* them.'

'You have no—'

'I *see* it,' interrupted Greer, 'in your eyes.'

'Why deny it, then?' added Tuan.

Oran held his silence, considering all options. There were none; he could not deny it.

'And, I suspect you are partially responsible for its misplacement,' Tuan persisted. 'Therefore, the Elliyan now order you to bring your son to us; besides, is it not *your* duty?'

Oran shook his head in defiance.

'And there lies the truth!' he threw back. 'I know you can't take him from me, despite your reluctance to admit it. I will give up my son when *I* am ready—and not by your command. We have time yet.'

'If that was so, Lord Oran, then I would gladly give you it.' The sound of the Ushabti speaking his name was magnetic, luring his attention to him. 'The threat is—to our great misfortune—all too real. It must be stopped.'

'As you are so reluctant and determined not to give up your son, willingly,' sniped Tuan, 'then we must come to an arrangement.'

'What kind of *arrangement*?' Oran retorted, now suspicious.

'A vital one!' added Greer. 'If we are all to survive.'

Oran stared into the faces observing him as they waited for his reaction; he gave them none.

'I assume, by your silence,' said Tuan, 'that you are willing.'

'That all depends …'

'We will allow your son—what precious time we can afford—to stay with your family. But there is something *you* must do in return, to earn that time.'

'And if I refuse?'

'I would not recommend it,' Tuan hit back—the tone in his voice low and hostile.

'Then what *must* I do?'

'You will search for the one who keeps Magia Nera's amulet,' Tuan maintained. 'And when you find them—*destroy* them!'

'Destroy them?!' Oran blurted, craning his neck forward, his eyes telling, full of apprehension.

As they scrutinised his response, a contemptuous grin appeared on Tuan's smug face.

'Behold! The admission,' he sneered, addressing the others. Greer shook his head in annoyance.

Oran regretted not speaking sooner. *The past always finds its way back,* he thought, reminded of Rosalyn's grim warning; he should have taken heed of it. He heaved a sigh, longing to see her.

'Who is it?' Lothian then asked, breaking his thoughts.

Oran's eyes flashed towards the Great Warlock. *Who?* Inside, panic struck him. *Think!* He then shrugged.

'It is most likely that the one who possessed it is long dead,' he lied, sensing the need to defend *her.* 'I'm sure of it; it was a long time ago. Besides, how do we know it has not fallen back into Magia Nera's hands? And, if that is so, remember … he is no longer of *our* kind. It would prove difficult to find him; perpetual darkness is now his Realm. He reigns over it.'

'There is probability in what he says,' said Lothian, defending the High Warlock.

Again, Oran was aware of Greer's watchful eyes as he stood defiant in his deception.

Tuan mused over the possibility, before addressing Greer. 'Send word to the Servitor,' he said.

'The Servitor?' Oran enquired, narrowing his eyes.

'They must be informed,' Tuan added, 'to be mindful of your family's comings and goings, from now on.'

'You mean—you *still* spy on them?!' Oran's face flushed crimson while, inside, he struggled to control his anger.

'It is our priority now, to protect your son.'

'Tell me his name!' demanded Oran. 'This *spy*, who knows my life.'

'With regret, we cannot reveal the name,' said Lothian.

'Why not? Surely, I have the right to know.'

'Not quite,' said Tuan, maintaining his smugness. 'For we made a solemn vow to her.'

Oran's eyes widened. 'Her?!'

Quiet and subdued in his detachment from the emotion dominating the Hall, the Ushabti continued to watch with a keen eye as Oran's heavy footsteps echoed; he paced to and fro, searching his mind for the traitor. He then paused briefly in front of the pillar dedicated to the memory of his lost friend.

Damn you! he cursed the Elliyan, inside, for neglecting to inform him of Tekkian's passing, then felt the guilt of his absence. Had he known ….

'We are all allies in this together, Lord Oran,' said Lothian, interrupting his moment of reflection. 'Even the Servitor and—' Lothian stopped himself. '*They* are not your enemy.'

In their male-dominated world, the possibility of the "spy" being a woman was inconceivable to him. He mused over it, regarding his elders. 'An unlikely source!' he admitted, sliding his eyes towards Tuan. 'And a clever move on *your* part, no doubt.'

The Great Warlock smirked, tilting his head in the admission of his plan.

'May I ask her name?' he inquired, his tone falsely polite and probing.

'What is the importance of a name?' Greer questioned. 'She has been keeping a protective eye on your son. Her duty will be fulfilled when he is placed into our care, before entering his new life,' he added, acknowledging the Ushabti.

'Do I know her?'

'Once a vow has been made, it cannot—'

'And will not be broken,' said Tuan, interrupting Greer—obstructing Oran's persistence. 'Try as you may, Lord Oran, you will not hear it from those present.'

Bound by the Elliyan laws, Oran sensed defeat in his inquiry, secretly vowing to seek out the spy—and deal with *her* himself. Reluctant, he nodded in agreement.

'Good,' Tuan responded, satisfied. 'The time in which your son—'

'Gill,' Oran snapped. 'His name is Gillis. If he is to be our ruling Magus, you will speak his name with respect.'

Oran's insistence surprised the three Warlocks, who sought the others' approval, with the exchange of a subtle nod.

'If you wish it,' said Lothian, on their behalf.

'Aye, I do. Although, what I truly wish for appears to be no longer possible.'

'And, for that, we are sorry,' Lothian replied, glancing at Tuan, whose face retained its disapproval of any apology. 'We know how much you desired a mortal life. Perhaps this could have been so, if …' Lothian's voice trailed as he slowly lifted his shoulders.

'I feel no shame in it,' Oran stated, defending his past. 'I was simply weary of the fight. For centuries, I—*we*—have fought too many battles, seen much bloodshed, and witnessed innocent people die, needlessly. Is it so wrong to desire a peaceful life?'

'There is a great evil coming, Lord Oran,' Greer warned. 'It must be stopped.'

'And without our kind, secretly protecting the mortals,' Tuan reminded him, playing on his emotions, '*they* would not survive.'

Insulted by his superiors' ploy to emotionally blackmail him, Oran, however, knew it had worked. Also, Tuan was right; the mortals would never survive—should they fail them.

'Therefore, from this place,' said Tuan, raising his voice of authority, 'you will go to the Realm of Ockram—'

'Not before I see my family,' Oran cut in, adamant in his request.

'We cannot afford to waste time.'

'I want to see them before I—'

'Your wants and needs have long expired!' snapped Tuan, approaching him with intent.

150

'Then find another!' Oran lashed out, clenching his fists, determined not to make things easy—Tuan bringing out the worst in him.

The two Warlocks stood face-to-face in defiance, eyes blazing.

'I will not do this!' he insisted. Oran now turned to the Ushabti, who had been absorbing every word. 'Do you hear me? I refuse!'

Greer moved to step between them, then stopped, when the Ushabti raised his hand, preventing it.

The Ushabti then turned his intense gaze on Oran until their eyes locked—the pressure mounting in the High Warlock's head. Oran tensed, closing his eyes tight from the pain of his energy being drained. His body shook, along with his racing heart. A blinding light flashed through his mind, as realistic images played out their scenes of death and devastation. Faces, both strange and familiar to him, battled against an enduring force. One by one they fell, defeated.

He saw his son challenge the unknown force, ready to strike it down. Clutched in *its* hand, for all to see, the Shenn glowed in its true magnificence. It was a warning—a display of power—letting one and all know who ruled. The image of the bearer was distorted. Oran struggled to see, letting his subconscious guide him. A gradual sense of clarity began to unveil their features. But as quickly as they had appeared, the images were torn from his mind. He breathed in deeply, gasping for air.

'Lord Oran?!' Lothian cried, going to his aid.

The High Warlock's wide-opened eyes stayed fixed on the Ushabti. Had he seen the face, or had it been shown to him with discretion? He was unsure, and yet …

The Ushabti raised his hand, placing it gently on Oran's crown. The Warlock felt the surge of energy gradually re-enter his weakened body, welcoming its return as his heart resumed a steady beat. With eyes still engaged, he began to understand the Ushabti's forewarning.

'Now you see why you must go.'

Oran nodded, grasping the full impact of what he had to do.

'Your task will be a difficult one,' the Ushabti warned. 'Yet, I am confident. The Shenn waits for its true Master … as do I.'

151

With nothing more to say, the Ushabti smiled warmly at Oran before taking his leave of the Great Hall of Eminence. The Warlocks watched as he faded into the haze of light, returning to the place where he would wait in revered silence.

With a clear understanding, Oran turned to his fellow Lords. 'Can you guarantee the safety of my family—while I'm gone?' he asked, his voice firm and unyielding.

'Be assured of it,' Lothian replied.

Oran felt comfort in the Great Warlock's words. If there was one person he trusted, it was Lothian; his word was governed by truth.

'Although I've no choice,' he told them, 'I am willing. Now, what must I do?'

'The portal will take you directly to Ockram,' said Tuan, relieved there would be no further objection; he now had the High Warlock's undivided attention. 'Your amulet will guide you. Let us hope the bearer of the fifth still resides there. If not, you must find them; Shenn's power *will* grow stronger, over the time we have left—eventually leading them here. We cannot risk that. It *must* be prevented.' Tuan paused for a moment of thought. 'Perhaps … it *is* wise, after all, to leave your son in the safety of his surroundings … for the time being.'

Oran smiled with a sense of self-satisfaction.

'But remember, Lord Oran, your son—Gillis—is now the priority. Nothing must stand in the way of him taking his rightful place, here, in Urquille. Stop this threat. No matter what!'

No matter what! Tuan's words echoed as they registered in his mind.

Torn between his past and his son's future, Oran desperately hoped *she* was still not the bearer. His thoughts raced with visions of them in conflict. And, should their paths cross, on the journey he was about to undertake, he questioned his ability to destroy her, despite his orders. However, if the opportunity presented itself … Could he? Would he?

Chapter Eighteen

Balloch: 1630 - Three years later - Late Autumn

'I told you not to go far!'

The young woman stopped and raised her hand, shielding her eyes from the glaring sun. 'Gill!' she cried, searching through the gaps in the trees for a mere glimpse of her young brother. Instinct told her he was near. Still, she preferred him to be in her sights. She looked down towards the loch, beyond the tree line, observing two familiar figures at play, by the water's edge.

Satisfied, she smiled before making her way to them. Then something caught her eye. She hesitated, catching sight of a dark shape moving swiftly, just beyond her view. Narrowing her steely-blue eyes, she stared through the foliage, waiting …

She saw nothing—not even a sound for her to follow.

Shrugging, she dismissed it, concluding it to be nothing more than a wild animal. But as she turned to call her brother, again, she had a sense of being watched. Quickening her pace, she cast off any foolish notions.

Eleanor Shaw stepped out into the openness of the loch. Looking above, she squinted at the dappled sky—the sun's hot rays still penetrating through, onto her bronzed skin. Closing her eyes, she inhaled the late morning air, filling her lungs with the freshness of the water and surrounding beauty.

'Nori!'

Her eyes flickered open at the sound of her name. She waved, acknowledging him.

'Will you come with us?' her brother pleaded.

'No, lad,' she replied. 'I think you are old enough to go hunting on your own … as long as Rave is with you,' she added, throwing him a mindful look.

'Are you certain?'

'Go!' she urged. 'Give me peace, and be sure to—' She had not completed her sentence, when the boy and his loyal companion scurried by before disappearing into the woods. 'And don't go far!' she called after him, rolling her eyes.

Eleanor approached the waterline, removing the light-blue shawl from her waist. Although the day was hot, she had taken it for one purpose only: to use as a comfortable, makeshift cushion for herself. Folding it carefully, she placed it on the ground, then sat on its softness before removing her mochs. She dipped her toe, checking the water's temperature, then smiled. Content, she let her feet slip gently into the coolness of the loch.

Laying back, she stretched out her tired body, releasing all her tensions; her limbs felt weary after the week's work—helping her mother at the Burgh. Rising early most days, she assisted with the baking of scones, bread, pies and tablets, for their stall in the village. But, for now, she was contented, stealing herself away from the bustle of the market, to enjoy the peace of the loch's surroundings.

Calm and relaxed, she let the heat of the sun bathe over her before rising. Though convinced she was alone, Eleanor still could not help but cast a wary glance about her, feeling the need to protect her modesty. Now, certain no one was watching, she clutched the length of her skirt, raising it to her shapely thighs. Before tucking the hem into the belt, around her narrow waist, she removed the item attached to it, tossed it back beside her shawl, then entered the water, as far as she'd dare go.

Worn from the heat of the day, Eleanor's long, fair hair began to weigh heavily on her. As she caught its thickness, before tying it above her head, nature's soft, warm breath brushed the nape of her neck, then glided down over her, swirling around her bare legs. She watched how it made the water dance and sparkle like tiny jewels, as it travelled over its surface.

Cupping some water in her hands, she threw it over her round, sun-kissed face—the glow of summer radiating its youth and vitality; and as the water trailed down her front and back, she languished in its cooling effect. Refreshed by its purity, she could not help but repeat the glory of it, in awe of how something—in its simplicity—could arouse the senses.

Leaning back on her custom-made cushion, Eleanor absorbed the beauty of nature's garden. Although late September—and the sun already displaying subtle shades of gold and amber as leaves still clung to the branches of overgrown trees—summer had decided to lengthen its stay. Therefore, she was determined to enjoy its reign for as long as possible, before its inevitable surrender to the winter.

Suddenly, Eleanor jolted and sat up—uneased by the sense of being watched again. Promptly lowering her skirt, she glanced over her shoulder. Her eyes followed the crest of trees ascending the hill behind her until they reached the top. There, alone and domineering, stood Balloch castle.

Though unoccupied, she had a sense of the old, residential fortress looking down at *her*, commanding her attention, and shuddered at its ominous presence. And despite the countless taunts and dares from her young brother, to do so, she had never ventured near it—not even as far as the courtyard.

Almost three years divided brother and sister: *there lies the difference!* she concluded inwardly—the bravery of a sixteen, "almost seventeen", year-old—as he regularly pointed out—compared to her, nineteen. Displaying little or no fear, Gill enjoyed relaying stories he had collected from their neighbour, Heckie Grant—especially the more effective and sinister ones. Heckie—a renowned Bard in the village—was a descendant of an ancient line of storytellers. And Gill adored him, hanging on his every word.

"According to Heckie," he once informed her, in *that* foreboding tone he loved to use when taunting her, "there are *strange* goings-on up there. He says it's haunted, by the ghost of a woman."

Eleanor had sensed an element of truth behind the tale. More than once, she had heard of the wrongful death of a local woman—burned at the stake over the death of a child. He had been the youngest of three, born to a wealthy English family who had resided at the castle, almost a century before. A sickly child, since birth, the woman had been called upon occasionally, to tend to his needs.

When the bairn became dangerously ill from a winter sickness, the woman made a potion from local herbs to ease his pain. Known for her healing skills, the expectations had been that the boy would see a full recovery. Yet, despite all her attempts, the child finally lost his battle when the fever took its toll, taking him from his parents. The poor woman, in all her innocence, had tried—through the best of her knowledge—to help the dying child. Distraught, and influenced by claims of witchcraft, the parents had the woman put on trial, leading to her demise, before they returned to England … or so the story went.

"… and Heckie says, on the night of every new moon, the cry of a woman and a child can be heard, coming from within the castle walls. Also, Heckie says an old man, from across the great sea—from a place no one has heard of—lives there, alone, with all his wealth, and no one to share it with, waiting for the return of his lost love. And Nori—do you know what else Heckie told me?"

"Aye, right," she would always reply—even if it didn't make sense—and slowly nod, amused by the numerous expressions on his face as he relayed the tales in one sweeping breath—engrossed in every word. Eleanor learned to control her laughter, displaying feigned looks of shock and horror, so as not to offend her brother. However, it only encouraged him further—no thanks to their neighbour.

Eleanor grunted and rolled her eyes, casting aside all notions of the castle being haunted. Feeling the tiredness on her eyelids she lay back, once more. Listening to the trickling of the water, as it softly lapped against the edge of the loch, she slipped into her world of daydreams, tutting and smiling to herself. *Heckie and his silly tales.*

Heckie Grant and his wife, Blair, were loyal friends and had been for as long as she could remember.

156

Blair, like her husband, was as large as life, as was her frame. A woman of staunch pride, she loved to wear a bodice, showing off her ample figure, without a care in the world. She paid no heed to what people thought and possessed a tongue as sharp as a blade. Her crowning glory was a thick, mane of black hair with strands of silver—visible from root to tip—and worn down in a bid to hold on to her youth. Her hazel eyes were warm and kind, like her features. And though Blair was of middle age, she retained a certain youth in her character, too.

Unlikely in their pairing, husband and wife were inseparable. Eleanor recalled how her grandmother, Onóir, shared the story of how the couple eloped at the age of sixteen, before fleeing to Balloch—making it their home.

Eyes still closed, Eleanor smiled, romanticising the idea of the couple's bold escape.

They, however, had not been blessed with children—Blair believing it to be their punishment for running away. In acceptance of their fate, the couple simply got on with life, until years later, when nature changed its mind, giving them a son. Eleanor called to mind the story—the night William Grant came into the world. Great celebrations were had at The Ferry Inn that same evening—the men providing Heckie with tankards of mead and pats on the back, congratulating him for, "fathering a bairn … at last!"

The child—their only one—grew up loved and protected. William looked up to his father, hoping, one day, to be just like him—spending his time constantly trying to prove his worth.

"Auch! Sure, what's the hurry, laddie?" Heckie would say.

But the boy had inherited his mother's stubborn streak, attempting tasks he was not quite ready for. Taking the axe—he regularly carried for his father, when permitted—Will had taken it upon himself to chop some logs, to show his parents how strong he was. But in his attempt, the weight of it had proven too much, and the oversized tool fell from his small hands onto the wood, showering him in splinters.

Several had gone into his hands as he tried to protect his eyes. Wanting to avoid a scolding, he attempted to remove them all … except for one. Satisfied he had prized out every splinter, the boy returned the axe to its place, saying nothing of his failure. Six days later, at the raw age of twelve, he was *dead*. Heckie and Blair were beside themselves with grief, along with the whole village—it, too, mourning the untimely loss.

It eventually came to light what had occurred, by the boy's admission, before he died: the stray splinter had made its way into his bloodstream, secretly rotting away. The infection eventually turned poisonous, spreading its death sentence throughout his young body. By the time the physician laid his hands on him, it was too late—Heckie throwing the blame on himself.

"I should never have let the lad near the damn thing!" he had repeated, before destroying the weapon in question.

"Dinnae blame yourself, *mo gaol*," Blair had told him lovingly. "He was just a wee bairn, trying to be the man his father is—no different than any other lad. 'Twas an accident."

Two years had passed, since, along with Heckie's acceptance of his innocence, and eventually the sparkle returned to his saddened eyes, bringing the couple closer.

Eleanor was fond of the husband and wife, appreciating the close relationship they shared with her own family. While she helped her mother at the market, Blair occasionally popped in, to keep Onóir company.

Her grandmother's health had deteriorated in the last year, more than she would admit, prohibiting her from accompanying them as often as she would have liked. But the elderly lady was not ready to give in to the cruelty of old age.

"Off with ye," she had insisted that morning. "And enjoy what's left of this late summer; it may be taken from us, tomorrow."

The boy, Eleanor realised, still relishing in the warmth of the sun, would be seventeen in less than a week. No longer regarded as a *boy*, he would soon be a man, with more expected of him. Mournful of the thought, she vowed to make the best of his diminishing youth before things changed.

Her thoughts were then disrupted by the distant sound of that same *boy* and his dog, triumphantly calling out to her. She grinned. *We shall eat well, tonight!* she told herself; it was clear, by the excitement in his voice and Rave's constant barking, that they had been successful.

Eleanor cherished their precious time together. It was the one day in the week they could call their own—hers to relax, while he went hunting with Rave—the pathetic creature he had found dying in the street—almost two years ago—at Balloch's annual Horse Faire. She could still hear his boyish pleas, to their mother.

"Please, can I keep her?" he had begged, cradling the weak pup in his arms.

The Faire had, as usual, been a hive of noisy activity. The constant sound of horse-drawn carts and raised voices had blanketed the animal's dying whimpers from distracted ears—except for Gill's. Being his elder, Eleanor had always kept a close eye on her sibling. Out of habit, she had turned to check on him, only to find him on his knees, by an abandoned three-wheeled cart. Her curiosity had drawn her to his side, having seen him retrieve something from behind one of the wheels.

"We can't leave her to die, Nori!" he had told her, wrapping the pup in his good shirt.

"Her time looks short." The defined tone from their mother's voice had, at the time, struck her hard. She had noticed, as Gill grew older, her mother's leniency towards her son had grown less.

"Let me keep her, Maw. I'll make her well again," he had pleaded.

"I doubt she will—" Her mother was stopped by the lad's tears and quivering lip.

"Let him at least *try*, Rosalyn," their grandmother had intervened, taking his side. "Have a little faith in the boy."

Won over by her own mother's persuasive words, Rosalyn finally gave in. "Then she will be your responsibility, Gillis Shaw," she had told him. "But, be mindful … she may not survive."

Despite their mother's objection, they were thankful for the hound's timely arrival. The dog became a welcome distraction after their father's disappearance while helping him to come to terms with the death of his closest friend, William Grant.

For more than a week, he nursed the hound back to health, rarely leaving her side. From then on, that had been the way of it—the constant companions, secretly grateful for saving each other.

Eleanor's thoughts then wandered back to the Horse Faire in Balloch; it was the highlight of the year—a national institution. She felt a tingle of excitement and looked forward to the upcoming one, in a couple of days.

Despite having few nice things, she contemplated what to wear— something special—a sure way to catch a lad's eye. She knew her mother would alter and add to something she had worn before, without the other young lasses in the village noticing. Indeed, Rosalyn Shaw was quite the clever one with a sewing needle, rarely failing to disappoint.

The Faire attracted throngs of people from all over. They came by horse and by boat to trade, in exchange for large sums of money. Stall-holders travelled overnight, staying for more than a day—enticed by studded tents selling an abundance of beer and whisky. Vendors with their stall furniture on carts, along with candy men, cobblers, saddlers and bakers—selling jam-stuffed Roly Polies—were a spectacle to the eye. And children, who saved what little money they had for the big day, would make it stretch as far as it would go, their eager eyes and rumbling stomachs dying to indulge in all the delights on sale.

Every year the Faire grew, attracting larger numbers from further afield—the small village almost bursting at the seams from its increasing visitors. Mr Walker, the local Ferryman, always had a time of it, trying to cope with boats crammed with horses and people—the increased workload forcing him to enlist extra hands to help with the passage, from sunrise to sunset. But at times the journey proved too hazardous, resulting in the occasional incident—one in particular, leading to a tragedy that was talked about for years after.

One boat did capsize, resulting in the deaths of several passengers. Eleanor recalled the panic it caused at the time. But she and her brother had been whisked away by their father, sparing them the visual trauma of the incident. It seemed the body of a Highland drover had been the only one not recovered from the loch. And it was said—courtesy of Heckie Grant—that the drover's dog had managed to reach land. For two days after, the poor animal ran along the shoreline howling, in search of its Master … or so it was said. Therefore, every year, since the incident—and before trading commenced—the victims were remembered in a moving ceremony.

Most of her memories of the Faire had been wonderful. However, they did not attend the year their father allegedly disappeared—the same year William had died. And it was almost decided *not* to attend, the following year. But as time passed it was thought, by her grandmother, that the Shaws and the Grants should resume going.

"Do not deny them the joy of the Faire," she had heard her say in conversation with her mother. "The children need something to look forward to."

And so, it was agreed. But Heckie, still consumed by guilt, refused—as part of his self-punishment. He had, however, insisted his wife attend and, despite her reluctance to go without him, the stubborn woman was eventually won over by her husband's persuasion.

It was that same year, when Rave entered their lives, that Farrow departed Oran's.

Somehow her father's horse had found its way home, after six months. It was clear the poor steed had been through the wars, by its dishevelled state. She recalled her mother's reaction when Farrow emerged through the trees, towards their house, without his Master in tow. Her mother had found herself in a state of utter confusion and dread, on seeing the Albrecht sword still attached to the saddle; she had seen her snatch the weapon, and then conceal it from them. For her father to be without his prized piece … It played on her worst nightmares. She had wanted to admit to seeing the weapon, but changed her mind when her mother had spoken to them, later that night.

"It is unlikely your father will be returning to us."

Her mother's words had been cold and defined. Gill, not understanding her meaning, had forced Eleanor to ask the questions—for both their sakes.

"Are you telling us ... Paw is ... *dead?*"

Dead! Dead! Eleanor felt a chill in the heat of the sun, recalling the moment she'd spoken *that* word in front of her mother and Gill. The coldness of its true meaning was absolute and had stayed with her ever since.

"Perhaps," had been her mother's blunt response, after a long pause.

"Then nothing *is* final," she had bravely replied, expecting a scolding.

But, instead, gripped by anger and sadness, her mother had stormed off, refusing to discuss it again. She recalled the look of heartbreak and utter confusion on her young brother's face. In all his innocence, he had tried to understand his mother's reaction. She, on the other hand, had thought it cruel of her, to detach herself from the subject, leaving her children in the dark.

But there was always someone she knew they could talk to—the most ardent listener of all: their grandmother.

Farrow's strength and vitality were renewed in no time, and his return had provided them with some comfort. Still in the prime of his life, the steed, however, had caught the eye of many. Her mother had wanted to keep him—in the hope her husband would come home. But with each passing day, week and month, hope had faded, and their belts grew tighter.

"You can't sell him!" she had protested to her mother.

"What alternative do we have, Eleanor?"

Gill had pleaded continuously to his grandmother, to intervene. But Onóir's silence had told them she had agreed with her daughter's decision.

"You know how things have been since I was forced to let your father's business go. Gill has neither the skill nor knowledge to manage it. When he comes of age, he will have to go to Eddin, to look for work. The earnings from a market stall can barely sustain four adults."

Eleanor knew it had secretly broken her mother's heart—the idea of having to part with her husband's—their father's—beloved steed.

"Needs must!" had been her final say on the matter.

The memory of that day was still vivid in her mind. Onóir, feeling unwell, had chosen not to attend, and remained at home with Rave, while they attended the Faire to say goodbye to Farrow, secretly hoping there would be no takers. But a steed as fine as Oran Shaw's had not gone unnoticed.

The sight of her mother, that day, reluctantly leading the horse into the pit of hungry traders, would never leave her.

She had held on to her brother's hand tightly, as the crowd circled with added interest. No time had been wasted in bidding. She could still hear their raised voices, desperately haggling to out-bid their competition, their volume increasing in a threatening manner—such was the interest—each generous bid growing higher and higher. It had been overwhelming yet terrifying. She remembered the crowds' angry frustration as her mother's grip refused to let go of the nervous horse, fearing the steed would bolt, hoping she would change her mind.

Her mother had looked hard into the eyes of those who had challenged her, seeing nothing but intent and malice. It was evident they would not treat the steed with the respect it deserved. Feeling threatened, her mother had turned, intending to leave, when a familiar voice spoke—their saving grace.

"I would gladly take him, matching any price they offer."

"Sold!" her mother had blurted, handing over the reins to Kai Aitken—the new landlord of The Ferry Inn. Later, when queried about her choice, her mother had simply replied; "I saw humility in his eyes, Eleanor. He will care for Farrow, as we did."

Angry protests of dissatisfaction and displeasure had ensued from the other bidders, who had felt hard done by, remarking; "How typical! A local, selling it to one of their own."

"It is decided!" she had yelled, finding her voice again. "Now good day, gentlemen."

The crowd, finally accepting their loss, eventually made their way towards The Ferry Inn, unaware of the irony in it.

Kai Aitken stood almost six feet in height, and lean with it. She gave him thirty years, maybe more. Though regarded as not being particularly handsome, his features, however, were striking. His dark hair—always worn neatly tied back—emphasised his well-groomed beard. His warm, brown eyes distracted from his pale skin, and when he smiled, his face came to life. She had detected a faint accent, surmising he was from the south. The clothes he wore were of the finest quality, and made from fabric she did not recognise. She imagined they were from somewhere foreign—somewhere exotic, perhaps.

Kai had fallen upon his occupation by mere chance. As a traveller, passing through, he had taken it upon himself to stop at The Ferry Inn for food, and a drink of local whisky. Ned McGregor, the previous proprietor of the establishment, had grown long in years. No longer able to control any ensuing brawls, his courage had begun to shrink. Because of it, word had spread beyond the village, attracting unwanted visitors. She knew, if her father had been around, he would have tackled the trouble-makers. She smiled to herself, visualising him doing so, with Heckie Grant by his side. But even *he* had lost interest, since his son's death, refusing to take another sup. And, because of their absence, it had only been a matter of time before the locals were driven from the Inn by the scandalmongers.

Kai had been sitting, minding his own business when four bothersome strangers happened upon the Inn. Though boisterous, he chose to ignore them, until they turned their sights on young, Sarah Butler—the maid. The four, however, after consuming large quantities of whisky, had been no match for Kai, who produced a claymore and dirk, threatening the instigators. A fight broke out, it leading to gravely injuring two, minor injuries to another, and a final warning to the remaining perpetrator—never to return.

Forever grateful to the stranger, Ned had then invited Kai to lodge that night … and the next … and another, his ongoing stay eventually leading to his purchase of The Ferry Inn.

164

Kai permitted Ned to stay on, rent-free, allowing the old man to retire comfortably. It had been the most welcomed gossip, quickly spreading among the villagers and luring them back, within a day.

Above the Inn's door, Kai had placed an unusually oversized axe, as a warning to anyone passing over his threshold, to be mindful of their behaviour—should they choose to enter.

Little was known then, or since, about the unlikely, new proprietor … nor did anyone ask. Eleanor recollected their first proper introduction, sometime after. She and Gill had been in awe of the unsuspecting hero as he chatted with their mother, about his unexpected purchase of their father's horse. They had been sharing a joke about something or other when she had noticed the scar, lining his throat.

She recalled her embarrassment when he found her out. Yet, despite her mortification, she had been determined to enquire: "Who did *that* to you?" she had asked, to her mother's horror.

"Prejudiced fools!" he had muttered, without thought, it had seemed. The comment had confused her, at first, but he'd been quick to apologise. "There are some in this world who know nothing but ignorance and prejudice, Eleanor," he had said. "They feel it their duty to rid it of those of us who are … *different* … and who don't share *their* beliefs."

"Eleanor Shaw!" her mother had snapped. "Do not pry into the affairs of others."

She smiled inwardly now, recalling the added shock on her mother's face when her brother's curiosity then got the better of him.

"What happened?" Gill had asked, his expression wild with expectations of another blood-curdling tale while relishing the thought of sharing it with Heckie.

"Gillis Shaw!" her mother had snapped again, preparing to drag them home, while begging forgiveness for the rudeness of her two children.

"Shall I tell you, Gill?" he had said, turning and winking at their mother. "I would hate to disappoint the lad."

Her mother had held her tongue, keeping them in suspense, then, with a sigh and a nod, finally surrendered her approval.

"Well, it was some years ago," he had begun, smiling at their eager faces. "Two of those … bigoted souls, crossed paths with this condemned one, deciding the world would be a better place without him. I was unarmed at the time—more fool I. Hence the reason I am never without *this*."

She recalled their expressions when he patted the hilt of the large sword, peeping over his shoulder at them.

"They placed a rope about my neck, thinking I should be hanged for my crimes of passion. As they hauled me up …"

In her head, she could still hear the loud gasp that came from her brother, as his mouth gaped in disbelief before asking; "And then?!"

Mortified by her inquisitive son, Rosalyn closed her eyes and shook her head.

Holding back his laughter, Kai continued with his story: "As I watched my condemners ride away, it seemed the weight of my body was too much for the piece of string they had called a "rope." The impact of hitting the ground caused me more pain, I must admit. And *here*, as you have seen, is my battle scar. However, to my real misfortune, I was rid of all my possessions."

"Not quite *all*," she had told him. "They failed to take your life!"

"Indeed!" he had replied, smiling gloriously at her. Despite Kai's purchase, Farrow somehow continued to find his way home, regularly. She laughed to herself, recalling her mother's annoyance, each time the horse reappeared on their doorstep—and afterwards—always insisting the steed was returned to its new owner.

Eventually, Kai bowed to the losing battle, letting Farrow stay where he truly belonged. A vow was made to pay him back, but he had refused, instead offering Eleanor a position as a maid, at The Ferry Inn.

At first, her mother had refused, insisting it was, "Out of the question!" But after leaning on her grandmother's softness, the old woman's influence had finally won over, and it was agreed; "Only on weekends." Thus, allowing her to be more involved in the local gossip—which she reported back if anything was particularly scandalous.

Meanwhile, Kai had settled into his new position as though he had done it most of his life.

Perhaps he has, she mused to herself, shifting her weight, to adjust her shawl, before settling back into her daydreams.

Little was known of his origins. Despite it, he became a good friend to her family, taking Gill under his wing like an older brother. She noticed how skilled her sibling had become in archery, not to mention his use of a sword—almost matching that of their father's. *Paw would have been proud.* Thinking of her father, again, she hoped her mother would pass on his sword to Gill. *No doubt, when he comes of age,* she assumed, and yet there'd been no mention of it, since …

No one had questioned Kai's privacy—until the night the *stranger* walked into The Ferry Inn. She shuddered, remembering the unpleasant incident. Burdened with full tankards of ale, she had been tending to two elderly locals. She recalled the moment the individual stepped across the threshold, ignoring the notable "warning" above the door. There had been malice in his demeanour; it reeked from his pores.

At first, Kai had not seen him, until her reaction alerted him to the unwanted guest. She would never forget the look on their faces as their eyes fell on one another; the stranger looked as though he had seen a ghost, while Kai's expression had been one of shock.

The silence that killed the locals' chatter had given her cause for concern, at the time. She had surveyed the stranger as he moved cautiously towards the serving counter—eyes fixed on the proprietor. It was clear they had known one another.

Kai, a man of integrity, had kept his poise as the *stranger* approached him. She recalled all eyes watching them with expectation. Ignoring the heaviness in her hands, she had waited in anticipation, as the landlord drew some ale for the unwanted visitor, sliding the tankard towards him. In the meantime, one of the impatient elderlies had swiftly relieved her of his ale, supping on it, hoping they would see Kai draw his sword. The silence had frightened her as the tension mounted. She remembered how the stranger stared into his drink, before spitting on the contents.

"I'll not drink *that* from the hand that poured it," he had sneered, casting it away.

"Then I invite you to leave this place—sir," Kai had returned.

"Hah! Sir, you say? Aye, that's it! *Know* your place!"

"I suggest you leave—*now!*"

A deep rage, she had never seen before in Kai's warm eyes, had forced her to step away from the looming threat.

The *stranger* stood back, laughing, before turning to address his eager audience. "Do ye know who—*what*—he is?" he had said, raising his voice.

The Inn had remained silent—the onlookers unsure, eyeing one another.

"I'll take that as a "no", then." The *stranger* then strolled around the open space, sneering into the faces of her friends and neighbours. She recalled the moment he chose to stop, his grey, lifeless eyes falling on hers.

A chill went down her spine, still haunted by his lecherous stare.

"Leave her be!" Kai had yelled, moving closer.

"Have ye asked yourselves why he has no wife or bairns to speak of?" the *stranger* had said, in his thick, northerly accent.

She could still remember the smell of stale whisky from his breath when he leaned towards her. His skin was like that of leather—parched from the elements that nature had inflicted on it. And his face—it had been born with the indented scars of a disease that had latched itself to him as a child. She could never have envisaged him bearing such innocence.

"I have no care to know, or enquire," had been her brave reply.

"Ah, but a fine young lass like yourself would give him no pleasure at all. Is it not a crime in these parts? I should imagine the—"

She could still hear the scream that erupted from inside her when Kai held his dagger across the reprobate's throat.

"I will match that which you inflicted on me, as a constant reminder of what you *stole!*"

The *stranger* had struggled to breathe, and she was certain, by the look of revenge on Kai's face, he had intended to slice his throat. But Kai had seen the terrified look in her eyes and chose to release him. Tension had gripped the onlookers as the *stranger* cradled his throat, his bulging eyes, wild with rage.

"I thought you surely *dead!*" he had croaked.

"As you shall be, if you do not leave this place," Kai had threatened, before leaning into his ear. He had whispered something to him. What that was, she never knew; she had always been afraid to ask. But it was as if he had delved into the depths of their soul, for as he released his final grip on him, the *stranger* had stared back at Kai, petrified, before promptly taking his leave.

Even now, thinking back on it, she still wondered what had passed between them.

When he had left, Kai turned to face the villagers. The Inn had been particularly busy that evening—full of the gossip mongers Ned McGregor had warned him about, before taking his post. He had become accustomed to their wagging tongues. However, despite those warnings, she had noticed, for the first time, on that occasion, his struggle to speak, prompting Ned to volunteer as spokesman.

"Is it true, lad?" he had asked gently. "What he implied?"

Everyone had held their own as Kai lowered his head. She recalled him taking a deep breath, which seemed to lengthen with every passing second. He lifted his head, without shame, and then stepped into the centre of his establishment. It had been the bravest thing she had seen anyone do, that day.

"It's true," he had admitted, with an air of pride. "And, if you wish, I shall leave Balloch, for good. I will return this Inn—the place I have grown to love—to Ned ... which will, again, play into the hands of those who brought nothing but gloom on it."

His words had had no threat or malice in them, his caring nature only providing them with the grim reality of what would happen—had he been forced to leave.

That night had been a reminder to her—regardless of idle gossip—how loyal the villagers were to those who looked after them.

They had all looked to one another for guidance, waiting for the first to speak. Protected too long from the outside world, she had learned the brutal reality of what happened to those whose preferences were regarded as unchaste and immoral. She realised, then, how grateful she was for her unprejudiced upbringing, choosing to be the first to support him.

"I see no harm in it," she had defended him, trying to conceal her shyness when everyone looked at her in surprise.

She'd beamed, seeing the relief on Kai's face when he provided her with one of his infectious smiles, while forced to wait in the quietude of his Inn, for further response.

"I second that!" Ned had added, punching the air with a determined fist.

"Sure, you'll no hear a word spoken against the laddie from me," another had voiced.

She remembered the swell of pride when, one by one, they had stood in defence of their landlord, bursting with laughter as the aptly named, Alastair Boyd, had to say his piece:

"Aye! Agreed. Sure, if it were not for him, would we be sitting here this day? And I'm certain many of ye would miss his heavy hand when pouring a dram for us. Aye, I'll be keeping wheesht, as will me missus."

"A true word spoken from a *true defender of mankind*, Alastair," Ned had remarked.

Chapter Nineteen

'*eleanor!*'

She jolted.

Torn from her thoughts and memories, Eleanor quickly sat up, looking around her. She was still alone. 'Gill?'

Her brother was nowhere to be seen.

Tilting her head slightly, she listened, narrowing her eyes.

All was still.

She then looked down, seeing the loch's flat surface, noting how it mirrored the perfect blue sky above—the wind's sudden absence now making it feel increasingly warmer.

She now felt thirsty, regretting leaving the water skin with Gill. Shading her eyes from the watery sun, she searched for the boy and his dog. *Where are they?* she thought, wiping the sweat from her brow.

'Gill!' she cried, her raised voice carrying through the serenity of the day, it disturbing a host of sparrows nestled among the shady branches.

There was still no sight nor sound of her brother.

Strange. Frowning, she placed her fingers in her mouth, prepared to whistle for him.

"That's not very lady-like!" her mother had said, the first time she did it—and with great success, too.

"Ah, but effective," she had returned.

"And whom, may I ask, taught you?"

"Blair."

"Blair Grant?!" her mother had replied, stunned by the revelation, at first.

"Aye, and why not?" she had challenged.

But when her mother had paused for thought, smiling to herself, it was clear she had been impressed by another of their neighbour's "talents"—gathering local gossip, also, Blair's speciality. "Why not, indeed!"

As she took a deep breath, ready to whistle, she heard her name being whispered again.

'*Eleanor!*'

She stopped, realising it was *not* her brother.

'*Eleanor!*'

Rising sharply, the heat of the day took its toll; dehydrated, her head became light, forcing her to reach out for something to hold. As the weight of her body tumbled towards the hard ground, she felt the strength of someone's hold, breaking her fall.

Dazed and confused, Eleanor found herself seated in the shade of a tree, cradling her head in her hands, waiting for the world to stop spinning.

'Nori! Nori! Are you all right?' her brother cried, taking her hand, while Rave barked continuously into the woods. 'Enough, Rave!'

The dog ceased immediately, returning to her Master's side.

'I am, thank you,' she said, patting Rave on the head. 'If it had not been for you, I'd have injured myself. The sun's heat is—' Eleanor stopped when her brother frowned and drew his head back—the confused expression on his face clear. 'It *was* you—who caught me—wasn't it?!' she then queried.

He slowly shook his head, offering her a drink.

'I found you here, like *this*.'

Accepting the water skin she placed the tip to her lips, instantly feeling the quenching benefits of its cool contents, on her parched throat.

Rising, he smirked as she gulped the water to its last drop. 'Better?'

'But it *had* to be you!' she insisted, handing it back. 'Who else could it have been?'

'Perhaps the hero in your daydreams,' he teased, rolling his eyes.

Eleanor scowled and looked up at her brother, ready to scold him, then hesitated. Tilting her head, she narrowed her eyes. *He looks … different?* she mused, as though he had suddenly come of age—all grown up. Almost.

For his sixteen years, Gillis Shaw reached an impressive height—four inches above six feet. Like his sister, his skin was tanned by the unusual hot autumn. His dark, hazel eyes lit up when he smiled, softening his notable, maturing squared features. Wanting to rid himself of the last of his youth, he had decided to let his black, wavy hair grow, constantly pushing it behind his ears while he got used to its new length. Also—thinking it would make him more appealing to a certain young lady—he had decided to add to it, by growing a beard. However, Eleanor would often mock him over the faint, bristled shadow on his chin, telling him how it would take years to grow.

Eleanor observed his clothes; they barely fit his broadening frame now—the cuffs of his faded, black shirt, stretching halfway up his muscular forearms. She noticed a tear on the shoulder, where he had overstretched the worn material. A glance at his scuffed, brown breeches told her they would part from his toned legs, soon enough, if their mother did not intervene with her sewing needle. Also, his body had seemed to take on a new strength of form. She surmised it was due to his over-enthusiastic displays of archery skills—clearly to impress his young beau, Meghan Downy, who lived at the far end of Balloch.

'What are you staring at?' he slowly asked, casting his sister a sideward glance.

'Oh! 'Tis nothing …' she answered, her voice trailing as she reached out for him to haul her up. 'Are you *certain* it was not—'

'Aye, positive,' he said.

A thought then occurred to her. Opening her hands, she looked down at her palms. There were no cuts or grazes.

'Then look!' she said, holding them out. 'See?! Had I hit the ground, there'd be—'

'Nori—you've been deceived by the sun,' he said, interrupting her again. 'Nothing more.'

She frowned at him, her lips pressed together, still determined. 'I heard someone say—no—whisper my name—more than once.'

Gill gave her a dubious look as he folded his arms and dropped his head.

She glared at him, still frustrated by his doubt. 'I tell you, Gillis Shaw, I know what I—'

'Do you not think Rave would have sensed the presence of a stranger?' he debated, turning to pick up the three hares, whose lives he had cut short.

Eleanor pulled a face, seeing their evening meal dangling from the piece of knotted rope—eyes bulging and lifeless. She cringed when an image of her grandmother, skinning the hides, entered her mind. She had tried it once—at her mother's insistence—but the mere sight of the blade, slicing into its dead body, made her stomach churn.

'Then *what* was she barking at?' she challenged, pointing at Rave.

'You *know* how excited she gets when we're hunting,' he replied, dismissing her daydreams. 'She's a hound—she'll bark at anything.'

Eleanor pursed her lips as doubt closed in. *Perhaps he's right,* she thought.

'I must admit, Eleanor …' he added, his tone now serious. 'I saw and heard nothing. You have my word.'

Shrugging it off, she smiled, feeling a little silly. For the first time, *she* felt like the younger sibling. He had been the one she'd looked after, protecting him from things he was not yet ready to experience. The *boy* was slowly passing into the fortitude of maturity. It was apparent a great change was taking place—one she was reluctant to accept.

'I've something to share with you, Nori,' he suddenly whispered, distracting her, his eyes wide with excitement. 'Can I show you?' he then added, nodding, encouraging her.

She drew her head back, raising her brows, throwing him a suspicious look.

''Tis no daydream!' he quickly stressed.

'Aye, right,' she said, rolling her eyes while observing the twinkling tell-tale sign in his. Then, for a moment, she saw the welcome return of the *boy*—eager to tell his older sister another story.

'I *hate* it when you say that!' he snapped.

She blinked, surprised by his brief outburst.

'I am more than aware, the stories Heckie told me—when I was younger—were nothing more than that. But this is different, Eleanor. Let me prove this one is *real*.'

She looked into his pleading eyes, trying to grasp his honesty, knowing he was serious when he used her full name, then saw him chew his lip as he waited patiently for her to show genuine interest.

She sighed. 'Right, then,' she said, pulling on her mochs. 'Lead the way!'

Setting their evening meal aside, Gill checked his bow and dagger before setting off at full speed, back towards the loch, with Rave and Eleanor at his heel.

'Slow down!' she called out, finding it difficult to keep pace; it only seemed a short while ago since she could outrun him. *When did he learn to run so fast?* she thought, trying to catch up.

In the distance she heard Rave's over-excited bark, followed by Gill's raised voice, telling her to "Keep up!"

Eleanor suddenly stopped, hearing the snap of branches, a few feet behind her. She swallowed, trying to catch her breath, then held it a moment, listening—the sound of her heavy breathing echoing loudly in her head.

'Nori!'

She spun, reacting to her brother's voice, then jumped back, to find him standing a few feet from her. She gasped. 'How did you …?'

'I've been calling you,' he said. 'What are you doing? Never mind—hurry—it's this way! We must be quiet from here. We don't want to frighten it.'

Giving her no time to reply, he took his sister's hand, leading her close to the water's edge. Then, raising a finger to his mouth, he motioned her to be still. 'Rave!' he called to the hound, lowering his voice as she noisily lapped up the cold water. 'Come!'

The dog crouched by their side, attentive and obedient.

'What are we looking for?' Eleanor whispered.

Gill remained silent, keeping a fixed eye on the far side of the loch. 'Just wait,' he urged, hesitating. Rave released a low growl from the depths of her stomach. 'Wheesht!' he snapped, placing a hand over her snout. 'There!' he said, pointing. 'Can you see it?'

Eleanor cupped her hands, shielding her narrowing eyes from the glare of the water, searching for whatever "it" was. She then caught the movement of a white horse, casually grazing near the water's edge, on the other side, minding its own business.

She frowned. 'It's a horse,' she said, stating the obvious.

A knowing curl appeared on the side of his mouth.

''Tis *just* a horse, Gill,' she then insisted, tutting and rolling her eyes.

'Aye,' he replied. 'But no *ordinary* horse.'

Staring at him, she waited, her patience wearing thin. 'Well?' she finally snapped.

''Tis the Kelpie!' he revealed.

'No!' she gasped, throwing her hand over her mouth, afraid it might hear her.

He grinned from ear to ear at her reaction, slowly nodding.

'Impossible! The water horse is nothing but a myth … isn't it?'

'Some would believe so,' he replied. 'But *I* know different; I've *seen* it—' He stopped, contemplating whether he should tell her exactly what he had witnessed—and on more than *one* occasion.

She narrowed her eyes. 'Seen what?'

He frowned, chewing on his lip again, before deciding to share his *secret*. 'See its mane, Nori?' She nodded, mouth gaping. For once, he had her undivided attention. ''Tis dripping wet, and covered in seaweed. *That* is how you know, and—'

'Who's that?' she blurted, observing a man approach the horse, from behind. 'His owner?'

Gill pulled an awkward face before looking into his sister's naive eyes.

'What is it?' she asked.

'Surely, you've heard the tale …' he said.

She stared at him, trying to recall it, her sudden, sharp intake of breath then signalling the realisation of what was about to happen to the unsuspecting stranger, across the loch.

'Oh, Gill! You *must* do something!' she begged, grasping his arm. 'Help him!' Her blue eyes widened, horrified, as she rose to alert the stranger, while Rave broke into a resounding, frenzied bark as if to warn him. 'Do something!' she then cried, seeing the stranger mount the Kelpie. Frantic, she began waving her arms, calling out across the calm waters.

''Tis too late!' Gill informed her.

She then stopped, knowing he was right. To the ignorant, the white stallion was seen as a prized trophy—worthy of a hefty price. And with nothing to mark its owner, the horse was there for the taking—if found roaming free.

'Only a foolish man would interfere,' Gill remarked, in a cold, flat tone.

Eleanor glowered at her brother, his calm observation telling her he *had* seen it before. It seemed the "boy" had just proclaimed himself a "man." The younger Gill—she once knew—would have taken a huge risk, and swam the loch.

'Is there nothing we can do?' she said, desperately hoping he would intervene.

'He is beyond our help'—he grunted— 'or another's, for that matter.'

It was and had always been a game of deception, on the creature's part: allowing its victim to mount it and take control, letting them believe they owned the upper hand. The Kelpie would then canter along the shoreline, at the stranger's command, biding its time.

Gill and Eleanor looked on, helpless, as the creature took pace, increasing its speed to a threatening gallop, while the restless stranger battled to stop it. Then, recognising his foolishness, he attempted to jump free from its hold—but was unable to do so.

'Jump!' Eleanor screamed.

The doomed man looked sharp, hearing the voice of desperation cry out to him. Panic gripped him as he frantically tried to free himself from the creature's bareback.

The Kelpie's long, mane wrapped itself around its victim's wrists and legs, securing its hold on the reluctant rider, before leaping into the murky depths.

Eleanor stood speechless, as the creature took its victim to his final resting place, still watching, until the rippling water calmed itself again, as though nothing had happened.

Gill felt an element of regret shroud him as he looked into the terrified face of his sister. Rigid with fear, she stood transfixed, in a state of disbelief.

'Nori,' he said, in a calm voice.

When she failed to hear him, he placed a comforting hand on her shoulder. She flinched.

A tear fell on her flushed cheek as she turned to him. 'We should have done something, Gill!' she whimpered. 'We could have—perhaps—even *tried.*'

'Believe me when I tell you, Eleanor,' he began, wiping the tear away, 'there was nothing we could have done. He was doomed from the moment he looked into the creature's black eyes. No man could have saved him.'

'Nor boy,' she snivelled.

Shaking his head, he forced a crooked smile, understanding her meaning.

'Why did I have to see it, Gill?'

'I'm sorry, Nori, but I did not bargain on that man being there.'

'Do you think we know'—she hesitated, unable to shake the image of the stranger being dragged to his death— '*knew* him?'

'Who can say?' he answered, raising his broad shoulders. ''Tis unlikely. Perhaps it was someone who had fallen on hard times—who saw an opportunity to prize himself a fine stallion. A fatal error on his part, though.'

She sighed heavily. 'But the guilt I feel is …' Her voice drifted, unable to express it.

'Do not let it consume you, Eleanor. After all, we didn't know him.'

For a moment she stared at him, dismayed at how unperturbed he seemed by the incident. There was something heartless in what he had said, and yet, deep inside, she was ashamed to admit he was right. *Still and all* … A spark of anger ignited inside her.

'How many times have you seen it, Gillis?!' she demanded. 'And why did you neglect to tell me?!'

A feeling of self-reproach engulfed him; he watched the familiar tilt of her head and raised eyebrows as she waited for his explanation.

'I *have* tried … many times!' he implored, with outstretched hands. 'But I was sure you would not believe me … and …'

'And?'

'I didn't want to frighten you, knowing …'

She glared at him and leaned forward, urging him to continue.

'Knowing how you like to bathe in the loch,' he blurted, diverting his eyes.

Eleanor drew her head back in surprise, then looked away, slightly embarrassed. But the thought was quickly cast aside as she grasped the grim truth behind the myth. It was there, written on her face for him to see.

'*Now* do you understand why I held back from telling you?'

'But … that could have been *me*, Gill!' she cried, cupping her hands over her mouth.

'No, Nori, you were always safe! I assure you! It never would have approached you!'

Eleanor's eyes glared as she pointed her finger towards her guilt-ridden brother. 'I have just seen an innocent man—'

'How do we know he was innocent?' he interrupted, in a vain attempt to humour her.

'Gillis Shaw! How *could* you?!'

The young man hung his head in a brief moment of shame.

'That poor man was taken to his death by that—that—*creature*, and you stand before me in a calm and amused manner … assuring me of *my* safety! This is one tale where you have my undivided attention.' With hands on hips, Eleanor began tapping her foot on the pebbled ground—the continuous sound of tiny stones being crushed beneath her foot, gradually grinding him down. Aware his sister carried the same temperament as their grandmother, he thought it best to change the subject.

'It will be dusk, soon,' he blurted, looking up. 'And Maw will be waiting. I promised her—'

'No, you don't, Gill!' she snapped, wagging her finger, knowing she would prevail over him.

He sighed, surrendering defeat. 'Be patient, a moment,' he said, turning to leave.

'Where are you going?' she called, intent on following him.

'To fetch our supper. I left it by the tree, where you fell. Wait here, with Rave.'

Shaking her head, Eleanor watched him disappear through the trees.

'Come with me!' she ordered the hound, turning to face the loch again.

Gill was right; the early signs of dusks' approach were visible now. She looked across the sky at the paling blue and orange light, following the setting sun as it gradually faded behind the distant Highlands. Tiny speckles of light began to wink down from above, announcing the coming of night. The days were growing shorter.

She felt an unexpected chill in the air, after the deception of the day's heat. It was, after all, late autumn. Her thoughts returned to the stranger, wondering if he had had a family—a wife and children, perhaps—and the devastation they would feel when he would never return home. She could relate to it. There would be no proof of his disappearance, unless the loch gave up his cold, bloated body. She shuddered at the idea of it happening to her, or someone they might know. But Gill's assurance of her safety seemed definite in *his* mind.

Feeling the brush of the cool, evening air, she released her hair, letting it fall over her shoulders, then thought of her shawl. 'Let's fetch it, Rave!' The dog leapt, wagging her tail back and forth.

As they made to leave, Eleanor heard the resounding snap of a twig behind her, and turned, saying, 'Gill, forgive your sister for being so—' She stopped short, convinced she had seen a movement among the trees.

Rave growled, cautiously lowering her head. Tail pointed straight, the dog hunched forward, ready to pounce.

'Stay!' she whispered. 'Gill? Is that—'

The swift, dark movement caught her eye, again. Watching and waiting, she carefully guided her hand to the belt—where her dagger usually hung—before noting its absence. She quickly gathered her thoughts, cursing herself for foolishly leaving it beside her shawl. She listened for the noise again, sighing with relief when she heard nothing further.

'A feast fit for a king, eh, Nori?!' Gill shouted, appearing from her left.

Eleanor's stomach almost heaved when he proudly displayed the three lifeless hares, swaying under their dead weight.

Rave ran to her Master's side—the hound always excited to see him, regardless of time.

'Here,' he said, handing his sister her shawl and the precious dagger. 'Maw will string you from the highest tree—should you lose *that*.'

Returning the small weapon to her belt, Eleanor felt the comfort of its presence.

A prized possession, the dirk had been a family heirloom. Despite its lengthy inheritance, no one seemed to know its true age or origin. Handed down through the female line, the women had one unique trait in common: they were all left-handed. And on her eighteenth birthday—as was customary—Eleanor's mother had passed the dagger on to her.

Eleanor kept the blade sharp, regularly, polishing the silver and gold fittings along its centre. A single sapphire crowned the pommel. The grip was fashioned with bog oak, and small gold studs were embedded in the throat of the weapon. Engraved on the back of the blade, read the initials of some of its previous owners. She glanced, with pride, at the space beneath the "R.S" where her initials "E.M.S" had been recently placed.

"I will gladly engrave your name on it when you reach that age," her father had promised. But his disappearance prevented him from ever doing so, and when Kai offered, she handed the dagger to him, without a second thought.

'What do you know about it?' Gill asked.

'Huh?' she returned, momentarily confused.

'The Kelpie?' he reminded her, rolling his eyes.

'Only what I've seen here, today.

Gill hesitated before asking, 'Are you *certain* you want to—?'

'Aye, go on,' she cut in, now eager to listen. 'Tell me!'

'Well, 'tis also known as the shape-shifting water horse,' he began. 'And I confess ... I *have* seen it take its victims to their watery grave ... more than once. And Nori, the victims are always men, according to Heckie. It seems the Kelpie never lures a woman.'

'Ah, now I understand your assurance of my welfare,' she replied. 'I suppose it is a comforting thought ... in the light of things.'

'They venture near lochs, streams and rivers. 'Tis said, they can take the form of a woman, to lure its victim ... Although ... I've never witnessed that. But they truly are a magnificent beast, Nori—and I can understand why a man should want to—'

'Did you say, *they?*'

'Aye. I've also seen a black one,' he added, his eyes dancing with excitement. 'And, what's more ... I've seen it up close.'

'Really?!' she said, raising her brows as she leaned forward with added interest.

He slowly nodded, rather pleased with himself.

'But how are *you* still here to tell the tale?' she queried, musing over his words. 'And if Maw finds out, she will—'

'But she *won't*, will she?' he said, looking at her with an air of innocence.

Eleanor found herself staring back at the face of the *boy* again, knowing he could win her over. 'Only if you promise not to take such idiotic risks like that again.'

'I shall do my very best,' he replied with a sideward grin, before pitching his kill over his shoulder. 'Time to go!'

Eleanor's mind filled with curious notions as they began their journey home, urging her to ask; 'But why has the creature not lured *you*—if you say you've seen it closely?'

'That,' he stated, 'is something I do *not* know. I've been close enough for it to coax me—several times—but it just seems to … *ignore* me.' He shrugged.

She regarded him when he gave a short laugh.

'Perhaps the Kelpie finds me too alluring.'

'Like Meghan Downy?' she retorted, mocking him.

Gill kept his silence, displaying a mischievous smile on his face. 'I can't understand why it pays no attention to me,' he remarked, letting her know he was unwilling to discuss his young beaux. 'But, whatever its reason, I'm extremely thankful for it.'

'And yet, you've risked it, Gill.'

'Nothing, but the natural curiosity of a young man,' he returned.

'And a foolish one, at that!' she mumbled.

He ignored the remark.

Darkness began its slow descent on them, as they made their way towards the incline, beyond the trees. Eleanor suddenly felt uneasy.

'Can we go the long way?' she asked, slowing her pace.

He stopped, sensing the nervousness in her voice, and looked to where the castle peered down at them.

'Through the woods?' he said, turning to her. 'But you hate going that way.'

'I know,' she replied, nodding. But …'

'They're just old tales, Nori,' he explained, dismissing them with a wave of his hand. 'According to Heckie, it's not the dead we should fear …'

'I know, but still …' She hesitated, trying to avoid looking up at the castle's lonely, forbidding courtyard, sensing it was watching their every move.

Gill, feeling the pang of hunger, released a long, heavy sigh, and shook his head.

'The long way it is, then.'

A streak of silver suddenly flashed through the distant sky. Rave barked when Eleanor jumped. She grasped her brother's arm. Gill smiled and looked up, seeing the heavy layers of black and grey clouds hovering beyond, against the slate-coloured sky.

'I doubt it will come to anything, Nori,' he surmised, attempting to calm her anxiousness.

Eleanor always feared the wrath of a thunderstorm, since the time they went fishing with Heckie and Will. She was no more than ten, at the time, and Gill on the eve of seven. The storm had seemed to roll down from the Highlands, its intent to assault itself on the world. Heckie had lost control of the small boat they were in—almost capsizing the vessel. The waves crashed over the sides, threatening to sink it. Lightening had flashed dangerously close, illuminating the loch's choppy, black waters. Traumatised by the incident, she had refused to leave the house for a week—and vowed to never set foot in a boat again.

'It will be fine,' he said, taking her from her thoughts.

'Do you think so?' she asked, keeping her eyes firmly fixed on the far-off sky.

'Aye,' he answered with confidence. 'The lightning is beyond the Highlands, so don't worry yourself.'

As they walked the long detour back from where they came, avoiding the castle, Eleanor moved closer to her brother, giving her a sense of comfort until the bulging eyes of the three hares forced her to step away.

Together they strolled in temporary silence, save for the sound of their footsteps, pounding the dry ground beneath their feet. But above the noise of each step, an unusual emptiness pressed down on her, bringing her attention to their surroundings; it was strangely quiet as if they were the only three in existence.

She looked down at Rave, to see if she had sensed anything. However, the hound—her grandmother described as "that nose on legs"—was too preoccupied with the kill of the day—watching the hares as they swung loosely over her Master's shoulder. But the momentary distraction was not enough, to avoid the eeriness that now crept up from behind. Aware of the ominous chill closing in on her, Eleanor shuddered, feeling its unwanted presence.

Don't look back! Don't look back! she kept telling herself. But it was unavoidable; the temptation was too much.

She turned her head.

There, from the castle's keep, she swore she saw the flicker of a pale-yellow light, blinking at her.

Chapter Twenty

'o you *really* want to go this way?' Gill asked as they approached the threshold of the woods. When his sister failed to respond, he turned to see her staring back at the castle.

'Eleanor!' he snapped.

'Certain!' she replied eagerly, spinning round to face him.

'So be it!' he returned, looking to the night sky. 'And look!' he added, pointing up. 'We even have the full moon to light our way. So, there's nothing to be afraid of.'

She followed his gaze, in awe at the spectacle high above them, trying to blank the sinister thoughts preying on her weakness.

'Does the moon look'—he stopped, then tilted his head— 'brighter than usual?'

''Tis always brighter at its fullest, Gill,' she replied, casting him a peculiar glance.

'True, but … see how clear the markings on its surface are,' he said, pointing directly at it. 'It was the same, last night. I've never seen it so … *illuminated!*'

Eleanor looked higher, stretching her neck, her mouth opening wide. 'Aye, so it is,' she agreed. Then, letting her eyes wander, she added; 'And look how crowded the sky is with stars.'

'How many do you think there are?' he said, keeping her mind occupied from sinister thoughts.

She frowned, shaking her head.

'They must be infinite. Too many to count; it would take forever!'

'Look!' he then whispered, pointing. 'Did you *see* that?!'

She gasped. 'I did! Blair once told me, every shooting star we see, is a soul passing into the next world. 'Tis sad, but a beautiful thought.'

'Well, Paw told *me*,' he challenged, 'they are restless, lost souls, waiting to be plucked from a never-ending journey of perpetual suffering.'

'How awful!' she exclaimed, staring at him, horrified at the notion of an eternity of pain and anguish.

He laughed.

'Don't be fooled by myths and legends, Nori. See them for what they are—*shooting stars*. None of us truly know what waits for us, beyond death.'

Eleanor's mouth fell at his unexpected statement; she had never heard him speak of such things—things she could only imagine coming from an elder. It was at that moment she realised: she was saying goodbye to the "boy."

'Rave!' Gill suddenly called, watching his dog race ahead into the stretch of trees before them.

'I think she's hungry,' said Eleanor, finding her smile again. 'I believe she can smell Maw's cooking from miles.'

'I can sympathise with her,' he replied, hearing the rumbling sound coming from his stomach. 'I'm starved, and these hares will not cook by themselves. Best be on our way. And if Maw scolds us for being late, I will lay the blame entirely on you, Eleanor Shaw.'

They quickened their pace, keeping a watchful eye on Rave's shadowy silhouette, pouncing away in the distance—the moon highlighting the whiteness of her paws and the tip of her tail. Every few moments she stopped, glancing back, making sure the hands that fed her were close behind. And, when satisfied, she turned to resume her position as *leader of the pack*.

Eleanor smiled at her display of loyalty.

'Do you think Paw is still alive?'

The unexpected question made her stop, catching her off-guard. Eleanor was lost for words at her brother's enquiry. She could not recall the last time he had asked, concluding, he had accepted his father's demise—and the issue no longer up for discussion.

Gill turned to meet his sister's stunned look, and waited.

'Gill …' she began, approaching him, her mind racing, unsure of what to say.

'Be honest with me, Eleanor. Do you believe he is—?'

'No!' she returned, in a solemn, flat tone.

He drew his head back, surprised by her bluntness. 'Well, *I* do!' he retorted, turning brusquely, to resume the journey home. From behind, he could hear her light footsteps trying to keep pace with his long stride, as he stomped on.

'I—I'm sorry, Gill,' she pleaded, catching up with him, breathless. 'But—but you *did* ask me to be honest.'

Gill stopped abruptly and turned to his sister, throwing her a disgruntled look. For a moment the two siblings stared at one another, biting their tongues on the unspoken subject. Then, rolling his eyes, Gill shook his head and walked on, grunting beneath his breath.

With heads hung low, they walked on in subdued silence—the seconds dragging, as Eleanor searched for something to say.

'Why now—after so long?' she finally asked.

Gill, eyes fixed on the ground, sighed. 'I—I'm being foolish, Nori,' he mumbled. 'Pay no mind.'

'Tell me!' she insisted, staring up at him, still doing her best to keep up.

Aware of his sister's persistent and determined nature, Gill slowed his pace then took a deep breath. 'Because … I *sense* him … and have, for a while now. At first, I banished all notions of his return from my mind but, of late … they persist, and torment me.'

Eleanor knew she had to be sensitive in her response, knowing he was on the edge of seventeen—a difficult age for any young man. And, without his father to guide him through to manhood, it was evident her brother's coming of age was causing him some concern.

'They never found his body,' he added, feeling the need to remind her.

'Gill, you know how it is when they go to war. Nothing is guaranteed. That's the way of it. It was the same when *my* father died.'

'But, did they not find *his* body?'

'Aye, but—'

'And you *were* only a wee bairn. It was a long time ago, Eleanor.'

'Perhaps,' she said, slightly annoyed. 'But it does *not* make it easier.'

'I believe it does,' he retorted, convinced. 'When there is a body to place in the ground, it gives closure to those left behind.'

Yet again, Eleanor was stumped by his words, admitting to herself the truth behind them. She opened her mind to the possibility, letting it gnaw on her thoughts.

'Think about it, Nori,' he continued, combing his fingers through his thick hair. She detected a hint of excitement in his tone as he insisted on relaying his observations. 'Paw was presumed to be another "victim of war." But I don't recall an official announcement. Do you?'

She shook her head, sceptical.

'In fact,' he continued, 'there *was* none!'

Keeping an eye on her footing, Eleanor listened intently, nodding, as her brother continued in his deductions.

'And tell me this, Eleanor …'

She looked up at his tireless and determined face.

'Have you, in all honesty, seen Maw mourn his loss?'

'*That* is unfair, Gill,' she replied, annoyed at his suggestion that their mother could be so cold and distant.

'I …' He hesitated. 'I've discussed it—briefly—with Onóir.'

Eleanor did a double-take; she could not believe he had just referred to their grandmother by her *name!*

'Granted, she was none too pleased,' he continued, 'but I could see it in her eyes.'

'See what, Gill? And do you not think it disrespectful that you should call her by—?'

'I suspect she may agree with me,' he cut in.

Eleanor groaned.

'Gill, I *saw* the sadness in Maw's face when he did not return,' she said, growing frustrated by her brother's theories.

'Aye, saddened, I would agree … but mournful? I don't think—' Gill stopped dead, and glanced around. 'Rave!' he yelled, his voice bellowing through the forage of ghostly trees. He then listened for his dog's response.

Nothing.

'She's gone ahead, Gill. She knows the way.'

'Not as well as our usual route,' he replied, casting her a knowing glance.

Feeling the pang of guilt being placed upon her, she called out; 'Rave!'

Overhead, a night owl hooted in response to their calls. Gill pursed his lips, ready to whistle when they heard a distinct noise coming from their far left. As they turned to call out, in its direction, Rave came pounding towards them. Gill spun round to greet her, discarding all other sounds, praising the hound for her obedient return. However, Eleanor remained still, her eyes focused, elsewhere.

'What is it?' he asked, noting her fixed stare.

'I think there's someone following us,' she said, placing her hand on the neck of her dagger. 'The bushes over there twitched,' she added, pointing with her chin.

'Tis just a wild animal, Nori.'

'Do you think I am not familiar with the sounds of the woods, Gillis?'

Detecting the aggravation in her voice, he moved to her side, following her gaze.

'The sound I heard was not Rave. She came from the other direction—towards home. I've heard it several times, today. It is no wild animal, Gill. What I heard was—' She stopped, seeing the scepticism in his raised eyebrows.

Gill lowered his head slowly, throwing her the same look he always gave, when in doubt. 'Well?' he said, in *that* cynical tone she hated.

'I heard … footsteps—I think!'

He looked at her, pressing down on his lips, trying to contain his laughter. Quite often she would wield her dagger at him for his taunting. He was more than aware of her skill, of the small, deadly weapon—but, also, equally mindful of her empty threats. His father had taught her well in its use, regarding her as a "most attentive student."

He recalled his words, during one of their lessons: "You must only use it, Nori, when you feel your life—or the life of another—is threatened; but most important, when your brother teases you."

'Footsteps, you say?'

Eleanor nodded.

'Are you *sure*?' he enquired, detecting concern in her determined eyes.

She lingered a moment, checking her thoughts with a seed of uncertainty. 'Almost.'

'Almost!' he retorted, sniggering at her. 'Until you are confident of it, *little* sister, your assailant, I should imagine, is nothing more than a wild animal, or that imagination of—'

'*Little* sister!' she cried, in an act of horror. 'I'll show you how *little* I can be?' she added, swiftly removing the dagger, resting on her hip. She wielded it before him, while he raised his hands in a display of feigned terror.

'Ah, so you still insist on acting on Paw's advice, I see.'

'Aye, I do,' she said, threatening him in jest. 'And always will.'

Rave danced around the siblings as they continued to tease one another, barking at intervals, as though joining in with their humorous taunts. Gill, eventually proclaiming defeat, threw his muscular arms around his sister. She felt a strangeness in his strong embrace; there was something different in it—something different in *him*.

'I will miss all this, Nori,' he said, his voice tinged with sadness.

Eleanor stepped back from him, and tilted her head with pleading eyes. 'Must you go to Eddin?'

'You know I have no choice. I'm expected at the castle at the end of this month, to sign for duty.'

'I must admit,' she replied, detecting an air of finality and acceptance in his tone, 'you don't appear to be troubled about going.' She held his gaze until he felt compelled to turn away from her probing look.

'I swear I heard Maw's voice,' he said, promptly changing the subject. 'She sounds angry. Step lively, lass!'

Eleanor narrowed her suspicious eyes, aware her brother was coveting a secret. 'There *is* something you're not telling me, Gillis Shaw!'

'We're late, Nori!' he replied, over his shoulder, starting to run.

'Tell me what you're hiding!' she demanded, struggling again to catch her breath, as she raced after him.

Gill stopped with such abruptness, she nearly tripped over herself.

'Promise me you won't tell them!' he said, lowering his voice, as though protecting his words from absent ears.

Eleanor nodded sharply, then stepped closer, eager to hear what he had to divulge.

'I am not going to Eddin alone.'

She drew her head back, baffled.

'Meghan is coming with me.' He watched his sister's face stretch in absolute shock. 'We *are* both of age,' he stated, intent on not being swayed. 'No one can stop us!'

'Her father will do his best to—as will Maw, and if Paw were here, he would—'

'But he's not, Eleanor,' he snapped. 'And we shall be well gone by the time they notice our absence.'

'It seems you have it all planned out.'

'Aye, we do. Now, make the vow!'

'Vow?' she asked, scowling at him.

'To stay quiet—for the time being, at least.'

Eleanor hesitated, reluctant to keep the secret.

'Say it!'

With a heavy sigh, she closed her eyes. 'I promise.'

Content by her word of honour, Gill smiled. 'All will be right, Nori. Trust me.'

Forced into secrecy, she knew she had no option. It was too much to absorb—the burden he had just placed on her. But she would use the time they had left, doing her best to make him see sense.

Wanting to avoid further inquisition, Gill marched ahead with the three hares still dangling over his broad shoulder. However, Eleanor, worn out by the day's revelations, slowed her pace, her thoughts racing with each sluggish step.

Suddenly, Rave howled and leapt forward, telling them they were a short distance from home. She glanced up, just in time to see her brother's form pass through the familiar opening ahead—joining the path, which lead to their house—the brightness of the full moon bathing him in a ghostly hue, before he disappeared from view.

Unable to comprehend what her brother had told her, she was now relieved he had gone ahead, leaving her to digest the changes life was about to deal out. She was simply at a loss. He had put her in a difficult position; how would she conceal it from them all? And as for Meghan Downy's protective father …? That concerned her, too.

Think, Eleanor! she warned herself. *Before you get back—before you look into their faces, pretending everything is normal. How could you, Gill?! How could—* She halted as she stepped into the clearing, her heart beating with apprehension. She had heard it again. *That sound!* She held her breath, daring to peer into the trees, beyond the clearing. She felt surrounded—not by nature's eerie presence—but by something else.

'There!' she whispered, spotting a shadow moving rapidly between the trees. Now fully alert, she concentrated, letting her instincts guide her. She turned swiftly at the sound of dry leaves being disturbed from behind. It seemed impossible, how quickly it moved. She heard it again—this time—from another direction. Her head began to reel, trying to follow each rapid footstep.

Eleanor narrowed her eyes, focusing hard on one place. She jumped, seeing the sudden movement of a dark figure before it blended into the shadows. She swallowed, her hand shaking as she slowly removed her dagger from its sheath. Another sound came from behind. She turned, catching the figure again, then gasped, when another joined the first.

The two shapes stood in the moonlight shadow of a large tree, concealing their forms.

Gripped by fear, Eleanor was unable to move.

"Run! Run!" the voice inside her screamed.

'Who—who are—?' Her words suddenly failed, when the sight of a third—and much larger figure—appeared, throwing her into a frenzied state. She opened her mouth to scream, but nothing came out.

One of the figures then slowly began to move towards her. She quickly glanced back in the direction of her home. Through the thicket of trees, she could see the flickering of her mother's night flame guiding her, filling her with renewed hope.

"Don't look back!" the voice cried again. *"Run to it, Eleanor!"*

With each anxious breath, and her instincts telling her what she should do, her curiosity, however, provoked her to stay, despite the unknown threat. But when the sound of their footsteps loomed closer, from behind, she jolted and held her breath.

"Don't look—don't—"

As Eleanor slowly looked over her shoulder, three dark shapes emerged into the clearing.

Chapter Twenty-One

The Realm of Meddian: 1630 - (Central Europe) - Late Spring

The Warlock lay silent in the dim light of what he referred to as his "temporary abode", focusing hard on the spider spinning its web, over and over again, until it succeeded. He had become acquainted with its constant comings and goings, discovering it, too, had habits and routines—no different from man. There was a pattern in its methods, which had played on his curious mind, bringing his attention to the familiar movements of his captor.

Each day, or night—he could not tell, hidden away from the world— the arachnid crawled from its hide-out. He noted how its entrance and exit changed regularly, surmising it was its way of fooling a predator, of sorts.

'It seems we are all creatures of habit, my little one,' he told it, rising from his small but comfortable bed. 'However, unlike *you*, I intend to release myself from these walls, with no intention of returning.'

Despite his imprisonment, Oran complimented his captor on the layout of his chamber. Small, yet adequate, he wanted for nothing, except his freedom, which regularly became the subject of bargaining— one he was unwilling to trade. His incarcerator had surrounded him with the familiarities of a home they once shared. The hand-made silk rug— beneath his feet—hailed from the Realm of Saó, in the far east. He recognised its pattern, curious as to how *they* came upon the luxurious item; it was rare, and solely commissioned for royalty.

A beautiful rosewood, huanghuali, low-backed armchair was his only seat. Acquired from the same Realm as the fine rug, he had tormented her with complaints of its discomfort. Thinking the added luxury might loosen his tongue, she promptly provided him with a silk cushion—to ill effect.

The small, writing table, he knew, had once resided in the Realm of Kah-luan—west, across the big ocean. The walnut and mahogany finish on its elaborate surface and carved legs screamed opulence. He grunted at the irony of it: being allowed a writing table … without its implements. In their place, lay the works of a particular playwright she had claimed to have met while "on her travels", surmising they were original.

And when he inquired—as to how they came into her possession—the reply had been; "William insisted I have them—before a fever claimed his untimely death! Such a great pity. We can only assume his greatness … had he lived longer!"

Oran had detected the threats between her lines—the hidden reminder of how vulnerable *he* was while confined to his "prison." And yet, there was no doubting that the luxuries bestowed upon him were a vain attempt to draw what information she could from him. However, in the fourteen months of his imprisonment, not once did he waver.

How could I have been so negligent? He scolded himself, reliving in his mind the irresponsibility of the error—his error—which lead to his present state.

After his impromptu departure from Elboru—on the Elliyan's insistence—he had, after a lengthy search, picked up her trail in the far reaches of Ockram, in the south. But he had been too late. It was evident, from the trail of destruction left behind, she had moved on.

Each village he came upon had indicated her presence, leaving behind a disturbing undertone. He had seen it in the villagers' eyes as he listened to their mourning, for the mysterious loss of a number of their young men. He had overheard some of the local gossips utter a name he had once been associated with.

At first, he had sneered at their small-mindedness, before realising the truth behind their *myths*. He recalled witnessing the burial of a young woman of abstinence, her tragic demise shrouded by a sinister motive. He then later discovered the innocent victim had been stabbed clean, through the heart.

He had taken great care in concealing his identity, the closer he drew to his goal. Keeping his distance, he had taken the form of a wild animal—the kind no one would pay heed to. It had been a necessity, at the time, as he was unarmed and unaware of her powers; he had to avoid the risk of being found out.

I should have had the Albrecht, he regretted. *Damn them!* But despite his frustration, he realised the sword would have provided him with little or no protection, after witnessing her powers in Triora.

Over time, he had noticed a pattern in her behaviour and movements. With each departure, taking her to pastures new, her company grew larger. Also, she was never alone; she was always accompanied by the two females—one, small in size and frame—the other, matching the stature of a man. He mused over where he had seen *her* kind before—convinced she hailed from the high north, beyond the boundaries of Urquille.

He had maintained his distance while secretly scrutinising her notable growing legion.

It soon came to light, they were not willing recruits, having witnessed it through the eyes of his camouflage—a young stag.

The small female would frequently leave the company, for a short time. He had taken it upon himself—in the early light of one morning—to follow her in the guise of the buck, such was her swiftness. Twice, she had seen the wild animal, paying no mind to its presence—too preoccupied with something else.

A young man—no more than the age of his son—walked alone in the early mist of dawn, his long, wavy, black hair wet by the dampness. Upon his person, he had carried a satchel over a grey, heavy cloak. Little did he know his well-worn, thick, brown leather boots would become his fatal distraction.

The curious buck watched from the brush, as the lad paused to remove one of his boots; some tiny pebbles had made their way through the sole, causing him discomfort. It was then—as he leaned forward to return the boot to his aching foot—she pounced. Her frenzied attack had been swift; he doubted the young man knew what had happened.

He had watched—with added curiosity—as she hovered over the lifeless body, preparing her next move when something distracted her. That was when she had seen it: the wild animal—the one that had been watching her.

She had caught him off-guard, prompting him to flee. But as he fled, he heard the rustling sound, before the hunter's snare had hoisted him into mid-air.

The young woman with the long, chestnut hair then approached him, leaving her victim behind stretched out on the lonely path. Wiping the fresh blood from her mouth, her pale-red eyes looked up at the young stag, its lack of fear in its imprisonment intriguing her.

She had stared at him a while, regarding him with interest, and when their eyes finally met, he had noticed the obvious change in hers; they were now deep, and dark—a vague reminder of someone else.

"*Te vad!*" she had whispered. "I see you!"

He had been surprised by the softness of her tone and gentle demeanour, after witnessing the vicious attack on her victim.

When his attempt to free himself from the netting failed, he had then contemplated returning to his true form but found he was unable to. The female then glanced back at the young man lying dead on the path.

"*La naiba!*" she had muttered under her breath, frustrated, before turning her attention back to him. "He should have lived! You distracted me, and it is too late to find a replacement. My Mistress *will* be disappointed. I think it is only right to show her *who* is to blame. You, my little *curiozitate,* are coming with me."

Still caught up in the netting, she had then cut him down before hauling him away, her physical strength surprising him; it was incomparable to her small frame.

He would never forget the overwhelming feeling of the unknown power that engulfed him, when the female took the "helpless buck" into the presence of her Mistress—the great strength emanating from her, weakening him. He recalled the moment when she looked directly at the wild animal, with curiosity, her familiar face devoid of all emotion.

"And what do we have—"

The instant her eyes latched on to his, it was evident she knew exactly to whom she was addressing.

"Looking for me, Oran?"

It was the last thing he had remembered—staring into her knowing eyes—before waking to find he had been transformed back to his true form. He had, at first, been confused by his surroundings, noting the lavish furnishings. It was when he glanced up at the small window, observing the grotesque iron bars crossing its opening, he had then understood their meaning.

But all was not as it seemed; he had detected something else— something familiar—something unseen to the eye. He had felt its ominous presence. His instincts had warned him to take heed, drawing his attention towards the locked door; the space between him and it was unusually wide, arousing his suspicions.

Cautious, he had paced back and forth across his personal space, contemplating it. After much deliberation, his curiosity had urged him to approach the door, when his instincts made him stop. However, uncertainty coaxed him to step closer—taking two more steps—before he had felt *it*: the tingling inside his body, warning him of a familiar force. But he knew he had to brave another step. He *had* to know.

As he drew closer, he had felt its defined energy strengthen in a threatening manner. But it was when he stretched out his hand, its burning influence had forced him to wrench it back, letting him know what he was up against.

"Do you think this invisible barrier can keep me here?" he had muttered, reaching for his amulet. But trapped in the confinements of *her* world now, he quickly discovered his amulet had been drained of its energy. Despite several attempts to break the barrier, all his efforts had proved worthless.

It was at that moment—and for the first time in his life—he had felt utterly defenceless and powerless against her might.

He had become her prisoner.

'How could I have been so stupid?' Oran muttered to himself, dismissing the memory; he had wallowed in self-pity for long enough.

He stared at the emptiness between himself and the heavily-bolted wooden door. He still had mixed feelings as to whether to accept the locked door as a compliment, or an insult. He then noticed the lanterns hanging on each side; they would soon dwindle, eventually needing to be replaced.

His powers had diminished greatly since finding himself in her company. The reunion had been indescribable. Her features, save for the eyes, were exactly as he remembered yet more intense. And she had not aged a day, since … *Since Lucia*, he thought. It was clear, by her sustained youthfulness, there had also been other victims to satisfy her obsession. The image of the young servant's charred remains crept back to haunt him—the guilt of her demise having never left his thoughts.

Beneath his loose shirt remained the one item the Sorceress did not remove from his person. Oran was aware she still possessed the other amulet, however, several attempts had been made by Kara to obtain his. He surmised that the Valkyrie may have wanted it for herself. He grinned, recalling the frustration on her seething face when it scorched her hand.

Despite claiming ownership of the one the Sorceress had stolen from Magia Nera, it pleased him to know she still lacked the knowledge of the amulet's true purpose. Hence the reason he was still alive—hence the reason for his comforts—in the hope she could coax it from him.

"I know something of great importance draws close, Warlock," she had said, sneering at him. "For *you* to come in search of me, after all this time, leads me to suspect the urgency of it."

With each pressing enquiry made upon him, his return was silent and had remained so, ever since. But now her visits were becoming more frequent. At times, she would venture to his holding alone, while on other occasions, she'd be accompanied by her two servants. He grinned, staring at the space before him; she had almost tempted him. Almost!

Removing his amulet, he held it to the fading light. The jewel within its centre now gleamed; its brightness had intensified since the last time he looked upon it. He could now clearly distinguish its yellow colour, clear in the knowledge it would continue to radiate until it reached its fullness: the day his son would come of age.

Closing his eyes, Oran delved into his memories, searching for *them*. He could see Rosalyn's face vividly, and wondered if she had forgiven him for his disappearance. It had been his choice to keep her in the dark—for her safety—for the safety of all his family.

His thoughts turned to Eleanor. She would now be in her twentieth year. She had developed qualities like her grandmother, during her adolescence—no doubt taking them with her into womanhood. He mused over the possibility that she may have claimed a husband—even become a mother.

I could be a grandfather now! he thought. His heart ached at the idea of it, giving him hope, encouragement and determination.

And then there was Gill, his son. In the next few months, he would be …

Unwilling to be tortured further by his thoughts, he cast them away.

Time to act! he told himself. There was still time—not much—but enough to complete his plan.

His hopes now rested on the source he had befriended.

Three individuals had been selected to tend to his needs—changing shifts at random. Thanks to his little spider's movements, he had carefully noted their habits and routines, engaging in regular conversation with them, in a bid to become familiar with their character.

Oran paid particular attention to their changing personalities, noting, as time went by, they appeared to come into their own—some more than others. And, by those observations, he soon discovered which one he could best acquaint himself with.

The younger, he surmised, had been a recent addition to her legion. Wild and reckless, his time spent watching over his prisoner was unpredictable; it was evident, by the young recruit's unease, he preferred to be somewhere else than confined to his assignment.

The second had once been like the younger, their differences divided by time. He discovered his name was Dakkus—and could not be trusted. His pale, brown eyes—unlike the redness of the *younger* ones—warned him of betrayal. His face was round, his lips full and prominent, and his black skin had lost its richness, becoming grey over time.

Oran had noticed his habit of running a hand over his head as if searching for the remnants of the hair that had once belonged there. Constantly suspicious of the Warlock's casual questions, Dakkus had been—and still was—reluctant to share any information, making it clear where his loyalties lay. Therefore, Oran kept their conversations civil and cautious.

The third hailed from the Realm of Saó. The great warrior—a Samurai—had been under her bond for almost sixty years. There was something mature and tranquil in his demeanour. His skin was olive in tone yet retained a hint of its darkness. Oran saw trust and honour in his dark-brown, almond-shaped eyes.

His thick, straight black hair matched the length of his spine, and the front was pulled high off his forehead and caught in an elaborate top-knot, on his crown. His garb was simple yet striking: a long, black kimono, making him look taller than he was. His torso was sturdy and muscular, and visible through the upper, patterned part of the kimono. The wide sleeves hung loosely, midway down his sinewy arms. From the waist down to his sandaled feet, the gown was made of rich, black silk. A thick crimson sash, about his waist, housed a large, curved sword that clung to his left side. On the opposite, a small, lethal dagger peeped out; though barely visible, its presence was noteworthy.

Reluctant, at first, to discuss his past, the Samurai had been content to engage in intelligent conversation with the Warlock, and it soon became apparent that the warrior had clung to many of his human qualities, enabling Oran to determine his temperament and character.

Oran enjoyed the calming influence of the Samurai's company and, over time, had begun to detect hidden meanings in their discussions, eventually leading to an element of mutual trust. It was what compelled him to finally make the bold move.

"There is something I would like to share with you."

That was how it started.

Oran knew his own words were of immense risk at the time of his asking. He recalled the lengthy silence, staring into his ward's dark eyes as he waited for his response, fully aware of the consequences—should their conversation be passed on. But his intuition had told him differently.

"You have my trust, Oran-san," came the reply—eventually—followed by a sharp bow.

It was at that moment, the Warlock knew he had judged his new ally well. Oran then braved revealing his identity to his ward, with the understanding he was of influence, and could perhaps help him in some way. Concerned it may not be the case, the Warlock had limited his information, at first, for fear of being subject to betrayal.

"There is another who could also be interested," his ward had revealed.

"*Could* be?" Oran had replied, with immediate regret; he needed reassurance.

"He is my loyal friend—against *her* wishes. But … there is nothing she can do to influence it. She relies on her best. She relies on *him*."

"Can I trust him?"

"He is no betrayer. But his temperament is fuelled by his stolen past. I, however, have been more accepting of the life I have been forced to lead. I have kept my humble beliefs locked inside, which have been my guidance and saving grace. It was difficult for *him* to accept his fate, in the beginning. But the years I gained on him, helped in his adjustment to the life inflicted on us. Despite our cultural differences, we formed a unique bond under the forceful one of the Sorceress'. She did everything in her power to separate us, but failed."

The ward had then proceeded to tell Oran his confidant's story, letting him form a picture in his mind. He had then assured him of his support, though nothing was guaranteed.

"Take care in your conversations with the others who tend to you," he had warned him. "*They* will surely betray you. I will speak with my colleague and return with his reply."

Since their conversation, Oran had waited daily for news, but none came. He paced the small space of his holding, watching the door with unease. It had been more than a week, since, and still, the ward did not appear; his routine had, in the past, comprised of two visits in one week—sometimes three. He also noted the younger, restless one had now been replaced by another, and when he enquired, Dakkus had simply stared back at him with distrust:

"You not entitled to explanation, Warlock," he had replied, in his broken English.

Oran paused, catching a glimpse of his own face in the plain mirror, hanging on the bare, stone wall. The item looked out of place among the splendour of his furniture.

"Every time you look at it, it will be a reminder of what you were," *she* had once commented, seeing him stare at his reflection.

Her remark had had a sense of victory about it, making him feel somewhat defeated by her. Had it not been for his amulet … He imagined the probability of it. But a mere glimpse of its gold chain reassured him: there was still hope.

Oran sat on the edge of his bed patiently waiting for the return of his confidant—certain of his visit. The minutes felt like hours in the hum-drum of his silence. He began to second-guess his decision to trust the warrior. Doubt slowly seeped in, playing on his insecurities. Perhaps he *had* been found out—or even betrayed …

No! he told himself, rising from his bed. *I sensed no betrayal in him.*

Oran approached the ornate little table, feeling the need to occupy his mind from the negative thoughts fighting to influence his thinking. He handled the playwright's works, contemplating which one to read … again.

'You will have to do,' he said, picking one up before returning to his bed.

Lying back, he flicked through the worn pages, more than familiar with the story.

It was the tale of the tragic Prince who feigned his madness, to bring to justice the perpetrator who had murdered his father. The crime had been committed by the hand of his mother's new husband. The young Prince eventually proved his stepfather's guilt, but at a cost.

No matter how often Oran looked over the pages, the story had the same ending: the Prince dying tragically, along with those he loved and hated.

He sighed, returning to the first page when the faint echo of distant footsteps caught his attention. He looked sharp towards the door, listening. Had he imagined them? He held his breath a moment. He could now hear their distinct sound, descending towards his chamber.

Prominent in their approach, they were footsteps he did not recognise.

Oran rose, his adrenalin beginning to surge. Doubt provoked his thoughts again as the footsteps drew nearer, their sturdy march confirming they did not belong to his ward—the Samurai's being much lighter and rhythmic. Concealing his amulet, he regarded the great door, feeling agitated. With eyes fixed, in apprehension, he joined his hands together as though in prayer, then raised them to his mouth … watching and waiting …

He hesitated, drawing his head back when the footsteps suddenly ceased, on the other side. The fading light from the lanterns forced him to strain his eyes; it would not be long before their flames extinguished.

'Why are you waiting?' he whispered, in the lingering silence.

He flinched at the sound of the large, iron key being slowly turned in the lock. He cast a sideward glance when the light from one of the lanterns flickered before going out. The key ground as the hand that controlled it prolonged its turning. Oran moved closer, with caution, ready to meet the individual on the other side.

The lock clicked, signalling their entrance.

When the door was pushed towards him, Oran held his breath. But as it opened, it invited a draught, extinguishing the second flame, instantly plunging them into darkness.

Chapter Twenty-Two

The great door creaked as it swung wide, revealing a shadowy figure in the space between it and the long, dark corridor beyond. Oran had no knowledge where the passage led, or of his placement within the walls of the citadel, where she had chosen to reside; nor did he care, at that moment.

The individual who now entered his holding, concealed their face behind the flaming torch in their hand. Oran surmised, by their silhouette, they were male—and as tall as he. Nothing was said as the figure re-lit the two lanterns, illuminating his surroundings once more. The Warlock squinted as his eyes readjusted, then focused hard on the unknown visitor, who remained with his back to him.

'Where is Asai?' he blurted, with a sense of unease.

Placing the torch in its walled bracket, its bearer lingered before turning to face his prisoner. Cautious, he approached Oran, then stopped within inches of him, conscious of the invisible barrier dividing them.

Standing in complete silence, they regarded one another. Oran dared to step closer to the barrier, mindful of its precarious presence, aware of its fatal purpose—should he touch it. He stopped abruptly. Eyes wide open, his lips parted slightly, as a familiarity about his guest struck him. *Where have I seen you before?* he thought.

In the awkward silence, Oran strived to retrieve the memory of where they had met. It suddenly dawned on him: they *never* had. The images forced on him by the Ushabti now returned as his reminder. He had seen this face in the battle—as shown to him—and yet could not recall their role: *Ally? Or rival?*

Frustrated by his visitor's unnerving stillness, Oran wondered how long it would be until the silence was broken. The wait was short-lived.

'So, you are the Warlock,' *he* commented. His voice was low and lacking emotion.

'I am,' Oran replied, lifting his head slightly.

His visitor turned, fixing his wary eyes on "her guest" as *she* referred to him. 'In my mind,' he continued, slowly pacing back and forth, 'I had formed an image of you, and I must admit, Warlock—'

'Oran,' he snapped. 'My name is—'

'I am rather disappointed.'

Oran raised a brow at the insult placed upon him, then watched as his guest surveyed the chamber with a keen eye.

'She *has* kept you well in your standards,' he sneered. 'It appears you are of some importance to her.'

'Do not be fooled by what you see here before you …' Oran paused, hoping he would reveal his name; it did not come. 'And, do not judge your friends' notion of me; I believe he is a good—'

'Man?' he interrupted, with a hint of sarcasm in his tone. 'Take my advice, Warlock, you should not be fooled by what *you* see.'

Oran took a step back to observe his guest, all the while still searching for his face in the image shown to him by the Ushabti.

'Tell me, Warlock,' he went on. 'What, precisely, *do* you see?'

Oran observed him closely. They stood almost at eye level. He then noted his striking features: his hair was black and unusually short; his piercing, green eyes stared back at him like glowing emeralds; his cheekbones were high and obvious; his lips full and perfectly shaped, and he wore a stubble. Oran then lowered his eyes, observing his clothing; it was that of a hunter's. His leggings were made from buckskin—dyed black and tucked neatly inside dark-brown leather boots. His long, sleeveless waistcoat was the colour of oxblood and made from thick leather. About his waist, he wore a wide belt where his sword or knife would hang. Oran was under no illusion; it was evident his guest had no use for them at that given time.

Oran could not help but notice the array of old and new scars on his visitor's bare arms—some, thick remnants of deep wounds, others, mere scratches. Had they been concealed, Oran would not have known he had seen many battles; also, there were no visible scars on his face, save for the tiny puncture wounds at the base of his neck—clearly visible when he turned.

'Well? Have you made your assumptions, Warlock?'

'You're not like the others,' Oran stated.

'No—*they* are young and impetuous,' he replied, rolling his eyes. 'And too easily led.'

Oran sensed annoyance in his tone, speculating he had little or no time for them. 'Am I to presume it is the reason why their guard on me is changed regularly?'

'Changed? No,' he returned, with a slight grin. 'They are … *replaced.*'

Oran narrowed his eyes, confused by his tone; it was one of permanence.

'Do you know who'—he lowered his eyes, then grit his teeth with distaste, having to admit his unwanted disposition— '*what* we are?'

'I have my theories,' said Oran.

'I assure you, it is *no* theory, Warlock,' he retorted. 'Asai, it seems, has neglected to tell you all the facts, relating to our ongoing presence here.'

'Somewhat,' replied Oran, recalling the sadness behind this individual's story.

'Then let me enlighten you. We—I—am what the mortals refer to as'—he sighed, loathing the mere thought of uttering the word— '*Dhampir.*'

Oran stepped forward, taking a closer look.

'But you look so …'

'Human?'

The Warlock nodded.

'It is because of my age—as with Asai—we did not succumb to the foul side of our character. We were—*are*—stronger than the *younger* ones, and well taught in battle. Those who are clever—as few as they are—have been fortunate enough to retain many of their human qualities.'

'Am I to assume, Wareeshta did *this* to you?' said Oran.

'How did you know?' he asked, with a sideward look.

'I saw her—once,' he began, before briefly relaying how he had witnessed her attack on the young man with the stone in his boot.

'She and Kara are bonded to the Sorceress.'

'Willingly?' asked Oran.

'I have my misgivings,' his guest replied. 'According to their Mistress, Wareeshta is the one with the *true* gift. She has been more than useful … to put it mildly. You see, her mother was human, her father—'

'*Undead!*' said Oran, cutting in.

'You are aware of them?'

'I've had my dealings with their kind—in the past—however, I have seldom come into contact with …' He hesitated, not wanting to insult his guest, but on reflection, chose to return it. '… *Dhampir.*' Oran caught his sideward glance but held his gaze. He would not be intimidated.

'Those who become Dhampir,' his guest continued, 'are unwilling victims. If they are young, their human qualities can be controlled by the more powerful and sinister side being forced on them. It is their newly acquired powers that entice and excite them, at first. They are lured into a false sense of invincibility. Many give in to its trap, eventually losing all self-control.'

'Therefore, destroying themselves?' Oran surmised.

'No. They grow weaker until every human quality they once knew has been taken from them—pushed to the depths of their subconscious—never to be reawakened.'

'Have you ever tried to escape?' Oran enquired.

His visitor approached him, drawing apart his waistcoat. 'Do you see these scars, Warlock?'

Oran observed the thick, pale lines scattered across his exposed, lean torso.

'Too often I have tried, to the point of death.'

Lifting his head slowly, Oran stared at him, confused.

'I see, by your expression, you wonder how I am still alive?'

Oran shook his head.

'No man could endure, nor survive the multiple wounds I see before me,' he replied.

'This is true. But I am no mortal. I have felt the pain of each wound inflicted on me. I can recall every sword, dagger and arrow that has entered my body. It is ironic that, in her captivity, I have tolerated more inflictions than on the battlefield of mortality. In other words, it is not so easy to destroy us.'

'*She* did this to you?' said Oran, unable to comprehend the brutality of the woman he thought he knew.

'It does not matter who, or how, for I ceased in my bid to escape long ago. From the moment Wareeshta administered her "gift" upon us, we, too, were bonded to the Sorceress. We cannot leave. We cannot touch her.' He lowered his eyes in a moment of thought, and smirked.

'What amuses you?' said Oran.

'Did you notice the scar below her—'

'Left ear?' he interrupted, nodding.

'I am impressed by your observation, Warlock.'

Oran bowed, acknowledging the compliment.

'It was a … *gift* from Asai,' he revealed. 'A true Master of his kind—one skilled in the art of the sword. I have great admiration and respect for him.'

'And yet, *he* still lives?'

'Against Kara's wishes. The Valkyrie would see us both "dispatched" had she her own way. This is why we need to be wary of her. Also, Kara's behaviour, of late, has become unpredictable, and something of a burden to the Sorceress.'

'In what way?' Oran enquired, leaning forward.

'Have you asked yourself, Warlock, what happens to the younger Dhampir? Why they are *replaced*, and never seen again?'

'Perhaps … because they lack the experience of a gaoler?' Oran joked.

211

His visitor shook his head, unable to see the wit in the Warlock's reply. 'Kara bores easily,' he said. 'She seeks amusement, targeting the young and … more willing Dhampir. They have appetites she is quite happy to satisfy. At first, the Sorceress turned a blind eye. But it was when their numbers began to diminish, it came to light who the perpetrator was.'

'Kara,' said Oran.

'Not all, but some of her willing candidates are … *discarded*—when she tires of their company. She regards them as weaklings. Think yourself lucky, Warlock.'

'Lucky?'

His guest grinned.

'That you are *old*.'

'That's twice!' said Oran, gritting his teeth.

His visitor tilted his head, puzzled.

'You have insulted me … twice!'

Unphased by Oran's comment, he shrugged before continuing. 'It seems Kara is not to be left alone in your company. It is my belief the Sorceress holds a place in her heart for you.'

'And, it is *my* belief,' Oran suggested, 'you may be her surveillance.'

The Warlock recoiled when his guest lunged forward—the invisible barrier between them glowing its warning, as they felt its surging heat.

'You think I have come to *spy* on you, Warlock?!' he snarled, his eyes wild with fury. Offended, he turned on his heel.

'Forgive me!' Oran blurted. 'I had to be certain of your reliability. I beg you to … stay?'

His guest hesitated, his hand wavering over the door handle, sensing the Warlock's pleading eyes on him, from behind.

He turned, his fingers curling into a fist.

'What do you want of me, Warlock?' he asked, his face hardened with frustration.

'Your help,' Oran replied, keeping his voice low and calm.

'You think you can trust *me*? A Dhampir?'

'I see your human qualities,' said Oran. 'They outweigh the other. I saw it in Asai, too. You both cling to a past that's buried deep inside—one you still crave.'

He watched his visitor's expression soften to one of reflection. Leaving him in his thoughts, Oran mused over his own memories, for a few moments. 'I know and feel your pain,' he then stated, his voice soft and sympathetic.

His visitor glared back at him. 'You cannot begin to know how I *feel*, Warlock.'

'The fact that you "feel" is a reflection of who you truly are—who you once were. I believe we can be of assistance to one another. I believe—should the opportunity arise—you and Asai would give anything to be free of your bonds. You would never again have to fight for *her*, against your will.'

His visitor paced the stone floor, his thoughts racing as Oran's words churned over in his mind.

'I can help you,' revealed Oran.

He stopped. 'You?! Help me?!' he said, sneering under his breath. 'And what of my colleague, Asai? Look around you, Warlock. Have you forgotten where you reside? You are a prisoner among your grandeur.'

The Warlock smiled at him. 'Listen to me,' he began, maintaining his poise and patience. 'This is no ploy on my part. I *can*—and *will*—help you both … in more ways than one.' The Dhampir lifted his head, raising a curious brow, then narrowed his eyes. Oran knew he had to risk it. *It's now or never!* Taking a deep breath, he added, 'I will help you both escape.'

His guest drew back, his piercing eyes wide and staring at the Warlock. Oran regarded him, concealing his smugness, as the cynical look was wiped from the Dhampir's face.

'Is this true?' he asked in a firm voice. 'For you are in no position to make vows you cannot keep.'

Turning his back on the Dhampir, Oran approached the plain, little mirror and stared at the image reflected back. 'It is a reminder of who you once were,' he whispered, echoing *her* words.

'Who you once were?' the voice behind him repeated.

'Foolish words!' Oran answered, turning to face him. 'I am a High Warlock of the Elliyan, bonded to the vows we make to whom we offer them. Ask what you will, and I shall share with you all I know.'

'Do you know the one thing I fail to understand, Warlock?' he put forward in disheartened confusion. 'The senseless killings we are forced to perform. There seems no logic in it. She strives to prove how powerful she is. And for what? Vanity? For vain she is. Our lives are nothing more than an endless journey of pointless battles. Our job is to simply … *kill* for her.'

'You say, you know nothing of her purpose?'

The Dhampir moved to respond, then hesitated; his eyes darted across the stone floor as if searching for something—perhaps a memory. He looked at it, momentarily confused.

Frustrated, he shook his head.

'No—she reveals nothing—not even to her personal aids, although …'

'Tell me!' Oran urged, prompting him to recall the memory, anything that may prove helpful to his plan.

'I have noticed, since *you* have been here, there is no talk of leaving. We never stay in one place for too long, and yet we remain here. But of late, she appears agitated. Asai brought this to my attention. Her attempt to mask it only ignites and feeds our curiosity. In our discreet observation of her, we have become suspicious. Something is afoot.'

Oran nodded as he listened with appreciation. A brief stillness washed over the chamber as a glimmer of trust passed between the two, signalling the Warlock to speak.

'Then let me tell you this,' he said, aware of what he was about to tell the stranger in his company. 'I know her plans. I know her intentions; they are aimed at my son.'

The Dhampir scrutinised Oran's face, searching for a hint of deceit; he saw none in his eager expression. Convinced by his honesty, he promptly turned, retrieving a small, wooden stool from the shadow of a corner. Placing it in front of the Warlock, he sat on it—straight and focused—resting his hands on his knees.

Oran had surveyed the Dhampir's actions with a sense of accomplishment, noting the added intensity in his green eyes. Maintaining his gaze, he now waited for him to speak.

'I am Reece,' he finally revealed. 'And you have my attention ... Oran.'

Chapter Twenty-Three

The woman stole herself from her inquisitive company, having ordered them to remain; she needed to be alone for a while. The route to her quarters had become *too* familiar, antagonising her more with each passing day. She grew restless and was eager to move on.

Inside, she cursed the Warlock for retaining his silence, even though she had given him everything he required—within his means. She had been nothing but civil and patient with him, and yet was *still* unable to win him over. She recalled a time when a mere glance would entice him to their bed.

Her secret visits to him had proved uneventful, and fruitless; even the promise to remove the invisible barrier had failed to loosen his tongue. However, lately, she had noticed a difference in his demeanour; there was an air of duty about him. Though slight, it was enough to provoke her thoughts. But time was pressing, and it grieved her to admit—should desperation take its hold—that Kara may have her way with the Warlock, after all.

Needs must! she thought. *You will regret your silence, Oran!*

The long, narrow hallway, leading to her solar chamber, stretched before her. Though well lit, she knew herself capable of finding her way in the dark, should the need arise. She had chosen it with care, to give her privacy when needed. The hallway led to a small passage, taking her to the steps leading up to her rooms, near the citadel's *Keep*.

In constant awareness of Wareeshta's lurking presence, she paused every few paces, glancing back over her shoulder.

She was still alone.

The large, oak-panelled door greeted her. Throwing one last cautious glance, she hesitated before inserting the key. Shut away from her aids, and the continuous sound of clashing blades, she sighed with relief on hearing the heavy door close behind her. However, she was still reeling at Kara's suspicions, when she had ordered the Valkyrie to increase their training.

"How dare you make enquiries!" she had snapped, before taking leave of them. And, to make matters worse, she had sensed Wareeshta's reluctance to make use of her "gift." It was all beginning to wear thin on her patience. As loyal as they were, there were times she was repelled by her two servants—and their company was not always sought.

Still, they have their uses, she reminded herself—until such time their services would no longer be required. But Wareeshta's gift had been her trusty ally; without it, she would not have her soldiers. *Just a few more,* she thought, then she would be prepared. Perhaps she *would* keep Wareeshta after all … for when the *real prize* came into her possession. If forced to choose, the young, female Dhampir would be her favourite.

Cast out from society for being "different", Wareeshta had had nowhere to go after the death of her father. Knowing her lineage would follow her throughout her timeless life, the young Dhampir had no option but to leave the home she had once called, Romania.

It was when their paths crossed, that she had found Wareeshta lost and broken with brain fever, caused by the sudden loss of all she had known. She had felt sorry for the poor creature, taking her into her care. It was through close observation, of the unusual, young woman, she eventually discovered her remarkable "gift." For saving her life—and sanity—Wareeshta vowed to serve her "Mistress" in any way she desired. But she had detected goodness lurking inside the Dhampir— no doubt inherited from her mother. It concerned her.

And then there was the Valkyrie. Kara was unique, in that her skills were next to none. Nothing phased her. When looking into her pale, grey eyes, she saw resentment and fearlessness, which was disturbing, in a narcissistic way.

She was aware the Valkyrie was becoming increasingly difficult to control—feeding on her anger. Despite it, Kara trained her soldiers well, dominating them from the start. Some, however, were immune to her charge. The behaviour of two, in particular, irked her, rousing her suspicions; she felt their eyes watching her every move.

Time, she sensed, was running out, offering her no alternative but to reveal her intentions to her servants. The mere notion of sharing it with Kara frustrated her. She had been aware of the Valkyrie's attempts to take the Warlock's amulet from him, noting the tell-tale scar on the palm of her hand. At least, she had given up on *that*.

However, the Valkyrie soon became distracted by the *younger* ones, her arrogance driving her insatiable appetite towards them. Already, another three had to be replaced in a short space of time, forcing Wareeshta to venture out into the suspicious world of mortals. It was now becoming a laborious task, trying to find young men.

Her spacious chamber opened out, welcoming her back into its sumptuous surroundings.

Decorated with mementoes of her wide and varied travels, some remarked upon them as "trophies" rather than souvenirs; she shrugged such descriptions off as insults.

Her most cherished item was the first to greet her. Carved from rare, golden-threaded wood, the ornate stand housed a large circular mirror, made from the finest bronze. Cast with a central square of decorated archaistic motifs and raised nodes, it hung with perfect precision, to match her height.

She came across it in the Realm of Saó, after taking the castle of Odani, much to the annoyance of Asai; he had claimed it to be from— what he had called—his ancestor's *Ming Dynasty*. From the instant her eyes fell upon its uniqueness, she claimed it as her own. It soon became her loyal and dependable companion—never lying about her beauty. But in the honesty of its constant presence, it also reminded her of her weakness.

She moved slowly towards its highly polished surface with dread. The subtle signs of ageing were there for her to see—although she was certain no one had noticed them.

'One more should suffice before we leave,' she told her mirrored image. 'And she will be the last.'

Stepping away, she paused, then looked towards the large, gothic window. Rays of strong sunlight streamed in, brightening the room. With the nearing of summer, she could feel the warmth of the stone walls generating their heat. She welcomed it, and the silence from beyond her window, telling her they had ceased training, for the time being.

She observed the Moorish-style, ebonized wooden table, standing alone beneath the window. When the light shone in, it highlighted the tortoiseshell, mother-of-pearl and bone inlay of its surface. Inlaid spindle legs, with open arabesque window panels, supported its raised bordered top, which contained a central carved drawer with pure gold handles. She knew, by a single glance, whether her servants had been curious about its contents; lucky for them, it had remained untouched.

Passing her four-poster bed, she moved with ease towards the long, burgundy drapes that covered one wall in its entirety.

"They retain the heat in this dismal place," had been her reply when Wareeshta once admired their lavish beauty.

'Part!' she commanded now. Her order was plain and effortless. The heavy drapes glided apart with grace and elegance, revealing a large, arched ebony door, its latch having seen centuries of wear.

'Unlock!' came her second command. She watched as the key turned itself. 'Open!'

The Sorceress stepped back as the panelled door reached out, letting her into the hidden room it concealed. The dim, white glow, emanating from within, drew her into its centre. Small in size, the secret chamber was walled with black, wooden panels of unknown figures carved into their centre. They were of no interest to her; it was the item nestled on the pillar, made from red, lacquered wood, which held her attention, its perfect sphere dominating the chamber, allowing her to see with true sight: *the crystalline orb of vision.*

She approached it with keen interest. No more than the size of a man's head, she could see into its core with clarity.

It had been a gift—one she acquired from an Orbist. She had been told of a magician who created magic, to the requirements of his client. Hidden away—in the far reaches of Ockram, in the southern hemisphere—she had sought him out. The raggedy little man, haughty in his bearings, was somewhat eccentric, choosing to live alone in the forbidden red caves of Alucard. The hazardous journey had taken her five months, on horseback.

She recalled the curious meeting: his long, white hair fell to the ground, almost covering the filthy rags on his tiny frame. At times, he carried its length upon his thin arm with every thought-out movement. It had been the strength of his power, having never been cut. His skin was grey—for the want of sunlight—and when he spoke, his sunken mouth babbled words she found difficult, at first, to understand. Yet, for all his oddities, he warmed her heart with his toothless smile.

She had visited him many times in his isolated little world, until he provided her with what she needed, along with the orb. In return, she gave him a gold ring inlaid with fine rubies. But it was the gentle kiss she had placed on his forehead, before departing, that became his greatest treasure. Her mouth twitched, recalling the moment.

'Show me!' she then commanded, her eyes narrowing as the light surged, displaying an image of the Warlock.

As long as the orb glowed, he could not escape. It was the one thing holding him captive, behind the invisible shield. There was no way above, through or around its force. She had contemplated ridding him of it, giving him the free movement of the citadel, with constant supervision—naturally, a bribe to entice information from him. But her instincts dictated otherwise when she thought of Kara.

'What to do with you …?' She raised her joined hands to her mouth as she mused over him. She tapped the tips of her slender fingers together, watching him lounge over the literary works she had left him. She continued to stare, pondering on a solution when a shard of light caught the corner of her eye. Drawing her attention away from him, she lowered her hands, focusing on the tiny light escaping between one of the panels. Her inquisitive mind pulled her closer, questioning why she had not noticed it before, and when she last looked upon it …

A year? she thought. *Perhaps longer?*

Reaching for the two panels, masquerading as doors, she slowly opened them.

Her eyes widened with excitement, as she looked upon the object still hanging from the place where she had left it; the precious stone within its centre was now sparkling with increased intensity. She noted its colour had changed—lightened—to a shade of pale yellow, and that it exuded intoxicating energy.

Lifting its heavy gold chain, the amulet swung, mesmerising her. She felt the heat from its energy wrap itself around her fingers, enveloping her hand, gradually spreading upwards. But for all its beauty, it was not "the one" she truly sought, adding to her frustrations. She frowned, pursing her lips, before marching back to the orb.

'I will force it from you, Warlock!' she raged, gritting her teeth. 'You *will* tell me where the Shenn is, or so help me I shall—'

'My lady?'

The sound of Wareeshta's wary voice alerted her. Aware the Dhampir would be waiting—perhaps even listening—she quickly returned the amulet to its hiding place, away from prying eyes. Leaving her secret behind, she promptly re-entered her chamber.

'Come, Wareeshta!'

The Dhampir cautiously entered her Mistress's domain with a sense of discomfort. She noticed the Sorceress appeared restless, refusing to engage in eye contact with her. Wareeshta stole a discreet glance around the chamber, before speaking.

'I have found two more, my lady,' she said. 'But they are not as *young* as the others. At least it will be their saving grace from—'

'Where is she?' the Sorceress snapped, expecting Kara to be close behind.

Wareeshta's lack of response betrayed the Valkyrie.

'This is impossible!' she cried, turning away. 'I have had enough! Kara tries my patience!'

Wareeshta's mouth gaped at the sudden outburst, having just witnessed a rare display of emotion; it was evident her Mistress could not bear the Valkyrie's presence much longer. She shared her sentiments. But it would not be easy to rid them of Kara's unwanted company.

Born of royal blood, Kara hailed from the far Norse lands—beyond the ruling of Urquille. She had been a product of close inbreeding, so as not to taint the royal lineage. But with every passing generation of close ties, came great risks. Some of her ancestors had been subject to insanity, leading to periods of unknown turmoil. It was unfortunate for the female—born of a sister and brother—when the signs began to emerge as she grew into her own. She possessed an evil within, displaying brutality, and was shunned by all—even their greatest warriors. It was when she came of age she discovered the *realms of men*, enjoying the "delights" of their company, much to the disdain of her parents; she had risked breaking the royal line. Banished from mingling with "mere mortals", Kara retaliated and ran away, leaving behind the mutilated corpses of her mother and father, without a shred of remorse.

She then fell into the company of a malicious old woman named Pökk—said to be Loki in disguise. Scarred by hate and mistrust of mankind, Pökk lured Kara with promises of great powers. The old woman bestowed her with the gift of flight, by providing her with a magnificent pair of white wings. Her weapon—a lance, fashioned from a single, thick piece of Obsidian glass—gave her the added strength of three men.

As time wore on, Kara grew uneasy in Pökk's company. The old woman became demanding and violent, inflicting her powers on the Valkyrie she had created. She had intended to embroil her captive into a plot of revenge. But Kara refused to do her bidding, plunging the old woman into a distorted rage, revealing her true identity—Loki.

He demanded she fight alongside him—against their Gods—to claim the throne of Aesir, as his own. She recoiled from such an impossible task, refusing to give in to his wants and needs. And so, for her rejection, he chained her to a tree, leaving her to rot; and there she remained—alone and starved of company and food—for days.

The Sorceress recalled how she and Wareeshta came upon Kara's lifeless body—slumped in the freezing depths of winter. Thinking her dead, they took it upon themselves to bury the "wretched thing."

But there had been a hint of life still left in the Valkyrie; a slight ruffle of feathers in one of her wings had told them she was alive. Where her captor had disappeared to, they never knew; he had simply vanished, leaving no trace behind.

Kara recovered with remarkable speed and, in a short space of time, her true potential began to emerge. And as the Valkyrie's new strength grew, it soon became clear that she would also be of use to her; Wareeshta would provide her with soldiers, while a willing Kara trained them. It could not have been more perfect.

It all seemed to go according to plan, until an unsettling feeling began to seep in, forcing her to watch the Valkyrie through cautious eyes. Kara's interest in the young, male Dhàmpir had given her cause for concern, noting how, occasionally, one would go missing—then another. Therefore, she had Wareeshta spy on her comings and goings. It did not take long for her to discover the cause of their disappearance.

She remembered the Valkyrie's savage reaction when she had warned her against her antics; that was when her true character surfaced. Kara then began pursuing Wareeshta, pleading with her to change her "like the others" so she could be as powerful as them. But the Dhampir refused, throwing Kara into a crazed frenzy, spewing threats of retaliation.

The Valkyrie became more arrogant and disagreeable, threatening to leave. Something had to be done; she could not unleash the unpredictable creature into a world she had intended on taking for herself. Then Kara's hostile behaviour became bold, threatening her plans further—when she asked Wareeshta to escape with her. The Dhampir declined, avoiding any explanation for going. But Kara's persistence eventually dragged the hidden truth from her, making Wareeshta confess: any notion of leaving was unthinkable; they simply could not.

"I am, and always shall be, bonded to her," she had overheard Wareeshta tell the Valkyrie.

"Willingly?" Kara had mocked the silent Wareeshta, in return. "It seems not! You fool! Unlike you, I will be a slave to no one."

But Kara, in her haste to leave, had failed to see the fate awaiting her.

It was at that moment, she then knew, she had to take matters into her own hands, forcing her to intervene in the threatening conversation between her servants.

It happened with such speed the Valkyrie had no sense or knowledge of the change that had taken place … until she attempted to flee.

"Leave, then!" she had urged the Valkyrie. "I challenge you to!"

She recalled the smirk on Kara's face as the Valkyrie stood grasping the weapon she had named "Obsidian" in her hand before her attempted departure. Then she and Wareeshta watched when the Valkyrie recoiled, crying from the pain being inflicted on her with every forced step, as she tried to leave.

She had relished in knowing—the more Kara fought against her—the more the crushing pain would grip her insides. If the Valkyrie had persisted, it would have taken a matter of seconds for her to collapse, before falling into a fatal coma.

She had seen it many times; none more so, than with Reece. In the beginning, he could not accept his bonding, making countless attempts to escape, his stubbornness taking him to the edge of death. Eager to stop him, Kara became the willing volunteer, engaging with him in countless fights—Reece taking the wrath of her sword, every time.

Disrupted from her thoughts, the Sorceress was forced to abandon them, hearing Wareeshta's movements about her chamber. The Dhampir paused when their eyes met.

'What are you doing here, Wareeshta?'

'I have brought you—'

'Yes, of course! I remember. You know what to do.' The Sorceress regarded the open door of her chamber. 'Where is she?'

'She is … with Tam,' Wareeshta replied, observing the irritated look gradually appear on her Mistress's face. 'But do not fear, my lady, he is a worthy opponent against her strength.'

'For now,' the Sorceress grunted, her mood turning to one of annoyance. 'No! I *cannot* and will not lose another to her. I swear she does it, not for her pleasure, but to try my patience. I must congratulate her,' she added sarcastically. 'If I do not act now, she will surely dispatch him. Tam has the qualities of a leader. I need him. I need them all … especially now.'

'Shall I look for—'

'Do it!' she snapped. 'The time has come to inform you of my plans.'

Warreshta stood to attention, sensing something was about to happen. Her curiosities were recently awakened, due to their prolonged stay in the one place. She was sure it was connected to the captive below; their presence was clearly of some importance.

'Go!' she shouted.

The Dhampir spun round, about to exit—

'And, Wareeshta …'

'Yes, my lady?' she replied, turning again—eager to please.

The Sorceress sauntered towards her with menace. Staring down into the Dhampir's deep-brown eyes, she leaned forward with intent, her tone now flat and calm when she spoke:

'I fear nothing!'

Chapter Twenty-four

'I risk it all,' Oran began, closing his eyes, reluctant to show his fears.

'Then take it,' Reece urged, sensing the Warlock's concern. 'You have my confidence.'

'Do I?'

'I assure you of it.' His attempt to smile at the Warlock proved difficult.

Oran grinned, feeling a little comforted by his effort. 'Asai said you are loyal to your word.'

'Know this War—Oran,' he started, his tone resuming its seriousness. 'If we are to be of service to one another, we must render it so. No secrets.'

Oran hesitated, holding the Dhampir's intense stare. 'No secrets,' he said, nodding in agreement.

'Then I shall begin, by putting your mind at ease. I have no loyalty to L'Ordana.'

Oran looked directly at him, a little startled. It was the first time he had heard the Dhampir use *her* name; when he did, he spat it out, with venom.

'If it were not for the bond, she has inflicted on us,' Reece continued, 'I would have destroyed her, on our first encounter.'

Oran remained focused, listening to Reece's every word, secretly relieved he had not killed her. He witnessed the hatred felt by the Dhampir, sympathising with him as he continued relaying his thoughts.

'And, believe me, I have tried … several times. This curse—this bond we endure—is impossible to break. We are living a prolonged death. It will be centuries before the Grim Reaper points his beckoning finger. I cannot lie when I tell you, there are times I would gladly welcome him.'

'*Centuries*, you say?'

'Because we are half-human, our hearts continue to beat, but at a slower pace, prolonging our lives. Our blood pumps through our blue veins. We feel pain, and yet endure its effect, briefly. Our strength and speed have their benefits, I grant you, but ...'

'You would trade it all for freedom.'

Reece paused as traces of memories interrupted his thoughts. 'I have forgotten how long I have been this way—nor do I care to remember. Those whom I once knew, from my past life, are now gone. I would have nothing to return to.'

Oran opened his mouth to speak, then hesitated, when the Dhampir rose from his seat.

'It was *she* who killed my wife!' he blurted.

'L'Ordana?' Oran replied, inwardly shocked by the revelation.

Reece shook his head.

'The Valkyrie was the perpetrator,' he said, adjusting one of the lanterns. He stepped back, making sure it was aligned with the other. 'She took great pleasure in informing me of her intentions. So, there is one thing I seek in all this ...'

'Retribution,' Oran replied, as though reading his mind.

The Dhampir turned to meet his look.

'You may have it yet, Reece.'

'*That* will prove difficult; we cannot touch L'Ordana's servants. She protects them both—especially Wareeshta—from a potentially fatal attack.'

'From *you*, in other words,' Oran stated.

A slight curl appeared on the corner of Reece's mouth. 'Among others,' he said. 'But, unfortunately, the "blood whore" is rarely away from her Mistress.'

The Warlock passed him a sideward glance, intrigued.

'She is the *key* to our freedom,' Reece revealed. 'If ... *when* Wareeshta dies, our curse goes with her, allowing us to return to the way we once

227

were. We would then continue to age—naturally—as was intended, from the day of our birth.'

'Then there *is* hope for you?'

'Perhaps. But Wareeshta is seldom alone. A rare opportunity once presented itself to me; a momentary lapse in her guard spurred me to stab her—in the back, no less. The coward's way.'

Oran raised a brow, surprised by the Dhampir's admission.

'When desperation takes its hold,' said Reece, shrugging, 'there is no controlling one's actions. As you can see, by my ongoing presence … I failed. My dagger did not even come within a foot of her.'

'Did she suspect you?'

Reece nodded.

'I remember the slight turn of her head, acknowledging my attempt. She did not flinch or retaliate in any way—save for the smirk on her face.'

'And, no doubt, you were punished for it.'

'I was prepared for the consequences of having to face Kara's blade, yet again. But it never came. It seems Wareeshta chose to keep it to herself.'

'How interesting,' Oran remarked, 'which leads me to suspect …' He paused, contemplating what Reece had just told him. 'Wareeshta may still retain some of her human traits, choosing to conceal them from the others. It may be her weakness, which would prove quite useful.'

'This life,' Reece stated, returning to his seat. 'I have known it longer than that of my mortal one. I struggled for years to accept it; I still cannot. But I have learned perseverance.'

'With Asai's help?'

'It is thanks to him that *we* did not succumb to dominance.'

'We? Am I to assume there are *more?*'

'There is another—Tam. He has not been with us long, but he is young and sturdy.'

'And you trust him?'

Reece nodded.

'Tam has been easily led by Kara, but he is now more than her match. You will see when you meet him.'

'If I had known …' started Oran, doubt now creeping in.

'He *can* be trusted,' Reece assured him, determined to prove his colleagues' worth. 'We must forgive him his wants and needs, ignoring them while he is willing to help us. We know the risks are great, however, it has its advantages, in that, the Valkyrie *favours* him.'

A knowing grin appeared on Oran's face as he grasped his meaning.

'I see you understand,' said Reece.

Oran smiled, amused that the Dhampir still maintained some sense of humour, beneath his cold exterior.

'Now,' he continued, 'time for truths! How, precisely, do you hope to *free* us?'

'I do not *hope* to,' the Warlock returned, shaking his head. 'I *intend* to. *This*,' he added, indicating to where the invisible barrier divided them, 'can be removed.'

When Reece sprung from his seat, Oran flinched at the Dhampir's sudden movement—the obstacle between them glowing dangerously at his closeness.

'How long have you been imprisoned here, Warlock?' Reece snapped, his eyes widening.

'I'm not quite—'

'And this *information* only comes to me now!'

Oran rose, raising his hands. 'Reece, you must understand—'

'Understand what?!' he retorted, his voice growing louder.

Oran noticed the Dhampir's inflamed eyes—them contrasting with the burning anger appearing on his pale face.

'I, among others, have suffered in ways you cannot conceive—devoid of all hope. And yet, stowed away, beneath *our* feet—right *here* under our noses—lay the secret to our escape. All this time, and—'

'I had to be convinced of the reliability of my chosen confidants; after all, you are—' Oran stopped himself, then took a deep breath, '*Dhampir*—not entirely trustworthy.'

Reece pulled himself up to full stature, breathing deeply, to take control of his temper. He could not comprehend the Warlock's comment, knowing he loathed the term. He felt taunted by it.

'And tell me, Reece,' Oran commented, 'What of your emotions?'

The Dhampir glared at him, confounded.

'How do you … *feel*, now?' The Warlock scrutinised the Dhampir with curiosity until, eventually, his clenched fists gradually loosened. He then saw Reece's shoulders fall, his body begin to relax, as his heaving chest slowly returned to its normal, rhythmic swell. Reece closed his eyes and inhaled, seeking calm. Slowly, he opened them again; they had returned to normal.

'Point taken, Warlock.'

'Oran,' he said, reminding him. 'If we are to be allies, we must address one another with respect. Agreed?'

'Agreed.'

For the first time, since his captivity, Reece allowed himself to feel hopeful. He had accepted the longevity of his extended life, storing his emotions from harmful influences. And now, the individual standing before him, observing his every move, had begun to unlock them. The lucid feeling returned, urging him to trust the Warlock. As his thoughts tempted him further—with images of great possibilities—he neglected to notice Oran remove the object from beneath his shirt.

Oran held the amulet out towards Reece—the sound of the heavy chain dropping from his fingers, borrowing his attention. The Dhampir watched as the precious item swayed to and fro, holding his gaze. Oran noticed the reflection of the diamond's pale-yellow light, in his green eyes. They widened with recognition, drawing on the Warlock's curiosity.

Though still conscious of the surging energy between them, Reece inched forward. He waited until the amulet stopped swaying, and tilted his head. 'I have seen this before.'

'The Sorceress?' Oran enquired, to confirm his assumptions.

'Yes, but how did you—'

'I was there when she stole it,' he interrupted, relieved it remained in her possession.

'You *knew* her?' said Reece, bewildered by the unexpected confession.

'Aye, a long time ago,' he began. 'She had another name, then—Kristene. She had been left alone after her mother was wrongfully burned at the stake. I had feared for her safety, perceiving she, too, may be convicted of sorcery, by those who condemned her mother. Unfortunately, my suspicions were realised.'

'They were going to *burn* her?'

'Not quite. She was condemned to the witch's drowning. To my shame, they almost succeeded.'

'And to our misfortune,' Reece muttered.

'Do not judge her yet, until you've heard her story.'

The Dhampir sighed, reluctant to learn more about the one who had sentenced him.

'Unless you have more pressing matters to attend to, Reece, I urge you hear me out. It is important to our task, and that you realise what you—*we*—are up against.'

The Dhampir nodded, encouraging him to continue as he took his seat.

Grateful, Oran proceeded.

Reece listened intently, absorbing everything being relayed to him, interrupting at intervals with questions of enquiry:

'How long did you know her?'

'Years.'

'Were you—'

'Aye, we were—but she was *different,* then—a good person.'

Somehow, I doubt that, Reece thought. 'Where did you live?' he continued.

'In different places—over time.'

'How did you survive?'

'Oh, we had our "means", allowing us to live a life of luxury.'

'Clearly,' he said, eyeing the grandeur the Warlock was being kept in. 'What happened to change her?'

'Her amazing ability to learn spurred her cravings. She was eventually lured away from me. I'm to blame, though, for the foolish error of my ways.'

'You?!'

'I confess, it was my neglect that drove her into the misguidance of another. However, *I* did not make her what she is today.'

'If it was not you … Who, then? For the woman you once shared a different life with is not the same as the one who rules this citadel.'

'The blame falls on another—a Warlock. I was acquainted with him, for centuries.'

'It appears we follow the same path of longevity,' Reece remarked.

'Perhaps. But, unlike you, it is part of who we are. We are *born* to it, therefore, are in acceptance of our fate … until we fall into the company of mortals.'

'Do you mean … when *love* seizes you?'

'There are those we meet on our long journey, who find difficulty in understanding it. It is, for this reason, why some of us choose to lead a life of solitude.'

'Unlike you,' said Reece.

'Needs must!' Oran returned, with a grin.

'And not a selfish trait, on your part?'

Oran sighed. ''Tis a burden of my weakness, I must confess.'

Reece considered his reply, envisaging the eventful life the Warlock must have led, to have brought him to where he was now. 'This other *Warlock* you speak of …'

'We fought many battles together, side by side,' said Oran. He grunted. 'We thought him dead—a presumption regretted by those who believed it. He had sought Kristene out, in secret, striking when the opportunity presented itself. I did not suspect a thing; I was too preoccupied, elsewhere.' The Warlock continued to reveal the chain of events that had finally led to their parting, in Triora.

'It was *then* she stole it?'

'Aye, after murdering my young servant girl.'

'So, that was when it began,' Reece assumed, slowly nodding to himself.

Oran tilted his head. 'I don't—'

'Are you aware she has taken the lives of many others, since then?' said Reece.

The Warlock's mouth fell in disbelief. '*Many*, you say? How many?'

'From my understanding … one for each year. She believes we are ignorant of her "needs." I have seen the subtle signs of ageing when they are not met on time. She sends the Valkyrie to "employ" a servant girl—one who is young and incorrupt. She then takes her into her confidence and …'

'Is never seen again,' Oran presumed.

'Her eyes betray her deed; they take the colour of the victim she has chosen. That is when we know what she has done. Her renewed youth matters to her a great deal.'

Oran shook his head, his thoughts still plagued by the image of Lucia's charred remains.

'You disagree with me, Oran?'

'I believe she's preparing herself,' he replied.

'For what?'

'For something she is not yet familiar with.'

Reece lowered his head, patiently waiting.

'The amulet she stole came from the individual who made her what she is—the Sorceress you are now acquainted with.'

Reece narrowed his eyes.

'It contains something of immense value,' continued Oran.

'Which is?'

'A *secret*,' said Oran. 'One she is desperate to acquire, which, at this time, is proving difficult for her.'

'Because *you* refuse to reveal it.'

Oran nodded.

'She'll not hear it from *my* mouth,' he said, determined. 'But I do not doubt it, Reece; she knows something is stirring.' The Warlock suddenly threw his head back, laughing.

'And this is amusing, because …?'

'Do you know that she visits me in secret?' said Oran.

'Impossible!'

'Even her servants are ignorant to her secret rendezvous with me. Though clever, she also has her underlying weakness.'

'That "weakness" being *you*,' Reece stated, folding his arms.

'Indeed,' Oran replied with a smugness that failed to amuse the Dhampir. 'At first, it was a game. She would visit me in a vain attempt to extract what information she required. It helped to pass the time. Also, I relished the thought of observing the seething look on her face, when I declined her offers.'

'So *that* explains her changing temperament,' Reece commented, slightly irked.

'Forgive me,' Oran begged. 'But I assure you, the games have ceased. I see the desperation in her eyes. She *will* persist. But, no matter what, I will—I *must*—protect the amulet's secret with my life.'

'And this … secret?'

Oran regarded him. 'In time, you will know it.'

'And *his* name?'

Oran glanced at him, momentarily confused.

'The one who is to blame for her ruin—the one who *stole* her from you?'

''Tis a name I've not spoken … in a long time.'

'Then speak it, now!'

Oran pondered over the name and everything associated with it. The mere idea of uttering it again repulsed him. It was as though he would be inviting the individual into the chamber. Before he realised it, the name he abhorred slid from his tongue into their presence:

'Magia Nera.'

The sound of melting candle grease hissed as it dropped into the lantern's flame, breaking their lingering silence. Reece cast a quick eye at the flickering flame before speaking;

'Do you know where he is?'

'No,' Oran replied, with certainty. 'Nor have I any desire to know it.'

'How much does she know?' said Reece. His enquiry was blunt.

Oran lifted his brows, detecting a sense of urgency in the Dhampir's voice. 'She is aware of the amulet's importance, but not of its true purpose. Timing is everything. 'Tis the "where and when" that matters—and she has no knowledge of either.'

'Yet,' Reece retorted.

The Warlock hesitated, staring into the Dhampir's intense eyes, suddenly disturbed by the menacing tone in his voice. Oran felt a sudden pang of regret infuse itself in him. He tried to swallow, but his throat was dry from their conversation. A feeling of dread then took over as Reece maintained his stare on him. And then he saw it—the smirk crawl across the Dhampir's face as he slowly rose. Sensing an unpredictability in his demeanour, he followed Reece's movement with growing fear and apprehension.

The Dhampir stepped closer, grinning.

'Well then … my friend,' he began, 'it appears your *Kristene*—our Sorceress—may yet unravel your *secret.*'

'I—I don't understand,' said Oran, his unease growing, fearing the Dhampir's betrayal.

'It seems she, too, harbours a secret—one *you* are clearly not aware of.'

'What do you—'

'This fine citadel,' Reece interrupted, 'houses—not one, but—*two* Warlocks.'

Chapter Twenty-five

'You took your time!'

Wareeshta's wary eyes flashed between her Mistress and the Valkyrie, as the tension in the luxurious chamber mounted, dampening its beauty.

'Well?!' cried L'Ordana, turning to meet Kara's insolent stare.

The Valkyrie played on her Mistress's surging anger before choosing to speak. 'I was … detained,' she returned, smirking to herself.

L'Ordana lunged forward, her stormy eyes displaying hate as she grasped the Valkyrie's throat. Wareeshta promptly stepped aside, avoiding the confrontation.

'I swear it, Kara!' she sneered, tightening her grip.

The Valkyrie glared down at her, demonstrating her lack of fear, as she felt the rhythmic tap of the long, sharp nail on her Mistress's right thumb, threatening to puncture her skin.

'No, my lady!' Wareeshta pleaded, reaching out to stop her. 'You *know* you need her.'

Kara felt the lethal pressure on her throat as L'Ordana pressed harder. The Valkyrie knew, if provoked further, the Sorceress would drive the nail into her artery; she remained staunch, refusing to give in to the threat.

'I beg you!' Wareeshta persisted, her hand still outstretched.

The Sorceress wavered, contemplating it, before releasing her hand from Kara's throat, leaving the deep indentation of her nail behind. She then turned away, repelled by the Valkyrie. It was clear there was no love lost between the two. Wareeshta was aware of the familiar pattern between them. It had always been that way; they fight, releasing hidden tensions, and then return to the order of duty.

The atmosphere in the chamber gradually subsided. L'Ordana kept her back to her servants, her thoughts filled with ambition yet fused by uncertainty. Her eyes blinked continuously in thought as she chewed on her lip. Composing herself, she turned to address the two faces scrutinising her from behind. She paused, glancing at the rug they stood on; Wareeshta followed her look, with interest.

'Come with me,' she then insisted. 'It is time.'

L'Ordana drew back the large, ornate rug with a sweeping gesture of her hand. As it retreated—on her command—Kara and Wareeshta stepped aside, intrigued, its graceful movement holding their fascination. For all the occasions she had been in her Mistress's chamber, Wareeshta considered why she had failed to notice its hidden purpose. Why would she? It was never brought to her attention, until now. A single glance at Kara's furrowed brow told her she, too, was oblivious to its secret.

There, beneath its splendour, a grey, paved stone floor looked up at them. There was nothing unusual about it; the citadel was layered with them. The Sorceress approached it and raised her hand. Then, in a forward motion, she extended her arm, silently commanding the floor back, without touching it.

Kara and Wareeshta eyed one another as the floor grinded away from them, its low crumbling sound announcing its opening. Slowly it inched back until it could go no further.

Equally curious, the two stepped forward and looked down into the darkness as it peered up at their eager faces, waiting to invite them into its hold.

'Follow me,' L'Ordana beckoned, making her descent.

The steps, at first, gave the illusion of reaching out into the unknown, then lead them down to a passageway—sufficient for them to walk side by side. The walls were lined with large, brass torches, clinging to their sturdy iron brackets, igniting—one by one—as the Sorceress came into their presence. It was at this point Wareeshta became aware of the extent of her Mistress's hidden powers.

'Where are you taking us?' Kara enquired, reluctant to proceed.

'I want to show you something,' said L'Ordana.

'A trap?' she sneered.

'How tempting,' she muttered, turning her head to acknowledge the Valkyrie's comment. 'But, alas! No. My priorities lie elsewhere. Now, take one!'

Following her order, they each removed a torch before watching their Mistress fade from view into a steep decline—the deep steps proving treacherous and slippery. With every tread, the stench of dampness rose to meet them. Wareeshta recoiled from its potency, her senses heightened by the unfamiliar territory.

The Sorceress stopped at the base of the steps and raised her torch, displaying the space in front of them; it spread out into a large cavern. Kara extended her light towards its centre, illuminating the mirrored surface of an underground lake. Tiny embers from the flame ignited as they fell on the water. She looked up, straining to see the opposite side.

'Thirteen down—thirteen up,' L'Ordana stated when the set of steps came into view.

'Why thirteen?' asked Wareeshta.

'Why not?' she replied, lifting her shoulders. 'It seems fitting; this citadel reeks of bad luck.'

'What is up there?' Kara questioned, pointing her torch.

'The way we came down mirrors the way we shall go up.'

Her two servants stared at her.

'But first, we must cross this lake.'

'You make it sound like a difficult task,' said Kara, in her derisive tone.

L'Ordana returned a scathing smile at the Valkyrie. 'I beseech you to *try*.'

The Valkyrie's eyes narrowed, regarding her with suspicion.

'Be wary, Kara, for this lake is poisonous,' she returned, extending her arm. 'Look!'

The Sorceress lowered her torch, as close as she dared, tapping it gently. Blue, toxic flames spurted up as the falling large embers touched the surface. They stepped back, avoiding potential contact—the strong smell of sulphur filling their nostrils.

'Cast your flame into this lake,' she warned, 'and we will not live to see another day.'

Handing her torch to Wareeshta, the Sorceress stepped forward, away from the inquisitive aids, her feet within inches of the deadly lake. Closing her eyes, she stretched out her hands—both palms facing the low, flat roof.

'Rise!' she commanded, her voice echoing throughout the dank cavern.

Quivering ripples of water fanned out in pursuit of the other, growing larger as they raced to the edge. The water continued to surge, pushed up by what was concealed beneath. What appeared to be a stone-cobbled footbridge, emerged into view, rising no more than a foot above the surface. It stopped, without order, water continuously flowing down its slimy sides, eventually subsiding into droplets.

'We must wait for the water to calm itself before proceeding,' she warned them.

Kara noticed three sizable rats scurrying along a ledge, away from the threatening lake. She thought it strange, how few there were. 'Surely, in this miserable place, it would be heaving with them,' she remarked, pointing to the rodents.

'Their numbers *have* somewhat declined,' the Sorceress replied.

Kara turned her attention to a subdued Wareeshta. 'Why so silent, Dhampir?' she taunted. 'Is there something you *know*?'

'I am as ignorant as you, Valkyrie,' she returned.

Ignoring them, L'Ordana snatched her torch from the Dhampir, and stepped out onto the bridge, closely shadowed by her two servants. The light emanating from the torches guided their way, safeguarding their footing. In the distance, the tilted steps—similar to the ones they had descended—waited for their ascent.

On reaching the other side, the Sorceress mounted them, without hesitation.

'Thirteen!' Wareeshta remarked when they reached the top.

Kara rolled her eyes.

They stepped up into an extended passageway—its length, longer than that of the previous—then continued into a straight, gradual incline, until the passage changed direction, leading them through its winding route.

'What *is* this place?' Kara insisted, her tone becoming impatient; she sensed they were being led upwards—back into the citadel. She received no reply. Snubbed by her Mistress, she moved to repeat the question, when the shape of a door came into focus. Carved from the rock, which held it in place, it was clear its purpose was to keep something hidden from view.

On their approach, L'Ordana motioned them to stop. Raising her torch, she slowly guided the flame over its high-arched frame—a red glow following her line. The heat seemed to melt away the fine divide between the stone door and wall.

The Sorceress stepped back. 'Ascend!' she commanded.

Shards of rock fell away as the door climbed into the ceiling above. Wareeshta and Kara's eyes surveyed its gradual disappearance, wondering how it was possible.

Turning to face them, L'Ordana smirked at the expressions on their faces before inflicting her warning: 'You speak to no one of this,' she cautioned. 'For I will not be lenient—should either of you reveal what you see. Make your vow … or suffer my wrath.'

Wareeshta was the first to nod, for fear of it. Kara breathed deeply, her eyes regarding the space where the door had been. Aware the Valkyrie was trying her patience, the Sorceress inhaled deeply, hiding her agitation.

'It is my curiosity that tempts me in,' she eventually stated, sliding her eyes towards her Mistress.

L'Ordana stepped into the blackness of the doorway. She hesitated.

'Something prevents you from entering?' sneered Kara, from behind.

'I am contemplating whether to "dispatch" you now, Kara,' she retorted. 'Or to leave it to another,' she added, leaving their sight.

'Why do you antagonise her?' Wareeshta voiced, shuffling by Kara. She was growing tired of her constant taunts.

Unperturbed, the Valkyrie followed the Dhampir over the threshold and through its darkness, to find her Mistress staring at something … waiting … But for what?

L'Ordana placed her torch into a perfectly carved wedge in the limestone wall—the flickering flame throwing light on their unusual surroundings: the chamber resembled a large dungeon, though clearly housed someone who was residing there; it looked lived in.

Their means were basic but sufficient. In the corner, the single berth looked as though it had never been slept in, while a simple wooden chair nestled beside a tiny bench, resembling a table. Kara thought the holding surprisingly dry and airy. Looking up at the far wall, she noticed an oval window, big enough for a large animal to come and go. Through its emptiness, she noticed the veil of night had descended.

'Who … "lives" here?' asked Kara, as her eyes surveyed the chamber.

L'Ordana released a long, heavy sigh. 'Why now?' she uttered beneath her breath, before deciding to leave. Frustrated, she turned— the anger visible on her dead-pan face.

'We are leaving, my lady?' Wareeshta queried.

'I misjudged my timing,' she replied, sweeping by her servants. As they moved to follow their Mistress, Wareeshta hesitated, hearing a shuffling sound from behind.

'Come to return what is rightfully mine, *Bella*?' said the voice, stopping them in their tracks.

The three females spun round to find the dark, figure grinning back at them. He slyly turned his head, waiting to hear her reply, but was met by silence. 'I thought not!' he added, in his thick accent.

Magia hesitated and tilted his head, catching a smirk on Kara's mouth. Then, as she lowered her head towards him, her wanting eyes fixed firmly on his, he knew why; he had caught the allure of her overpowering scent—and she knew it. As it grew stronger, weaving its way, trying to manipulate his senses, he was then alerted to her ploy. Had he been weaker, he would have bowed to her wants and needs as the sweet smell of lemon oil entered his system, its magnetic effect trying to lure him. However, he was far from weak; despite her attempt, he was unaffected by it, though aware of its influence.

So, you think you can capture me with your scent, he thought, smirking back at her.

Kara, seeing his reaction, lifted a brow, enticed by the prospect of this unique challenge. Drawing her tongue across her sensual lips she inched closer, ignoring L'Ordana and Wareeshta. But when he rolled his eyes and shook his head, the idea of it vanished, injuring her pride; it was clear he was immune to her. Insulted, Kara made to move towards him, but the Sorceress stepped up, preventing it.

He smiled, amused by the intervention, and yet sensed an underlying tension between the two.

'If you value your life, Kara,' her Mistress warned, 'I suggest you keep your distance.'

The Valkyrie threw her a curious glance. 'He is a threat?'

'The "threat" is the invisible barrier dividing us. It keeps him within his holding.'

'But the window …' said Kara, pointing to its openness.

'Your beautiful Mistress,' he began, 'allows me to enter and leave of my free will.'

'Within your boundaries,' she reminded him.

'But, of course,' he returned with a modest bow.

'Who is he?' Kara whispered, in her Mistress's ear.

'This *shall* be interesting,' he said, referring to the Valkyrie's question.

L'Ordana's eyes remained fixed on him with scepticism. 'You look well,' she commented.

This time he addressed her with a sweeping, complacent bow.

'… considering,' she then added, grunting.

Disgusted, he rose to his full stature, glaring at her with his burning, red eyes. 'Where is it?' he snapped.

'Safe,' she replied, in a calm and collective tone.

He composed himself, somewhat relieved to hear it.

'… for now, at least!' she added, unable to help herself.

His sudden, swift movement caught them off guard. 'If anything should happen to it,' he snarled. 'I—'

'Then you know what you must do, Magia.'

'And should I *choose* to tell you, would you return the item to me—its rightful owner—and guarantee my release?'

'Its rightful owner?!' she remarked, amused by his insolence.

'*Sì!* Then we would both have what we want— *Arrivederci!* — *Goodbye!* —and may our paths never cross again. It is as simple as *that!*'

'Nothing is simple in *our* world, Magia Nera. Surely *you* realise that. If you think, for one moment, I could trust you—let alone release you—then you are mistaken.'

He paused, gripping his hands behind his back before turning to face the open window. Kara surveyed the two rivals with interest. It was obvious they had shared a past.

'Be mindful of *time*, L'Ordana,' he began. 'It is our greatest foe. There is nothing we can do to slow its creeping hands. We scurry about, striving to keep up, knowing how it prevails in the end … regardless of *who* we are.'

Inside, L'Ordana was screaming. She detested him and his smugness, but knew he was right; the march of time *was* pounding its way towards her—and running out.

'Steady your heart, *Bella!*' he simpered, turning back to her. 'For it betrays and ages you.'

Conscious of his meaning, she felt the urge to touch her face, displaying her vanity. Her hand twitched, tempted by his cutting remark. But instinct prevented her from doing so.

'You *have* aged, *Bella*.'

Her mouth fell at his continuous insults in the presence of their company.

'And your eyes—they lack … spirit! I preferred it when they were sultry and inviting.'

Trying to ignore him, she turned away from his malevolence and glanced around. Something dawned on her. She looked to where Wareeshta had stood. The Dhampir was nowhere to be seen.

'Step out from the darkness, *piccolo Mio*,' he urged.

Wareeshta came forward from the doorway, where she'd been hiding. He surveyed her with insight, making her cautious. He now inspected L'Ordana's servants with quick scrutiny, before making his assumptions. He imagined he could now read Kara's intense thoughts, as the Valkyrie's images entered his mind. A smug grin appeared across his mouth; she looked away, still reeling from his insult.

'And what of *you*?' he asked, his attention returning to Wareeshta. 'Are you like *her*?'

L'Ordana followed his playful interaction with her servants, with annoyance; the mounting aggravation from his constant games was taking its toll on her, the more he persisted.

'No, you are nothing like her, *little one*,' he said, slowly shaking his head. 'True?'

Wareeshta lowered her eager eyes, relishing in the bond she knew they secretly shared.

'Are you thirsty, Warlock?!' L'Ordana snapped, through gritted teeth, reminding him of what he was. Her eyes were wide with rage.

'I am … remarkably well. *Grazie!* The rats are—surprisingly—agreeable to my palate.'

Pity they did not poison you, she thought, as she watched his tongue glide over his upper lip.

Observing him, Wareeshta felt her senses rise, as their arcane blood pumped through her veins.

'He is a Warlock?' Kara quietly asked, creeping to her Mistress's side.

'At your service,' he answered, hearing her speak his true title.

L'Ordana stepped closer, regarding him. 'He, too, shares Wareeshta's *gift*,' she revealed, 'in more ways than one. Many have tried to slay him over the centuries, but failed.' She lingered as they exchanged knowing looks. 'I thought *I* had succeeded.'

'You?' Kara exclaimed.

'We were once acquainted—a long time ago—before taking our separate paths.'

'Regretfully,' he added, pulling a solemn face.

244

'And, because he could not bear to be parted from his "*Bella*", he came looking for me.'

'And here we are,' he said, mocking her. 'Reunited, once again.'

'The "reunion" was a mere coincidence,' L'Ordana continued, ignoring him.

'I have no recollection of it,' Kara stated.

'Why should you? He was *my* concern—*my* challenge.'

'One, which you failed in,' he added.

'I thought I had destroyed him,' she went on. 'My mistake; I neglected to make certain he had been dispatched *properly*. And because of my error he … lived. Regrettably.'

'How did you—'

'Snare him in the end?'

Kara nodded.

'After a year—convinced I was rid of him—the familiar signs of his presence began to re-emerge; I then knew he would not give up searching for me. Therefore, I sought *him* out, at his most vulnerable time. However, having failed to instil the fatal blow it, unfortunately—'

'Rendered him, more dangerous,' boasted the small voice from behind.

Magia Nera smiled, his dark eyes staring into the ardent face of Wareeshta, her eyes glowing with excitement, in the dim light.

'Leave us!' L'Ordana snapped at the Dhampir.

Disregarding the order, Wareeshta continued to embrace his captivating gaze. Alerted to the growing energy between them, the Sorceress threw out her arm, pointing it at the Dhampir. Too preoccupied with his presence, Wareeshta failed to see the warning sign, before being slammed against a wall.

Unable to conceal her satisfaction, Kara smirked—only to have it then wiped from her face when she caught his hostile stare.

Stunned by the unrepentant blow, Wareeshta stumbled to her feet, glaring at the Sorceress with resentment.

'Do not make me ask you again, Wareeshta,' she warned, maintaining her threat.

The Dhampir cast an unforgiving look at her Mistress, before finding Magia Nera's attentive eyes. He acknowledged her with a subtle nod; she returned it, before cowering from the dimness of the chamber, back into the darkness.

His taunting laugh grabbed L'Ordana's attention.

'Remember who keeps you alive, Warlock!' she cried.

'I do not intend to forget … *Witch!*' he returned, with added insult. 'And lest *you* forget … remember who holds the knowledge you so desperately seek.'

Sickened by his constant observations, the Sorceress struggled to control her temper. Resisting the need to clench her fists, she felt her distaste for him battling to escape. No, she could not display weakness in front of him. And then there was Kara's smug arrogance to consider. The Valkyrie would be more than content to take advantage of any sign of her weakness.

L'Ordana then detected Kara's strong scent as she dared to step closer.

'If he does not give you what you need, Sorceress,' Kara whispered in her ear, 'there is always the *other* one. If you would only let me have my way with him …'

L'Ordana caught Magia's curious reaction; he was now alert with interest.

'The other one?' he enquired, moving within a breath of the barrier.

His inquisitiveness gave her a sense of control. She lingered, savouring the moment, before casually answering; 'An old acquaintance of ours,' she revealed.

An old acquaintance? he thought, narrowing his eyes. He looked sharp when it dawned on him. 'No!' he retorted, drawing his head back. 'How can this be?!'

'You are not the only one who came searching for me,' she said, teasing him. 'It was almost … too easy. *He* underestimated my powers. Because of his past sentiments, he practically offered himself as my prisoner. How *could* I refuse?'

Kara stood motionless, absorbing all she could while taking pleasure in the rivals' mutual distaste for one other.

'Where is he now?' Magia asked, stepping dangerously close. There was an urgency in his voice.

It begged her to question it: *Could he be threatened by his old nemesis?* She decided to play him. 'He has been most helpful,' she replied, sauntering back and forth, exchanging the occasional playful look.

He grunted. 'Just like your heart, *Kristene*, your eyes betray you.'

She halted, slowly turning her head to meet his smug expression.

Kara eyed them, baffled. 'Who is Kristene?' she remarked.

'Do not call me by that name!' L'Ordana hissed, taking no notice of the Valkyrie. '*She* no longer exists.'

'I would not count on it, *Bella*,' he returned, adding to her frustration. 'Tell me—has Oran *told* you yet?'

In a moment of weakness—having heard his name—she lowered her eyes briefly, forgetting herself. She blamed his taunts for distracting her.

Her hesitation answered his question. 'But of course not!' he said. 'Why else are you *here*? And why does your servant beg you to—'

'It is only a matter of time,' she cut in.

'How brightly does it now shine?' he asked, pressing her further.

The Sorceress remained quiet, racing ahead of his thoughts and questions. She needed to maintain her calm while she mused over her situation; also, to stay mindful of Kara's lingering presence, as more came to light.

In her keep, she held two Warlocks. Both knew the secret of the amulet. She wanted that knowledge—whatever the cost—yet neither would speak. It became apparent she would have to make a bargain with one of them.

But which one? she asked herself.

Magia watched, amused, as she churned away at her thoughts.

'Perhaps … if I could *see* it?' he suggested, in a coaxing manner.

'No!' she retorted.

'I could be of some assistance.'

She tilted her head, narrowing her suspicious eyes. 'I think not!'

'If we agree to trust each other, again, L'Ordana,' he began, 'I can help you to take this world and shape it into the one you desire.'

There was a familiar softness in his voice. She recalled its soothing influence from their past. Her face softened as it tempted her.

Noticing the subtlety of its effect, Kara, once again, bent her Mistress's ear. 'Can you trust him, Sorceress?'

L'Ordana flinched at the Valkyrie's unwanted closeness. 'Keep your distance!' she growled, stepping away.

Magia grinned at the fiery exchange, gradually discovering flaws that could prove useful. He paced his chamber in a slow, menacing stride, watching them.

'Tell me!' she demanded, her voice vibrating with intensity. 'How long do I have?!'

When he turned towards her, she breathed hard as his eyes penetrated hers.

'We both have something we need from one another, *Bella*. Let me stand by your side while you claim revenge for your scarred past.'

'Where is the Shenn?!' she cried, her impatience mounting, making no effort to conceal its infringing effect on her beauty, as the faint lines of ageing showed themselves.

Seeing it, motivated him further. 'It is clear you *have* been unsuccessful, in extracting what you desire from Oran.' He paused for thought. 'I cannot recall the last time I … No matter.'

'Oran would die rather than betray his oath,' she retorted.

'I am quite aware of that little fact,' he said. 'Yet, confused.'

'How so?'

'Why do you keep him alive, when he refuses to speak?'

'And in such splendour,' Kara muttered.

He cast the Sorceress a vexed glance. 'How interesting! I suspect you still harbour a tiny ember for him in that cold heart.'

L'Ordana pursed her lips, furious. Clenching her fists, she felt the pain of her nails dig into her soft skin. 'When the Shenn amulet is mine,' she informed him, her threatening words slow and defined, 'Oran will bow to me. He will have no choice. And when I am satisfied, I will gladly destroy him … personally!'

Kara threw her a disgruntled glance, feeling denied the opportunity of performing the act.

'There is a poetic tone in your words, L'Ordana,' he remarked, as he conjured up images in his mind of Oran's demise. 'It reminds me of "Alighieri." However, you must *find* it first.'

You must find it first, she thought, hearing his frustrating words repeat in her head. He was right; she could not do it alone. Also, he claimed the added advantage of knowing that. She slowly raised her eyes, meeting his.

Holding her gaze, Magia silently waited for her agreement—the reluctant nod of her head finally telling him he had won her over.

'Kara!' she said, staying fixed on him. 'Give him what he *needs.*'

Satisfied, Magia Nera turned away, grinning to himself; he was done with her … for now. Staring out into the darkness he contemplated the night, waiting for the Sorceress and her aid to leave. And as they left the chamber, he overheard her parting words to the Valkyrie:

'Find me another girl!'

The echo of his low, sinister laugh could then be heard, following them.

Chapter Twenty-Six

'Where is he?!' Oran demanded, astonished by the Dhampir's disclosure. 'Where is Magia Nera?!'

A small movement caught Reese's quick eye; he had surveyed the little spider, scurrying about between them, undecided in its direction. The Dhampir's speed was so swift Oran barely glimpsed the movement of the dagger—putting a sudden end to the arachnid's journey.

'I thought you were unarmed,' he stated, taken aback by his unexpected action.

The Dhampir disregarded him. 'I find it strange …' Reece began, observing its little body spasm beneath the tip of his blade, until it ceased, 'after all these years—despite my affliction—I still abhor these unsightly creatures.' He lifted the dagger to his eye level, inspecting it closely, then shuddered at its grotesque appearance.

'Your emotions betray your human side, Reece,' Oran remarked, observing his annoying scrutiny of the lifeless spider. The Warlock rolled his eyes with growing impatience. 'I think we can safely assume it is dead,' he snapped. 'Now, where is Magia Nera?'

'Locked away,' said Reece, discarding the spider from his blade.

'Are you certain?'

'You have my word on it,' he answered, returning the dagger to the inside of his boot.

'Where does she keep him?'

Reece considered Oran's persistence. 'It seems your past acquaintance with him is one of importance—causing some urgency.'

'*This* is the reason,' Oran conceded, acknowledging his amulet. 'You say you have seen one like it?'

'Once.'

'When?'

'When he came looking for her—creeping into the citadel like a ghostly shadow.'

'You *saw* him?'

Reece shook his head.

'Asai saw him first; he sees things others fail to. He brought it to my attention—and so, we followed him with intent.'

'To destroy him?'

'Naturally. However, he somehow slipped past our guard.'

'Magia Nera is clever, Reece. He deals in the dark arts—some, even I am unfamiliar with.'

'Perhaps,' said Reece. 'But he was no match for *her* that night. We followed his foul scent, which took us to her chamber. We overheard their conversation; it was clear they had met before. She presumed him dead, but it seems he had returned to claim what was rightfully *his*. She spoke of "the light in the stone." He refused to discuss it, demanding it was returned to him; however, she was determined to keep it.'

'But how did he become her prisoner?'

'Their conversation became heated when he insisted on seeing the amulet. She teased and mocked him, before exhibiting it in front of him. Threats were made. Despite my distaste for the Sorceress, we are bound to protect her. Given the unwanted choice, I would prefer to be under *her* command than that of the Valkyrie's.'

'So, you felt it your obligation to intervene,' Oran stated.

'An obligation that would have led to punishment, had we failed to meet it. We had no choice but to intervene; therefore, we were compelled to enter her chamber … without permission. It was then I caught a brief glimpse of the amulet before she concealed it on her person. I recall her anger at our "intrusion", as it was put.'

'Does she know you saw it?'

'No. The presence of her unwanted guest had distracted her.'

251

'Another advantage, in our favour,' Oran remarked.

'I thought his appearance … strange, at first,' said Reece. 'He was none too pleased with our timely interference. His shared anger revealed his true nature, arousing our suspicions. It soon came to light what he truly was: one whose preference is the night.'

'Making him more dangerous than you realise.'

Reece smirked. 'Not while he is imprisoned in a dungeon, beneath this citadel … beneath her bedchamber.'

'Her bedchamber?!' said Oran, stunned by the revelation. His eyes slid from Reece as he shook his head, muttering, 'a convenient arrangement, indeed.'

Reece's mouth twitched, detecting the taint of jealousy in the Warlock's tone.

Oran then grunted. 'No doubt *her* idea.'

Reece nodded.

'After we imprisoned him, we were sworn to secrecy.' He hesitated, studying Oran's mood, for a moment. 'Do I sense a hint of—'

'Have you seen him, since?' said Oran, cutting in, hoping to avoid any further unnecessary questions.

'I have seen and heard nothing more yet I am aware he still resides there. It is my understanding he, too, continues to disregard her demands.'

'Something tells me,' said Oran, 'that Magia is unaware of my presence.'

'We cannot presume that,' said Reece. 'After all, she *is* desperate. We must consider the possibility that she has told him.'

'If so, then she will play him, in the hope he gives her what she wants. She has accepted that I will never tell her the secret. I am now her lost cause.'

'For which you may be destroyed, then,' Reece stated.

'She would not—'

'Desperate times call for desperate motives,' said Reece, as a grim reminder. 'Do not presume you are indispensable—because of the past you once shared with her. She has promised you to Kara, if all else fails. And nothing would please the Valkyrie more.'

Oran looked away before his thoughts brought him back to his amulet. Reece regarded the Warlock as he caressed the precious item, his eyes becoming distant. The Dhampir parted his lips to speak, but hesitated, noticing the sombre look on his features. Detecting his sadness, Reece felt an underlying sympathy for his new ally, and lowered his head; it moved him in a way he thought he'd forgotten. Oran glanced up, catching the Dhampir's rare moment of emotion as he slowly nodded, as though in understanding.

A wave of relief then shrouded Oran with confidence; at last, he felt Reece had accepted his words in simple faith. He was grateful for the Dhampir's patience and self-control, imagining how difficult it must be for him, after so long in captivity.

Oran took a deep breath. 'It is time,' he said, 'to share the amulet's secret with you.'

'Thousands of years, before our time,' Oran began, 'there was a High Warlock—one of reputable intelligence, and a great visionary.'

'A visionary?' Reece enquired, shifting in his seat, trying to make himself comfortable.

'Aye, one who envisaged what would become of our world—should it be taken by those for whom it is not intended.'

'Such as our mutual acquaintance?'

Oran nodded.

'Such as *she*. Therefore, he sought a way to protect it. He was well-learned and accomplished in the knowledge of magic—in all its good and evil. The medium through which he acted was an ancient power: *Heka*.

'I am not familiar with it,' said Reece, drawing his brows together.

''Tis only known to Warlocks.'

'And its meaning?'

'*Magic*,' Oran revealed. 'It was by this means he used it to acquire power from the universe. It promised dominance and prosperity. And it is *that* very power which is contained in the amulet.'

Reece cast a confused glance at the item clutched in Oran's hand.

A suspicious grin appeared on the Warlock's mouth. 'This is not "the one" she seeks. The amulet I speak of is called the Shenn.'

'A greater one, no doubt.'

'Much greater,' said Oran. 'The High Warlock had his most skilled craftsmen find him a precious stone—one surpassing all others. After a long and treacherous search, they found one of exquisite beauty and size—mined from the mountains of the red lands—hidden deep in the southern Realm of Ockram.'

'A diamond?'

Oran nodded.

'Its colour was of the deepest blue—extremely rare. The stone was concealed by the craftsmen in an undisclosed place, where they had it cut, perfecting its brilliance. Its shape resembles a tear. The loyal craftsmen then created a magnificent amulet to house the stone as its centrepiece—fashioned from the finest yellow gold, with in-lays of lapiz-lazuli and carnelian, on its outer rim. He then ordered them to fashion six more—smaller in size—their centre stones cut from the remnants of the precious diamond.'

'Its size must have been immense,' Reece commented.

'Aye, unique in size *and* colour.'

The Dhampir stared at the Warlock's amulet, studying it. Even in the dim glow of the chamber, its cut and clarity were dominant. 'If the stone's original colour was deep-blue,' he quizzed, 'how can you explain its present state? It shines like—'

'The sun?' Oran interrupted.

Reece nodded.

'When his craftsmen completed the amulet, the Warlock took it to the great pyramid of Khufu—in the north of Ockram. He was accompanied by six high priests—each wearing one of the six amulets created for them.'

As Reece leaned closer to inspect Oran's, the Warlock held it up.

'The seven entered a secret chamber—carved within the inner sanctum of the pyramid. All that exists inside is a black, granite sarcophagus and four small shafts—carved into each wall—designed to run from inside the chamber, and out into the world above. It was here—surrounded by his high priests—he placed himself inside the sarcophagus, wearing the amulet. Through the power of *Heka*, he conjured the energy from the centre of the universe. Then drawing it through the shafts, into the inner chamber, he seized its power, by locking it within the amulet's diamond.'

Reece shook his head, sceptical. 'An impossible feat!'

'Nothing was beyond him,' Oran stated. 'His powers were relentless. As the energy filled the sacred chamber, the stone absorbed its life-giving force, changing its colour. Overwhelmed by the magnitude of its immense, and unknown, power, the Warlock tried to remove it, but was cast down by its dominance.'

'He died?'

'Not quite. He regained consciousness within a few days. The initial impact it had on his body had simply been too much. His newfound strength grew beyond anything he knew, proving difficult for him to master its influence. He then proclaimed himself as the first Magus, changing his name to "Lumeri"—after the great scribe and prophet, who lived thousands of years before. In his new name, he vowed to protect the world from harm, knowing he had the power to do so—along with the aid of five others.'

'Were there not six?' Reece queried.

'Unfortunately, one of the high priests stood in the way of the light when it entered the chamber. Its immense heat consumed him—and the amulet he wore.'

'A life, for a life!'

'Who knows?' Oran replied, shrugging.

'What of the other five?'

'Together, they formed the Elliyan: a *council* of Warlocks who would remain loyal to the Magus and his prophecies. Through his visions, his concern for mankind disturbed him. In them, he saw a sinister threat which stank of brutality and death, silently waiting for him to drop his guard. He feared the mortals' ignorance of an unknown force would be their downfall—should they not be protected ...' Oran paused. 'You must understand, Reece, we originate from a different age, long before your explorers sailed the great oceans. Malevolent threats have been lurking for thousands of years, waiting to hurl their terror, in the hope we become complacent. Although we reside in the same world as yours, *we* continue to recognise it as it was named, by Lumeri: "As was then— so shall it remain."'

Reece frowned, confused.

'It is simply a loyal and ancient tradition which we have taken with us through time—and shall continue to do so,' he explained. 'Lumeri then divided the mortal's world into *Five Realms*. The newly proclaimed Warlocks were allocated one each—to watch over and protect. They were then sent out with willing followers who would be loyal to their cause. It was Lumeri's belief, that they could live peacefully among the mortals, provided they concealed their true identities. They were encouraged to integrate with them, to live normally, while secretly protecting them from sinister threats. Some took wives, who would bear them children, while others chose a different path.'

'*How* different?'

'They became skilled mercenaries.'

'Were they mortals?'

Oran hesitated. 'Somewhat.'

'You seem uncertain,' said Reece.

'These *followers*—akin to medieval knights—were exceptional, bringing their unique qualities to the attention of the Warlocks. They had a natural ability to master the skill of battle. It was, for this reason, an elite number of mercenaries were formed, to protect the Elliyan. They are known as the "Bullwark"—believed to be a secret legacy, left behind by Lumeri.'

'They still exist?'

'Their numbers evolved—and continue to do so. And as the centuries passed, the lineage of Warlocks also grew. This world—in which you once lived, Reece—slowly became one with ours. To this day, the mortals are still unaware of our presence; we have learned to adapt well within their company.'

'I am curious, Oran.'

The Warlock regarded the Dhampir with equal curiosity.

'Have you ever been … complacent? Have mortals ever known the *immorality* you describe?'

'Apart from their weaknesses, no. The mortals have always been spared, due to our intervention. I would be lying if I said there have been no "incidents". Of course, there have! During troubled times. Thankfully, though, they were unaware of any … minor mishaps. But, despite them, the peaceful times have outweighed the troubled ones, and we have always kept a constant, watchful eye while maintaining our true identities. We can be thankful for man's blissful ignorance.'

'Surely, your loved ones *must* have known,' Reece speculated.

'They do,' said Oran with melancholy. 'Because of the longevity of a Warlock's life, we, unfortunately, outlive our loved ones. Therefore, we take it upon ourselves to share our hidden secrets with them. If the mortal is willing to share her life with a Warlock, it's only right she should know.'

'What became of …?'

Oran smiled when Reece paused, then frowned, trying to recall the name.

'Lumeri,' he reminded him. 'He became obsessed with the Shenn's power, to the point where it finally devoured him. It is thought he *allowed* it to.'

'Something tells me, *you* have a different opinion.'

'He was young and unwilling to restrain it. He ruled for nigh on seventy years, but his eccentricities paved the way to his downfall. It is vital that Magus and Shenn find their *balance*. I believe his naivety and ignorance may have led to his destruction.'

'And the fate of the amulet?'

'On his death bed, the Elliyan gathered. When the Magus released his final breath, they witnessed the light in the stones' centre had faded to black—as did the other five—signifying his demise.'

'So, the power of the amulet died with him,' Reece stated.

'That had been the way of their thinking. With its lustrous beauty lost to the darkness of death, it was considered worthless. Therefore, after much debate, it was decided to take the Shenn to a secret place, after which, the Warlocks would return to the lives they had built. Yet, unknown to the Elliyan, it simply lay dormant.'

'Dormant?'

'The five Warlocks parted ways, thinking they were at peace, taking with them—as a reminder of their past—the amulets given to them by their Magus. For years the items remained hidden away. True to say, it was a peaceful time … until a son was born to one of them.

'The very moment his father watched him enter the world, screaming innocence, something drew the Warlock back to his past—back to his amulet. He was not prepared for what his eyes would see.'

Reece stared with growing understanding as Oran's story unfolded. Finally, it dawned on him. 'The stone came to life!' he blurted.

'You are quite perceptive, Reece,' Oran remarked.

'What became of his child?'

'The Warlock's discovery played on his inquisitive mind, prompting him to keep a vigilant eye on his only son, *and* his amulet; he sensed a connection. With every passing year, he noted its inner light growing stronger. Instinct warned him to send word to the other four. With each reply came the same response: "The stone is reawakened!"

'A meeting then ensued, with the decision to retrieve the Shenn from its secret place. To their amazement, it, too, had come to *life!* Unable to determine a reason, they failed to see the connection, therefore, its mystery was left to the passage of time, which would prove fatal.

'When the Warlock's son stepped from childhood onto the threshold of adulthood, a change came about. The young man suddenly came into his own, his strength slowly increasing, day by day, and at a remarkable pace. His father became curious yet anxious for his welfare.

258

'Intrigued by his son's changing character—and convinced the amulet was the source—the Warlock voiced his opinion to the Elliyan. However, thinking the Warlock wanted the precious jewel, for his own benefit, they rejected his suggestion. But the Warlock's inner voice urged him on; he believed all was not right.

'Intuition returned him to his amulet, again. When his eyes looked upon it, the centre stone radiated its inner, blinding yellow light. He was now sure, beyond all doubt, its great energy *was* influencing his son, adding to his concerns.'

'Was it killing him?' said Reece.

'This was the Warlocks' theory, leading him to consult the Elliyan once more with his conclusions, insisting that the Shenn was responsible for his son's "condition." But still, they refused to listen. Determined in his beliefs, he retaliated by stealing it. He simply *had* to know.

'But when he returned home—on the day of his son's coming of age—the Warlock was shocked to discover his son had fallen into a deep slumber, from which he could not wake him. He was confounded by it. He watched in dismay as he stood over his waning son, helpless, convinced he was dying. With the Shenn held tightly in his hand, he became aware of its expanding heat. His distraught wife's cries of mercy for her son spurred him into an act of selfless devotion for them both. "'Damn them all!'" he was claimed to have said, before placing the sacred amulet into his son's limp hand.'

'Did he survive?'

Oran observed the intense interest Reece displayed, proving the Dhampir still held his human abilities.

Oran nodded.

'The amulet returned to its former magnificence, finding its balance while restoring the Warlock's son.'

'So, they *found* one another,' said Reece, implying the outcome.

'The Shenn was merely finding its way, unbeknownst to its new Master and the Elliyan. It had chosen their ruler.'

'What did the Warlock do?'

'He returned to the Elliyan with his son.'

'The new Magus,' said Reece.

Oran smiled. 'The Warlock had discovered the amulet's true purpose; however, the Shenn was still in its infancy. They had been unprepared and ignorant of the extent of its powers. Time, it seems, had been their silent enemy.'

'Did he live as long as the first—Lumeri?'

'He survived—no more than two years—much to the Elliyan's disappointment,' said Oran.

'And his mother's dismay,' Reece added.

'It is said, her broken and unforgiving heart took her to an early grave.'

'And the Warlock? Surely, he did not forgive them.'

'You would assume it. But this was not the case. United in their thinking, the Elliyan drew on their conclusions. After the stones lost their light, yet again, it was agreed they would always wear their amulets, to avoid repeating the same mistake. And yet, they still had no way of knowing *who* would be the next, or *when*. Their only guidance was to be prepared. It was then decided, whoever should sire the chosen son, the Elliyan would groom the child for his future role. His powers would be nurtured—as would his skills—to perfection, enabling him to accept the Shenn's challenging forces.'

'How long did they have to wait?'

'It was presumed, the next son—born to a Warlock—would be "the one." Years passed, and with them the births of others; but still, the amulet's stone remained dormant. Even to this day, we do not understand *which* makes the unwanted choice: The Shenn? The universe? We simply don't know.'

'Unwanted?'

'It is ironic in that it should be an honour to have one's son chosen to be our great Magus. Yet, with such an honour comes great risks … and doubts.'

'Did they learn by their mistakes?'

'In time,' said Oran. 'The Shenn, along with its "siblings", as Lothian affectionately calls our amulets—'

'Who?'

Oran smiled to himself, as he thought of his fellow Warlock. 'One who has a good heart,' he commented, before continuing. 'Aye, they learned. And when the Shenn came to life again, no time was wasted. They knew they had to study it carefully, to gain its knowledge. And, as agreed, when the child entered his tenth year, he was taken, and prepared for his future role.'

'Taken from his parents?'

Oran shook his head.

'Not quite. The child must be given up … willingly. He cannot be forced. That was—*is*—the way of it.'

'Have any been … unwilling?'

'No,' said Oran, holding the Dhampir's gaze. 'Not until now.'

Chapter Twenty-Seven

Reece drew back, staring at the Warlock, having detected his underlying scepticism throughout his story, urging him to ask: 'Why do *you* disapprove?'

Oran looked away. 'I have heard of the Elliyan's methods of training; they are somewhat … cold and detached. When the child enters his training, he must be pure of heart—and have committed no crime. However, once they have prepared him, it seems as if those very traits are replaced by an element of arrogance, stripping him of his youth and the life he had known among mortals. I feel—if he is to protect the mortals—it is important he maintains a true understanding of their ways. This has not always been the case. I believe this influences his bond with the Shenn.' Oran shrugged. 'Then again, I may be wrong. As with the first Warlock, I have my theories, too.'

'But *did* they succeed?' asked Reece, trying to justify their methods.

'It took time for Magus and Shenn to find their balance. But, under a watchful eye, he went on to become a great ruler, as did his successors. He ruled with the wrath of iron, under the same name—Lumeri—for over two hundred years.'

'A long time,' Reece commented.

'Some have ruled longer. Their lifespan is determined by the respect they show the amulet. Unfortunately, some were not so successful—by the methods of their ruling; *I* blame the Elliyan.'

Reece moved to speak, then hesitated.

'Ask it,' he urged the Dhampir.

'Had the first Warlock's son failed to bond with the Shenn, what would have become of him, and the amulet?'

'It is thought the Shenn may have taken back the energy it was giving him … but that has long since been dismissed as a myth, as he did bond with it. But there was a slight problem; he did not know how to control it. You see, the bond between a Warlock and his amulet is paramount. Regardless. We are *one* with them and, therefore, must respect them, as they are linked to the Shenn.'

Reece scrutinised Oran's. 'Yours is one of the *five*?'

'Worn by my ancestors,' he said, with pride, 'and handed down through the generations. They differ, somewhat, from the Shenn,' he added, displaying the back of his. 'See this?'

Reece dared to move closer, then drew back, feeling the barrier's surging energy.

'These hieroglyphs—carved by ancient hands—identify the Realm of Urquille, which belongs to me, as it did my forebears.'

'What does the Shenn look like?'

''Tis larger. Carved on the back, are the nomen and prenomen—the two names identifying …' His words drifted as he lost himself in a moment of thought, contemplating his amulet in silence.

'Identifying …?' Reece prompted, eyeing him with suspicion.

Oran looked sharply at him, before continuing. 'Identifying the "one" who will wear it—his common name, and the name he takes when the Shenn becomes his.'

'Lumeri,' said Reece.

Oran slowly nodded, his face growing sombre.

The Dhampir sensed the Warlock's inner torment, as his deep secret finally emerged in the quietude of the chamber; it was etched all over his face.

'*Your* son?'

'It is with heartfelt sadness that Gill will not wear mine. I knew his fate the moment he was born.'

'Where is the Shenn now?' asked Reece.

'Under the safe protection of the Ushabti.'

Reece tilted his head. 'What—or who is the—'

'Its Guardian.'

'I see,' said Reece, slowly nodding. 'But do you not fear your son might share the same fate as the first Warlock's son?'

'No!' Oran replied, defiant. 'We now have a better understanding of it, and besides … history has not repeated itself, since then. My concern is that my son and the Shenn find their balance *when* united. He will soon reach that time in life.'

Reece drew his brows together, confused.

'But I prepared him, as best I could. He has a good heart, and will make a—'

'You mean—you never gave him up?!' Reece suddenly realised. 'When it was *expected* of you …?'

Oran stared back at him, aware the Dhampir had completely misread him.

'Do you—did you have children, Reece?'

The question was unexpected and, for a moment, Reece did not know how to respond.

'No,' he said, at last. It was all he could say.

'I—I'm sorry,' said Oran.

'Why? I fail to understand your pity for something I have never experienced.'

'Then forgive me, but you can never truly know the bond a parent shares with their child. You would do anything to protect them. I could not take him from his mother and give him to *them*—and at such a young age, too—which is why *I* chose to train him, and why I took my family away.' His gaze hardened. 'No, *they* would have to wait. When *my* son becomes Magus, he will rule with goodwill—and devoid of arrogance.'

'*If* your son becomes Magus,' said Reece, fearing time was running out for the Warlock.

"If your son becomes Magus."

The words resonated deeply in Oran's mind as he held the Dhampir's look of uncertainty. Sudden desperation spurred him to relay what Reece needed to know: the vow he'd made to his wife and the agreement with the Elliyan. But as his reasons unfolded, the Warlock began to see the true error in everything he had done—and the possible consequences of it.

'What will happen if the Shenn falls into the wrong hands?' asked Reece.

'It would be catastrophic to us all!' said Oran, feeling the burden of his regret. 'I thought I could make it right—find a way to hold on to our son. That's what I told her—my wife.' He hesitated, shaking his head in annoyance. 'I foolishly believed I could find another to take his place. How wrong and selfish I was to *assume* it. I can't avoid it. I'm the one at fault for everything that has gone wrong.'

Reece regarded the Warlock intensely as his deep guilt was finally exposed.

'I did not bargain on *this,*' Oran continued, looking at his surroundings. 'Everything changed the moment *she* took me as her captive. I have put my son at great risk, because of ...' He sighed and shook his head.

'Because of your principles,' Reece stated.

'As well as my stubbornness,' said Oran, lowering his head in shame. 'I'll not deny it,' he added. 'And now, the real threat lies within the walls of this citadel. L'Ordana wants the Shenn. If my son fails to bond with it ... then it is there for the taking. I must get to my son before *she* finds him—convince him of the vital role that awaits him.'

Reece quickly drew his head back, in disbelief.

'You mean to tell me ... he does not know?'

'Another selfish mistake on my part,' replied Oran. 'I did not predict my present situation, which is why I pray my wife has told him—for his sake. If so, I hope he willingly accepts his role—because the Elliyan cannot force him to. But I know my son ... *and* my wife'—he looked at Reece with fear in his eyes, and shook his head— 'and my instincts tell me different. If I don't get to him—persuade him—then L'Ordana will.'

'If this is her intention,' said Reece, 'and, as you refuse to give her what she needs, it is most likely she will turn to your *mutual* acquaintance for help.'

Oran rose swiftly, pacing the chamber in deep contemplation, stretching his fingers continuously, showing his frustration. It was a valid point Reece had made. Given the opportunity, Magia Nera would work his charms on her again, with his irritating thick accent, luring her into his way of thinking—should she let him. Oran now had to assume each was aware of the others' presence ... He paused at his little mirror again, searching for inner guidance.

Realising his disposition, Reece felt compelled to help the stranger, who, in the short time of their acquaintance, had become his ally. 'What can *we* do?' he finally asked, catching the Warlock's eyes looking back at him, in the mirror.

'Help me escape from here.'

'**e**scape?!' cried Reece, rising, as Oran turned to face him. 'Believe me when I tell you, Warlock'—he shook his head vehemently— 'if I cannot leave this forsaken place, it is extremely unlikely *you* will.' He paused. '*Here*, the Sorceress controls everything and everyone.' He approached the Warlock, drawing dangerously close—the growing energy dividing them, warning of its menace. 'Look at it!'

Oran stared, feeling its ominous surge of death willing them to touch it.

'It was *she* who created *this*,' said Reece, feeling its heat. 'And it is *she* who only has the power to remove it.'

Composed, and appearing unconcerned by the fatal barrier, Oran raised a finger, commanding the Dhampir's attention. 'Not quite,' he replied.

Reece threw him a sidelong glance, raising a brow.

'Though we may be her prisoners,' Oran went on, 'it is *here* we shall help each other.'

'How?' said Reece, unconvinced.

'I make a solemn vow to you, Reece—on my son's life—may he live long enough to experience it. Should you do as I say …'

The Dhampir's brows shot up at the Warlock's suggestion.

'… I will free you from this place. Time is marching towards Gill's coming of age, when he will turn seventeen. We still have a few months yet. He must be brought before the Elliyan, who are waiting for him.' He hesitated. *I only hope I've prepared him enough*, he thought, reluctant to openly admit his possible failing.

'It is my fear L'Ordana may soon discover its secret, and take it—perhaps even …' His words trailed, recalling the images the Ushabti had shown him. 'I will not let my son die by *her* hand. Nor shall I let his mother mourn for the son who is on the brink of discovering his new life.'

'If you say you can *free* us … then we will do what we can,' Reece told him.

'We?' said Oran, momentarily forgetting the Dhampir's colleagues.

'I cannot do this alone. If you seek my help, it will involve Asai and Tam.'

'I must confess, Reece, I have my misgivings about Tam and his "arrangement" with the Valkyrie.'

'He *can* be trusted,' Reece voiced with staunch determination.

Oran felt difficulty in accepting his word. He sighed, making no effort to hide his reluctance, but Reece held his look of doubt, in support of his colleague.

Realising the Dhampir's defiance, Oran felt he had no choice but to surrender to it. 'If you insist!' he finally agreed, before detecting the sneer of victory on his ally's face. 'Now, listen carefully … First, you must go to L'Ordana's chamber—where you will find another—'

'There is no other chamber,' Reece interrupted, with certainty, prepared to challenge him again.

'Ah, but that's where you're wrong, my friend.'

'I am in no doubt of it, Warlock,' Reece persisted, his frustration mounting again. 'I know this, for I—' He stopped, as a vivid reminder of a particular *rendezvous* teased his thoughts. He shook his head in annoyance, attempting to cast it away.

Oran tilted his head and laughed.

Reece grunted with disgust. 'It is an encounter I would rather forget.'

'Yet, we are still *men*, making it difficult to resist. True?'

Reece cast him a searing, sideward glance. 'How do you *know* there is another chamber?'

Oran grinned. 'Because she told me!'

Reece stopped, his green eyes sparkling in the dim light. 'Why tell *you?*'

'Because she cannot help herself. I'm her prisoner, and she is under the pretence I will remain so … until her choosing. Yet, hidden beneath her cold exterior lurks much weakness.'

Reece hung on the Warlock's words, waiting …

'She is sentimental and—'

'Inconceivable!' the Dhampir snapped back, refusing to believe the Sorceress was anything *but* sentimental.

'Am I not alive?' said Oran, pointing out the obvious.

'You have a high opinion of yourself, War—'

Oran glared at him.

Reece rolled his eyes. 'Oran.'

'You forget, Reece, I *know* her. I see it in her eyes when she looks at me.'

'And her other weaknesses?'

'I taught her the good ways of our magic before Magia Nera changed all that. She was a bright student, eager to show what she had learned.'

And eager to please her teacher, no doubt, Reece thought.

'And though she had imprisoned me,' Oran continued, 'she still could not help but boast of her triumph, by throwing everything I had taught her in my face. I can still see the complacency on *hers* when she said, "Shall I tell you how I know your movements, Oran"?'

Reece narrowed his eyes. 'How could she possibly know *that?*'

'Because she watches me—from that hidden chamber.'

Reece quickly glanced around him with a sense of unease.

'Perhaps she even watches us *now*,' said Oran.

Suddenly the Dhampir felt the need to remain still. Seeing this, Oran threw back his head, laughing. 'Sit, my friend,' he insisted, gesturing towards the seat.

'Is it possible she *can* see us?' Reece enquired, cautiously sitting as his eyes surveyed the chamber.

'*See*—but not hear,' Oran stated.

'I fail to understand …'

'In her bedchamber, there hangs a long set of heavy drapes. Have you seen them?'

Reece nodded, listening attentively.

'Good. Behind them is a great window. This, however, is an illusion, to fool the inquisitive eye. Instead, you will find two wooden doors.'

'Sealed?'

'No, but only she can enter.'

'Our first obstacle,' said Reece.

'You may think it,' said Oran, smirking. 'But remember, it was *I* who tutored her. And I can teach another. All they require is an open mind.'

'And what shall we find in this … chamber?'

Oran regarded the Dhampir for a moment, before stepping back. Reece tilted his head, suspicious, as the Warlock grinned from ear to ear. Slowly, Oran spread his arms wide, as though in self-adoration.

Reece's mouth gaped. 'You?!'

Oran laughed out.

'Now you do mock me, Warlock!' Reece retorted, jumping to his feet, his body tense as rage began to take over again. 'No one can be in two places at one time.'

Seeing the Dhampir's rising anger—the veins in his throat pulsate as Reece ground his teeth—Oran dropped his arms. 'Forgive me, Reece,' he begged, realising the delicate line between his conflicting emotions. 'It was not my intention to mock you.'

'Then, do *not* try my patience,' he warned.

Oran lowered his chin. 'I shall do my best.'

Reece grunted, sliding his eyes away. 'How can you be here … *and* there?'

''Tis an illusion—a mirage—a deception. Call it what you will. It is her way of keeping a watchful eye on me.'

Reece stared at him. 'Then this changes everything!'

'Why should it?' Oran replied, shrugging. 'She can't hear our conversation.'

'She may question it, though.'

''Tis unlikely; has she questioned the conversations I've had with the others, who are sent to tend to my needs?'

'Not that I am aware.'

'Shall I tell you *why* Reece?'

'Do I have a choice?'

'Although Kris—L'Ordana needs you and Asai, for your skills, she sees *you* as nothing more than a servant—bound to her for as long as she sees fit. She thinks you are simply an emotionless object, used to fight her battles.' Oran paused, hearing the Dhampir grind his teeth, as he continued to glare back at him. It was clear Reece was feeling the insult, of the perfect description of his miserable life.

'And this, my friend, is another advantage.'

Reece narrowed his eyes, sceptical.

'She sees *me* as her vital source while holding a sentiment that runs deep. I believe the young woman I once knew as "Kristene" is still very much alive inside our Sorceress.'

'And keeping *you* from Kara's clutches.'

'Let us hope so,' said Oran.

'But if she watches us …'

'Until now, Reece, you have acted naturally—or as natural as you can—towards *me*,' said Oran. 'However, you may bring attention to ourselves, should you remain … *so*,' he added, raising his chin, indicating his reluctance to move.

The Dhampir breathed out, trying to relax.

'And we must be vigilant,' Oran stated, 'if we …' He stalled, regarding his ally—the two lines of doubt gradually appearing between his brows.

'What is it?' said Reece.

'I don't doubt your word when you assure me of Tam's loyalty,' Oran started, 'but … I feel it necessary to limit his knowledge—for now.'

Reece frowned, vexed by the Warlock's persistence to question his companion's loyalty.

'As a measure of precaution … you understand.'

'If you *insist!*' the Dhampir mumbled, unable to hide his annoyance.

271

'And, as much as I do not wish to insult you again, Reece, I think'—he hesitated, taking a deep breath— 'that Asai is the right choice—to undertake the first task—if we mean to escape.'

As he contemplated the Warlock's advice, Reece glanced over his shoulder towards the door, having noticed the light in the chamber had dimmed. 'I agree,' he promptly returned, to Oran's surprise. 'Asai maintains a calming demure—one of disciplined control—unlike me.'

'I applaud you for recognising it,' Oran replied, with admiration. 'You have retained so much of your human traits, Reece—more than you know.'

'They have been hibernating for far too long,' he returned.

'Then, my friend, it is time to reawaken them.'

When Reece rose, Oran followed him with observant eyes; the Dhampir appeared content and accepting of his plan—despite being aware of the immense risk—having taken him into his confidence. Nonetheless, he felt it was a great accomplishment, having done just that.

'Your light will soon fade,' Reece stated, taking note of the torches as he approached the door. 'I will send Asai.'

As the Dhampir made to leave, he wavered. Then, turning to face the Warlock, he frowned, narrowing his eyes, reminded of something. 'The *first* task, you say?'

Oran grinned.

'What is the second?'

Chapter Twenty-Nine

A sai's presence in Oran's chamber contrasted greatly with that of his previous visitor. The great Samurai's engaging character returned Oran to a feeling of restfulness, giving him hope. His movements had a sense of ritualistic purpose. Oran could not help but admire the gracefulness he displayed, in the simple act of sitting on the same seat his friend had occupied, during the previous hours. Before doing so, he bowed respectfully to the Warlock. It was evident they had made the right choice.

'He has referred to you as our *"Tomodachi"*,' Asai began. 'It appears you have made a great impression on him, to call you our "friend".'

Oran raised a brow. 'Now I feel I have truly accomplished something.'

'We have a long path to tread, Oran-san, before we can claim self-praise.'

'Indeed, we do, Asai. And are *you* prepared to walk it?'

'From the moment I was bound to *her*.'

'Then begin by taking note of her movements,' Oran began, 'until such time you are satisfied with her habits and routine. Let's just us hope she keeps to them.'

'We are all creatures of habit, regardless of who—or *what*—we are,' replied Asai, answering his concerns. 'It is instilled in us from birth.'

''Tis logical to assume it,' said Oran. 'Nevertheless, we cannot *presume*. She is extremely clever.'

'She cannot maintain her guard with consistency,' Asai stated. 'We have already been observing her nervous movements.'

273

'But of course!' Oran exclaimed, recalling what Reece had told him. 'She is becoming *distracted*. 'Tis only a matter of time before she succumbs to it.'

'What would you have me do?'

'Monitor her increasing visits to her chamber where, secretly, she visits Magia Nera. You are aware, no doubt, of his lingering presence, beneath her rooms?'

'*Hai!*' the Samurai returned, with a sharp nod.

'If her aids are not to be seen about the citadel, then they are likely to be with her. It is *then* you must enter her chamber … alone. Once inside, you will see a long set of drapes. Behind them is a glass window.'

'Glass?'

Oran nodded.

'You will simply walk through it.'

Asai frowned.

'Do you fear you will fall to your death, Asai?' Oran watched the Samurai's confused expression soften to a smile.

Raising his forefinger, he wagged it at the Warlock. 'Ah! You mock me, Oran-san.'

'And you hold your humour well, Asai.'

'It is difficult to do so within these cursed walls. But, since Tam has come into our trust, he has brought with him a … *strange* humour; he claims to have inherited it, from his roots. His acquaintance has been quite refreshing. His family's loss has been our gain. They, however, would not forgive me for making such an admission. It is shameful guilt.'

'How did he end up here?'

'By misfortune,' said Asai. 'He was in the wrong place at the wrong time. Wareeshta had already chosen her *victim*, only to be disturbed by Tam. He intervened, to save the individual's life. Perhaps he should have left them; his interference led to their final demise. And, as they were of no use to her "dead" Wareeshta felt it was Tam's duty to *replace* him.'

'Do *you* trust him, Asai?'

'I have been expecting you to ask me this.'

'No doubt Reece told you to say yes.'

'On the contrary. He asked me to be truthful.'

'Then you *do* trust him.'

'*Hai!*' The reply was defined, and honest.

'Then your word is good enough for me,' said Oran.

'So, what lies beyond this … *window?*' Asai then enquired.

'An illusion, making one believe it offers a view,' Oran replied. 'Keep an open mind. Pay no heed to what you may see, and you will pass through it with ease. Remember, it is simply an illusion, nothing more. Do *not* be fooled by it.'

The Samurai nodded in understanding.

'You will then be met by two great doors—I will instruct you how to open them—which will take you into her secret chamber. There, you will find an orb.'

'An orb?'

'Aye, 'tis what keeps me here. *I* had told her about its existence, but never imagined she would go to such lengths to find the Orbist. Yet again, I ...' He sighed then, casting away his assumption continued; 'Also concealed inside the chamber is an amulet.'

'How will I find it—if it is hidden?'

'Trust me, my friend, it will let you know of its presence,' said Oran, removing his.

Asai narrowed his eyes from the stone's radiance.

'The one you will find is similar to this one. She stole it from Magia Nera—a long time ago.'

The Samurai nodded.

'Ah! Now I begin to understand,' he replied.

'The amulets are bound together,' Oran went on. 'You may call it our *means of communication.* When you take it into your hand, I will know it is in your possession. I will sense it, as will you. Hold the stone to the orb; it must touch it. That is when their energy and power will fuse.' He stalled. 'But, whatever you feel, do *not* let it go. Do you understand?'

'Clearly,' Asai returned, confident of his ability to succeed. 'It will enable me to call on their combined forces, to break our bonds.'

'And what of the other Dhampir? Will it also release them?'

'If I choose to speak their names—which is not my intention. But we must be alert; when the bonds are broken, there can be no delay. The opportunity given to us will be short. We must remain one step ahead of her, otherwise, she will discover our plan and make us suffer the consequences.'

'It may be weeks before we escape,' Asai informed him.

'I am aware of it,' said Oran. 'Time is what is important here, and if we need it … then we must wait until it is right. In the meantime, we must find our route of escape.'

'I discovered a maze of passageways,' Asai casually revealed. 'It was some time ago—by chance,' he added, recalling the time when he had to rescue one of his colleagues from the complex labyrinth. 'We have Tam to thank for it.'

Oran's eager eyes lifted. 'Where?'

'Beneath the citadel. But I am wary of it; it has its risks, and *we* cannot venture beyond our restraints.'

'Let that be my concern,' said Oran. 'I vowed to free you from them … and I will.'

The Samurai stared intently at Oran, evaluating everything he had instructed him to do. Rising, he bowed, signalling his departure.

'I have every faith in you, Asai,' Oran then stated.

'Do you require the amulet she stole from him?'

Oran stared at him, musing over what he had asked, reminding himself; *We need all five.* Confident the Samurai would be capable, he replied; 'Take it! We will be long gone before its absence is noted.'

'As you choose, Oran-san,' he answered, bowing again, then turned to take his leave.

'But …'

Asai stalled and looked back at the Warlock.

'… there *is* something else.'

276

L'Ordana stood alone in her chambers, quietly thinking to herself. Moving towards the hanging window, she felt the heat from the sun's rays filter through. The looming summer was finally making itself known; the woods and forests were already bulging with new life after the buds of spring had opened themselves, to embrace it.

It would be perfect.

She paused, catching her image in her mirror. Edging towards the polished surface, she leaned closer to consult its honesty. Something was not right in her appearance. The eyes staring back at her were not as they should be.

'You should be deep-blue,' she whispered, recalling the young maiden Kara had "employed" into her service, recently. It was the first thing she had noticed and admired about the girl.

"They are exquisite—like sapphires!" she had remarked, before whispering in her ear, "Did you know, child, the eyes are the window to the soul?"

After the girl had served her purpose, L'Ordana glorified in her renewed youthfulness. Turning her head slightly, from left to right, she scrutinised them, detecting the taint of hazel. Raising her hand, she let her fingers glide over her flawless skin, barely letting them touch it, for fear of damaging its perfection.

Perhaps, it is only the light, she thought, reassuring herself.

She then looked sharp, hearing the distinct sound of hasty footsteps, descending towards her chamber. *Damn you!* she cursed them, for the untimely distraction from her inspection. Rolling her eyes, she sighed and then rose, stealing one more glance of herself in the precious mirror. But as she turned, ready to bid them "enter", her attention was briefly drawn to the painting on the wall. Immortalised on canvas, it seemed as if the *Boy*—holding the bowl of fruit—appeared to stare at her, as though he kept a secret. Curious, she moved to investigate, then jolted when the door of her chamber was flung wide open.

'They have gone, my lady!'

Chapter Thirty

Balloch: 1630 - Mid-Autumn.

Run!' her inner voice yelled. But intuition still prevailed, urging her to remain. Confusion now seeped in, feeding on her anxieties, aware of their steady approach.

Looking back, over her shoulder, Eleanor snatched one last glance at her mother's nightlight as it waited to guide her home. She turned, longing to run into the embrace of its haven, but felt her head at odds with her heart, their conflict deterring her from doing so. Dread began taking its hold, tormenting her mind with wild notions of—*No!* she screamed inside; she could not let it. Then instinct took over. Acting on it, she gripped her dagger, keeping it from their sights.

Glancing up at the starry sky—as though searching for intervention—she held her breath and listened.

They stopped.

Unable to hear their movements she hesitated, hoping—praying—they had left. Discretely and quickly, she returned the dagger to its sheath, taking the brave decision to turn around, to confirm her speculation.

'Please be gone—please be—' Eleanor tried to scream.

Nothing came out.

Reece, Asai and Tam approached the young woman with caution—sensing her fear—while disregarding her failed attempt to conceal her weapon from them.

"You must reassure her, and bring him to me, safely. Protect them, whatever the cost."

Oran's request—before parting ways—raised itself in Reece's mind, reminding him of the vow he had made.

"You have my word," had been his reply.

Eleanor stood staunch and defiant, watching the three strangers intensely.

An admirable trait, Reece thought, considering her dismay and uncertainty.

They could hear her heavy breathing, playing in time with her racing heart. The three warriors looked at one other with concern.

Reece raised his hand slowly, signalling his two colleagues to wait. He edged closer, watching her as her eyes leapt from one to the next, monitoring their every move. He then paused, now raising both hands in an act of defence. 'Do not be afraid,' he called, remaining still. 'No harm will come to you. I promise.'

Eleanor stared up at the three figures, struggling to visualise their true forms in the moonlight; it seemed to emphasise their eerie presence, its sinister glow illuminating their skin, resembling fine porcelain.

Gill was right! she realised. The moon *was* unusually brighter; she could see it now. But that was the least of her worries.

A small cloud crept across the moon's wide face, gradually shrouding her in darkness. She stepped back, keeping fixed on her unexpected company as her eyes readjusted; the tallest of the three stepped forward, in unison with her.

'No, Tam!' Reece blurted, with an underlying threat.

'Who—who are you?' she called out, her nerves now visible, through her wide-set eyes and the trembling in her voice. 'And—and why have you been following me?'

'How long have you known this?' Reece asked, impressed.

To her surprise, his tone—although clear and precise—was pleasing to her ear. However, they were still strangers—and a threat. 'You will get nothing from me,' she declared, with false bravado. 'Nor have I anything to give.'

Eleanor caught a faint smile on the mouth of the strange-looking one with the almond-shaped eyes, and curiously long, satin-like hair.

As she parted her lips to speak, the tall one moved closer again; when the moon crawled out from its cover, she gasped, catching a glint in his pale, red eyes. Again, instinct told her to pull the dagger from her belt. Holding it out in a threatening manner, she was unaware of her error; it was *still* in its sheath.

Pre-empting her move, the three warriors subconsciously wielded their weapons at the same time—Asai and Reece joining Tam in one blink of her eye.

Eleanor jolted, letting the dagger slip from her hand, but then caught it, holding it so tight it ached. Despite her anxiety, she felt comfort in its energy—stored from the hands of a past era that once held it—instilling her with the strength to face her foes. Raising it slowly, towards Reece's face, she swallowed her fear and stepped forward.

'Who are you?' she asked him, her voice now calm and strong. But in her effort to hide her fears she was betrayed by her continuous turning of the dagger wielded in her left hand, its rotation catching his eye.

The three warriors stood armed and ready—not by *fear*—by *way of rule*. Reece motioned Asai and Tam to retreat, while Eleanor's ongoing pivoting of the weapon drew him in.

'Where did you get that?!' he inquired, pointing at the dirk. While his tone was composed, his face, however, told a different story, as he held the weapon with his eyes.

Eleanor second-glanced him, perplexed by the unforeseen question. She disregarded it, keeping her silence.

Reece, realising her intention was to ignore him, felt his frustrations rise. 'I asked you a question!' he said, lifting his eyes, his manner now firm and demanding. '*Where* did you get that dagger?!'

Tam and Asai caught each other's eye, intrigued by the thought-provoking reaction between the two, and yet they were curious about their friend's sudden interest in the girl's weapon. With a subtlety that went unnoticed, Asai lowered his katana, followed by Tam, who threw his claymore over his shoulder, back into its sheath.

''Tis none of your business,' Eleanor retorted, feeling more protective of her inherited piece. 'Let it hold no interest to you ... not that you *need* it,' she added, referring to the broadsword in his hand.

His eyes lowered, resting on the dirk again.

Following them, she checked her weapon. *Oh no!* she realised, now noting her error, and cursed herself. Then, below her eye-line, she saw the head of a dagger peeping out, from inside one of his boots. Her heart raced, fearing her sharp tongue would be cut out by it.

She then looked up into the green eyes, standing out from the veil of night, as they continuously stared at her dagger. Then, as Reece raised them to meet hers, Eleanor instantly found herself lost behind their intensity, only to be met by his silent plea.

To ease her fears, he slowly returned his sword to its belt, his face softening as he cautiously extended his arms towards her.

'May I see it?' he asked, with a politeness that startled his colleagues.

Tam raised a brow, still confused by his friend's uncharacteristic behaviour.

Eleanor looked down at the stranger's opened hands, observing the distinct, thick scars lining his palms. She shuddered at the thought of what might have crossed over them, as he waited with uncertainty. She considered him again, now detecting a sadness in his patience. Something—a feeling of pity, perhaps—she could not say—compelled her to hand over the dagger. Eleanor felt its residual energy leave her, as she finally placed the weapon into his waiting hands.

It was then, at that moment, when Asai observed the unexpected tenderness between the two strangers, and yet he was in no doubt—both were blind to it.

'Thank you,' said Reece, before looking down.

Inside, he began to shake at its familiar touch. He felt its inner strength reach his core, injecting him with renewed hope. He let his hands wander over the leather sheath, to its pommel, where the moonlight enhanced the true clarity of the blue sapphire staring up at him. He grinned as an image of it being thrust at him stirred a hidden memory—one he thought long forgotten. Shaking his head, he turned to his colleagues, to show them.

When the stranger turned his back on her, Eleanor sensed unease, feeling completely vulnerable without the daggers' comfort to drive her. Clenching her fists, she fought against the urge to flee. *Not without my weapon!* she thought, prepared to fight for it. Feeling a sudden tightness in her throat, she coughed. The three Dhampir paused then peered down at her anxious face.

'Please?' she asked, her voice shaking. 'Can … can I have my—'

'Yours?!' cried Reece, moving towards her with added interest.

Eleanor stepped back, almost stumbling.

'Aye, 'tis mine,' she snapped, finding the courage to stand up to his overbearing height. 'Now—now give it back!' she demanded, throwing her hand out, her face stern and determined.

'How long?'

Her brows knitted into a confused frown. 'What do you mean, how—'

'How long have you had this?' he pressed, raising the dagger to her eyes. 'Or did you *steal* it?!'

''Tis mine!' she hit back, reaching for the dirk.

'So, *you* say,' he returned, drawing it away from her.

'It is, I tell you! It was handed down to me on—'

'The day you turned eighteen,' he blurted, acting on another memory. 'As it has always been done—for centuries—along your female line.'

Eleanor clapped her hand over her mouth in disbelief—the wide-eyed look of astonishment on her face, confirming her lineage.

'How do you know that?' she mumbled.

The sound of the dagger being torn from its sheath made her jump. Reece drew it up to the moonlight, searching for its identity. There, in the depths of an autumn night, Reece's lost past returned, displayed again in all its beauty for him to see. For decades, he had tried desperately to cling to memories—ones that were being slowly erased by captivity and war. But now, as he stood staring at the dagger, they seemed to be finding their place again.

'Reece-san!' Asai moved to his friend's side. 'What is it?'

'Can you see them, Asai?' he asked, holding the weapon out, to show his friend. 'True, some are worn but—to me … they read as clear as the day they were put there.'

The Samurai nodded, observing the small weapon.

Engraved at the base of the blade, the tiny initials of the young woman's female line, stretching back more than two hundred years, finally stood out. Reece scrutinised the serrated blade carefully, then paused, his heart momentarily skipping a beat.

'There you are!' he whispered to it—the reflection of his piercing eyes, coveting the initials "O.M.". But his frustrations were raised further when he unexpectedly did not know how to truly react to seeing them again.

'Whom do you speak of?' Eleanor enquired, edging near him, her voice soft and inquisitive.

Feeling left out, Tam stepped closer, equally curious.

Reece turned to her. 'These initials, here,' he then quizzed, pointing to "R.M.". 'Who do *they* belong to?'

She cast him a hesitant stare, reluctant to disclose the bearer's name.

'I beg you!' he urged, touching her arm. 'Please, tell me!' He *had* to know.

She flinched at his unexpected touch; though cold, it was soft. Closing her eyes, hoping she would not regret it, Eleanor finally released the name:

'Rosalyn Molyneaux.'

He leaned closer, staring at her in earnest. 'Molyneaux, you say?'

Eleanor swallowed. 'Aye, it was her maiden name. But now, it's Shaw. She is my mother.'

Reece Molyneaux fell to his knees and kissed the blade cupped in his scarred hands. It was as though his mind and body had been lifted free from the burden of his captivity, releasing all his emotions at the same time—forbidden emotions that had been seized by the evil still threatening them. And, for the first time in years, he felt a flutter of happiness—something he thought he could never have again. But no,

284

it was still there, deep inside him—now drawn out, by the blade of a dagger he thought lost forever.

Eleanor, struck by pity for him, reached down to return the kind touch he had shown her, but stopped herself; she felt awkward, and there were questions she needed to ask him, regarding the dagger still clutched in his hand. *Her* dagger.

Sensing her approach, Reece composed himself before rising. Her eyes followed him as he stepped back, taking her in.

Asai and Tam looked on as the two regarded one other with intense scrutiny.

Reece held out the blade, pointing to it again. 'And *these?*' he asked, with apprehension.

'"E.M.S."?' she replied.

He nodded, waiting, his eyes still fixed on her.

'Eleanor Molyneaux Shaw. It came to me almost three years ago. But I am at a loss, sir, to understand how—what is—' She stopped when he abruptly leaned in.

Searching her face for some recognition, it suddenly became clear to Reece. Even in the dead of night, he could see it: the same intensity and colour in her eyes—the same he had known in his wife's. Convinced, Reece nodded as he reached out to touch her.

'Please, sir,' she pleaded, inching back, prepared to run. But when the unexpected presence of Asai—now standing behind her—prevented it, her fears were heightened once more. 'Please—tell me—who *are* you?'

Seeing her distress, Reece stalled; he had disregarded *her* feelings. 'My name is'—he hesitated, smiling down at her— 'Reece … Reece Molyneaux.'

Her eyes widened as the realisation of his words enveloped her.

'I am your grandfather, Eleanor.'

Chapter Thirty-One

A tense silence devoured the small group, as the shock of his declaration rendered them all speechless. The surrounding woods seemed to fall into an unearthly quietude, wrenching Eleanor from the impact of his revelation.

'How can that be?' Tam queried, sharing a confused look with Asai.

Reece stayed fixed on Eleanor, unable to stop smiling, scarcely believing the words he had just spoken. *Am I truly staring into the face of my … granddaughter?* he asked himself. *How is this plausible?* But the more he looked at the young woman, standing in front of him, he knew there was no doubting her lineage.

'I see *her* in you,' he revealed, moving closer.

Eleanor pulled back from his advance, speechless. Reece stopped short, as though waking from a dream; the magnitude of his disclosure had momentarily made him lose sight of his senses. Eleanor then proceeded to step away, her mouth gaping as she slowly shook her head, in dismay.

'Wait!' Reece begged, observing the look of denial on her face.

'No!' she then blurted. 'This—you—are not real. 'Tis impossible!'

Asai, in a vain attempt to encourage the young woman, stepped forward. But as soon as he moved, she promptly turned on her heel.

Eleanor felt as though her heart would swell and burst, from the effort of her escape. Tempted to look back, she thought better of it, choosing to stay focused on her mother's guiding flame.

'Please, don't let them follow me!' she pleaded to the unknown force she called on to help her.

She ran along the little path—worn by the tread of footsteps she and her brother had made over the years—thankful for its familiar presence, and followed it until their house came into view. Breathless, she stopped, quickly glancing back, when a sudden hot chill came over her. It was then she became aware of it. She looked down at her empty hands.

'Oh no!'

Watching her pale silhouette vanish from sight, Reece stood speechless—completely at a loss—unsure what to do. He began pacing across the small clearing, his eyes pinpointed to the place where she had disappeared, his mind racing and crowded with notions, as doubt crept in.

Asai stepped forward, listening to the rustling of her hasty steps as they faded away.

Reece halted. 'What if I am mistaken?' he stated to his confused colleagues. He looked down at the dagger still clutched in his hand. 'This *was* my wife's, Asai,' he insisted, brandishing the dirk. '*These* initials— "O.M."—I know them. She had told me the dagger's history.' He let out a short laugh. 'And *she*—the girl—is also left-handed …'

Tam and Asai looked at him, still baffled.

'… as was my wife!' he added, rolling his eyes.

'Just a wee coincidence … perhaps?' said Tam, acknowledging the blade.

'*This*, is no coincidence, Tam,' said Reece. '"O.M." are the initials for, Onóir Molyneaux—my wife. The girl even looks like her!'

'Shall I bring her back, Reece-san?'

'Aye, we'll find her,' Tam added.

'No!' Reece retorted.

His two colleagues sensed an air of tension rising from their friend. The softness they had seen in his face, for the first time, gradually altered to distorted anger. Reece forced the blade back into its sheath, piercing its base. Tam gave ground to his colleague, not knowing what might ensue.

Reece tilted his head back, inhaling the dampness of the cold, night air; it had no effect.

From the depths of his stomach, the weight of his rage forced itself to the surface, as years of agonising heartbreak and depravity fed his rising anger.

Having witnessed his friends' wrath in battle, many times, Asai recognised the signs when fury took control of Reece. Even he—his most loyal confidant—could not prevent it, realising he would have to do something before its influence took hold.

'Reece!' His voice was firm and adamant. 'Do not let it in, my friend.' He moved to his side, prepared to do what was necessary. 'Not now that you have found the future you were denied.'

Reece raised his head, staring into the Samurai's deep-set eyes. 'She lied!' he snarled, through gritted teeth.

At that moment, the Samurai could feel the energy of the immense hatred his friend was feeling for the Valkyrie; it was like no other.

'The whore lied to me! Kara had me believe my wife was *dead!* She even revelled in telling me how Onóir pleaded with her to "take her life"—such was the torture she claimed to have *enforced* on her. And *I* foolishly believed it. I had no reason not to. She also took pleasure in displaying the green shawl I last saw my wife in. It had blood stains on it! How could I *not* believe it?!'

'You know how she is, Reece,' Tam remarked, recalling the Valkyrie's persuasive powers. 'Open your mind to her, and she'll have you believe anything that pours from her vile mouth. She's quite convincing.'

Reece's eyes slid towards the Highlander. 'As *you* are more than aware.'

Tam hung his head in shame. His encounters with the Valkyrie had been all too easy for her; after all, he was young and had been tempted by her seductive lure. At first, he could refuse her nothing; she had possessed him—used him for the wants and needs of her sexual desires. And, with the ability to control his thoughts with her sweet scent, it had left him with little or no recollection of it.

Had it not been for Reece and Asai's intervention—teaching him to refuse her advances—it was only a matter of time before she would have dispatched him—like the others. But the more Tam refused, the more it enticed her; however, it eventually became an advantage in their escape. Although unpredictable and dangerous, the game they had played with the Valkyrie had been worth it in the end.

'Forgive me,' Reece begged, conscious of Tam's remorse. 'I sometimes forget how vital you were in our escape.'

'Auch! Sure, 'tis nothing to forgive, *mo charaid*. Ye have every right to vent your anger.'

'But not on my friends.'

Tam acknowledged his colleague's apology with a simple nod, illustrating his respect for him. The gesture was promptly returned.

'I must go after her,' Reece decided. 'Can you imagine what is going through *her* mind? She has a right to know. There is so much to explain.'

'And much to learn,' Asai added.

'And, besides,' Reece started, looking at the dagger in his hand, '*this* needs to be returned to its present owner.'

'Then let us not waste any more time,' Asai stated, making his way in the direction Eleanor went, with Tam by his side.

'*Is* it possible, I wonder?' Reece asked, as his colleagues started towards the nightlight.

They turned to meet his bewildered face.

'That *she* is still alive?'

'What does your heart tell you, Reece-san?'

'I am afraid to ask it.'

'Then, my friend, your answer waits beyond those trees.'

Eleanor threw herself at their wooden door, fumbling for the brass-ringed handle, then pushed it wide open. The three family members stopped and stared as she slammed it shut. Burying her head in her arms, she held it closed against the outside world.

Rave jumped up, barking, as though calling for her attention. Eleanor spun round to see the curious faces of her mother, Gill and grandmother gaping at her. Unable to control her heavy breathing, she could not find the strength or composure to release her words.

Suddenly her world seemed to slow down against her racing heart. She glanced around: her grandmother appeared motionless in her comfortable old chair, by the fire, and yet the book she had been reading seemed to slowly glide towards the wooden floor—dropped by the abruptness of her entry; she saw Gill reach for a sly piece of loaf, but the slowness of his movement seemed to take a lifetime, while Rave took longer than usual to greet her; her eyes then flickered to her mother, whose head slowly tilted as she steadily dropped her hands onto her hips.

'Where have you been, Eleanor Shaw?!' her mother snapped, bringing her back to them.

Rosalyn began the irritating tapping of her foot on the floorboards, letting her daughter know how annoyed she was at her lateness. At the action, Gill rolled his eyes, shaking his head, then continued chomping on the bread he had been warned not to eat before their evening meal.

Eleanor, ignoring her mother, moved to the small window near the door, heeding caution. Peeping out, her eyes darted, searching for the strangers beneath the shadow of moonlight. Save for the prowling of a local, wild tom cat, rummaging for scraps in their yard, she saw nothing.

'Eleanor!'

Still ignoring the sound of her mother's voice as it launched into;

"Did I not tell—"

'Nori?' the old woman interrupted, her voice soft and concerned as she retrieved her book—putting it aside—before rising from her seat. 'What ails you, lass?'

Eleanor turned and stared at her grandmother—the swell of tears and panic visibly building. Lost for words, she bit down on her quivering lip. *How do I tell you?* she thought, feeling a trickle down her cheek.

Though in the twilight of her years, Eleanor saw youth in the lines that had seen decades of struggle and hardship. Her grandmother had been a survivor, refusing the hands of marriage from those who had offered her and her child a respectable life—after being left alone without a husband.

"There was, and, is, no other I could love, more than *he*," she had told them, her heart remaining true and honest to his memory.

'Oh, Grandmaw!' she cried, throwing her arms around Onóir. Eleanor then saw the blur of her mother's concerned face, through her tears.

Casting aside her anger, Rosalyn rushed to Eleanor's side.

'What is it?' she asked, placing a tender hand on her daughter's shoulder, perturbed by her distress.

'Nori?' Gill had now joined them, his guilt mounting for having left his sister alone in the forest.

Eleanor pulled away from her grandmother.

'He—' She stopped, short of breath, trying to release the words as she looked from one face to the other, as they stared back at her, wondering and waiting …

'He said'—her eyes then moved to Onóir's— 'that he was my *grandfather!*

Chapter Thirty-Two

The three arcane figures lingered on the fringe of the woods, contemplating their approach to the lonely house staring back at them. The moonlight—in its contrast with the night fire—brought life to the structure. Above the flame, a cluster of moths fluttered wildly, their prominent, *Silver Y*-marking, glinting pale-gold against the firelight, as they, too, waited for an opportunity to enter the lodging.

Hidden away from the outside world, the dormer-size abode was adequate—enough to house an average-sized family. The ground lodgings bore two glazed windows—each throwing out a warm glow from behind its lattice. The exterior—clad in wood—was coated with a terracotta plaster, with beams of horizontal timber crossing paths with their vertical match. It was clear, from first impressions, the abode was well maintained.

'Oran chose his location carefully,' Asai stated, beneath his breath. 'Had it not been for the girl, we may never have found it.'

'I hear voices,' said Reece eagerly. 'Two?' he surmised, listening intently, in the hope of recognising *one* in particular.

'Three—for certain,' Asai replied.

'And a dog, it seems,' Tam added, inhaling deeply.

Reece cast the Highlander a wary eye. 'Be mindful of the company we are about to meet, Tam.'

The swift movement of a cat, chasing a mouse, distracted him from the enticing scent of the individuals behind the door they were about to pass through.

'So …' Tam cleared his throat, swallowing his temptation. 'What do ye propose to do, now?'

Reece surveyed the black door; it seemed to beckon him. Taking one hesitant step, he paused. 'Bearing in mind, I have just been threatened by my … *granddaughter*, with the dagger—once owned by my wife—' He stopped and shook his head, trying to comprehend it. 'I'm baffled! What do *you* propose I—we—do?'

Tam grinned. 'Well, we could knock on the door … or…'

'I think not, Tam!' Reece returned, throwing him a disapproving look. 'Breaking the door down is not the way to introduce ourselves.'

'You are certain the dagger *is* your wife's?' Asai enquired. 'The girl may have found it, or, dare I suggest, stolen it—claiming the weapon as her own.'

Reece stared at the house, recalling their chance meeting. No, he was in no doubt of what he had seen. Shaking his head, he looked at the great Samurai.

'She has the same fighting spirit—and I see Onóir in her blue eyes.'

'Then, if your convictions are true, my friend, why do you hesitate?'

'Because, I am …' He wavered, scouring through his confused emotions.

Rolling his eyes, Asai muttered something in his native tongue, before snatching the dirk from Reece's hand. They watched as the Samurai strode, with grace and confidence, towards the house. Then, with one soft knock, he entered, sending the heightened voices behind the door into stunned silence. Not even the dog stirred.

Seeing the hunting dirk in the stranger's hand, Gill gaped at his sister and pointed.

'*This* is your grandfather?!' he cried.

Asai's striking presence took precedence over the household; it was only then, as he stood in the glow of their home, that Eleanor truly noticed him. Never had she been confronted by another, whose poise and unusual features captured the attention of—not only her—but the rest of her family.

Gone now was the sinister threat created by the shadowy darkness of night. She now noted the slight warmth in his face, telling her there was nothing to fear. But there was something else about him— something striking and unique: his aura—and she could *feel* it.

The Samurai bowed—in respect of their home—while holding the hilt of his katana. As he did so, his sleek, black hair fell before him like thick strands of satin.

His audience stood speechless, until Rave's sudden outburst of barking roused them from their silence, hurdling them into a sudden state of realisation.

'Rave!' Eleanor snapped.

Asai threw the hound a sharp look at which she retreated, whining, before shrinking away to her hiding place—beneath the table where their meal still waited above, on its surface.

'Who are you?!' Gill demanded, outraged by the treatment of his dog. 'And what have you done to her?!'

'She knows her place,' Asai replied, his voice calm and confident. 'The dog will come to no harm. You have my word.' The Samurai then turned to Eleanor, his face softening as he held her gaze for an instant. 'I came to return *this* to you.'

Rosalyn and Onóir looked on, dumbfounded, as Eleanor moved towards him.

Keeping her eyes engaged with his, Eleanor reached out, letting him place the dagger into her small hand. She glanced down when his cold hand touched hers; it was the slightest of touches, and yet she was conscious of its discerning impact. She felt compelled to smile, and nodded in return.

But the moment was rudely interrupted, by the dagger being wrenched from her hand. Eleanor jumped as Rosalyn pulled her away, stepping between them. Removing the blade, with precision, she wielded the sharp weapon in front of the Samurai. In an instant, Gill was by his mother's side with a red-hot poker he'd snatched from the fire.

Asai surveyed the dirk, intrigued, then raised a brow. 'It seems there *is* truth in what he says,' he remarked, his tone serene and complacent, noticing how Rosalyn brandished the dagger with her left hand. Rosalyn shared a confused look with her son.

'Why are you here?' Gill demanded, holding out the poker, its tip still smouldering.

'And what do you want?' added Rosalyn.

When Asai moved slightly, Rosalyn, with a steady hand, jerked the dagger at him. The Samurai straightened his stance until his eyes met Gill's. He surveyed the young man, recognising the similarities between father and son.

'I *will* use it!' Rosalyn threatened, despite having no plan. 'Keep back, I say, or I will thrust it through your heart.'

'No, Rosalyn!' cried Onóir, looking on in horror, as she threw her protective arms around Eleanor.

Reece looked sharp at Tam—the wide-eyed look of recognition in his eyes, raising his hopes; he had *heard* it: the voice from his past, telling him it was no longer a fading memory.

Reece felt the beat of his heart urging him forward. *I know it is her!*

His response was immediate.

The sheer force inflicted on the door almost tore it from its hinges, as he suddenly appeared on its threshold. Rave rose from her hiding place, barking uncontrollably at the intrusion of yet another stranger to her domain. Asai glared at the hound, silencing her once more.

But Reece failed to hear the commotion as his eager eyes searched the room. At first, it seemed crowded with the throng of people. His search darted from one, dumbfounded individual, to the next, until his desperate eyes finally found hers. The same blue eyes he fell in love with—more than a lifetime ago—now gazed back at him through the perplexity of their spectators.

Tam hovered at the doorway, unnoticed, watching, as Onóir released her hold on Eleanor. For a brief moment, a rush from her past youth flooded her ageing body, as she recognised the face of her husband. A surge of renewed energy filled the house, as Reece and Onóir's worlds were reunited, against all the odds.

Onóir closed her eyes, shaking her head.

'No, 'tis a dream. You *cannot* be here. 'Tis beyond belief!'

'Open your eyes, Onóir,' Reece begged, in the purity of his defined voice.

Shocked, Rosalyn threw her hand over her mouth, letting the dirk slip from her grip.

Onóir's eyes flew open when the dagger struck the floor. Frightened he would fade from sight, she reached out, holding his gaze.

Reece lifted his hand to hers, feeling their energy merge as their fingertips touched. It was more than she could bear. She felt the room, and everything in it, spin.

Once again, Onóir Molyneaux found herself in the arms of her husband.

Her senses were first awakened to the aroma of the pork flory, which Rosalyn had cooked earlier for their supper. The tapping sound of Rave's excited paws, pacing the floorboards, told her the dog was impatient about something.

Onóir gradually opened her tired eyes, reluctant to step out of her dream, then felt the cool hand of another, holding hers.

'Are you well, my love?' the same voice from her dream asked.

Her eyes sprung to life, to see him smiling back at her. She looked up from her old chair suddenly aware of all the concerned faces staring down at her.

Reece touched her face, reassuring himself she was real and not an image conjured up in his mind. In his eyes, he did not see the cruelty of time in her features, but that of the young woman he thought lost for more than four decades.

'I thought I'd dreamt it,' she whispered to him. 'Oh, tell me you are real, Reece.'

'I feel the softness of your skin,' he replied, forgetting the company surrounding them. 'I still see the richness of youth in your blue eyes, as I had done, the moment I first saw you.'

'I never felt your loss,' she informed him. 'I told myself you were still alive.'

Reece closed his eyes. 'While I thought you were …'

'Why would you think that?'

'Because I was told by another. I saw the blood-stained shawl.'

Onóir gathered her muddled thoughts, trying to understand his meaning.

'Your mother's green shawl?'

Her eyes widened as the old piece of clothing came to mind. She had retrieved the item, treasuring it, after her mother's death; its lingering scent had made her feel close to her. 'I had wondered what came of it,' she said, then slowly lifted her shoulders. 'But the blood was not mine.'

'No?'

She shook her head, her winsome eyes still fixed on his.

'And all this time you thought so?'

'To my shame,' he replied, lowering his head.

'Who could do such a callous thing?'

'Another, whose words are difficult to deny,' Tam interrupted, stepping into their company.

Onóir's eyes filled with tears from the pain and heartache that had been planted in their thoughts and memories.

Lifting his hand, Reece wiped them away. 'But … the blood?' he enquired. 'If it was not yours …'

'The day you left, I watched until you were gone—out of sight. But I could not help myself. In my reluctance to let you go, I followed the path a little. But you had gone. On my return, I came upon two foxes, fighting over a dead bird. When I intervened, it was clear they had inflicted each other with countless wounds. One ran into the woods, leaving the other dying.'

Reece slowly nodded, recalling the injured fox.

'Of course!' he said. 'The blood on the shawl belonged to one of them. And, naturally, you tended its wounds.'

'Aye,' she returned. 'I removed the shawl, before burying the poor animal, and simply forgot about it. It was a couple of days before I noticed its absence, and when I went back to search for it, it was *gone!*'

'It matters no more,' he said. 'I am here now, and I intend to never let you go.'

'The one consolation I can give you, my love, is the fact I have never been alone,' she said, looking up at Rosalyn and Eleanor. He slowly rose to meet them, formally. Standing a head above Rosalyn, he looked down at her anguished face.

'This is Rosalyn—your daughter, Reece. She was the hope that kept me alive.'

He drew back his head in wonder. 'I had no idea you were—'

'Nor had I,' Onóir assured him, 'until the time presented itself.'

Reece was struck dumb by the enormity of his wife's revelation.

Tam smirked at Asai, amused by their colleague's loss of words. Aware of his sharp tongue, they had seen Reece survive the taunts and crudeness of others, and yet it took an old woman to silence him.

Rosalyn struggled to find the words; she had accepted a life without a father, and now here he stood, a mere breath away. 'But how can this be?' she blurted, cupping a hand over her mouth. 'You look so ...' Her words trailed, as she tried to justify his youthful appearance.

'It is a long story—and no fairy tale—I assure you,' he responded.

'I can't comprehend it,' she said. ''Tis unbelievable! How can I begin to call you—'

'Reece *is* your father, Rosalyn,' Onóir argued. 'And Eleanor's grandfather. And though I, too, have no understanding of it,' she continued, 'I am telling the truth. I *know* my husband.'

'Then ... *how?*' asked Rosalyn, eyeing him as he regarded her son.

Reece drifted from her questions, reluctant to answer. How could he even begin to explain what had happened to him? Then there were the reasons: why and how he came to arrive where he did, with his unusual friends. Avoiding the question, he returned his focus to Onóir.

'How did you cope?'

'With great difficulty,' she began. 'I was ignorant to childbirth. If it had not been for the kindness of Marian Drew, I dread to imagine … It was she who helped bring your daughter into the world. I prayed for your return but … when the days turned into weeks and months, and a year had passed, without a word, I had to accept my new responsibilities. Do you remember the Drews, Reece?'

'I do, now,' he said, seeing their faces in his mind. 'They were good people, and he a fair landlord.'

'They helped as much as I would allow, but pride won me over. I chose to return *here*, to Scotland.'

He recalled the conversation from their past. 'As I had *instructed* you.'

'You remember?'

He nodded, smiling with pride at her bravery.

'And I shall always be indebted to Mr Drew, for the kindness he showed us. He took charge of my affairs; I was in no fit state to deal with the selling of what little possessions we had. What money we made, he matched it to pay for our safe journey. Before we parted, he vowed to keep an ear to the ground for any sign of your return, so he could inform you of our location.'

Reece sighed, sparing a thought for the landlord he had once called *friend*—now long passed.

'Every day I waited for news,' she went on. 'But in my expectations, I failed to notice the swift passing of time. I watched Rosalyn grow from a child into a young woman. I stood alone at her wedding, while she made her vows to a soldier. It grieved me to see them so young and happy in their short time together.'

'At least Malcolm lived to share *his* daughter's life in her first six months.'

Onóir glared at Rosalyn's sudden bitterness.

'Well, 'tis true, Maw. When Malcolm died, at least his death was confirmed by his superiors. I saw his mutilated corpse with my own eyes. It sickened me to the pit of my stomach, plaguing me with nightmares for months in the aftermath of it all. Aye, I've had my fair share of death, but I buried my first husband, knowing, in time, I would have closure. I moved on with my life … as *you* should have done.'

'How dare you!' Onóir snapped, in retaliation. 'You cannot presume to understand how I truly—' The old woman suddenly keeled over in a spate of coughing, erupting from deep inside her weakening lungs. In an instant, Reece was by his wife's side again, concerned.

'You are ill?' he enquired.

The room became a sudden hive of activity as they shuffled about to assist Onóir—Gill reaching for a jug of water, while Rosalyn, consumed with guilt, joined Reece, by her side.

'What ails you, Onóir?' Reece insisted, giving her a sideward look.

Pre-empting her daughter's explanation—given her heightened emotions—Onóir interrupted. 'Oh, 'tis nothing for you to concern yourself with,' she replied, dismissing her symptoms. 'Age has simply caught up with me,' she added, accepting a drink from Gill. She slowly sipped the soothing contents, letting it ease her pain while observing him closely. *Unlike you, my love*, she thought.

As her grandmother spoke, Eleanor stole a fleeting glance towards Asai. Convinced it had gone unnoticed, she swiftly diverted her eyes, before he could return it.

'Forgive me,' Reece begged, taking his wife's thin hand. He looked at her. 'You are so cold.'

Rosalyn reached for the thick, blue woollen blanket lying draped behind her mother's chair.

'Thank you,' said Onóir, exchanging the subtle, warning glance with her daughter. Rosalyn understood the plea in her mother's eyes. The old woman was dying, and only *she* knew it. The infection in her lungs had spread beyond its limits—her one comfort being, the treatment given to her by the local spaewife, to ease her suffering. She had secretly fought it, determined to stay alive, in the hope that, one day, she and Reece would be reunited. *If not in life—then in death—should fate allow it,* she had told herself.

'You are the cure to my ailments, Reece. It will pass,' she lied.

'So, what do I call you?' Rosalyn blurted, distracting him; it was all she could say, to avoid his further enquiries into Onóir's illness.

Reece considered his wife, with scepticism. He was not convinced.

'Are you not going to answer your daughter?' she said, acknowledging Rosalyn, who was looking down at him, wringing her hands together, her nerves beginning to get the better of her.

Rising to his full height, he turned to her. 'Call me—Reece—all of you,' he replied. 'Besides, I think it strange you should call me—'

'Father?'

He hesitated, not wanting to offend her. 'Because I am … *younger* than you.'

'Which I fail to understand,' she returned. 'Yet, here you are.'

'Indeed,' he said, struggling inside to think of a way to justify it all. He looked around, stalling. As he did so, he cast another quick, suspicious eye towards Gill, drawing on his conclusions; there was no doubting who the young man's father was. Seeing this, Rosalyn moved to confront him further, but was prevented by Onóir—silently pleading with her daughter to *wait!*

Reece then let his eyes wander, taking in their surroundings: the kitchen and hearth-room were warm and welcoming—a far cry from what he and his two colleagues had been subjected to, for years. The oak, trestle table—where the cold, evening meal now sat—had signs of woodworm in its legs. Rave remained huddled beneath it, nosing at the piece of meat Gill had baited in a small mousetrap, in a corner next to it. Above the high, wooden fireplace—decorated with elaborate gouging on the sides—Reece noticed a shelf. Hanging from its tenon pegs, he thought he recognised the pieces of familiar crockery. A faint curl then appeared on the corner of his mouth. He glanced at Onóir, her eyes afraid to leave him.

'I couldn't bear to part with them,' she stated, lifting her narrow shoulders.

He then slanted his eyes, noticing another item from their past, sitting alone in a corner: a plain, heavy-panelled chair—made of oak—with a box below the seat. Though worn from years of use, and darkened by the smoke from the fire, it was still recognisable. On it, rested a large basket of dried flowers.

'Aye, *that* too,' she added. 'I remember how you used it—to clean

301

your boots. I was offered a good price for it, but every time I looked at it, I saw you sitting there—from my memories.'

'There is so much to tell you,' he whispered, turning to his wife. 'And so much I would not dare reveal.'

Onóir felt the rise of her aching lungs, once more, and tried desperately to hide it. Rosalyn reached for a small, brown bottle. From its contents, Reece saw her count the drops as she mixed the solution with Onóir's drink.

'It eases her cough,' Rosalyn casually informed him, keeping her eyes diverted.

'Then start from the beginning—'

The three colleagues turned abruptly at the sound of Gill's authoritative voice.

'—if you please.'

Reece now regarded the fine, young man, leaning against the hearth with his arms folded, his tone full of doubt and suspicion. He disliked it. 'You have your reservations?'

'Do I not own the right?' Gill retorted.

Rosalyn stared at her son, taken aback by his scepticism. There was a time she would have intervened, by scolding him for his brashness. But an element of pride stopped her from doing so. Her son had taken it upon himself to protect his family against the intrusion into their home. *Just as it should be,* she thought.

'I would not deny you it,' said Reece, shaking his head. 'This is your home. You have *every* right.'

'Then I urge you to justify your … *presence*,' Gill insisted.

Reece shared a hesitant look with his colleagues. Asai tilted his head forward, acknowledging his friend. Taking a deep breath, Reece slowly exhaled, carrying with it the word he loathed, from his mouth:

'*Dhampir.*'

The three women looked at one another, wary; there was a malevolence about the word when uttered, filling them with fear.

'Reece?' said Onóir, her brow creased, baffled by the unease it gave her.

Aware of her concern, he turned to explain but was abruptly cut off.

'It means—he—*they*—are not *human!*' Gill blurted, taking it upon himself to reveal their true identity.

All eyes turned on the three Dhampir—the growing uneasiness bringing with it a vulnerability within the room. Rave raised her nose, sensing the tension.

'Is—is this true?' said Eleanor, edging towards her brother.

'Do not be frightened,' Reece begged, keeping his voice calm, in a bid to reassure them.

'*What* are you?' asked Rosalyn, trying to conceal her nervousness.

'They are half-human—half …' Gill's words trailed off.

'Half what?' Eleanor queried, looking up at her brother, her mouth gaping.

'There is a part of them that is …' Gill hesitated, searching for the word. '*Undead!*'

Eleanor paused, recalling the stories her brother used to tell her. Her eyes grew wide as she became aware of his meaning.

'Undead?!' cried Rosalyn, inching away from Reece. 'I—I don't understand.'

'I thought that was just a myth,' said Eleanor, glaring at her brother.

A deep, low growl suddenly came from beneath the table. Rave snarled, her fevered eyes focused on Tam. Slowly, the hound crawled forward, her teeth now visibly exposed, and hackles raised.

Sensing the restlessness of his dog, Gill wrenched Eleanor back. The young woman stumbled over his feet, giving him a disgruntled look.

'Look at him!' Gill shouted, pointing at Tam. 'Look at his eyes!'

Rosalyn's mouth gaped when she saw the frenzied look on the young, Dhampir's face. Asai and Reece had detected the rising agitation in the Highlander's demeanour, hoping it would subside. Conscious of his colleague's weakness, Asai swiftly drew his katana, making them jump.

Rave leapt forward.

'Leave us!' yelled Reece.

Chapter Thirty-Three

The sound of Reece's bellowing demand sent his defiant colleague from their company, leaving Rave and her family closed off from the dead of night—and looking for answers.

'What just happened there?!' Rosalyn demanded.

Asai cast Reece a cautious glance.

Reece turned, meeting their dismayed faces, while Rave paced back and forth across the foot of the door, nose down, following Tam's scent.

'What is it *she* sees, that we don't?' she added, pointing at the hound. She hung on his silence, waiting for an explanation.

Ignoring her, Reece promptly returned to his wife's side.

'A crowded room makes him feel … uncomfortable, at times,' said Asai, attempting to justify the Highlander's actions.

'Uncomfortable?!' Rosalyn persisted. 'What exactly do you mean by *that*?! I saw it with my own eyes; he looked as though he wanted to—' She struggled to say it, let alone think it.

'—kill us!' Gill casually stated, appearing undaunted by the incident. Aware of Eleanor's presence behind him, he turned, catching her steal another glance off Asai. 'I won't let any harm come to you, Nori,' he remarked, glaring at the Samurai.

'This is too much!' Rosalyn admitted, shaking her head. 'I will *not* have my family threatened.'

'You will soon have all your answers, Rosalyn,' said Reece, with a trace of sympathy in his voice. 'I understand and sense your frustration, but ask that you trust us and remain patient. Everything *will* be clear, but now I must see to Tam.'

'Do what you will,' she snapped, turning away from him.

Onóir's eyes beckoned to her husband's. Patting his hand, she smiled, acknowledging the door. As she watched him make his hasty exit, the candles in the room flickered when the door slammed, sending a deep chill of *déja-vu* through her.

Reece stepped out into the darkness, pausing, then looked over his shoulder. *Did that just happen?* he thought, taken aback by those who dwelled in the house—whose threshold he now stood on. *Are they truly my family?* He looked at his hand, still feeling Onóir's lingering touch.

It was real. *They* were real.

He looked up at the night sky; it was clear and vivid. He noticed the thick clusters of stars, their light fading as the moon took precedence. He narrowed his eyes against it, damning its brightness; it was nearly blinding.

Stepping away from the house, and its chattering voices, he looked around the quiet yard.

I warned you, Tam, he thought, as he searched for his colleague.

Several paces away—on the verge of the woods—he saw a small, solitary outhouse, imagining his comrade would be there, nursing his guilt.

Two small windows stared at him on his approach. Inside, it was pitch black. He then circled it, discovering a small door facing a wall of ghostly trees. He noted the thick, iron lock hanging from its bolt, drawn securely across its front—to deter unwanted visitors, no doubt. Thinking he saw movement within, he moved towards one of the windows, stalling, when the paleness of a familiar face reflected back at him.

'The moonlight betrays our true form,' came the strong voice emerging from the woods.

'We are what we are, Tam,' said Reece firmly, turning to confront him, his grievance visible in his deathly pallor.

Tam swallowed hard, his throat parched and tight. 'Look at me, Reece!' he began, through gritted teeth. 'I did not ask for *this!*'

Reece lunged at Tam, forcing him against a tree; clumps of dry leaves rained down on them, against the force of their impact. Despite his greater size, Tam's efforts to struggle against his peer's firm grip failed miserably.

'Did I not warn you?!' Reece threatened, glaring into his pale, red eyes, as his hand clamped the base of his throat. 'I swear it! Should any harm come to them, I will "dispatch" you myself. I have just found the life I thought lost, and will not lose it again—because of *your* negligence. Do you hear me?!'

Tam blinked, acknowledging the threat. It was the first time he had seen Reece display his anger, towards his friends—and with such persistence, too.

Reece loosened his grip slowly and turned away, knowing the young Dhampir would not retaliate. 'You must control yourself, Tam. I will not allow any errors on your part—or mine, for that matter. You have my final warning.'

'We Brodies are a proud clan!' the Highlander retorted, defending his character. 'I am a son of Alexander Brodie, Chief of Morayshire. We do not threaten those who fight alongside us. My father would curse me if he thought it. I would *not* harm them.'

Reece regarded his colleague; there was an unwavering strength of purpose in Tam's eyes, and honesty in his words, telling him the Highlander was just in his reasoning.

'Accept my apology, my friend,' said Reece, displaying the hand of friendship. 'I am aware of your loyalty, and should *trust* you …'

Tam placed a reassuring hand on Reece's shoulder. 'I know and feel your frustrations,' he said. 'But I am on *your* side.'

'And I yours,' said Reece. 'Sometimes, I forget I was once like you.'

'Then you understand my difficulty when I try to contain my emotions,' said Tam. 'It has been too long since I shared the company of …' He paused, refusing to use the *term* others of his kind had no respect for.

"They are nothing more than *mortals*—weaklings in our eyes," Dakkus had once remarked.

"Aye, right—as *we* once were," he had reminded the other Dhampir.

"Perhaps," Dakkus had replied. "But you will forget, soon enough, *fair one.*"

But Tam never forgot; he reminded himself every day, fighting hard to hold on to the precious human qualities hidden inside. 'It has simply been too long, Reece.'

'There is not much for our kind in this, Tam, which is why we must take the journey alone, or guide each other. The latter gives us hope, no matter how little it offers.'

'I feel my soul is at a constant battle,' Tam admitted, 'fighting the evil that conspires against its goodness.'

Reece looked up into the shamed face of his friend with understanding. 'It will always be a battle until we can rid ourselves of the cause—which is my intention. But, for now, you must keep fighting it. Do not let the evil consume the good I see in you.'

Tam nodded. He had become accustomed to the unwanted company forced upon him, denying him human contact. And now, the suddenness of being thrown among "mortals" again, was proving to be an arduous task. *And so many, at one time!* he thought. It was overwhelming. The small, confined space of the house had overpowered his senses, driving them into a frenzy of uncertainty.

Despite it, he knew he would not have harmed them.

'I shall do my best, Reece.'

'And while *I* do my best to trust in you,' said Reece, 'I think, for now, you should remain in open spaces—by my side, or perhaps ... in the company of—' He stopped when Tam cast him a sideward glance, narrowing his pale eyes. '—or perhaps not.' The two warriors grinned at the personal joke associated with Asai, aware the Samurai would not find it amusing.

'Now go!' Reece urged. 'Do what you must, and do not stray far. I sense ...' He paused, listening to every sound and movement his heightened senses alerted him to.

'You sense something?' Tam prompted.

Reece hesitated. 'No,' he replied, dismissing it. 'However, I think *your* senses have dulled from the lack of nourishment. Go!'

Making his way towards the forage of trees, Tam stalled and then turned to his friend. 'I swear to you: no harm will come to your family.'

Reece smiled back at the Highlander before he vanished from sight.

Family, he thought. There was something comforting in the word. Still, it would take some time to get used to; nonetheless, he would gladly embrace it.

In his moment of reflection, Reece was interrupted by his perception—aware of a presence behind him. He tilted his head back, inhaling their scent.

'Is my wife dying?'

Rosalyn froze. *How the hell did he know?* she thought.

'Well?' he persisted, turning swiftly.

She flinched at his rapid movement, suddenly finding herself face-to-face with her father's scrutinising eyes. His sudden closeness had been unexpected, throwing her off balance. Her shawl fell from her shoulders when the lantern she was holding, flew from her hand. Reece moved quickly. Rosalyn stared, amazed, as he promptly retrieved the items before they hit the damp ground.

'Thank you,' she said, accepting them from his outstretched hand. She glanced down at the lantern; its flame still burned.

'I need to know,' he insisted, returning to his inquiry.

'No—no, she's not dying,' she replied, ashamed of her lie. Keeping her mother's secret from him had not been her choice. Nevertheless, she had to respect Onóir's wishes.

Reece turned to consider his daughter's response. She felt his eyes study her but held his gaze. She had had plenty of practice, from when her children quizzed her about their father. At first, it had proven difficult, but time had been a convincing teacher.

''Tis an inflammation of the lungs,' she blurted, hoping to sway any further questions. 'Age slows her recovery. But no doubt she will soon feel the benefits of your presence. Already, I've seen the brightness return in her eyes.'

'Let us hope so,' he answered, glancing over her head at the house. 'Now I have found Onóir, I intend to never leave her … for whatever time she has left.'

Rosalyn's mind raced, chewing on the words she feared would slip out, searching for a diversion. 'Is it true—what Gill said?' she asked, changing the subject.

Reluctant, at first, to answer, Reece hesitated, then looked down at her. It was then he saw it: the uniqueness in her eyes—one green, like his, the other deep-blue, similar to her mother's.

'Well? Is it?' she prompted.

Despite his apprehension, he felt it necessary to admit the truth behind the myth. 'All of it.'

Rosalyn peeped over his shoulder, staring into the blackness of the woods. He sensed her nervousness.

'How much did you hear?' he queried.

'All of it,' she said, meeting his gaze.

'You have nothing to fear, Rosalyn,' he assured her. In a subconscious move, he reached out to take her hand, pausing, when he caught her staring at the thick scars embedded in his palm: 'Reminders of a tormented past,' he remarked.

She hesitated.

'They cannot harm you, Rosalyn,' he added, stepping closer. 'May I?'

Denied the right—and love of a father's touch all her life—Rosalyn simply did not know how to accept it, now. Reece waited patiently for his daughter to take his imploring hand. She slowly looked up. As their eyes met, he saw her anxiousness.

''Tis not your scars'—she wrung her hands with uncertainty— 'but the realisation—' She flinched when he unexpectedly took her warm hand, placing it where his heart resided. She gasped, overcome by his first touch. Rosalyn was speechless—completely in awe of it.

'Can you feel it beating?'

She nodded.

''Tis slow,' she stated, finding her voice again.

'If I were "undead" there would be nothing. What you feel, here'—
he pressed her hand against his slow beating heart— 'is *life!* They tried
to wear us down—to a point where our emotions were virtually stripped
from us.'

'They?'

'The ones who inflicted this curse on us—against our will. We
learned to fight its dominance. It was important to hold on to what
made us human. And now that I am returned to the glory of the
company of mortals'—he nodded, relishing in the touch of her hand—
'I feel the better for it.'

'Is it true you—'

'Drink blood?'

Slowly she removed her hand from his, suddenly aware of its
coldness, her anxious eyes now glancing around, wishing she had Rave
by her side.

Reece smiled. 'It is a matter of choice—one I do not participate in.'
He heard her inward sigh of relief. 'I sleep, eat and drink, like any normal
man.'

'Then you must try some of Kai's mead,' she nervously joked, making
light of the conversation. ''Tis the finest, this side of the loch.'

He leaned in, drawing his brow together. 'Whom did you say?'

She drew back. 'Kai, he is—'

'Your husband?'

'No!' she returned, shaking her head. 'He is a good and loyal family
friend.'

'I see,' he replied, with a sense of relief; he did not relish the idea of
having to tell Oran his wife had remarried, in his absence.

'And what of Tam?' she enquired. 'He appears to lack *your* strength.'

'Tam is relatively new to this unfavourable way of life. It is—*was*—a
difficult adjustment for him. Without guidance, he would have lost
control. But thankfully, he has learned to remove himself from
confining situations.'

She glanced around, still unsure. 'Where ... is he, now?'

Reece diverted his eyes, deciding some things were best left *in the dark.* 'Clearing his thoughts,' he lied. 'I give you my word, Rosalyn—on everything I hold precious—he will not touch any of you.'

Rosalyn smiled gently at the man who was finally proclaimed as her "father."

An awkwardness divided their thoughts but was short-lived, by the crushing sound of leaves being stomped on by heavy, on-coming steps. She leaned forward, ready to draw Eleanor's dagger from the inside of her boot.

Reece grinned. 'You do not need it.'

The moonlight bathed Tam as his great figure came into view. Slowly he walked towards them, his stride long and heavy. Reece noted the content look on his friend's face. Tam acknowledged him with a wink.

Rosalyn observed Tam's looming presence. It was only then—in the open space—she truly noticed the Highlander.

Tam Brodie stood a good foot over Reece—who was already above average height. His fair, shoulder-length hair fell thick and straight, curling slightly at its ends. Like his counterparts, Tam's skin was pale. His face was large and square—a sign of strength—and its most notable feature was his peculiar broad nose. His pale red eyes played on her suspicions, making her ponder over their true colour.

She recognised his garb, noting, in particular, the vivid red tartan he wore—below the tanned, buckskin waistcoat, covering his wide torso—marking his clan. Even in the veil of the night, its colour stood out. His thighs were bare, displaying his brawny muscles. On his feet, he wore tanned brogues. Below the knees, short buskins of various shades were worn on the legs and tied above the calf with a striped pair of garters. About his waist, he wore a thick belt made of cowhide; it was fastened with a silver buckle with two sheaths attached—one on each side—each containing a dagger. And peeping over his right shoulder, the hilt of his claymore sword gleamed at her in the moonlight.

She surmised his origins were one of the northern clans, who lived near the Highland border—a valued warrior who, no doubt, was missed by them.

Tam sauntered calmly towards them, glimpsing the dirk in Rosalyn's hand. 'I am not your enemy, lass,' he stated, staring down at her.

'You are well, my friend?' said Reece, studying him.

Rosalyn detected a hint of warning in her father's tone.

'Auch! Aye,' Tam replied, catching her staring at his left ear, where a sizable piece was missing. He then smirked, unable to resist. 'One of the *younger* ones got a wee bit close.'

'Forgive me,' she blurted, embarrassed at being found out.

Tam threw his head back, letting out a great bellowing laugh, matching that of his frame. 'Forgive *me*, ma'am,' he retorted, bowing. ''Tis just a wee memento of a young lad's ambitions of great battles with his father's oversized sword.'

Rosalyn lowered her head smiling. In the face of their first meeting, she now sensed a warmth in the young Dhampir; it was clear he aimed to make amends, by the use of his wit.

'But now … I *am* truly thirsty,' he said.

Rosalyn swallowed and inched towards her father when Tam stared at her.

'Did I hear you say … mead?'

Her eyes widened. 'You … *heard* me?'

Reece smiled, rolling his eyes when Tam winked at her.

'Well, then,' she began, intent on setting her rules, 'if you are well enough to return to the company of our household, I ask that you keep your composure.'

'Aye! I will, ma'am,' he replied, with a single nod.

'Then … Eleanor will gladly supply you with some.'

'I thank you, ma'am. Oh, and ye'll not be needin' *that* while ye'r in our company.'

Rosalyn looked down at the dirk still in her hand.

'Ye have my word, lass.' With a final nod, he turned from them, quickening his pace at the thought of the sweet, honeyed drink quenching his thirst.

Reece felt his daughter's agitation subside when Tam's large frame disappeared through the door—Rave briefly barking on his entry, until quietness resumed once more.

'Onóir used to taunt me with it,' he told her, pointing at the dagger.

''Tis been in our family for centuries,' she informed him.

'And now it belongs to Eleanor.'

'How did you know?' she asked, her brow knitting tightly. 'And how did *he* come by it?'

'She told us,' he said, 'when we met in the woods. And *his* name is Asai.'

'When you ...' She shook her head. 'Something tells me, your meeting with my daughter was not by chance. I think it's time for more answers.'

Raising the lantern, she saw the log—Gill had neglected to chop—and sat as comfortably as she could, reminding herself to scold him, later; despite his age, her son was not too old for a telling-off.

Reece watched as his daughter rested the lantern and dagger beside her. And when she looked up, tilting her head at him, it was clear she was ready to listen.

'May I?' he asked, gesturing towards her choice of seat.

His settling presence beside her was overpowering. Never before had she been made aware of another's company. She could feel the strength of his energy pressing on her. Closing her eyes, she breathed deeply, then opened them, asking; 'How did you find us?'

'I confess ... it was no ... *coincidence,*' he said. She tilted her head to the other side, her eyes narrowing. 'None of this was by *chance*, Rosalyn,' he went on. She then slowly lifted her head. 'We were ... *sent* to find you.'

He sensed her racing thoughts as she turned to face him, her brow now furrowed, baffled by his disclosure.

'Sent?' she queried, her eyes now interrogating him. 'By whom?'

Chapter Thirty-four

'O ran?!'

Rosalyn jumped from her seat, glaring down at Reece; the hesitant look on his face said it all. Pacing back and forth, she tried to make sense of it. *My husband sent my father to*—her thoughts ran with her doubts. She stopped abruptly, disregarding her nerves, then threw her hands on her hips.

'And tell me, Reece, why is my husband not here?'

'It was his intention—'

'No doubt there were more pressing matters to attend to,' she snapped. 'Aye, that'd be Oran Shaw. I've not seen or heard from him in almost three years. My children had lost all hope, thinking their father was … *dead!* To be honest, even *I* had begun to believe it.'

Reece allowed his daughter to vent her anger on him. It had been her right. He opened his mouth to speak, but her persistent rage prevented it.

'When?! Where?! And'—Rosalyn stood back— '*how*, may I enquire further, are you *acquainted* with my husband?!'

Reece glanced at her gaping mouth; though shocked, it was Rosalyn's angry eyes that spoke to him.

'Our meeting was not a conventional one,' he began, 'but one of … uniqueness. We were held prisoner, by someone unwilling to part with us.'

'*Prisoners,* you say?!' she retorted. 'He lied to me, then!'

'No, Rosalyn, I assure you. Oran did not lie. He has told me everything.'

'Everything?!' she said, raising a brow.

'Well … as much as he needed, to win my trust. At first, I was dubious, but he made a convincing story. Little did we know, then, we would have more in common than we realised.'

'His family,' she stated, returning to her seat—beside him—her eyes focused on him.

Reece nodded.

'At the time, he had no knowledge of our connection, and I was not aware of your existence. He promised us freedom if we helped him escape. In return, he asked a favour of me.'

'That being?'

'The agreement seemed plausible, at first. We were two strangers seeking each other's help, from what seemed like a hopeless situation. He approved of my choice of companions, making matters easier. And so, it was settled: we would come here, complete the task, and then return to the remnants of our past—should anything remain of it.'

Rosalyn tried to take in what she was hearing yet remained confused and suspicious.

'It was difficult to find you,' Reece continued. 'It was, however, by *chance*, we came across Eleanor and Gill, near the lake. They were preoccupied and unaware of our presence, at the time; it allowed us to watch them while—'

'Then it *was* you!'

He cast her a sidelong glance, unsure of her meaning.

'I have sensed, of late, someone watching me—watching us—from a distance. But when I search for a suspect, I find nothing, and yet the feeling remains.'

'Then I must disappoint you; we are not your *spies!*'

'No?'

He shook his head.

'We only found Eleanor and Gill, on *this* day. We kept our distance until I was confident of their identity. Oran's description of Eleanor was precise—save for the boy; it was evident Gill had changed since his father last saw him. I was uncertain, at first; however, it was when I looked at him more closely—in the house—I saw the similarities. But, had I not been drawn to Eleanor—by her resemblance to Onóir—we may have continued on our journey. It was my *curiosity* that held my interest. She is quite the perceptive one; she sensed our presence.'

'Perhaps you *let* her.'

'Perhaps. I admired her bravery when she took it upon herself to challenge her three *strangers.*'

Rosalyn drew her head back and lifted her brows. 'Eleanor *challenged* you?!'

'Indeed. You should be proud. She is extremely resolute and protective of her heirloom.'

Rosalyn's eyes rested on the weapon nestled beside her and smiled with pride.

'Had she not drawn the dagger …' His words trailed at the probability of what may or may not have happened.

'I believe you would have found Onóir again—regardless,' said Rosalyn. 'Don't they say, "True love finds its way back?"'

'Until this day, I would have rejected such notions,' he said, glancing back at the house. 'I still have to remind myself Onóir is behind *that* door, waiting for me.'

'And waiting for answers,' she reminded him. 'Having said that—because of the time you have both lost—I believe she would rather spend it living in the present, and not the past.'

'Nonetheless,' he said, 'she is entitled to know.'

'As am I. And so, I ask you, once more.' She paused. 'Where is my husband?'

'You must understand, he had your interests and—most importantly— your safety at heart.'

Rosalyn rolled her eyes; it was typical of any man's justification, of something he failed to do, especially for a woman.

Not wanting to waste too much precious time away from Onóir, Reece briefly provided his daughter with the facts of what had happened to them: their imprisonment; the Sorceress; their escape. 'Oran intended to return to you, Rosalyn. You must believe that.' She frowned. 'But there was an item he had hoped to acquire—'

Her brows shot up. 'The amulet!' she blurted, cutting in.

'However,' he continued, 'things did not go according to plan after he came into possession of something else—something connected to his past, it seems.'

'If it's not the amulet,' she said, 'then, what is it?'

'A book … of sorts,' he revealed, shrugging.

'A book?!' she retorted, her eyes full of outrage. Biting her tongue, she looked away, her foot tapping uncontrollably, in an effort to control her anger before returning her attention to him. 'And this … *book* … What makes it more important than his family?'

'He did not say—nor did I ask.'

'Why not?' she snapped.

'It was of no concern to me,' he said. 'It assisted in our escape. That was all that mattered. Remember, there was, at that time, no knowledge of our connection. It did not matter to me what secrets the book might hold. Why should it? Time was crucial in our escape, therefore, our words were brief before we parted.

'Did he even mention us?'

'There was a message.'

Her seething face softened.

Reece sensed the anguish in her patience as she waited for him to relay her husband's words. 'He said, "Tell her I had no choice, but to return to the Elliyan".'

Her expression hardened, returning to anger. 'He's gone back to *them?!*' she cried, clenching her fists against the log's hard surface.

'He said you would understand. It is my belief, it had something to do with that book.'

'I know nothing about a book!'

'Oran was reluctant to go, Rosalyn. But it was clear the book was of great significance to him—for whatever reason—especially when the item came to him unexpectedly. The decision broke his heart; I saw it in his brooding eyes. "Our reunion must be postponed", were his last words to me.'

317

Filled with dismay, Rosalyn slumped beside her father, burying her head in her hands. 'Why now, Oran?' she mumbled, feeling dejected again.

'Do you understand why he sent us?'

She sighed. 'I fail to understand *any* of this,' she said, slowly raising her head.

'Fate and misfortune have brought us together. The task Oran asked of me, initially had no personal meaning. I—we—were simply returning the favour, after he gave us our freedom. No one could have foreseen this. But now I have found you, the responsibility weighs on me.'

'Well—my apologies for the *burden* inflicted on you,' she sneered.

'Listen to me, Rosalyn!'

She threw him a glance, lacking interest.

He ignored it, turning to her. 'Dismiss these notions from your mind. Everything has changed now. You are a burden most welcome—and one I intend to protect. And in the words of your husband; "Whatever the cost".'

Rosalyn forced an honest smile.

'He spoke of you with immense pride and, despite your misgivings, he *will* protect you.' Reece surveyed their surroundings, adding, 'I commend his choice of abode.'

The statement drew her attention back to him. Noting his strange observation of their location, she became suspicious.

'Oran concealed you well'—he stalled, considering his words—'from those who might wish to seek you out and interfere.' He watched her wary expression change as she began to grasp his meaning. 'You know of whom I speak?'

'Unfortunately,' she replied, her tone hard and defensive. 'But I know they cannot take him from me. My son must be willing—and I *know* Gill.'

'And it is because of *that*, Oran sent me,' he stated. 'Rosalyn, I am here to help you convince Gill of the importance of his role, then … to escort him to the Elliyan.'

As each reluctant word fell from her father's mouth, Rosalyn knew her day of reckoning had regrettably arrived. 'Why did it have to be *you*?' she asked herself, out loud.

'We had no way of—'

'I know,' she interrupted, sighing. 'Yes, I know. Sometimes it is natural to ask—what we already know—in the hope the answer will provide another explanation.'

'Despite your reservations, I am honoured to do this,' Reece replied.

'Must he leave me?'

'If he could have prevented it, Oran would have done everything in his power to do so.'

'I've looked upon this day with dread since Gill was born.'

'Do you regret—'

'No. Never!' she said, without hesitation. 'I could not part with him then, nor …' She sighed again, sensing defeat. Glancing at the night fire, she checked its diminishing flame; she felt exactly like it. 'When Malcolm—my first husband—died, we had been living in Eddin, choosing to stay on, after. I took employment at the castle, cooking for the soldiers; I had no choice. Eleanor was no more than six months. I worked, while Onóir looked after her. It was there—after a year or so— when I met Oran. I confess … I was rather taken by him.'

'So soon?'

'He was quite persistent and charismatic in his pursuit of me. Four times I turned him down. I felt disrespectful to Malcolm's memory.'

'Yet, you eventually married him.'

'Onóir saw something in Oran; it was she who persuaded me. Of course, she was right.'

Reece smiled, nodding his head slowly.

'As always.'

'We remained in Eddin. He was of high rank and I could give up work. Eleanor was on the doorstep of three when Gill was born. But Oran's joy was somewhat short-lived when he made the unexpected discovery. He kept it from me, for a while. But I had noticed a worrying change in his character. Our protection soon became his obsession, to

319

the point where he would not allow us to venture out into the busy streets of the city. His behaviour became increasingly erratic, eventually forcing me to challenge him. You can imagine my dismay when I learned of our son's fate, and what his birth represented. My whole world fell apart that day. Soon after, we departed for the quiet village of Balloch.'

'Concealing you from the world.'

'Aye, and we had a good life here until that strange boy made himself known to Oran.'

'What boy?'

She shrugged.

'Oran has a way of dismissing things he chooses to forget. I was aware they knew one other. No doubt, a messenger sent by *them*. Within a day, my husband was gone. He swore to me he would deny Gill's existence to them. That was three years ago. There has been nothing, since.'

'Then know that he denied it,' Reece informed her.

A faint smile appeared on her tired face, grateful for her husband's attempt to safeguard his family.

'… for all it is worth,' he added.

'Did they … *force* it from him?' she asked, fighting against rising images in her mind of her husband being tortured.

'There was nothing to—' Reece stopped, then looked away, contemplating the words he had just uttered.

Confused, Rosalyn tilted her head, frowning.

In the back of his mind, Reece could hear Oran's voice.

'All this time they have been watching us,' he then muttered, echoing the Warlock's words.

'Reece?' she prompted.

Looking into her eyes, he was in no doubt she was oblivious to his meaning. 'Forgive me,' he begged, shaking his head.

'What did you mean by that?' she pressed.

'It had only been a fleeting comment—I barely heard it and—'

Rosalyn jumped to her feet, quickly scouring the trees, as though someone or something was spying on them.

'I knew it!' she sneered, through gritted teeth.

Reece moved to her side, following her gaze.

'Is it the feeling you described—of being *watched?*' he asked.

'Aye. The first time I sensed it, I ignored it. But lately, I've noticed it more frequently.'

'Have you told the others?'

She shook her head.

He listened intently to the sounds of the night—the lack of wind making it easy. He could detect the soft tread of a deer, sauntering through the woods; two owls engaged in their unique conversation, while a distant fox wailed like a *Banshee*. He looked at Rosalyn. 'There is no one out there,' he said. 'Trust me, I would know it. And, had there been, I am certain Tam would have found them.'

'I've been so naive, Reece,' she admitted. 'I see that now. It was only a matter of time before they would catch up with us, despite Oran's good intentions. How foolish were we, to imagine we could keep our son from the Elliyan? In my naivety I had hoped—one day—Gill would marry and raise a family.' She grunted at the irony of it. 'He has a sweetheart, you know. He thinks I know nothing about her. She's a flighty lass—Meghan Downy—one who will keep him in check.'

Reece tried forcing a sympathetic smile.

She sighed. 'One who *would have* kept him in check. Oh, Reece, what do I say to him?'

Reece considered telling her Oran's hopes: that *she* might have told their son, in his absence. He then changed his mind; as it stood, the Warlock was in enough trouble with his wife.

At his silence, she said softly, 'How do I tell my only son that, everything he has known—all his dreams and aspirations—has been nothing but—' She grunted. 'I could curse Oran for bringing this upon me. *I* am the one who will have to look our son in the eye and tell him how his life has been mapped out, since birth. Believe me when I say— I do *not* relish the thought; it will not be easy. And he has not yet even come of—' Rosalyn stopped short. With a sharp intake of breath, she cupped her hands over her gaping mouth. 'Oh my—'

Observing the alarming reality and heartbreak manifest in her eyes, Reece jumped up.

'When?!' he asked, looking down at her.

'I had forgotten,' she mumbled. 'How could I have been so—'

'When?' he implored, his tone now urgent.

As her hands slid from her face, Rosalyn's pain was now clearly visible. Distraught, she slowly lifted her eyes—the tears already building. 'Gill comes of age … in *seven days!*'

Reece watched the tears of premature grief fill Rosalyn's tormented eyes; at that moment, she looked alone—lost and vulnerable—the child deprived of the love of an absent parent.

Lost in her thoughts, she neglected to notice her father's comforting arms, at first. Without thought, she returned the gesture.

The awkwardness he had felt was now replaced by the natural, paternal love, once denied. With each passing second, it made him feel human again, only to have it shattered by the contrast of their beating hearts; it was a grim reminder of *what* he was. Gradually, pulling away from her hold, Reece looked down and wiped the tears from her saddened face. She shuddered from his cold touch.

'Rosalyn,' he said softly. 'I have been denied a valuable part of my life. I did not see you enter this world, or watch you grow from child to woman. I cannot retrieve those years; I was not to blame. There is only *one* who is truly at fault—the *one* who will pay.'

'The Sorceress you spoke of?'

He nodded.

'Nor is she alone in her ambitions. Others have their sights on *the* amulet, in question, but there is only *one* who can own its great power.'

'Gillis,' she stated.

'The Shenn's rightful place is with its true Master—the Magus—*your* son.'

The true Lord, she thought, recalling Oran's story.

'While it belongs to no other—at this time—the Sorceress will strive to have it. Because of this, many would see her destroyed. But there is much to do, first. I vow to keep you all safe. I will help you speak to

Gill. You have my full support. But I suggest we tell him at first light; the burden of another revelation—such as this—might prove too much in one night. The gravity of his fate will have enormous consequences. We cannot predict his reaction, which is why you must stay strong and be prepared. I cannot stress how vital it is to take Gill to the Elliyan. They are preparing for his arrival as we speak.'

'But six days, Reece! That gives us little time.'

He raised his head to see the stars gleaming down at them; the night was spectacularly clear. However, it was the moon, with its bright ring, commanding his attention. Rosalyn observed his striking features as its unusual brightness highlighted them; the similarities were now plain to see.

'We have enough time, and I know the way. Much, however'—he pointed up— 'depends on *that*.'

She followed his gaze. 'The moon?'

'We are fortunate in that its cycle coincides with Gill's coming of age,' he said. 'It will guide us on our journey, however, we must reach Elboru by the final crescent—before the new moon,' he added, turning from her.

Left speechless, Rosalyn grasped her father's muscular arm, forcing him to stop as he made for the house.

'What will happen—should he fail to reach Elboru on time?'

He paused and stared down at her. 'You do not know?'

She shook her head, her eyes widening with visible fear.

'Perhaps—Oran had his reasons,' he replied. 'Still, he should never have kept it from you.'

His calmness forced her frustrations to the surface. Rosalyn pressed down on her lips as her eyes flared. 'Tell me!' she yelled, still clutching onto him.

'As long as Gill possesses the Shenn—by his birthdate—all should be well; no one else can touch it, then.'

'And if it is *not* claimed by him?'

'Then it is there for the taking. And the Sorceress wants it.'

Rosalyn loosened her grip, letting her arm drop to her side. The question she was reluctant to ask burned inside, and yet she had to know. 'And what of Gill?'

Reece stared at his daughter, his blank expression failing to achieve the certainty she had hoped for. 'We can only ... speculate,' he replied. 'But I intend to make sure he claims it. There will be no room for complacency in this venture. Prepare your words carefully, Rosalyn,' he advised, turning away. 'We leave in two days!'

Chapter Thirty-five

'I will live the life *I* choose!'

Gill's voice of retaliation wreaked havoc on the quietude of the early morning, carrying it with him beyond the walls of their house as he stormed out, leaving Rosalyn and her father staring at one another.

He stopped dead—the sound of his heavy breath drowning out the silence surrounding him. Gill ran his hands over his head as if protecting it from the world that was about to crash down on him. Looking up, he stared through the wide gaps in the trees and beyond, just in time to catch the fading glow of sunrise as the paleness of blue took its hold, announcing the arrival of a new day. The middle of autumn was still proving to be mild, fooling nature into thinking summer still reigned. But the signs were now plain to see: the golden ambers of the changing leaves and their struggle to hold on to their branches.

It had always been his favourite season—autumn; the simple pleasure of seeing ripe berries and apples, weighing heavily on their branches, as they waited for his eager hands to relieve them of their burden.

'Aye,' he reminded himself. 'We'll do that—today.'

'Do what, Gill?'

He turned to see Reece, and his mother's inquisitive face, staring back at him. He had failed to hear their approach.

'Go to Eddin—with Meghan Downy?' Rosalyn added, observing the growing wide-eyed shock on his face.

'How—how did you—'

'Your sister told me.'

I'll not forgive you, Eleanor Shaw, he told himself, turning away in disgust.

'Please, Gill, listen to—'

'I refuse a life that has been chosen for me! So, you can tell *him*, when they leave,' he argued, pointing at Reece, 'I'll not be accompanying them.'

'You have no choice,' said Rosalyn, her voice firm and determined.

'And should I refuse?' he threatened, watching his mother's reaction.

'Listen to her, Gill!'

Gill shot a persistent glance at the one who would dare order him. 'And now *it* speaks!'

'Gill!' Rosalyn snapped.

'Until this moment, *he* has stood by in silence, scrutinising—'

'It was not my place to tell you your fate,' Reece stated, interrupting Rosalyn.

'This is not *your* place at all ... *Grandpaw!*' he sneered.

'Enough!' cried Rosalyn. 'This house is ruled by *me*, and I will not have you disrespect any visitor—regardless of who they are.'

Gill marched towards his mother, his face red, seething with anger. Caught unawares, she gasped, recoiling from her son's aggression; it was the first time she had been forced to do so.

When Reece's quick intervention came unexpectedly, it forced Gill to step back—separating mother and son.

The young man glanced down at the Dhampir's hand, noting how it now rested on the hilt of his sword.

'Do not underestimate me,' Reece warned, lowering his chin. 'I will use it if need be.'

Gill slowly drew back, realising what he had just done, feeling ashamed of the aggression he had displayed towards his mother. 'How can you conceive that I would harm her?'

'How can I be certain you would not?' Reece hit back.

The flush of anger began to fade from Gill's face as he turned to his mother. 'Forgive me?' he begged.

Rosalyn's tired eyes softened when her son looked down at her. In his changing features, she still saw the innocence of the young boy, pleading for forgiveness for all his wrong-doings. Staring into his dark, hazel eyes, she could see nothing but love—tainted by hurt—knowing

326

he could never harm her. Unscathed, she stepped out from her father's protection—her one desire—to comfort her son.

'You are changing, Gill, through no fault of your own. I have seen it—and understand your aggravation. You *should* have been prepared for the journey you now face. The blame is not yours.'

The fear of not knowing what lay ahead now played on his frustrations; he felt vulnerable and weak, despising his father for making him feel that way.

Sensing Gill's inner torment, Reece moved to offer his goodwill—by way of an apology for his threat—then hesitated, hearing the faint voice calling him from the house. Without warning, he was gone from their company.

'Does he know?' Gill asked, watching Reece vanish behind the door.

'No—and we must keep it that way,' she warned. 'It's Onóir's wish, and we will abide by it.'

Gill looked towards the cloudless sky and inhaled. Nature was wide awake. He could hear the familiar melodic sound of the crossbill resonate above them while, down below, red squirrels scurried about, busying themselves in the foliage.

Rosalyn watched him absorb its wonder, as though observing it for the last time.

''Tis a perfect day for hunting red grouse,' he remarked.

Rosalyn drew back her head, startled by his statement; it was clear he was in denial of his fate.

'Aye, I'll take Rave with me. Where is she?' he asked, glancing around. 'And Eleanor, for that matter? Where is my *breach of trust*?'

'Gone to market—ahead of first light. Perhaps, when they return you could—'

'They? Is she with *him*?!' he demanded, frowning.

'If you mean Asai—aye, she is,' Rosalyn retorted, slowly placing her hands on her hips. 'What of it?' Her raised brow told him she would not tolerate his outbursts.

He snorted, imagining the curiosity of the villagers when their inquisitive eyes would meet with those of the peculiar stranger accompanying his sister. 'They'll not have seen *his* like before,' he replied, smirking. 'They'll be whispering behind her back.'

'Let them! Everyone harbours a secret, of sorts; our villagers are no exception. They'll keep their opinions to themselves. Did they not accept Kai? And, besides, I'm sure Eleanor is well able. If you are concerned for her welfare, I can assure you, she is quite safe. Reece has given me his word, and I trust it.'

'You *trust* him?' Gill stared at his mother, amazed at how easily the words flowed from her mouth. 'You have known him but for one night, and now you say you trust him!'

Mother and son held each other's gaze for a brief moment. Rosalyn knew he was right. She then looked towards her home—*their* home—where she knew Onóir and Reece would be engrossed in conversations of the past and present. Beside her, she could feel her son's anticipation, as he patiently waited for her reply …

'I trust my instincts,' she finally answered, turning back to him. 'I trust him. He made a vow to your father—to protect *you*—a stranger. Neither one of them could have foreseen this outcome. We've all been strangers, until now. While I understand how discontent you are by their sudden presence, I confess to welcoming it … especially now.'

'And what of the other one—with the mangled ear? I've not seen him since he indulged in some of Kai's mead … Where is *he*, now?'

'Tam is around, keeping watch. It is merely a precaution.'

'For whose benefit?' he retorted. 'Did you not see that look in his eyes?'

Rosalyn made every attempt to dismiss the image from her mind—trying to remain positive, for her son's sake.

'I know,' he added, rolling his eyes at her reluctance to answer. 'Reece has *assured* you.'

'I am content, knowing Tam is *our* ally. It seems we will need all the protection offered to us, at this time. Accept it, Gill. Accept *them*.'

Gill mused over his mother's words. As always, they made sense, considering the strangeness of his new circumstances, and yet, inside, he was struggling to accept the future he had known nothing about. A

328

picture of Meghan entered his thoughts. He recalled the beam of happiness on her face when they made their plans. Unknown to his mother, he had intended to join the forces of the royal army. He had received a letter from a Donald Mackay, to report for training by the end of September—after he turned seventeen. It had all been arranged; he and Meghan had planned to elope, before taking up his position. Feeling betrayed by his sister, he decided he would deal with her, later. Then something occurred to him …

He turned to his mother, to challenge her. 'Am I to believe Eleanor *knows?*'

Rosalyn released a long sigh. 'Since last night,' she admitted. 'I was unable to sleep. She found me by the remnants of the fire with Rave. It was not my intention to tell her … until I had spoken to you. But you know what your sister is like …'

'Unfortunately,' he muttered, remembering how she forced his plans from him, by threatening to tell Meghan's father … everything! The poor man would have been heartbroken, and devastated; he had relied on his daughter since his wife died—five years previously—from a weak heart. 'Aye,' he added, ''tis one question after the next with my sister. Her persistence is enduring until she's satisfied with her answers.'

'Even though they may hurt?' Rosalyn replied.

Gill's heart sank as he imagined his sister's reaction—when told her only sibling would soon be leaving her … for good!

'It was difficult for her to accept, at first …'

'She should wear my shoes,' Gill muttered under his breath.

'Do not misjudge your sister; she is stronger than you think. Give her time. She did not tell me your intentions out of spite, Gill. No—Eleanor felt it her duty.' Rosalyn hesitated. 'You know you will have to tell Meghan your plans have changed.'

'And how do you propose I do *that*, Maw?' he growled, seating himself on the same log his mother sat, oblivious to the chore he had forgotten to do.

Tempted to scold him, Rosalyn held her tongue. She then rose from her seat and looked down at him, her heart bursting, wishing she could remove his great burden. Instead, she would offer him the best advice she could give.

'Gill,' she began. 'How long might you have lived as a soldier? War claims many casualties. Did you want to make Meghan a young widow, like I was? I know what a difficult life it is. I dread to imagine the path I might have taken had I not met your father.'

He looked up, sharp. 'My father?!' he cried. 'Did he not desert us? And what will become of *him* now?' Gill's tone reflected the anger he felt for his father.

Rosalyn hung her head, shamed for her husband's actions.

A pang of guilt rested on Gill as he saw the tears well in his mother's eyes. With a reluctant smile, he rose, enveloping her in his arms. 'Do *not* cry for his failings, Maw.'

Rosalyn felt the pressure of his hold tighten as she struggled to breathe; it was clear Gill was unaware of his growing strength. She tensed at the strain of it, begging him to release her. He stepped back, apologetic.

'You must learn to keep your strength in check,' she advised, forcing herself to laugh.

Gill—on the other hand—did not find it amusing. Staring at his hands, he fought to understand how his newfound strength came to be. ''Tis all new and strange to me. At first, it was slow and gradual, but now I'm more than aware of its presence. It frightens me, Maw.'

'There are some, in the village, who would be jealous of you,' she said, trying to make light of it.

'I can *feel* it … inside,' he added. He then stared at her, his eyes intense with fear. 'What—what if I can't control it?'

'Now you understand why you *must* go,' she informed him. 'The answers and the help you seek, are with your father. Whatever grievance you have with him, I can tell you this: he tried with the greatest of intentions to hide you from the Elliyan. Oran did not want this for you. He would have gladly taken your place, or given it to another, had it been allowed.'

'So, is that why he taught me the skill of weaponry?' he asked, recalling their time together. 'He was ... *preparing* me?'

Rosalyn smiled, slowly nodding.

'Which begs the question ...'

'What?' she said.

'Did he *know* they were coming for me?'

Her smile faded. 'I swear it, Gill,' she appealed, on her husband's behalf, 'he did *not* know. If you are to blame anyone—blame both of us. We convinced ourselves, in our ignorance, *they* would never find us. Besides, I was not willing to hand you over ... not at such a young age. I couldn't do it. Maybe one day when you—'

'Have children?' he sniped. ''Tis now an unlikely ambition.'

Rosalyn was at a loss, knowing the planned future her son had hoped for was being cruelly snatched from his reach. And yet, she did not know the privileges allowed to the Magus. 'You cannot know this,' she said. 'While I'm not privy to it, I can only assume the affluent life that awaits you. Whether you like it or not, you *have* to go!'

Gill sensed the determination in her underlying concern. Again, she was right. *She's always right!* he thought, and it annoyed him. Finally, his mother's defiance triumphed over his stubbornness. He momentarily looked away from her. 'Will you come with us?'

Rosalyn blinked, stopping the tears from falling. Swallowing the words—she wanted to say—she placed a hand on his shoulder, seeking his attention, then looked him straight in the eye. 'I can't go. I think you know that. Onóir is too weak. She needs me here. I just hope she's with us long enough to see Reece again.'

'How can he leave her after such a reunion? I could not.'

'Gill, you are young,' she stated, resuming her place on the infamous log. It was then—on seeing it—he was reminded of his neglected chore. He diverted his eyes, pretending not to notice. 'Sometimes,' she went on, 'we are given choices which pave our future. True, in that they never seem to turn out the way we visualise them. Though, some are fortunate. This is how I see it for Reece and Onóir; their first parting was not their choice. But now, they have been given a second chance—however long it may last. Should this be their last day together, they are now aware of it—more than ever—enabling them to make choices.'

'I think I understand,' he said, drawing his brow together.

'You must admire their bravery.'

'I see it now,' he said, nodding, as he sat beside her.

'The war you so wished to fight—here—will pale in comparison to the one facing us all—should the Sorceress take what is rightfully yours.'

'Where does she—this Sorceress—reside?' he queried, with an element of doubt.

Aware he was not entirely convinced, Rosalyn decided it was time her son knew the brutal reality. 'We don't know,' she returned. 'But Reece suspects they may follow, sooner or later.'

'*They?*'

'She's not alone. The threat of devastation she could inflict upon a world of mortals is very real, Gill. Now you understand why your father was secretly preparing you for your role—whether it be one of peace or conflict. It is unfortunate that it should be the latter. I have no doubt you will make a great leader, son. But there is much to do before you leave, and we must be vigilant.'

'Vigilant?' Surely, we are not at risk—at least—not yet?'

Rosalyn hesitated, pondering over her reply.

He frowned at her unwillingness to answer. 'Well?' he persisted.

'I cannot be certain …'

'Out with it, Maw!'

'It seems … we are being watched.'

'Watched?! Where?! Who?!' he demanded, leaping up to scour the trees. He then reached for the axe, which had lain idle on the ground, beneath the log, and readied himself.

'I don't know,' she answered, fretting, as she followed his gaze, his sudden actions making her feel vulnerable and nervous—and so close to their home, too.

'How long?' he added, wielding the axe.

'"Always!"—that's what he said to Reece.'

'Who?'

'Your father,' she blurted. 'Even *he* is none the wiser,' she quickly added, before he could cast more aspersions.

Gill felt frustrated, not knowing their *spy's* presence or identity. His eyes darted, searching again through the shroud of trees staring back at him. 'Where are you, *watcher*?' he shouted, in the stillness of the morning. 'Show yourself, coward!'

The unexpected sound of something battling its way through the trees made them jump. It loomed closer. Gill shielded his mother, ready to defend her. But Rosalyn had already removed the dirk, prepared to use it; nothing deterred her from doing so when threatened.

'Here it is!' he whispered, tightening his hold as it grew closer—the anticipation in his voice spurring them on. 'Now!' he cried, hurdling the axe towards their potential attacker. As it left Gill's hand, the weapon found itself in another's grip.

Mother and son stopped dead.

'Your father taught you well, Gill,' Reece stated, returning the axe to him. 'And, I admire your skill,' he added, throwing a smirk at Tam, who had just emerged from the trees; the Highlander frowned, catching his colleague's look.

'Auch! The wee lad would have missed!' Tam argued back.

Rosalyn stared in disbelief at the swiftness of their response, while Gill stood amazed, in awe of it.

'I could have *killed* you, Tam!' said Gill, with an underlying sense of pride. But the overbearing presence of the Dhampir read differently.

Tam lowered his head. 'Hardly!' came his short, flat response. It was clear he was insulted, judging by the bemused glance he threw back at Reece.

Gill—rather pleased with himself—grinned from ear to ear as he leaned on his axe.

Noting the annoyance on Tam's soured face, Rosalyn winked at the Highlander; he frowned back, still unimpressed.

She then turned and, seeing the smug look on her son's face, grunted. 'As you are feeling so inspired by your actions, Gillis Shaw …' She nodded towards the axe. He looked at her, still smirking. '… you can put *that*—her eyes then slid to the idle log— 'to another use.'

Two eyes secretly looked on, undetected, as the small group shared in Rosalyn's joke, at her son's expense.

They smiled with contentment. The boy *had* been raised well and *was* prepared—more than he realised. As for Oran's choice of companions? They were exceptional.

Yes, it was time to inform the others … The Magus was coming!

Chapter Thirty-Six

'**T**is the day of our Faire.'

'Faire?' Reece echoed, reaching out to help his wife from their bed.

Although she ached, Onóir threw her husband a stubborn glance, telling him she was more than capable of standing on her own. 'Aye, Balloch Faire. We have attended every year'—she paused, recalling a memory— 'except for one—when young Will Grant died of ...'

Reece waited, with respect, as she struggled to remember.

'Auch! No matter,' she mumbled. 'Such a tragedy. Poor wee lad.'

He watched her slow movements as she dressed, without the awkwardness, nor the embarrassment, of her changed body. He adored her now as he did, then.

Onóir's small, but comfortable, bedchamber was simple for her means. An oversized throw—they had once shared—now draped over the sides, touching the rough, wooden floor. An average-sized coffer sat below the small window, which looked out onto the yard.

'Oran made it for me,' she stated, opening its lid.

Inside, the leftovers from their past looked up at him. 'Is that ...?'

'Aye, my wedding dress.'

He leaned over to touch the fine linen, its whiteness now tainted with age. But it was the blue, bobbin lace—woven across the bodice—that brought it to life once more, its colour still vivid, as though it had just been sown on. Beside it—and wrapped in a soft, yellow cotton cloth—the dry flowers he had given her that same day. She then removed a tiny, plain chestnut box. Handing it over, she waited for him to delve into its history. Drawing back the lid, he saw a thick curl of fair hair.

'It was beautiful when she was a bairn,' said Onóir. 'I kept it, hoping one day you would see it.'

Reece stared at the precious item she had retained for him, finding it difficult to believe Rosalyn was once fair; a mere glance at his wife washed away his doubts. To him—dark or fair—the small lock of hair was beautiful and dear to him. He let his finger brush over it gently, for fear of damaging it.

'"Tis yours now,' she said.

'Keep it for when I return,' he replied, touching it one more time. Their eyes rested on each other, for one intense moment, together silently mourning the loss of those precious years.

'When do you leave?' she asked, watching him go to the window, then.

Reece, opening it slightly, remained silent and distracted.

Throwing a woven blanket across her shoulders, she went to his side. He was watching Gill.

'See how he uses it—and with such ease, too,' he remarked.

Gill reigned his axe down on the infamous log with one hand, as though he was cutting moss. There was no pause or effort in his work. Reece glanced down at Onóir, noting the look of pride in the way she smiled at her only grandson.

'I wondered how long it would take him to get around to it,' she remarked. '"Tis one chore our grandson dislikes.'

A small rap on the door bid Rosalyn's entrance before she opened it: 'Is that mine?' she asked, seeing her mother return the familiar box to the coffer.

'It is hard to believe that lock of hair was once yours,' Reece remarked.

'Aye, and it will be again,' she grinned. 'Although … whiter in shade.'

'Whereas yours, my love,' Onóir added, 'has not changed, since that day.'

Reece carefully observed the two women as they scrutinised him. The cruelty of time was playing out its role. Where it had slowed for him, his wife and daughter—not to mention Eleanor—would succumb to it. *Time will take them all*, he thought, knowing he would eventually outlive them … except for Gill, who, no doubt, would live longer now, given his new role. *He cannot see his family die before him*, he thought. But that was the cruel reality of it; he would.

Closing his eyes, he saw Wareeshta's face, then drew on his plan. He would make her suffer first, then destroy her. Clenching his fists, he breathed deeply, trying to control his anger.

Rosalyn cast a worrying glance at Onóir on hearing the bones of his knuckles crack. 'Reece?'

Hearing his daughter's voice, his eyes flew open, releasing him from his mood. 'The Faire?' he blurted, reminded of something.

'Aye, we're going today,' Rosalyn informed him, 'and say what you will … I'll not deny my son his last one.'

'Nor would I,' he agreed. He turned to Onóir. 'Two days. We must leave in two—and no later.'

Onóir hesitated before slowly nodding.

'Do you have horses?' he asked Rosalyn.

'Just Farrow,' she said. 'We keep him behind the house—in his stable. He's Oran's pride, and I'll *not* part with him.'

'Although, from what I recall …' Onóir added, 'he will not part from *you*.'

Rosalyn smiled, calling to mind her failed attempts to leave the steed with Kai. 'No, Reece, Farrow stays. If you want horses, Balloch Faire will provide you with a fine selection. But I should warn you … it is a peaceful day … so you will have to leave *that* behind.'

Reece stepped back from the two women, feeling outnumbered; he saw what she pointed at and frowned. 'My sword stays with me!' he insisted.

On his objection, Rosalyn turned on her heel, leaving her parents briefly, before returning with a piece of clothing thrown over her arm. 'Then you will have to conceal it, to avoid unwanted attention,' she insisted, holding the garment out.

Reece took the cloak, with some reluctance, then threw it around his shoulders.

'I doubt Oran will mind,' she remarked, approving of the fine noir, damask cloak, now draped on her father's muscular frame. 'However, I do want it back.'

'It fits you well,' said Onóir, admiring her husband.

'A little too large, perhaps,' he grunted, toying with the garment to exaggerate its size.

'Nonsense!' said Onóir, dismissing him. ''Tis a perfect fit,' she added, smoothing it out across his broad frame, '… and should someone question your identity—'

'It is the least of my concerns,' he stated.

'We will say …' Rosalyn paused for thought, chewing on her lip. 'You are … a long-lost cousin of mine.'

Reece slid his eyes towards her after Onóir nodded in agreement. 'Surely, that is what they all say,' he returned, bemused.

''Tis none of their business,' said Onóir. 'Although, I suspect you will attract the attention of the young lasses; they see the Faire as an opportunity to catch a husband. So, be on your guard!'

Mother and daughter laughed out loud. Unimpressed by their shared amusement of him, he stared at his wife, demanding her attention. When she stopped and looked up at him, he kissed her tenderly. 'I am husband to only one.'

Rosalyn pursed her lips, fighting back the tears, then looked away, feeling intrusive in their private moment.

Taking his scarred hand, Onóir smiled, returning the kiss. 'I never doubted for one moment you were dead. To be handed this time with you again has made the stolen years melt away. The happiness and contentment I feel compare to no other. It is a feeling I will take with—'

'You must come with us!' he blurted. 'I have decided.'

Behind his back, Rosalyn was shaking her head at her mother.

Onóir closed her eyes. 'Should I go with you, Reece, the precious time you require for your task will be disrupted by my presence; I will slow you down. You have a duty to fulfil; Oran depends on you—we all do. So, I will hear no more of it.'

He opened his mouth to protest.

'But … I will gladly accompany you to the Faire,' she added. 'I wouldn't miss it.'

Onóir gave quite the convincing performance that all would be good. But, despite it, Rosalyn felt the aching of her parent's saddened hearts.

Reece looked sharply towards the window, detecting the distant sound of Rave's excitement. 'Asai and Eleanor are back,' he announced, returning to the window.

Rosalyn, joining her father, peered out. She frowned. 'I don't see—'

'Wait!' he said.

She looked up at him, confused, and when his mouth twitched into a faint smile, he pointed with his chin, prompting her to look again. And as she did, Rosalyn saw Rave coming into view—on the path's bend—bounding towards the house.

Together, they observed the two approaching figures engaged in conversation—Rosalyn noting her daughter's eagerness, by the lively gesticulation of her hands and her animated chatter. Now and then, Asai stole an interested glance, staring into her eyes for fleeting moments. He paused when Eleanor laughed out loud and pointed at Rave.

Reece grunted and smiled.

'What amuses you?' Rosalyn quizzed.

'It seems your dog has kept you busy during her younger years.'

Rosalyn threw a look at her father, unsure.

'It is, I confess, amusing,' he said.

'You can hear their conversation?'

'Clearly,' he replied. 'The quietness of your surroundings makes it easier.'

'We must be mindful of what we say in future,' said Onóir, winking at her daughter.

'Indeed!' Rosalyn returned, keeping a fixed eye on Eleanor. She also noted how the Samurai towered over her daughter—in a protective way—clinging to her every word. The two hesitated, catching each other's keen look. Rosalyn caught the awkward exchange—that of a couple who had suddenly become aware of each other.

'My interests are the same as yours,' Reece informed her, truthfully. 'Asai is a good man. It is the first time I have seen him smile like that, for a while; it is a wanting smile—not a forceful one.'

Rosalyn beamed with approval. But her moment of possibility was soon overshadowed by their grim reality. In a matter of seconds, the fading dream slipped from her thoughts. 'But they have no future together.'

Onóir closed her eyes, knowing her daughter was right.

'Then I intend to give them one!' Reece's declaration was defined and intentional.

The two women cast him a wary look.

'I intend to give us all a—' He halted. The continuous, methodical sound that had been in the background of his mind had ceased.

'Rave!' Gill's authoritative voice echoed as he summoned his dog.

The hound ran towards him, then paused, looking back at Eleanor and Asai. Contemplating her choice, she threw one more glance at Gill, before returning to the couple. Feeling betrayed, Gill stormed off, leaving the axe embedded in the remaining piece of log.

'I will not tolerate jealousy in this house!' Rosalyn stated, ready to follow her son.

'Wait!' Onóir called.

'Did you not see the way he scrutinised them, Maw?'

'Do not judge him,' said Reece. 'I sensed no jealousy.'

'You must remember,' Onóir continued, 'he has had his sister's company for nearly seventeen years. They share a special bond that is about to be snatched from him. I suspect he is frustrated by their impending separation.'

'That may be so,' Rosalyn returned, 'but *you* must remember what is being taken from him. He is about to lose the future he'd planned with Meghan. I fear there *is* a fit of underlying jealousy when he looks at Nori and Asai.' She moved to leave.

'The transition he is experiencing now is like no other,' Reece reminded her. 'As eager as you are to see him, I urge you to remain. Be patient with him.'

'Reece has a point,' Onóir agreed. 'Gill will calm down, soon enough.'

Rosalyn watched Eleanor play with Rave while witnessing the captivating smile on Asai's face; the Samurai was intrigued by her every movement, proving his interest in her daughter was sincere.

'Then *they* will stay here with Tam,' she decided. 'I want to avoid any confrontation which might arise in public. However, Gill still comes with us!'

Strained by the extra weight he had to bear, Farrow dragged the large cart along the dirt track, towards the Burgh of Balloch. With a little encouragement from Rave, Gill urged his father's horse up the incline, before leading the steed down into the village.

Rosalyn gasped at the throngs of people that had already accumulated. 'We'll have missed the memorial service,' she remarked, glancing up at her son, who remained peeved in his silence.

The usually sleepy village was flooded with young and old—everyone with a plan in mind: to hook or tender. The intention of the day was not to leave empty-handed—be it with a horse or potential husband. Regardless of which, the Faire held a purpose for one and all, however, Rosalyn and Onóir were no fools and were aware of the shrewdness of those hell-bent on a bargain.

The heaving numbers forced them to slow their pace as they made their approach—Reece making it his business to keep a vigilant eye. As he did so, he saw hostility in the faces of two individuals, their envious eyes regarding Farrow as the carriage trudged by.

'Just ignore them,' said Rosalyn, smirking at their resentment.

Unable to proceed through the mass of lively people, they finally drew to a halt.

Only one thing dictated the numbers attending—the weather. Rain had threatened, but the wind had carried the heavy clouds up into the

Highlands, letting the warm, autumn sun cast its welcoming rays over the Burgh.

Hordes of travellers continued to pour onto land from the ferry, placing increasing pressure on Mr Walker—the ferryman—who had luckily hired the usual extra hands to deal with the masses.

'I think it will be the largest one, yet!' cried Onóir, trying to be heard over the hum of excited voices.

Gill rose to his full height, searching through the crowd. Then, catching a glimpse of one of his friends, he jumped from the cart—without a bye or leave—commanding Rave to watch over it. Rosalyn glared after her son as he disappeared towards the Ferry Inn. She rose, tempted to call after him, but was thwarted by a voice of wisdom.

'Leave him!' Reece suggested, offering Onóir his hand to help her down.

When her mother dismissed his gallantry, with a wave of her hand, Rosalyn found her smile again. She had noted the glow of youth in her mother's face, since the arrival of their house guests. It seemed as though the love of life had rejuvenated her, making all the difference, giving her renewed hope for some form of remission. Every time her parents shared a certain look—the kind only measured by true love—she felt a pang of loneliness, and longed for her husband.

Beckoning her parents to follow, she casually strolled on, taking in the atmosphere. Now and then, Reece regarded the crowd, in the hope of catching the watchful eyes; he still sensed nothing. *Perhaps, Oran imagined it*, he thought, doubting the Warlock's suspicions.

The annual Balloch Faire was finally underway. The smell of bread and cakes mingled with open stoves, filled with fresh meat, cooking slowly. As the rising smoke danced on the gentle breeze, it attracted the high noses of hungry dogs, lurking about for scraps; they were rarely disappointed. The mixed aromas, however, barely masked those left by the increasing population of horses. Reece winced at the overpowering stench.

Oblivious to the goings-on of their peers, groups of children ran from stall to stall, trying to decide what candies to spend their precious coins on—the sugar-sweet tablets being their favourite. Reece spotted a young boy swipe a sizable piece, while his accomplice distracted the stall owner. He smiled when the two made their swift getaway, unnoticed. He'd forgotten what it was like to experience the normalities of a mortal's life, and how easily they moved with the luxury of freedom—something *he* had been denied, for years.

He felt restless in their comfort of it, asking himself: would he ever enjoy its simplicities again? But his thoughts kept returning to the matter at hand. He knew Onóir was ill—gravely ill—despite her vain efforts to conceal it. The little warning glances she had displayed towards Rosalyn were far from inconspicuous. But the one thing he did not know was how long she had left.

'So far, so good.'

Rosalyn's voice roused his thoughts back to them. He looked at her with absent eyes and a blank expression.

'No one is *staring* at you,' she added, noting his confusion.

'Why would they do that?' he replied, frowning. 'Have I not concealed my weapon?'

Onóir rolled her eyes at their daughter; it was apparent that Reece was unaware of his striking looks. Even in the brightness of the watery sun, his eyes stood out like emeralds.

'I think you will find *I* am not the only stranger here,' he remarked.

Rosalyn paused on his words, surveying her familiar surroundings. The Faire lured traders from far afield, and because of the wealth it invited, their origins were no longer questioned. She hadn't noticed it before until he pointed it out.

'You look, and yet fail to see,' he said pointing with his chin.

She stared at the peculiar faces, interwoven with the crowd, wondering exactly where they had come from.

'Do you think it is one of *them*?' Onóir suggested.

Reece slowly shook his head.

'I confess, I—' He stopped, listening, then turned to his daughter. 'Someone is calling you.'

Rosalyn stood on the tips of her toes, straining to see and hear above the rumpus, unable to find the face she sought. Reece pointed towards the Inn, where she finally glimpsed the hands of Blair Grant waving frantically, and mouthing her name.

With little effort, Reece encouraged his wife and daughter to join their neighbour, vowing to return.

'Do you … have the means to purchase?' Rosalyn quietly asked him, feeling somewhat awkward, having to do so.

'Sufficient ones,' he replied, feeling the presence of the small, leather pouch concealed inside his belt.

Relieved, she then pointed in the opposite direction. 'Ask for William Woodford. You will know him by the honesty in his eyes; there is no greed in them.'

He watched as Rosalyn guided Onóir away, waiting until they were out of sight. Content, he turned his back to wade through the mass of people, in search of the trustworthy face his daughter mentioned.

Reece felt the heat of the sun on his skin, thankful that its energy proved no threat to him. It prompted a thought: *Magia Nera can only travel by night.* He knew the sun's rays were the dark Warlock's lethal enemy, restricting L'Ordana's movements—should she be on their trail; he was certain of it. But, for now, he detected nothing sinister, giving him some solace.

He felt a sudden shove from the flowing crowd and looked around; it appeared to have doubled in size. He thought of Tam; the Highlander would never have survived the growing numbers; the temptation would have been too great. *How fortunate for them*, he thought, then realised Rosalyn was right when she insisted that he remain at the house.

Moving forward, he briefly checked the sword hidden beneath the cloak Rosalyn had lent him. He could almost feel Oran's presence from its luxurious fabric.

Searching through the crowd, the surge of voices—embroiled in ongoing conversations—was deafening to his ears: children playing noisily, while dogs joined in their games; bidders secretly outbidding each other before trading commenced; and women calling for their children, then scolding them on their reluctant return.

Where are their fathers? he wondered, then grunted. *Taking refuge at the Inn, no doubt.*

Young, local women beamed widely at him, making determined attempts to flirt. He smiled wryly back at them—not out of politeness, but as a feeble attempt to look "normal." He found it increasingly distracting. Feeling an element of discomfort, he blanked them from his mind as best he could. It was then—through the brief clarity he was allowed—he sensed a familiar yet unknown presence. He lingered on its movements, uncertain until it lost itself to the surrounding hubbub of the Faire.

A sudden thought occurred to him, prompting him to remove the leather pouch from his person; there were bound to be pickpockets—not that they would succeed in prizing themselves of his means. He then felt the pain of his guilty past as he checked its contents. Inside were some of the spoils of battles they had fought for the Sorceress. He had respected Asai's refusal to acknowledge the precious gems. But despite the Samurai's disapproval, Reece saw their necessity—should they escape. He recalled his colleague's reply:

"When I look at them, Reece-san, I do not see precious stones, only the blood of innocent victims who were prized of their wealth, and their lives. Use them as you see fit, but do not ask me to participate."

Although the feeling of guilt usually passed, it seemed to cling to him now. He had been aware of his human emotions resurfacing, since connecting with his family—and it troubled him, leading him to suspect that it could be the cause of his downfall …

There can be no room for weakness, he reminded himself, aware of the detrimental effect it could have—should he give in to his emotions. Reece knew he could not let them influence the task ahead, or he may be unwilling to proceed with it. This was not his only concern; he would also have to keep an eye on Asai—the subtle signs already there—Eleanor being the notable one.

An honourable man for my granddaughter—had the timing been right, he told himself, deciding it was for the best they were leaving soon.

The piercing sound of a bell, announcing the official start of trading, beckoned him to join the proceedings ahead. After several enquiries—followed by curious glances—he found William Woodford, who was already surrounded by conflicting faces of buyers, eager to part with their money.

Reece stood a good head above his competitors, his intense stare catching the attention of the horse trader. It was true what Rosalyn had said; William's methods were honest and, having seen the contents of the unassuming leather pouch, the trader happily parted ways with four of his finest steeds.

Pleased with the quality of his purchases, Reece returned to their cart to find Rave on full alert and snarling at any passers-by who came too close. But there had always been a rule of the trade: *"What's purchased will not fall into the hands of another, at the Faire."* Rosalyn's words had tried to reassure him after he had voiced his concerns. Nevertheless, he maintained his misgivings.

'Watch over them, Rave,' he said, tying the steeds to the cart.

The hound wagged her tail, only too eager to oblige. For a moment he held her gaze, his instincts telling him she trusted him. Then, without thought, he smiled, and let his hand glide slowly over her soft coat before rubbing her ear. The dog responded playfully by leaning into him, relishing in his affectionate touch.

Reece then paused, his smile fading, realising what he had just done.

'No room for weakness, Rave,' he whispered, removing his hand. 'A change of plan,' he uttered. 'We leave at first light. Some things are for the best.'

Turning on his heel, he marched towards the Ferry Inn.

The wide door was open, welcoming all visitors to enter, and sup. He looked up, observing the oversized axe above the door as if daring any poor soul to remove it. He could tell by the effects of nature it had not been touched in years, inviting him to muse over its curious history.

From the outside, he could see the public house was heaving with life; voices in fine tune sang along with a bagpipe and two fiddlers. People were in high spirits as the warmth of the day stretched out into what would become an unusually close and sultry night. No doubt the landlord would be wringing his hands at his tidy profit.

As he stood in the doorway, he observed the scene before him with reservations. Heavy tobacco smoke filled the air while women mingled with drunken men in search of a husband … or perhaps another's. *This is where my granddaughter works?* he thought, observing food being washed down with copious amounts of ale and whisky.

Struck by a fleeting memory, he wondered what it would be like to indulge in the gold liquid again; it had been a long time. Compelled by the thought, Reece placed one foot over the next—

He froze.

Everything around him ceased, as though suspended in time: no sound—no movement—save for one. He finally felt *its* presence.

'It's here!' he whispered, drawing his sword.

Reece searched through the motionless crowd until his eyes were met by another's, staring wildly back at him. He could see it now—the unknown source—in its true form.

The *Watcher.*

Chapter Thirty-Seven

The crowded Inn seemed frozen in time, failing to notice the two figures staring at one another.

'Can you not see it?!' Reece cried out, through the eerie silence.

The creature stood taller than Reece, its luminescent skin glowing as bright as the moon. Its oval face was one of perfected beauty. The creature's wide eyes were of the blackest onyx and shone like mirrors. Its hair, matching its eyes, hung down its long, slender back—tied in a single tail. If it wore clothing, he could not tell through its ghostly appearance.

Reece glanced around in disbelief. *Are you all blind?*

As the creature unexpectedly raised its thin hand to beckon him, the Dhampir lunged over the Inn's counter, before pointing his blade at its throat. With eyes blazing, he snarled into its tranquil face, his sharp teeth now exposed.

'You cannot kill that which is already dead!' it whispered into his ear. There was a hint of sadness attached to its peaceful tone.

Reece swiftly stepped back, keeping his sword propped towards his target. He glared at the creature, baffled by its words. 'You are not a—'

'Thankfully, no,' it replied, maintaining an unperturbed stare on its attacker.

'Are you the one who watches them?'

The creature paused, contemplating its answer. 'Somewhat.'

'Then *what* are you?' Reece snarled, through gritted teeth.

The creature smiled warmly, impressed by his assailant's tenacious ability to defend those he loved.

'Do not try my patience … *creature!*'

'I am not what you presume.'

'If that is so,' said Reece, maintaining his grip on his sword, 'then I suggest you share your secret … Now!'

'Reece?!'

The Dhampir failed to notice the familiar voice calling him, as the resurgence of life returned to the Inn. 'Who *are* you?!' he persisted, his voice loud and threatening.

Looking over Reece's shoulder, the creature's enigmatic smile found another's.

'You have toyed with my patience long enough. Now tell me—'

'Don't harm him!'

The Dhampir turned promptly, to be met by the stunned silence of every individual staring at him, horrified by his actions. He glanced back at the creature before facing his audience again, baffled, then realised that their eyes failed to witness what he saw.

'Lower your sword, Reece,' the soft voice implored.

Reece looked down at the outstretched hand. His mouth fell when he saw the worrisome expression on his wife's face, begging him to stop.

Distracted by her mother's voice, Rosalyn tore herself away from her heated discussion with Gill, to be by her side. 'What is it?' she asked, unaware her son had accompanied her, alerted to the disturbance.

''Tis nothing,' said Onóir, dismissing the incident with her hands.

'Are you blind?!' Reece cried, glaring at them, his frustration rising.

The effect of his fuelled anger began to unfold. Some grew uneasy by the strangers' assault on their favourite landlord, casually seizing what they had paid for, before discreetly leaving.

Whereas, the curious few—Alastair Boyd and his cronies—quite happily remained fixed to their seats. 'Do ye think the troubles are starting up again?' Alastair said to them.

Hearing his remark, Reece threw Alastair a scathing glance, forcing the old man to recoil.

Growing increasingly irritated by their naivety, Reece yelled out; 'Can you not see it?!' he argued, pointing to the creature with his sword.

Gill drew closer with an air of discretion. As he did so, Rosalyn caught the sly movement of his hand, realising her son also concealed a weapon—the glint of the familiar pommel alerting her to the fact he had smuggled the dirk from the house, after seeing her return it to Eleanor's coffer. His sister would be furious. She moved to retrieve it, but the distraction of her mother's continuous appeals to Reece heightened her concerns.

Confused by her father's altercation, Rosalyn stepped forward. 'Reece,' she began. 'This is Kai ... Whom I spoke of?'

The Dhampir drew back. '*This* is your ...' He shook his head, unconvinced.

Kai passed a troubled look to Onóir; it did not go unnoticed. Rosalyn now grew suspicious, sharing in her father's confusion; something was wrong.

'Please, withdraw your sword,' Onóir begged, concerned for Kai's identity.

But the Dhampir's refusal to back down brought with it grave concern, it disturbing his spectators.

'He is of no danger to us, my love,' she insisted. 'Please—Reece—you have my word.'

Ignoring his wife's pleas, he turned to his alleged victim once more. '*They* cannot see what I see. Reveal your true form *creature* or I shall do my best—despite what you say—to try and *kill* you ... again!'

'Again?' echoed Rosalyn. She turned to her mother. 'What does he mean?'

Onóir shrugged, shaking her head.

Reece glared at his wife. *She knows!* he quickly realised. 'Make it show its true form, Onóir,' he demanded.

All eyes turned on the old woman.

'Maw?' urged Rosalyn.

Keeping its poise, the *creature* looked at Onóir as though seeking her approval. The Inn held on to the breath of all who watched and waited. They lingered in anticipated silence as the seconds dragged on, observing every motion. Onóir's shoulders dropped in defeat. Closing her eyes, she then nodded with esteem towards her family's close friend.

Kai, the one who had fought against the odds to be accepted by society, stepped away from Reece, having felt the hurt of being called "creature." He was anything but. He glanced at the threatening broadsword suspended before him, knowing it could do him no harm.

Looking away, he now regarded the well-known faces peering at him, from across his counter. For years he had served them well. And now it pained him to see their questioning eyes and hear the suspicions in their whispers. As he stood in the place he regarded as his "haven" Kai Aitken prepared to be judged, yet again—only now, by the people who had initially accepted him into their lives.

'You do not need it,' Onóir whispered to her husband, urging him to withdraw his weapon.

'Show yourself!' Reece demanded, disregarding her. He was taking no chances.

All those present—save for one—fell witness to the slow manifestation of the *spectre*.

As Kai reluctantly uncovered his true form, his saddened eyes followed the gasps of disbelief being shared among his onlookers. Aware of their mounting tension, he looked to Onóir for guidance.

'There is nothing to fear of him,' she stated, addressing the nervous few who thought themselves brave, by remaining. It was the uncertainty of not knowing what might happen, that played on their imaginations. For too long they had languished in the welcoming atmosphere of their kind-hearted landlord. And now, with the risk of violence looming over them once more, it filled them with dread.

Word of the strange, ghostly apparition spread rapidly beyond the Inn. People outside clambered over one other, straining to see through its small windows. For once, they resisted the temptation to venture over the all-too-familiar threshold.

Gill stepped out in front of his mother, brandishing Eleanor's dagger.

Onóir scowled at her grandson in disgust. 'How dare you, Gillis Shaw!' she cried.

351

'Come away from it,' Rosalyn urged her mother.

'Ghaist! Ghaist!'

The ghastly word quietly resonated, until one brave voice cried out; 'Aye, 'tis a ghost!'

'No! 'Tis a demon!' a female voice added, from a dark corner. The woman—who had been entertaining another's "young" husband—then scrambled from the concealment of their little snug, escaping for fear of her life, leaving behind her misconduct.

Panic immediately followed suit.

Onóir glimpsed the sudden sea of hysteria as it unfolded before her weary eyes. Rosalyn's hand continued to reach out to her, still warning her to, "come away from it." Reece remained staunch, his sword now more threatening than ever. Onóir felt sickened by their ignorance. And yet, only one remained tranquil throughout … Their creature. Their ghost.

Her Kai.

'Enough!' she cried, above the chaos, exasperated.

The fury in the defence of her close friend dropped an unexpected heavy silence on the Inn. All and sundry stopped and stared at the frail, old woman.

'Why do you defend it?' Rosalyn sneered.

In a sinister move, Gill inched closer to his grandmother with intent. 'This is the Watcher!' he insisted.

Onóir shook her head in defiance.

'Is this true, Maw?' Rosalyn insisted, preventing her mother from any explanation. 'We invited him—it into our lives—our home, and all the while we have been fooled by this … creature's façade.'

'Do not call him that!' Onóir returned, gripped by rage. 'You will call him, Kai!'

Gill lowered his head with contempt. 'I think not,' he sneered.

Reece looked sharp, alerted to the same threatening tone the young man had used towards his mother that morning. He leapt forward, refusing to stand by and let Gill use it against another—regardless of his grandson's future role.

Gill jolted at the suddenness of Reece's swift intervention—the Dhampir now standing within inches of him.

'Step away!' Reece warned.

Gill held his stance, unprepared to back down. As they eyed one another, their audience struggled to hear the heated conversation between them.

'You are not yet the Magus, Gill. Until then, you do as I say.' The Dhampir's searing eyes burned into Gill's with deadly aim. 'Do I make myself clear?'

Adamant, the young man paid no heed, forcing himself past Reece— the unearthly strength of his force throwing the Dhampir off his guard.

Kai recoiled as Gill rushed forward, his face flushed and distorted in anger.

'You think you can spy on us?!'

Reece recovered instantly, only to find himself defending the creature.

'No, Gill!' Onóir was now straining to be heard. 'You cannot kill him!'

Ignoring his grandmother, he lunged forward, prepared to drive the dagger through it. 'He is not—'

'Stop!'

Gill felt nothing as he passed through the apparition, without causing it harm. Gripping him from behind, Reece forced Gill back to the ground. Shocked by what had just happened, the young man sat staring up at the *creature* in disbelief, as an uncertain silence engulfed the Inn.

Kai lowered his head in shame for having deceived them.

Slowly rising, Gill kept his wary eyes focused on the *creature* as it approached him. He drew back.

'He is a messenger of the Elliyan,' Onóir divulged, smiling at Kai. Her manner was apologetic to him as voices whispered and hissed on hearing the anomalous name.

Rosalyn approached her mother in a state of utter confusion. 'He's *not* the Watcher?'

Onóir, turning to her daughter, shook her head.

'No, Rosalyn'—she hesitated, struggling to take a breath— '*I* am!'

Confused and startled faces stared down at the unsuspecting woman. No one stirred.

Drowned by feelings of betrayal and mistrust, Onóir felt smothered by the crowd's stunned silence. Gradually she felt the walls of the Inn creeping in on her, along with their suspicions. Overwhelmed and exhausted, Onóir reached out for the hand of support, only to be met by prejudice.

Chapter Thirty-Eight

leanor's heart leapt when the door of their home flew open without warning. She had been in the process of lighting the evening fire. She spun, almost stumbling, her hand held firmly against her heart. As the sound of the door collided with a chair, it, too, alerted Tam and Asai, breaking their conversation in mid-sentence.

Gill stormed in, outraged, throwing himself into a chair like a spoiled child, moving awkwardly, feeling the discomfort of his sister's dagger pressing hard against his thigh, as though in protest. He would return it, later. He then glared at Eleanor, his anger fuelling, having seen his sister in the Samurai's company, yet again. He rolled his eyes, casting Asai a warning look.

Rising to question her brother's mood, Eleanor paused, seeing the dirk wedged into his belt. 'What are you doing with my—'

'Not now!' he snapped.

Tam shared a troubled look with Asai. Choosing to veer from a potential argument, between the siblings, a single motion of his head suggested they leave promptly; brother and sister failed to notice their swift departure.

As Eleanor moved to give her brother a piece of her mind, Rave bounced through the open door, unannounced, making her jump again. She then knew something was afoot when Rosalyn stormed in and marched towards her parlour. She watched, slightly perturbed, as her mother then made her anger known, by the noisy preparations of their late meal, uttering words of warning to Rave to, "Leave it!"

'Grandmaw?!' she cried, seeing Reece carry Onóir over the threshold, to her comfortable chair.

Ignoring the frosty atmosphere, Eleanor moved to attend to her grandmother, then hesitated, when she caught the lonely figure of Kai standing in the doorway, waiting to be invited in.

'Kai? Are you not coming in?' she asked, noting a sadness in his eyes.

'He's not wanted here!' snarled Gill.

Shocked, Eleanor gasped at her brother's insolence towards their friend. She looked to her mother, waiting for her to scold Gill, but Rosalyn continued busying herself with supper.

'As you wish,' said Kai, turning to leave.

'Wait!'

They turned to see Rosalyn standing with a ladle in her hand. Tears of cold broth fell in large droplets onto the floor but were promptly cleaned up by Rave, who had kept a fixed eye on the utensil. 'Close the door after you'—she sighed and rolled her eyes— 'enter.'

Gill rose to protest but was knocked back by the sharpness of his mother's glare.

Closing the door on the approach of night, Kai entered the place he had regarded as his second home. At that moment, he felt like the disloyal member of the family who had adopted him as their own. He glanced at Onóir—the most loyal individual he had ever known—and forced a smile; however, it quickly fell from his face when he sensed the hate emanating from Reece, who refused to leave his wife's side.

'I think someone had better start explaining!' Eleanor demanded, glaring at them all.

Wary glances were passed around, displaying reluctance to do so; Gill looked away as his sister caught his eye, while Rosalyn distracted herself by scolding Rave for almost helping herself to their food.

'Well?' Eleanor insisted, folding her arms.

'There must be no fighting among us,' said Onóir, casting a warning look towards her husband and Gill.

'Onóir is right,' said Reece, turning to address them. 'This is a crucial time for us, and whether we like it or not'—he paused, eyeballing Kai—'it seems we *need* each other.'

'Did *you* know about Onóir?' Rosalyn asked, joining them.

Reece stared at his daughter, puzzled, followed by looks of utter confusion from Eleanor.

'Did you *know* she was the *Watcher*?' she then prompted.

'No,' he returned, glancing at his wife, slightly vexed. 'I did not.'

'Watcher?' Eleanor echoed.

'It appears our grandmother has been … *spying* on us,' said Gill, in a scathing tone.

'A spy?!' she cried, disclaiming any notion of the accusation, as she looked at her frail grandmother. 'No! I don't believe it!'

'Aye, nor has she been *alone* in her activities,' he added, casting a disloyal glance towards Kai.

Eleanor turned her attention back to their friend—the man she also worked for. Watched carefully by her family, she moved quietly towards the lonely figure, who still hovered on their doorstep, and looked up at him.

'Nor is he *human*,' Gill blurted.

Eleanor gasped and stepped back, stunned by her brother's allegation, then instantly regretted it, seeing the expression of guilt and sadness on Kai's innocent face, making her feel empathy towards him. And yet, she was still at a loss …

Tired of her grandson's snide remarks, Onóir slammed her hand down on the armrest of her favourite chair. 'No more!' she cried. 'Do you hear me, young man?!'

Gill jumped at the old woman's outburst, lowering his eyes with embarrassment.

'Be mindful, Gillis Shaw, for that is what you still are—a young, naive man. You will continue to call him by his name—Kai. And you *will* treat him with the respect this family has always given. Kai is our ally—a friend of the highest regard.'

357

Reece turned his head slightly, smirking at his wife's tenacity. But with each outburst, he detected the weakening of her heart. The events of the day were taking their toll.

Aware of the signs of her failing health, Rosalyn snatched her mother's medicine from the sideboard and went to her.

Filled with apprehension, Kai looked on, concerned; he knew what to do yet was afraid to intervene. And so, he waited …

Soon, the heightened tension evaporated as Onóir regained her breath once more. ''Tis true,' she began, staring into their eager faces. 'I *am* the "Watcher", as you call it. And as for Kai?' She smiled at her confidante. 'Well, he is … *unique!* He is of the *Dreaocht.*'

Gill sat up, suddenly interested. '"*That which is unseen*",' he quoted, from one of Heckie Grant's stories.

They looked at the young man.

'I have heard of the *Dreaocht,*' said Gill. 'Heckie told me.'

'Then you will know of their origin,' Onóir replied.

'I don't understand,' Eleanor remarked, acknowledging her brother.

'Nor do I, for that matter,' Rosalyn added, equally confused.

Rising from his chair, Gill approached his sister. 'It means he is … like a spirit, Nori.'

Eleanor gasped. 'You mean he's …' She swallowed. '*Dead?!*'

'In a way,' Gill replied, shrugging.

Rosalyn raised her hand over her gaping mouth, unable to take her eyes off Kai.

Eleanor slowly turned to face him again, then narrowed her eyes; she could not help but see the faded scar circling his neck, it now standing out, despite his efforts to hide it. A deep sense of sorrow overwhelmed her as the sudden realisation of his plight hit home. Raising her small hand, she tenderly placed her finger on the stigma of his past. Kai remained perfectly still, allowing her.

'It seems they *did* take everything from you, after all,' she said softly, with tears in her eyes. 'How lonely and tragic for you, Kai.'

'Then how is it we can *see* him?' Rosalyn questioned her mother. 'And how did he end up *here?*'

'I have always known about Gill—since his birth,' Onóir began.

They all stared at the elderly woman.

'Everything?' Rosalyn returned, her eyes and mouth wide with disbelief.

'Aye. Oran confided in me when you doubted everything, at first. I was sworn to secrecy. He, too, had his weaknesses—regardless of his powers and abilities. Oran struggled with the burden of knowing he would perhaps lose his battle against time, not to mention your son. But he was determined to fight against it *and* the Elliyan—anything to protect Gill. That is why he moved us here—to the quietude—in the hope, one day, he just might defeat it—for Gill's sake.'

'How naive of him,' Reece remarked.

Onóir looked at her husband. 'Would you not have done the same, my love—even though you knew, deep down inside, you would fail and have to give up your child?'

Reece glanced at Rosalyn, recalling Oran's words: *"You would do anything to protect them."*

'You know I am right,' she went on. 'And it was no different for Oran; he was a father, protecting his family—and trying to protect his son from an unavoidable fate.'

She regarded Gill for a moment. 'This is no fault of your father's, lad. He would gladly have taken your place. Trust me when I say, he did all he could to prevent it.'

'Now do you believe us, Gill?' said Rosalyn. 'It broke our hearts.'

Gill felt the sudden pang of guilt eat him up as more truths came to light about his family—wondering where it would all end. The weight of his unknown burden swung before him, but it was only a matter of time before it would stop—and sooner, rather than later. Dread reached in, ready to take its hold when his sister's inquisitive voice snatched him from his encroaching dismay.

'How—and when—did you discover Kai's secret?'

'Soon after he took ownership of the Ferry Inn,' Onóir revealed.

'After Father left?'

'Three years ago,' Rosalyn stated.

Kai then stepped forward into the heart of the group, and looked at Onóir, seeking her approval to explain everything. She nodded, glad of it, feeling the tiredness seep into her weary body.

With a smile, he turned to address them all: 'I am of the Servitor,' he began. 'It is our preference of title; we do not like to be referred to as the "Dreaocht." Some would call us "the lost souls of Purgatory." It is a dismal place where the souls of those who are murdered—or who have nothing to live for—reside. There, they remain suspended indefinitely, until the powers that be decide their fate. I have met some who have been there for what seems an eternity, with no way out. It was through the Elliyan's intervention, we discovered they had the power to choose our providence.

'As death was not my choice, or doing, they plucked me from Purgatory, saving me from limbo—to use me as their servant. You can imagine my joy when I was allowed to resume my mortal form. However, I can return to my true state at the time of my choosing; it lets me move swiftly—should the need arise.

'Naturally, there are rules I must abide by. The ability to lie was taken from me unless my identity comes into question. It is only then I am permitted to …' He paused, recalling the term. *"Bend the Truth."* Although my life—as you would call it—is spent in their service, it is most welcoming to be allowed to walk and speak with mortals, again.

'From the moment you were born, Gill, it was my duty to secretly report to the Elliyan on your progress. Oran was unaware of my presence.'

'Surely not!' Rosalyn snapped. 'He *must* have known.'

'He …' Kai hesitated. 'He sees the Servitor as lowly spies; we are much more than that. Therefore, it was thought best to keep Oran in the dark; to inform him of my presence held a risk the Elliyan were not prepared to take.' He passed a knowing look to Onóir.

She nodded in recognition of his meaning.

'After Oran left,' Kai continued, 'I was ordered to protect his son. This proved somewhat difficult, from a distance. Without his father,

Gill would be vulnerable. And so, it was agreed, I was to return to the world of mortals.'

'Which is when you—conveniently—entered our lives,' Gill surmised.

'I must admit,' said Kai, reflecting on their first meeting, 'I was wary of Eleanor.'

'Me?' she responded, raising her brows.

Kai turned to her. 'You are more perceptive than you know, young Eleanor.'

'I am?'

He nodded.

'It was *how* you subconsciously questioned and looked at me.'

'But, of course!' she exclaimed, pointing to his scar. 'I thought it too deep—I mean—to survive a hanging, *and* you were quick to conceal it.'

'Indeed. And I was fortunate in that the young woman who was easily distracted, conveniently dismissed her suspicions.'

Eleanor lowered her head and smiled, before turning to steal a glance with Asai; it was only then she became aware of his absence and frowned with disappointment.

'Therefore, I had to find an ally,' Kai resumed. 'Someone I could trust—someone who had the trust of others. The moment our eyes embraced, I knew Onóir was my true confidante. But I needed assurance of her honesty and integrity, which is why I discreetly observed her for a while, before making my approach.'

'I always had a sense of someone watching me,' Onóir admitted. 'There was no fear in it; I felt … *safe*. Then, one day, I simply … *noticed* him.'

'That was when I made a point of befriending her'—he paused on the memory, smiled, then grunted— 'which did not go unnoticed, by the curious eyes of some of our villagers.' Onóir smiled back at him and nodded. 'But, despite the unusual circumstances surrounding my … *introduction*, I knew it was only a matter of time before I would convince her.'

Balloch: 1627- Three years earlier.

The old woman stopped amid the busy street she had tread daily for almost two decades; the sense of another following in her footsteps had intensified. She had noticed it for a while and, though sensing no danger, it frustrated her.

Surely, they would have made themselves known to me, by now, she wondered. But, when thoughts of her grandson entered her mind, she grew anxious. *Oh, no!* Perhaps *they* had finally come to claim him. *Not without his father!* And yet, she still felt unthreatened.

She surveyed the busy street. Despite her suspicions, she was relieved she was on her own. At the far end of the market, she caught a glimpse of Rosalyn and Eleanor, tending to their customers. Saturday was always bustling with life, especially when the weather was dry. And, as long as the fresh smell of her daughter's baking lured her customers into temptation, she knew Rosalyn would not be distracted by the ramblings of an old woman.

Onóir followed her instincts by observing all the passers-by; those she did not recognise, she knew had travelled from the other Burghs, to visit the market.

'Would ye be lost, Onóir?' Ned McGregor called, pausing on his way to the Inn, to tease her.

"He has an eye on you, Maw," Rosalyn would occasionally mock.

Though fond of the Inn's former landlord, Onóir made a point of keeping a safe distance; she had no desire to encourage a match.

'Away with you, Ned,' she returned, waving him off when something made her stop—her hand still suspended in mid-air—as her eyes were drawn to another's.

"Tis you!' she whispered, staring over at the kind eyes smiling back at her.

Kai Aitken nodded, acknowledging her.

He heard me! she realised, lowering her hand, observing his approach; he appeared to glide towards her, holding her gaze.

She looked up, connected to him now in new recognition. 'I had felt the eyes of someone watching me for some time,' she began, 'but I could not find them.'

'Do you see them now?' he replied, his tone calm and pleasant, as usual.

She nodded, smiling.

'As clear as day.'

It seemed, at that very moment, she lost all sense of time in his presence. It was as though they were alone among the liveliness surrounding them.

'You were in no danger, Onóir,' he assured her.

'I never doubted it.'

'And now you seek answers?'

'Aye, I do.'

Kai looked above and beyond where they stood, catching the odd curious eye. He grinned, dismissing them. Following his gaze, Onóir also paid no heed to the occasional glance; just the usual busybodies searching for local gossip to play *Chinese Whispers* with. Had she been of the younger, opposite sex, then, no doubt, there would have been plenty to set tongues wagging. It was no secret; everyone knew about Kai since *that* night when the stranger came into the Inn causing havoc, his accusations leading to Kai's admission of his "personal preferences." There had been another incident, too—before he took over the running of the Inn—the four instigators eventually "removed" by the skin of their teeth, just like the other. After that, things had calmed—thanks to his bravery—and no one judged him. But, somehow, she found it difficult to imagine Kai displaying such violence. Then again, when one's life is being threatened …

'Do you trust me, Onóir?' he asked, lowering his voice. His tone was adamant.

With tenderness he had not felt, for as long as he cared to remember, Onóir placed a hand on his, and leaned forward. 'You do not need to ask,' she reassured him with a wink.

'Then come with me,' he urged, 'to a place where we can speak—in private.'

Without question or hesitation, Onóir followed Kai, willingly, towards the Ferry Inn.

Even at the earliest part of the day, the public house was alive with its usual array of customers. Alastair Boyd raised his head from his third glass of whisky when he spotted Onóir entering the premises. He lifted a curious brow as if to question her business there—and so early in the day, too! —then promptly returned to his sup and heated debate with his three cronies as to the true height of their hero, William Wallace; he pointed at Kai, making comparisons, adding to their deliberations.

Apart from the "feuding four", as they were commonly known, no other sinner noticed the two figures slip from view.

Kai withdrew a small, ornate black key to open an arched door he had made from the old floorboards of the restored cellar. He then lit two lanterns, handing one to Onóir.

As they descended the stone steps, the smell of strong ale rose, overpowering her senses; she dismissed it as part of the ambience attached to the Inn.

Throwing light on the contents stored below, she glanced around. The cellar looked clean and tidy. She thought it unusual, considering it was the common belief that men were not usually accustomed to tidiness. Then again, this *was* Kai—one who took pride in his appearance. But, for now, her mind was focused on more pressing matters.

Kai begged her to take a seat on the steps. Onóir surveyed the small cellar: it was dry and stuffy—no doubt a different story during the cold and damp winter months. She imagined mice and rats taking advantage of its shelter when the seasons changed for the worse. Old barrels of ale lined the walls in perfect formation, like soldiers awaiting their orders, to quench the thirst of the folk above them.

364

'I have been watching you from a distance, Onóir—'

'So, it was *you*?'

'—but with good reason,' he quickly added.

Onóir waited patiently, ignoring the hard surface she was perched on. She remained composed and collective, ready to take in his carefully prepared words, letting her calming influence assure him of her trust.

'I have been informed you are aware of Oran's true identity,' he said.

Taken aback by his statement, Onóir sat up, wringing her hands in agitation, uncertain of her reply: 'How—how do you know…?'

'That he is a Warlock?'

She hesitated, then slowly nodded.

'I serve his *council*,' he stated. 'The Elliyan.'

Onóir pressed her lips hard, her eyes widening on hearing the name. It was then he became aware of her obvious recognition of his peers. 'Ah, I see you *are* aware of them.'

'Aye, more than aware.'

'Then, no doubt you wish to know … who *I* truly am?'

'That I would,' she said.

'I belong to the Servitor,' he started, before embarking on an explanation of how he came to be. As his truths poured out, Kai saw the tears well in her eyes as she tried to come to terms with his story. She winced when he revealed the thick scar lining his throat, beneath the wide braid of leather he wore, to conceal it; a fine thread of gold had been interwoven in a flamboyant design, making it a fashionable piece. She drew back, alarmed, at the sight of the scar's ugliness.

'No man could have survived—' She stopped.

The look of trepidation on Kai's face confirmed her growing uneasiness, as the realisation of his true state struck her hard. Her eyes widened, mouth slowly opening, quivering, trying to get the words out.

'They … *murdered* you!' she whispered, shocked to the core. 'Then you are a—' A sudden urge to flee grasped her, but when she saw the look of sadness in his eyes, instinct intervened, encouraging her to stay. He watched as she kneaded her hands together, carefully contemplating her decision.

365

'Please, *will* you trust me, Onóir?' he asked, again.

His vital question swirled about in her mind, screaming at her, demanding an answer. 'But you are …' Her voice trailed away.

'There is *nothing* to be afraid of. All I seek is your trust, Onóir. I rely on it. I rely on *you.*'

Her nervous hands stopped as she felt her body relax in the serenity of his presence.

'It is only right you know *who* I am,' he continued, taking two paces back. Kai then prepared to reveal his true identity, conscious of the risk he was about to take. Closing his warm, brown eyes, he stood motionless. Then …

As Onóir moved to address Kai she froze; her mouth gaped when the Elliyan's messenger began to change, his form slowly altering before her startled eyes.

The cellar glowed from his transformation, casting creeping shadows along the walls.

She closed her eyes from it, then slowly opened them, gasping, as the man she knew as Kai Aitken stood silent in his true form, waiting for her to collect her thoughts.

Onóir fought to grasp the strain of what had just unfolded, reminding herself over and over that it was her friend—Kai. *I do trust you … I do trust you,* she chanted inside, until her body and mind found peace, once more.

She swallowed. 'Kai …?' she whispered, rising cautiously. She edged forward, uncertain, reaching out to touch him, then swiftly withdrew her hand.

Overwhelmed by the spectacle of Kai's transformation, Onóir could not help but stare; he was taller, she noted, and his hair now longer and darker—almost black. Everything about him seemed exaggerated. She was sure he wore clothing, of sorts, and yet was unable to see them. But above all, she noticed the blackness that replaced the warmth of his brown eyes. There was now an emptiness in them—devoid of *life!* Despite it, though, she was simply mesmerised by him; she momentarily thought of Gill and how he, too, would marvel at it.

Kai grinned. 'You will not evaporate,' he said, reaching out.

She stared at his open hand as he motioned her to take it.

'Please?' he urged.

Feeling confident—and slightly foolish—she willingly accepted his hand of friendship, taken aback by its warmth and kindness. 'Forgive me,' she begged. 'For staring.'

Smiling at her through his familiar warmth, Kai maintained his comforting hold on her timid hand. 'I should imagine it is not every day you meet a—*my* kind.'

Feeling her apprehension and tension gradually slip away, Kai released his hold; she failed to notice the subtlety of it.

As Onóir looked deep into his lifeless, black eyes, trying to accept his true identity, she was suddenly overcome with pity for her friend; it was almost unbearable as she sensed the loss of a life that had been cruelly snatched from its prime. 'And the men who *did* this to you? What became of them?'

'They were eventually punished for what they did.'

Onóir narrowed her eyes, shaking her head. 'But—how can you be …?'

'Standing here before you?'

She nodded, still trying to make sense of it.

'Aye. When they …'

She recoiled in horror as he resumed his grim story, explaining, in more detail, the concept of *Purgatory*—the prison from where he had been seized.

'It is better to serve the Elliyan and abide by their rules, rather than share eternity with those who truly deserve imprisonment, in the torment that is Purgatory. Because my death was unjust, I was given a choice—one I was willing to receive. The Elliyan *allowed* me to … *live* again … so to speak.'

'As long as you serve them,' she stated.

'Had I chosen unwisely … I never would have met *you*?'

'But will you ever know peace?' she asked, with genuine concern.

'That is for the Elliyan to decide.'

'I hope, one day, they give it to you, Kai.'

'As do I. But, for now, I have a duty to Gillis.'

She gasped, lifting her hand to her mouth, hearing him speak of her grandson.

Kai, seeing the agitation return to her face, extended his hand towards her. 'I beg you to be patient,' he pleaded.

Overcome by emotion, Onóir took a deep breath, almost keeling over when a sudden pressure in her chest threw her into a fit of coughing.

'You are ill, Onóir,' he stated, inching forward.

She waved him away, calming herself.

'I sense the weight of your sickness. Do your—'

'No!' she croaked, trying to clear her throat. 'My—my family don't know. And I would like it to stay that way.'

He hesitated, reluctant, then nodded.

'As you wish. However, they shall know soon enough.'

She cast him a warning glance.

'Your condition will deteriorate in time, and you will have no option but to seek their help.'

'Perhaps,' she replied. 'Nevertheless, until such time, my secret remains with us.'

He leaned towards her, lowering his head in respect. 'You have my word.'

Kai proceeded to share all he knew with Onóir, giving her a brief history of the Elliyan and how Oran detested the Servitor.

'You mean—he has no knowledge of your presence, here?' she pressed further.

'He is aware of it now and has no choice *but* to accept it. When Oran left Eddin, with his family, the Elliyan were unhappy at his sudden departure. It was evident he was reluctant to return to his duties when it was required. He had, after all, made a bargain with them.'

'Aye, he told me,' she recalled.

'However, he did not predict the role born to his son. That is why he disappeared. Fearing he would break his promise, the Elliyan ordered me to find him, after he had failed to inform them of his son's birth. It was a lengthy search, taking longer than we anticipated.'

'*We?*'

'I was accompanied by Lothian—another Warlock, and willing volunteer. When we finally found Oran, we secretly observed his movements. He was content in his life—protective of you all—and notably attentive to the boy.'

'Surely, Oran *must* have known—sensed your presence.'

'If he had … then he chose to ignore it. Regardless of it, it was decided to leave him alone … for the time being, as there was no threat, then. I frequently returned, making sure things were as they should be. I must confess, I shared in Lothian's sentiments, having observed the close bond between you.' He hesitated, nodding to himself. 'Yes, we were right to leave Gillis in the capable hands of his family, despite the Elliyan's disapproval. But time eventually catches up—Oran knew this. And when it did, I was told to summon him. But I was disinclined to. I had'—he paused, smiling at her— 'grown *fond* of you. And, for my weakness, I believe the Elliyan were discreetly informed of this.'

'Someone betrayed you?!'

'It was … *hinted*, I might warn Oran.'

Onóir tilted her head, curiously. 'And *would* you have done so—warned him?'

'No. It would have achieved nothing but disaster, prompting the Elliyan to take precautions. Therefore, they chose another to do their bidding—Lorne.'

'Lorne?'

'He is also of the Servitor—one who took great pleasure in reminding Oran of his duty.'

'My impression of this individual,' said Onóir, 'tells me, you do not like him.'

Kai mused over his reply. 'He is what he is. But thankfully, it was *I* who was chosen as Gill's silent protector—stepping into his father's shoes … you might say.'

'Well, you have done yourself justice,' she said.

369

The Servitor slowly bowed, grateful.

Onóir moved to speak, then stalled, when a sudden thought entered her mind—something Kai had said. She sat up straight when it dawned on her. '"There was no threat, *then*",' she blurted, staring at him. 'That *is* what you said.'

Kai lifted his head, impressed. 'You *are* alert, Onóir. I was right to choose you.'

'Choose?' She hesitated for a moment, then did a double-take. '*Me*?!'

'All in good time,' he said.

Kai drew her inquisitiveness further as she hung on his every word.

'The Elliyan have power over one another,' he continued. 'Except for one. He is another Warlock—Magia Nera.' He sensed, by her blank expression, she had no comprehension of the dark Warlock's existence. 'I have searched for him, without success. Therefore, we think him … passed-on—to the next life—which would be to our advantage, should this be the case.'

'You seem doubtful.'

'Until I have seen his corpse, I can only assume he still lives. As for the remaining four—including Oran—the life of a High Warlock is not his own … nor is your grandson's.' Kai paused, noting Onóir's sombre expression. 'So, you *are* aware of the extent of his fate,' he said.

She sighed, then nodded in her sorrowful admission of it.

'We aim to protect his identity, for as long as possible,' he explained, sensing her pain. 'Although …' His voice drifted as he slipped into deep thought.

'Why do you hesitate, Kai?'

His lifeless eyes stared back at her in consideration. '*When*, precisely, does Gillis come of age?'

She frowned, confused, at first, then looked away, searching her mind for the answer he sought. 'Three years …' She paused, doubting herself. 'No, 'tis a little more.'

'That is when the challenge will prove more difficult.'

'Why?'

'The *amulet*.'

'The amulet!' she echoed, her eyes widening. 'I had forgotten.'

'From the moment of his birth, it sparked a potential threat—one that had been silently looming in the background. It caused no concern, at first; the Shenn amulet had just reawakened, and the Elliyan were the only ones aware of it. When Gillis reaches his full maturity, so will the amulet. They are growing together and must be united—bonded—when the time dictates. However, as that time approaches, both will prove easy to find.'

'Why is that?'

'The Shenn is Master over five other amulets—each one belonging to a Warlock—one you are well acquainted with.'

'Oran,' she stated.

He nodded.

'Theirs will grow in strength, guiding them to the Shenn …' He paused. 'But there is a slight problem: one is missing, and it is unfortunate that it should be Magia Nera's.'

Onóir gasped. 'Do you think he might …?'

'We do not know. But others would take the Shenn for themselves … whatever the cost. Whoever holds the missing fifth amulet will prove a great threat.'

As the information the Servitor relayed to her began to sink in, Onóir quickly gathered her thoughts. With all sense of fear of the ghostly figure before her now gone, she then stepped closer, folding her arms. 'Am I to believe,' she started, tilting her head, annoyed at the thought of someone threatening *her* grandson, 'that threat is … *here*?'

Kai nodded.

'Not only does it threaten our kind, but, also, that of mortals. The wars your soldiers fight against one another will pale in comparison to any dark power that is unleashed. It could mean the beginning of the rout of mankind. In other words: if the Shenn amulet falls into the wrong hands … this world would simply not survive its evil influence.'

'Do you think it will?' she inquired, raising her voice.

Kai looked up, listening, fearing his customers might hear them and come to investigate. 'Do not be alarmed, Onóir,' he said, keeping his voice low. 'We are privy to it. That is why I was sent here; Gillis needs a constant eye—a guardian. But I cannot do it alone, now that Oran is not here.'

She drew back her head, throwing her hands on her hips. 'And *where*, may I ask, *is* Oran?'

'He has gone in search of that very threat. He has been *ordered* to destroy it.'

'I must tell Rosalyn. She's been—'

'No! You cannot tell her, or anyone, for that matter.'

'Rosalyn is his *wife*! She feels abandoned—let down by her husband.'

'I sympathise with her—with you all. But we cannot risk it. The less who know, the safer you shall be.' He stalled, regarding her carefully, when she fell into silent contemplation. 'Do you understand the importance of what I am telling you, Onóir?'

She sighed. 'I am trying. It is a lot to take in, though.'

'I know,' he said, with understanding. 'Also … we *must* keep our silence. For now, at least,' he stressed. 'You have my word when I tell you, she *will* be reunited with her husband … when the time is right.'

Onóir mused over his words before yielding to an agreement. 'What do you need?' she finally asked.

'For you to keep a close eye on the boy,' he informed her. 'But you must continue to live as normally as you can; try not to bring attention to yourself, or me, for that matter.'

Onóir looked her friend up and down, lifting her brows. '*This*,' she said, indicating to him, 'will take time to get used to.'

'Then I shall remain in the form you are more acquainted and comfortable with,' he replied, returning to his earthly disguise.

She jolted at his unexpected change, then nodded with gratitude.

'All I seek in return,' he continued, 'is knowledge of his progression, over the next few years; the Elliyan must be made aware of it.'

'This, I can do,' she promised.

'Thank you,' he said, placing his hand on his heart. 'This is most reassuring—knowing he is being watched over. Also, it allows me to come and go, to relay all that you tell me to the Elliyan.' He then smiled at her through his familiar, warm brown eyes. 'I see how you dote on him—on both your grandchildren. Eleanor is quite protective of her young brother, despite how much they tease one another.'

Onóir narrowed her eyes, amazed by his knowledge of the siblings. But her concerns persisted, urging her to ask; *'Can* I tell Rosalyn?'

'No!' His reply was soft but firm. 'You cannot reveal who you are, even when tested. This place—that Oran chose—is a refuge for you all, especially Gillis. Nonetheless, we must conceal our purpose. The Elliyan are grateful and will not forget your loyalty.'

'They *know* it's me—even though *I* was unaware of it?'

'But of course!' he said, his infectious smile spreading across his face.

'I can imagine their surprise when you informed them of your choice—an old woman.'

'On the contrary,' he returned, with confidence. 'They saw *you* as the perfect candidate.'

'Aha!' She grinned, then winked. 'I am the *least* conspicuous.'

Kai slowly nodded.

'Who would ever suspect *you*?'

Chapter Thirty-Nine

'N ow, do you understand?'

Gill's eyes followed the shared looks of disbelief and admiration as everyone in the household stared at Onóir, speechless. His grandmother's ability to conceal her secret overwhelmed him with pride, in her loyalty towards her friend. He now felt an element of guilt, having listened to the account of her first meeting with the Servitor.

'I never would have …' He paused, lost for words.

'Imagine *I* would be capable of such a task, Gill?' Onóir replied, with a hint of humour in her voice.

He slowly nodded, ashamed.

'Maw always felt someone watching us.'

'And she was right,' said Onóir, smiling over at her daughter.

'When I think of the times,' Rosalyn started, 'when I was troubled by it. I even shared my concerns with you and still, not once, did you falter or betray Kai.'

'Onóir had given her oath,' said Kai, 'for which I am exceptionally grateful, not to mention proud. And now that Gillis lies on the threshold of manhood, his grandmother's duty is done.'

Onóir did a double-take. *It's what?!* she thought, taken aback, as it began to sink in—his meaning.

'Do not scold your grandmother for the vow that was placed upon her, Gill,' he continued. 'Instead, share in my pride for what she has done.'

Kai turned to Onóir and knelt by her side. 'Onóir Molyneaux,' he began, 'I release you from your vow. You have done your duty well. For that, I thank you—the Elliyan thank you. From this point on, Gillis is our responsibility.'

The old woman drew back, staring at her close friend, clearly put out by his unexpected announcement, before responding; 'And it was my privilege to serve *you*, Kai. But I refuse to be let go of my duty; Gill is of my blood, and I intend to watch over him until the day I—'

'As will I!' Rosalyn cut in.

'And me!' added Eleanor, quickly raising her hand, making a point of being seen and heard.

Gill proudly watched his family then laughed. 'How lucky am I to be the subject of such wanting protection?' he said, breaking the tension.

Observing the relationship his newfound family shared, Reece suddenly felt like an outsider. He became aware of something simmering inside him. But while he tried to share in their fellowship, he felt resentment towards the other man who had won his wife's heart—though, in a different way. It was plain to see that Onóir held a unique bond with the *creature*.

The creature! he thought. *No.* He was in no position to criticise, let alone judge Kai's form. And yet, he could not help himself. As he watched them smile at one another, he frowned, feeling the urge to tear Kai away from her side—to warn him off—in a feeble attempt to convince himself there was nothing to be jealous of. But it seemed the more he observed them the more difficult the restrain. Reece instantly felt insecure, having been denied the joys of human contact for so long. He had locked away the ability to display any emotions he may have once had. And now the frustration of unlocking those sentiments was proving arduous.

He abruptly rose.

'We must start our preparations,' he blurted, dampening the warm atmosphere.

Rosalyn glared at her father for his abruptness.

Reece glanced around, inwardly cursing his two colleagues for abandoning him, then looked at the door, noticing it was ajar—no doubt Tam's doing. *Traitor!* he thought, knowing his fellow Dhampir would be ear-wigging, from a safe distance. *And where are you, Asai?* He was unable to sense the Samurai's presence, surmising he was keeping a watchful eye on the woods. His thoughts swiftly turned to the journey ahead.

'Perhaps five!' he muttered, then began making a headcount in his mind. *Asai, Tam, Gill …*

'Five what?' Eleanor echoed, staring up at him, confused.

Reece turned and looked down at his granddaughter, contemplating the expression on her young face. And as her lips parted, ready to question him further, he spoke without thinking— 'There are *five* horses,' he informed her, bluntly. 'But we will *only* need four.'

Rosalyn stared at Eleanor, speechless, as her daughter looked to her for some kind of understanding, while Onóir threw a warning glance at her husband, stunned by his harshness; how could he have been so thoughtless, by disregarding his granddaughter's feelings?

'We leave at first light!' he then stated, with no understanding of the impact of what he had said.

'What—what do you mean, "at first light?"' Eleanor asked, eyeing him.

There was a momentary pause—weighed by guilt—before Gill released a long-winded sigh and said, 'In other words, Nori … *you* must stay.'

Eleanor turned to meet her brother's look of dread, his heart sinking as her resolute eyes glared back at him. She slowly began shaking her head in denial.

'No!'

Rave, roused by Eleanor's sudden outburst, barked and looked up, inquisitive—the occasional thump of her tail on the floor responding, aware of something happening. Her large ears lifted as she tilted her head from side to side, as though listening to a conversation she could never understand.

'You can't do this to me!' Eleanor argued. 'I'm *going* with you!'

One and all remained silent as they watched the unfolding heartbreak of the young woman about to be parted from her only sibling. Eleanor searched the sympathetic faces of those she loved, waiting for an explanation. Each, in their thinking, was in agreement with Reece, and yet were reluctant to voice their admission.

Eleanor felt deceived by her family's silence. Clenching her small fists, she fought back the tears. But the stabbing pain of her fingernails only reminded her of the hurt being inflicted on her broken heart.

Gill reached for his sister but, feeling betrayed, she recoiled from his embrace. 'It has always been you and me.'

'Nori—please—don't cry!' he begged, hating the idea of upsetting her. But it was too late; the hurt was done.

'It would have been an easier thing to accept if you and Meghan had eloped.'

Despite knowing his plans, Rosalyn still could not help but glare at her son, who threw his eyes skywards for being squealed on by his sister. But where was the justice in enforcing a discussion over his plans to move to Eddin with the lass? There *was* none; it would never happen. And so, she let the matter rest; it was her daughter's well-being concerning her now.

'You are braver than this, Eleanor,' he continued, resting his hands on her sunken shoulders. He had used her full name, taking on a more serious tone. It was evident someone had to break the news to her—him being the unwilling volunteer.

In less than two days, the unforeseen arrival of their "guests" had brought with them an ocean of emotions and changes—the reality of their presence still lingering like a dream. Only now, the *dream* presented itself with the awakening truth: they were about to embark on a treacherous journey that was unavoidable, leaving her behind. Eleanor found the inevitable parting simply unbearable.

'Nori!'— Gill shook his sister from her thoughts— 'Listen to me!'

Eleanor found her way back to him, her eyes brimming with tears, her bottom lip quivering.

'I know this will be hard for you; it is heart-wrenching for me. But you *must* stay. Onóir needs you—and I'll leave Rave here.'

377

'But the journey you're taking, Gill'—she shook her head, dreading the thought— 'it's dangerous!'

'Your sister speaks the truth,' Kai informed him, to Rosalyn's disdain.

'And I do not doubt it,' said Gill to his sibling, ignoring the others in the room. 'Even *I* can't envisage what lies ahead. But, Nori, if you go … you may never come home. Something must remain of our family. And I will be content knowing you are safe, here.'

Eleanor flung her arms away from his hold, in defiance. 'How dare you!' she cried. 'There was a time *I* was the one who protected *you*, little brother,' she sneered. 'And here you stand before me, handing out your insults, or have you forgotten that I am capable of defending myself?'

She reached forward, attempting to snatch her dagger from his hip; he stepped back, refusing to part with it.

Onóir glanced at Reece, silently calling for his assistance. He pretended to ignore her, choosing to let the siblings fight their own battle; he had his own inner conflicts to contend with.

Rosalyn moved to intervene but was prevented by Kai, who insisted they were left alone in their childish rivalry.

In jest, Gill raised his hands, recoiling from his sister's advance.

'Give it to me!' she demanded, despite knowing she would be unable to prize the weapon from him.

'No!' he teased, patting his thigh. '*This* stays with me until you have calmed down.' Looking down at her, he rose to his full height and folded his arms, raising the barrier between them, fuelling her anger.

Rosalyn closed her eyes, shaking her head; with so much at stake, brother and sister continued to behave like disruptive children. She would have to intervene. But as she moved to do so, the single, loud grunt from Eleanor told them what was coming … Turning on her heel, the young woman stormed from the house, pulling the door behind her.

Gill laughed in triumph. But his victory was short-lived when he turned to his mother and saw her head tilted. She was tapping her foot, too, which sent a warning to him. Gill passed a look to his grandmother, seeking her support; Onóir slowly shook her head, defiant.

'*Traitor!*' he mouthed at the old woman, then groaned. 'All right, I *promise* to return it before we leave.'

But in his moment of glory, after their brief battle, something told him they may never see each other again. Gill then sighed with regret for having taunted his sister. Plagued by more guilt, he decided to follow her. He would apologise, and they would discuss it like grown-ups.

Heading for the door, he halted, finding Reece blocking his path.

'Leave her!'

'But I must explain—'

'Leave the girl!' Reece insisted. 'She needs to work this out for herself. She is no longer a child—and *you* should know better.'

'He's right,' Onóir added, siding with her husband. 'Eleanor will eventually understand.'

Gill frowned at his grandmother; he felt deceived and let down by her—by them all.

'The "traitor" yet again, it seems,' Onóir confessed, feeling a pang of shame. Nonetheless, she knew it was time she stopped taking his side.

Gill looked back into the green eyes peering at him through their intensity. He now saw an honesty lurking behind Reece's stare. It was the first time he had noticed it.

'What about Onóir and Kai?' Rosalyn enquired, moving towards her father. 'How safe will *they* be?'

Reece and Gill watched her determined face as she stood—hands on hips—expecting answers.

'Kai will not be staying,' Onóir informed her curious daughter.

Reece let out a deep-rooted sigh. 'Then we shall need five horses,' he mumbled.

'I thank you,' Kai returned, his tone calm and diplomatic, despite being aware of Reece's dislike of him. 'But I do not require one.'

'Then four it is!' Reece promptly replied, his mood now brightening; the thought of spending their impending journey in the Servitor's company had not been appealing.

Onóir turned to her daughter. 'Therefore, it is important *we* make certain no one enquires of their whereabouts—or follows them, for that matter. Everything here must remain as it is.'

'*We?!*' cried Rosalyn, taking a deep breath.

The forewarning tone in her voice cautioned the wary faces staring at her.

'If you think I intended to stay,' she informed them in a slow, defined manner, 'then you are mistaken. We'll be needing *five* horses … as *I* shall be taking Farrow.'

Chapter Forty

eleanor threw herself out into the balmy night before finally giving in to her tears. Overwrought with sadness and fear, she failed to notice Tam loitering about in a vain attempt to avoid the family feud. Her mind was distracted—awash with anxious thoughts.

How will I cope without Gill? she thought. *And when did he suddenly become my protector?* She was unable to comprehend the change in her young brother—and in less than two days?! *Is that all it's been?* It felt as though their unexpected visitors had been in their company much longer; so much had happened since their arrival.

She felt the familiar tightness in her chest as she struggled to catch her breath, forcing her to stop at the edge of the woods. Leaning over, she tried desperately to control the irregularity of her breathing, before the burning in her stomach made its presence known.

Gradually the tension released as she relaxed into the rhythmic flow of life, once more. Wiping the tears from her flushed cheeks, she inhaled, straightened her body, then gazed up at the night sky. The lustrous stars winked down at her as if letting her know everything would work out. Closing her eyes, she made a wish. It was the one little secret she had taken with her throughout her childhood, carrying it on into womanhood.

She then recalled the story Oran had told her of the starry sky's "lost souls" and thought of Kai. She was in awe of their close friend yet sympathetic to his plight. *What a sad existence!* she thought, unable to imagine it. *But he seems content with his lot ...*

Reece entered her mind, next. Despite being her grandfather, she would not forgive him for the blunt way he had spoken to her. She then grinned to herself; it was clear—by the way he occasionally glared at him—Reece was envious of Kai's relationship with the family—none more so than the bond the Servitor shared with Onóir.

'Huh!' she quietly grunted, feeling a little unsympathetic. 'That's *his* problem!'

There was a warm stillness in the night air that had followed the humidity of the day, despite it being late autumn. Turning her gaze to the moon, she was forced to narrow her eyes against its glare; its unusual glow was still dazzling, lighting up everything below its domain—even though it had begun to lose its fullness. She looked down at the distinctive, eerie shadows it cast on the ground, catching sight of two hedgehogs rummaging about in the thicket of leaves, preparing for hibernation. They would soon find quietude in their long, lazy slumber ahead. She envied them.

Eleanor glanced back at the house, deciding to wait a while before facing her family again. Leaving it behind, she headed into the familiarity of their surrounding woods. The dry leaves beneath her feet crunched as she made her way through nature's territory, and when a sense of relief fell over her, she stopped and sat for a while, beneath a tree, enjoying the solitude of her own company.

'Why do things have to change?' she quietly asked the universe.

Her grandmother's words drifted back as she nestled her head against the tree: "Life is all about change, Nori; it is what moulds us, makes us who we are. From the moment we are born, it is inevitable. But we *do* have a choice—one which is ours to make. We can either fight or accept it and join its journey through life. It is wise to choose the latter."

Eleanor jumped to her feet. 'That's it! *I* will make a choice … *my* choice. And I refuse to stay!'

And so, it was decided; she would go back and simply *tell* them, whether they like it or not. She played out her speech in her mind. *I am going with Gill, and no one will change my mind.*

'Short and to the point,' she told herself aloud.

Committed to her decision, she turned to make her way back when the moon's light seized a glint of metal—enough to catch her attention. She hesitated, waiting to glimpse it again, quietly gasping when it began to dance and sway in perfect formation. Mesmerised by the beauty of its movement, she decided to seek it out, her curiosity enticing her.

The hoot of an owl announced her presence as she drew closer. She stopped; and when she did, *its* movement stopped, too. Unafraid, she moved quietly with confidence. But, despite her knowledge of her territory, she was unaware her movements had not gone unnoticed.

The sudden sound of a blade being slowly removed from its sheath reawakened her senses. She paused before promptly concealing herself behind a bush, rummaging through its branches to see.

Tilting her head, Eleanor scrutinised its owner's every move, in awe, as he handled and caressed the curvature of the sword with passion and respect.

He stopped—the weapon still in mid-air, its metal glinting under the moonlight. Thinking he had heard her, she held her breath, then slowly released it when he placed the sword on the ground. Her eyes then shot up when he unexpectedly removed the upper part of his kimono, revealing his bare torso. She looked away … briefly. Her eyes widened at seeing the outline of every moving muscle on his toned body. He paused again and, picking up the sword, raised the great weapon to the moonlight, displaying its true magnificence, before making it dance again in the elegance of his skilled hand.

When Eleanor gasped at the mastery of his expertise, Asai stopped and looked in her direction.

Embarrassed, having intruded on his privacy, she rose from her hiding place, and turned to leave.

'Come—join me!' he called. 'Your company is always welcome.'

Turning back to face him, Eleanor's breath caught at seeing him standing there, in full view—and half-naked. With his free hand outstretched, he smiled, beckoning her. She peeped over her shoulder nervously, knowing she would be completely alone with him now, under the blanket of night, without another soul watching them. She lingered, sensing the intensity of his presence.

Trembling inside, she edged towards him, hoping her nerves did not show.

Asai bowed, then encouraged her to sit on a fallen tree trunk, nearby.

She returned the bow—the awkwardness of it making her blush.

He smiled, approving of her attempt to acknowledge him as she cautiously sat on the uncomfortable surface. 'Will you permit me?' he asked, motioning to the space beside her.

She nodded, diverting her eyes.

Aware of her embarrassment, he covered himself again.

As he took his seat, she pretended not to notice when she felt his thigh brush against hers before space divided them again.

For a short time, they sat together in silence, conscious of one another—Eleanor clasping her fidgeting hands while he sat, poised, resting one hand on his sword.

Her eyes slid towards the sheen emanating from the blade. ''Tis a beautiful piece,' she finally remarked, plucking up the courage to speak.

Without a word, he held the weapon out before her. She gasped and then slowly stretched her hand, daring to touch its lethal blade.

'Be mindful of its sharpness,' he warned, his voice soft and melodic. 'It can sever the hand with one swift movement. It has been known to cut the skin without one knowing.'

Eleanor snatched her hand back, visualising its ferocity. But unable to resist, she leaned forward to inspect it further, her brow creasing with genuine interest. She noticed the deep engravings of unusual symbols—one, in particular, standing out. 'What is it?'

He smiled. 'A reminder of my home,' he said, subtly moving the blade away from her. His features softened as droplets of fading memories returned for a brief moment.

'Is it far—your home?'

'A great distance away—to the east. There was a time I could close my eyes and visualise it. Sometimes … I imagine I can smell the apple blossom tree. Its wonderful scent is intoxicating.' He closed his eyes, struggling to catch a mere glimpse of the memory he had fought to retain.

'Is *this* what you describe?' she asked, pointing to the small but perfectly detailed engraving of what appeared to be a flower.

'Ah! The lotus. It, too, hails from my home.'

'It's beautiful!'

He nodded.

'*Hai!* It is sublime in its simplicity, and its aroma … unique!'

'How long has it been—since you last saw one?'

'Almost six decades'—he looked away in a moment of thought—'no, fifty-seven years, to be accurate. It is a piece of my memory *they* failed to steal. It continues to remain *here* and *here*,' he added, pointing to his head and heart. 'I only have to look at my sword and I can see it vividly in my mind. It is something of great beauty, and yet it is so delicate to the touch like—' He hesitated, glancing at her.

Eleanor's eyes widened. Smiling, she looked away, discreetly fixing her hair while concealing her shyness.

'It is a pure and sacred flower,' he continued, arousing her attention once more. 'Each morning it emerges from the murky waters—from which it lies—before presenting its true, clean magnificence to the world.'

'Without a stain?' she asked, astonished by his description.

He nodded.

'Pure. It is one of many colours. I favour the white.'

She frowned, confused by his choice, compelling her to ask; 'Even in the splendour of colour, you choose the simplest?'

'Ah! But it is not simply the *colour*,' he said, raising his hand, 'it is *what* it represents.'

When she failed to respond, he looked directly at her, taking her with his glance, before continuing: 'Each distinct shade symbolises the choice of the individual. The white lotus stands for the enlightenment of the mind and spirit. It depicts the spiritual journey one has taken, in the hope they will find true happiness at its end. It is the one thing I seek … again.'

She turned to face him. 'Again?'

A vacant look fell on his flawless features, emptying him of all expression, save for the sadness in his dark, almond-shaped eyes. It drew her in, making her want to delve further into his mysterious world.

'Who is she?' she asked, attempting to hide the taint of jealousy in her tone.

It seemed an age had passed before he replied in a sombre voice; 'My wife, Ayumi.' He stalled, realising he had not spoken her name in all the time that had passed since their final parting. 'She died.'

'Oh!' Eleanor chewed her lip as the wave of guilt came crashing down. She searched for the necessary words to express her sympathy but was at a loss. Clearing the lump from her throat, she finally asked; 'When did she …?'

Asai inhaled deeply. Until that moment, he had only shared his story with Reece. Even then, his colleague had to force it from him. Nonetheless, it had been the making of their friendship. And now, as he sat beside his friend's granddaughter, he was about to do the same.

'Forgive me,' said Eleanor. 'I didn't mean to—'

'It was a long time ago,' he started, interrupting her. 'We were new to marriage. I came from a line of "Daimyo"—feudal lords of the Asai clan. Our home was the great castle of Odani. It was considered to be impregnable, and regarded as among the five greatest mountain castles … or so we thought. I had the honour of becoming a Samurai—a protector—following in my father's footsteps.

'Ayumi lived with my parents, inside the fortress. Her mother and father had long since entered the spirit world. Although we had survived many turbulent years, we felt safe within the castle walls, knowing we had our allies—the Asakura clan. But then came the great battle against a more powerful Daimyo—Oda Nobunaga. We were all but defeated. We struggled for another three years until the Asai clan were eventually eliminated by him.'

'If that is so,' Eleanor remarked. 'Then how are *you* here?'

'Oda was not alone in his battle for Odani. He had the aid of another. *Her* intervention forced me into this way of life, and on to this point in time.'

'The Sorceress?'

He nodded.

'It was our unique skills that attracted her to our kind; the Samurai is regarded as a prized warrior.' As he spoke, Asai removed a smaller sword, tied to a gold rope, attached to his belt. He held it out alongside the larger one. 'So different yet well-matched as equals,' he uttered.

'The one you first met is the katana—the sacred one—linked to my soul. It is the Samurai's ruling, that it can only be used as a last resort. As with most things in life, it needs its pair. *This*—the smaller sword— is called, wakizashi. Together they are "Daisho" meaning, "the big and the small"—the big for cutting—the small for stabbing. They are the perfect, deadly match.'

Eleanor watched, enthralled, as he admired them equally before rising, to give her a brief display of their unity.

'Only the most skilled warrior of the Kenjutsu—the great art of the Samurai sword—can wield both weapons at the same time,' he stated, continuing his display.

Eleanor observed the pride in his face while he spoke like he'd been transported back in time. She listened intently, letting him relive his past.

'Once skilled in this art, the Samurai knows he can go to battle with honour and pride. When he draws his sword, he intends to draw blood. As he attacks his opponent, his unique ability to rush his victim confuses them. It is *then* the Samurai strikes … without fail. But it is also his will to die a glorious death, by the blade.'

Eleanor gasped at the great warrior's revelations, though was saddened by them. 'Do you see this as your fate, Asai?' she asked.

Asai. He stopped and stared down at her; there was something in the way she had spoken his name—like a voice from the past.

'Asai?'

He continued to stare before the reality of his past failures returned. His shoulders dropped, recalling the horror of his defeat. Looking down at his precious weapons, he returned them to their resting place, before quietly resuming his seat beside her.

Her mind raced, thinking of what she would say next when something in the night sky caught her eye. She looked up; his eyes moved quickly, following hers.

In the far-reaching distance, to the north, they noticed a faint, green hue of light, through the wide gaps in the trees. It danced and swirled in a continuous flow, throwing its wonder across the night sky. They marvelled at its haunting, natural glow, before its abrupt departure.

'It was during that final conflict—to save Odani—when …' His voice drifted off.

'Tell me!' she urged.

'When L'Ordana interfered—along with her followers. She took some of Oda's warriors as her own. It seems even *he* was powerless against her, and was forced to take her side. She took the castle, along with everyone in it.'

'Your wife and parents?'

'Not quite.'

Eleanor stared as his face hardened and held her breath, desperate for him to continue.

'My father was a proud man. He would not let the Sorceress dictate his death, nor my mother's. "The right does not belong to the Witch"! I'd heard him say. He could not bear the thought of another taking such a precious gift. So, by the ritual of *Seppuku*, he took both his and my mother's spirit to the next world. Through his actions, it was easier for me to accept their demise. He had once shared his thoughts with me, in secret. His words live inside me as a reminder of his bravery. I can still hear him saying, "Should another threaten our lives, my son, and should there be no hope, I will not give our enemy the privilege".'

'He was thinking of you,' Eleanor stated, in awe of his father's bravery.

'And my mother; she, too, shared his beliefs—as did I. I watched them die with honour while guarding them.'

388

Eleanor's heart ached for his loss and feared asking him her next question. He spared her dread.

'Ayumi became separated from us amid all the slaughter. She fled the castle. I searched in desperation for her but was too late. I found her at the base of the escarpment.'

'Did she …?'

He shook his head.

'She was less fortunate. The Valkyrie—Kara—took it upon herself to … *execute* my wife.'

Eleanor tried fighting back the tears while hiding her fear as his tragic story unfolded. She wanted to reach out and comfort him but resisted the urge.

'My grief urged me on in battle, until I was the last Samurai, barely standing. I had fought with honour, choosing to die the same way. It was not *their* choice to make. As they sneered at my battered body, I fell to my knees and drew my sword before their very eyes, ready to follow my loved ones. I can still see the smirk on her face when I thrust the wakizashi *here*.' Drawing back his clothing he pointed, showing her where the sword had entered his abdomen.

Eleanor winced when she saw the thick, horizontal scar—the reminder of his failed attempt to join his loved ones.

'I waited for death to take me to them. But before I took my last breath, L'Ordana gave her order: "Give him to me." It was at that moment when Wareeshta stepped in, to do her dirty work. I no longer had the strength to defend or retaliate when she made her attack.' He sighed. 'I recall each agonising moment as everything I had known disappeared. I had become L'Ordana's servant—her battle armour—forced to fight against my will.

'When satisfied with her accomplishments, she simply moved on to her next potential victory. Death became her ally, continuously following her path of destruction. If it had not been for Oran, we would still be bound to the Sorceress—kept under her rule. It is better to live "free" for centuries than to be her prisoner, with the constant threat of death hanging over us.'

'Centuries?!' Eleanor cried, turning to confront him. 'Do you mean to say—you will live … *forever*, while those around you grow old and die?'

'I thought you understood,' he said.

Stunned, she sat up—eyes wide open, mouth quivering, unable to grasp the reality of her newfound situation. How would she cope, now, when her feelings for him were growing with every precious second spent in his company?

Chapter Forty-One

'eleanor?'

The softness of his voice, speaking her name, brought her back to him. It was the first time he had spoken it since their acquaintance; it melted her heart to hear him say it, even though ... She began shaking her head at the unfairness of it all.

'You must forgive me,' he begged, sensing her pain. 'It was *not* my duty to tell you. I assumed Reece would have—'

'No!' she snarled. 'He did *not* explain! There is much *they* failed to tell me. It was my understanding that now you're free, you would return to a normal life.'

'We *will* die ... eventually.'

'When the rest of us have long gone!' she exclaimed. 'It's not right. I—I cannot comprehend it.'

Asai looked into her anxious face as she struggled to stop the tears.

'Because we are Dhampir,' he went on, feeling the unenviable burden of having to explain the truth behind their affliction, 'our human side continues to exist. It clings to our beating hearts.'

Without warning, she felt her hand in his—the unexpected coolness of his touch making her heart jump.

'Can you feel it?' he whispered, placing her hand where she could feel the slow, unnatural beat.

Her mouth parted slightly as she stared at their joined hands and slowly nodded.

'If it beats,' he said, assuring her, 'there is *life*! And all life ends.'

'Aye, but—you are not ... *normal*,' she reminded him, reclaiming her hand.

'I have no doubt,' he continued, 'this heart *will* eventually cease. True, we are no longer bonded to the Sorceress, but we continue to be *what we are*—something that is not easily destroyed. When we suffer injury, our bodies have the power to heal swiftly.'

'But you said you will *die!*'

Asai could not help but smile at her innocence as she tilted her head and frowned like an inquisitive child, striving to understand the true meaning of "life."

'To die a natural death would be a glorious thing, Eleanor.'

Her cheeks flushed when he sang her name again.

'But there is only one who has the power to give it—the Sorceress.'

'And what of the others?'

'Wareeshta and Kara?'

She nodded.

'Kara's name lies on the tip of my sword … for good reason. *She* will be easy to destroy. However, Wareeshta remains under the constant protection and control of the Sorceress; L'Ordana relies on her "talents" as she affectionately calls them.'

'Why protect *her*?'

'When Wareeshta dies, only *then* will we know peace. In *her* death, she will take our curse with her, restoring life to us once more. As long as her poisonous blood continues to flow—'

'You will stay the same,' she quickly realised.

'*Hai!* Her blood runs through our veins, manipulating our own. When I choose to sleep, I can hear its constant reminder of her presence. It will be difficult, though not impossible, to destroy her.' He tilted his chin. 'Now do you understand?'

'I understand why you seek revenge for the loss you—all of you—have endured. But if you find it, will you bask in its glory, knowing you may die in the process, leaving those—' Eleanor stopped herself, biting her tongue before she said too much.

No, I can't tell him. Not now, she thought, lowering her head. *Where's the point in that, when we have no future together?*

'Revenge is there for the taking when the time presents itself,' he replied, aware of her growing concern and frustration. 'But, for now, other things take priority.'

Eleanor lifted her head.

'We must honour our promise to your father. Oran relies on us to escort Gillis safely to Elboru, where he—'

'Elboru?' she inquired, lifting her head at the familiar name. 'That's north of here.'

Asai hesitated, realising his error: he should not have told her where they were going, fearing she would want to accompany them. 'Our time is limited,' he then stated, wanting to sway from her curiosity. 'And you must not blame your brother. He did not ask for this burden. I see the way he displays his bravery in your presence; it is his way—a man's way—of concealing his fears. But, inside, the thought of leaving you behind tears him apart. He simply wants to protect you from the unknown evil he has yet to face. And make no mistake of it, he *will* see it, soon enough. This is why you must stay. He is simply … trying to do what is best.'

Eleanor closed her eyes, attempting to block out images of the times she and her brother had shared throughout their childhood. Discarding them, she finally came to understand those days were long gone; it was the here and now that mattered—*he* mattered.

Drawing on her newfound strength, she prevented the tears from coming. She was his big sister and had behaved like a spoiled child. *Time to grow up!* she told herself, prepared to do what was asked of her.

Turning to Asai, she was met by his patient gaze. She inched closer until they touched again.

'Promise you'll not fail, Asai?' she asked with resolve—the spark of hope and determination evident in her piercing, blue eyes as she held his look.

In the seclusion of their own company, they became oblivious to their surroundings, suddenly aware of one another.

Asai regarded her, momentarily unsure; there had been no other since Ayumi. From their first meeting, he had sensed Eleanor's energy, secretly choosing to reject it out of respect for his wife's memory. But now, in their closeness, it was reopening his world, drawing him nearer and melting away his apprehension.

Eleanor felt it, too—the rush inside—the anticipation of uncertainty. Letting her natural instincts guide her, she swallowed before slowly raising her hand. He responded by tilting his head to greet its warmth. She placed it gently on his cheek. Even in the balminess of the night, it felt remarkably cool; she barely noticed it.

As their eyes held each other, his then lowered, aware of her lips parting; Eleanor reached up, daring to place a delicate kiss where his waited.

Overwhelmed and surprised by the tender moment, she pulled away. 'Forgive my forwardness!' she begged, not knowing where to look.

Moved by her impulse, Asai now turned to her and gently took her head in his hands, holding her like the fragile flower he cherished. Fuelled by a reawakened passion and honesty, he willingly returned her gesture, refusing to let go.

It was her first. Throwing her arms around him, she felt her body respond in a most natural and wanting way—pressing against him, feeling him. Embraced in his tight hold, she urged him on—him letting her as he relished in the softness of her young body. But the silence of their private moment became disturbed, by the sudden awakening of nature from its sleep.

Asai stopped, his abruptness causing her to sway; he steadied her, then lifted a hand. 'Quiet!' he whispered, before rising sharply. His dark eyes darted from side to side, hunting through nature's habitat, suggesting something was not quite right.

'What is it?' she whispered back, moving to his side.

The Samurai stood staunch, remaining silent, ready to unleash his weapons. Eleanor noticed his hand hover over the hilt of the katana. She moved to question him again when he suddenly turned and bowed. She drew back, startled.

'Can you forgive my rudeness?' he appealed, smiling down at her.

As she opened her mouth to reply, he stopped her.

394

'I think it is time you return to the house,' he said. 'The others will be concerned.'

Eleanor raised her brows—confused by his apology—unsure of his meaning. 'Have I offended you, Asai?' she quizzed, feeling a little dejected.

Recognising her confusion, he motioned her towards him, to reassure her. She blushed, moving closer, then stalled when a sudden, flittering movement beyond him caught her attention. She leaned sideways, stretching her neck, to see what it was.

The dark silhouette of a large bird stopped and peered at her from a short distance. It lingered briefly on a thick, large branch—straining to bear its weight—before leaping high.

As she watched it take flight, Asai turned to see what had distracted her from him. They watched as it ducked and dived between the trees— the moonlight catching the sheen of its jet-black feathers.

'These ancient woods never cease giving up their secrets,' she stated, while they kept their eyes fixed on its movements.

'Why do you say that?'

''Tis unusual to see a black hawk,' she said, 'and one of *that* size.' She pondered on it a moment, then shrugged. 'Perhaps a female, although … I've not seen one like it before.'

'Never?'

'Ever!' she replied, shaking her head.

Suspicious, Asai observed its movements as it shrunk into the distance. Content with its departure he turned to her, noting her inquisitive frown.

Eleanor slowly tilted her head. 'However, something tells me, *you* may have seen one before,' she said, folding her arms.

'Perhaps,' he retorted, glancing over her shoulder. 'I think we *should* go!' he then insisted—on an instinct—pointing towards the house in his eagerness to coax her away.

Rolling her eyes and throwing her arms down in retaliation, she reluctantly agreed. She turned, taking a few timid steps, then stopped, aware he was not beside her. She glanced back, to see him staring at the sky, again.

'It's gone!' she called out.

'No,' he said. 'It is returning.'

She approached him, looking up. 'Are you sure?'

'Perhaps your unusual friend is equally curious about *you*,' he said, mocking her.

'Where is it?' she whispered.

Asai kept his silence as he listened to the crescendo of the bird's beating wings, as its speed gradually increased on its return.

'How did I fail to miss it?' he muttered beneath his breath. He quickly glanced at Eleanor. 'Wait here for me!' he blurted.

In an instant he was gone, leaving her bewildered.

Eleanor's imagination took charge of her thoughts as she dared to take a step in the direction he'd gone, having detected the look of unease on his face before he left.

"Wait here for me!" His words echoed in her mind as she contemplated returning to the security of her home.

She chewed on her lip, glancing back towards the house, undecided, then looked again to where he had gone. 'Where are you, Asai?' she quietly called, grasping her hands with growing concern.

She then paused, noticing it: the encroaching eerie silence; it was unnerving, as though nature had fallen into a lazy slumber, deserting her. But the quietness was soon disrupted by the sound of slow, beating wings, growing louder and louder …

'Asai? Where are—' She stopped dead as a cold breeze brushed over her from behind, sending a ghostly shudder down her spine. She felt it again; this time it was stronger, catching her long hair, making it dance about her face, disorienting and frightening her.

It was then she heard it: the familiar voice of instinct— *"Run!"*

Again, it cried out to her— *"Now!"*

Failing to obey her inner warning, Eleanor hesitated …

Her high-pitched scream rose above the tree line, desperately calling his name. Asai stopped dead as her cry reached out, searching for him.

Armed with intent, he turned and ran, increasing his speed to get back to her. But even then, he knew he was too late, and cursed himself for leaving her, to intercept the hawk. *I should have realised …*

Asai found himself, once again, at the place they had discovered their love for each other. However, the disturbing sound above him now penetrated and threatened it. Reluctant to do so, he raised his head, knowing what he would see. But nothing prepared him for the true spectacle. From behind, he heard Reece and Tam's approach; they had heard her, too.

Within moments, the three Dhampir were reunited, wielding their arms.

Above their heads, the Valkyrie hovered, sneering down at them. Grasped firmly in her hold was Eleanor—shocked and silent. Kara's other hand slowly raised, exposing a large dagger. She toyed with the sharp implement before placing it across the young woman's exposed throat.

The Valkyrie's huge, white wings were spread wide, keeping both of them suspended in mid-air, as they looked down at the gathered few.

Keeping its distance, though visible, the black hawk, Nakia, perched herself nearby, watching over the proceedings. She was waiting for her Mistress's prompt: to stay or leave.

Asai stared in shock as he saw the terror in Eleanor's eyes, pleading with him. A wave of revenge urged him to leap.

'No!' cried Tam, standing in his way.

Kara smirked down at them. 'I would take your friends' advice, Asai, or—' She stopped and glanced towards the house. The smirk then reappeared. 'It seems we are about to have a larger audience.'

After Reece and Tam's swift departure, Gill and Rosalyn acted on instinct and followed them into the woods, leaving Onóir, Kai, and Rave behind—the hound unimpressed, judging by the sound of her continuous howling.

The Valkyrie's grin widened when mother and son appeared, running into the small clearing.

Failing, at first, to see the spectacle above them, they stared at the three, armed Dhampir, confused.

Gill quickly glanced from one to the next. 'Where is she?' he asked, bemused by his sister's absence. When no one replied, panic hurled itself at him. 'Where is Eleanor?!'

It was then they heard the slow, menacing beat. And when a deep-set grunt came from above, Rosalyn and Gill looked up, unprepared for what they were about to see. Unable to grasp the reality of the new horror they now faced, mother and son froze, momentarily stunned by it.

'Oh, Eleanor!' Rosalyn sobbed, lifting her hands, trying to hide the terror on her face.

Gill stood, aghast, staring at the evil mocking them. Kara's physique was nothing he had ever seen before in a woman. Under the shadow of night, her long, braided hair seemed to glow. The breast of armour—she held his sister against—gleamed beneath the moon. The strength in her arms gripped her victim without effort, as her great wings continued to bear the weight of the two women.

Seeing her family, Eleanor reached up in a failed attempt to release herself from Kara's hold, only to be hampered by the steel bands protecting the Valkyrie's muscular arms.

From the depths of his fear, Gill's voice fought its way to the surface as his sister struggled within the creature's grip, desperate to escape.

'Eleanor!'

Chapter Forty-Two

'Wait, Gill!'

Reece stepped into his grandson's path. 'She will kill you without thought,' he whispered, staring into the young man's wild eyes. 'And, whatever happens, say nothing of your father,' he discretely added, before turning to challenge the Valkyrie.

'Then *do* something!' Gill answered back, through gritted teeth.

Reece searched for a solution to their unexpected predicament; as it stood, it was a hopeless one. The Dhampir was more than aware of Kara's capabilities. He noted how she clutched Eleanor like a prized possession. The reason returned, haunting him.

The Valkyrie playfully tapped the point of the dagger against her prisoner's throat, drawing on her spectators' anger. She eyed them individually. 'It appears the Warlock has deserted his three conspirators,' she teased in her low, foreign, raspy tone.

A shrewd glance from Asai warned Rosalyn to stay silent.

'He helped us escape,' Reece casually returned. 'Then we parted ways, without questions. His business was his own. I assume he returned to wherever he came from. However, it is no concern of mine,' he added, dismissing it. 'Now let the girl go!'

'Girl?' she retorted, eyeing Eleanor. 'This is no *girl* I hold in my grip!' Peering down at Asai, Kara leaned in and whispered in Eleanor's ear; 'Has he had you yet?'

The Samurai's face flared, hearing the Valkyrie's lewd suggestion.

Kara threw back her head, releasing a deep, intimidating laugh. 'I think not!' she then purred. 'You see, Asai is not like the others; he is … *unique!* Even *I* could not entice him.'

'She is of no use to you, Kara,' Reece persisted, ignoring her familiar taunts. Stepping forward, he lay down his sword, to the surprise of those around him. 'If you release her, I will go in her place.'

'Always the noble one, Reece!' she jeered. 'And why would *you* do that? What is this … *woman* to you?'

Gill could no longer contain himself, as he turned Eleanor's dagger over in his hand, feeling her energy. 'Let my sister go!' he demanded, raising the weapon.

Kara's eyes widened with added thrill. 'A doting brother, no less!' she remarked, turning a curious eye on him. She hesitated, regarding Gill with suspicion. 'You remind me of some—'

'Stop! I beg you!' Rosalyn implored, braving a step closer. 'If you are to take anyone, let it be *me*!'

'Not you, Maw!' Gill hissed, forcing her back. 'Let one of *them* go!'

Kara's brows shot up. 'And here stands the "mother!"' she said, 'pleading for her offspring. Quite the family gathering,' she added, relishing in the unfolding revelations. 'As brave as you are, to surrender yourself in place of your daughter …' Her voice trailed off until a curl then appeared on the corner of her mouth. '… you are too *old* for certain … *needs*.'

Rosalyn looked to Reece for an explanation of the Valkyrie's meaning, observing him share a worrying glance with his two colleagues.

'What does she mean?' Gill insisted.

Knowing Kara was revelling in her continuous goading of them, Reece knew they had to act quickly. He looked at Asai—whose eyes had not faltered from Eleanor—sensing the Samurai's growing agitation.

Caught up in a moment of self-indulgence, Kara's hand dropped from Eleanor's throat. The young woman reached up, wrenching the Valkyrie's long braid in a bid to distract her. Those below gathered closer as they watched, fearing what might happen should they choose to act. But Kara's reaction was too swift and strong for Eleanor. In the moments that passed, as she fought against her hateful enemy, Eleanor felt her strength wane from the overpowering heady scent, emanating from the Valkyrie.

Kara pulled back and, using the point of the dagger, forced Eleanor's face to meet hers. 'Do *not* try that again!' she threatened, reapplying pressure to her prisoner's throat.

A trickle of blood crawled down the side of Eleanor's neck; she felt its warmth seep into her bodice, staining her clothes as she met with Kara's seething eyes.

'Enough!' yelled Reece.

The Valkyrie ignored him. 'I should slit your throat open, and let you bleed to death in the presence of your precious fam—' Kara stopped dead, drawn in by Eleanor's striking eyes. 'But of course!' she exclaimed, now seeing the truth behind them.

She looked down at Reece then grinned. 'I see *your* eyes in hers—hidden behind the pretty veil of blue—subtle yet obvious. They share the same intensity as a rare stone. The resemblance is uncanny—now that I can see right into them.'

Kara watched those below eye one another. Sensing their heightened discomfort, she perceived she had stumbled on something they had wanted to stay secret. 'The eyes betray them, "mother",' she stated, then snorted, observing Rosalyn's frantic, silent pleas to Reece.

Kara turned her attention back to him. '*She* cannot be your wife, Reece—too young. And as for *this* little one,' she teased, continuously provoking Eleanor with the dagger. 'I—' She stopped, again. Her eyes widened, suddenly seeing the connection. 'Ah, yes! Mother and daughter are also … *your* daughter and granddaughter, Reece. It makes sense. But I see we are missing someone. Where is she? Where is your *wife*, Reece?'

'She is long dead,' he returned, without flinching.

Rosalyn glared at Reece for denying her mother's—his wife's—existence, before grasping his motive. But even in his denial, the Valkyrie maintained her constant mockery of him.

'Look at what I could have prevented,' she continued, referring to Rosalyn and Eleanor. 'Perhaps I *should* have disobeyed the Sorceress, and dispatched her anyway. Had she not been with child …' Kara's words drifted, regretting the lost opportunity. As she held his gaze, searching for lies, she saw nothing but contempt staring up at her.

'Time is such a cruel enemy, Dhampir,' she continued, satisfied with his reply. 'However, we must not dwell on it, and I am bored now. Besides, *she* is waiting for my return and is anxious to press on. I should imagine it is only a matter of time before we find the Warlock.'

'You know where he is?' Reece enquired, his eyes darting to Eleanor as she strived to keep her eyes open, fighting against the weight of tiredness.

'Not quite. But the other one has been more than helpful.'

'The other one?' he quizzed, trying to waste time. He inched closer, followed by his two colleagues.

Kara rose slightly, away from their subtle advance—the familiar curl on the edge of her mouth warning them of her intent. 'Your attempt to insult my intelligence, Reece, says little of your granddaughter's worth,' she said. 'You know precisely to whom I refer.' Anticipating their next move, she lifted herself higher into the night as Eleanor surrendered to exhaustion.

'Please, don't take her!' cried Rosalyn, watching her daughter slump in the Valkyrie's grip.

For a moment Kara lingered, catching the reluctant eye of another. With a nod, she then extended a faint smile towards the individual, before taking flight—leaving her cauldron of fear, dismay and anger behind.

All eyes followed the Valkyrie as the trees rose thickly above them. Together they stood speechless and defeated, watching until they could no longer see the movement of her great wings.

Reece jolted, then glanced around, seeing the shocked expression on everyone's faces. But it was several moments before something occurred to him: Asai was missing.

When a distinct sound distracted him, he looked sharp, towards the woods; he could hear his colleague's determined footsteps, fading into the distance. It seemed the most rational one among them had lost all sense of decorum.

No, Asai! he thought, abruptly leaving the others behind, desperate to catch up with the Samurai.

He then became aware of the faint steps of another, following him—Gill.

The pain of being separated from his only sibling had been heard, when Gill cried out after her—the young man then taking it upon himself to pursue them. However, Reece knew Gill was not quick enough to catch up.

Reece now pushed himself, fearing what was at stake: everything that was precious to him; everything that had been given back, and more. No, he was not going to let anyone threaten that … No matter *who* they were.

'Bring her back!'

Reece heard Rosalyn's cry reverberate from behind. To bring Eleanor back was out of the question—impossible! How would he tell her? He blocked it out … for now.

He then caught a movement ahead—Asai.

The Samurai was making ground on the Valkyrie—and fast.

Onward Reece forced himself, no longer hearing Gill's footsteps. *Good*, he thought, concentrating on his colleague, who was now proving difficult to catch. He *had* to stop him.

The space between them eventually tightened, drawing him, edging him closer … closer … closer until he was almost upon him—within an inch of his grasp. But when he reached out, Asai unexpectedly swung round—weapon in hand.

'No, my friend!'

Reece felt the Samurai's sword brush against him, cutting his cheek. On instinct, he reached for his broadsword before realising it was still on the ground back where he had left it.

Asai stopped abruptly, catching the last glimpse of the Valkyrie, his face grey with anger and distorted, concealing the defeat he was feeling inside.

'They will *kill* her,' he snarled.

Dismissing Asai's instinctive reaction towards him, Reece moved to his colleague's side, sensing his mix of emotions. 'No,' he said. 'Now that Kara knows who she is, Eleanor is safe.'

'For now,' Asai retorted, attempting to resume his pursuit.

Reece intervened, stopping the Samurai from doing so.

Asai drew back, wide-eyed, then bowed. 'Forgive me, Reece-san,' he begged, having seen the graze on his friend's cheek.

'It is just a scratch—forgiven and forgotten,' he said, placing a hand on the Samurai's broad shoulder, feeling the tension inside him. 'Listen to me,' he continued. 'I admire your courage and understand your wanting, but you know what will happen if we follow her. That is what Kara wants—to lure us back into L'Ordana's hold, knowing she'll have Eleanor to use as *bait*. She expects us to follow. But we are only three.' Reece shook his head. 'We cannot risk it—not knowing how many we are up against.'

Asai, woken to the truth behind what Reece had said, slowly nodded in agreement. 'What was I thinking?' he said, his shoulders slumping.

'You were thinking of Eleanor.' He paused. 'Trust me, we *will* get her back, somehow.'

'Easier said than done,' said Asai, looking over his shoulder. 'And how are we going to explain it to *him*?' he added, watching Gill plough through the bushes into their company.

Seeing them return without her daughter, Rosalyn ran to Reece and Asai, her distress marked by the look of dread on her face. 'Where is she?!' she cried, looking from one to the other. Faced with their wall of silence, she turned to Gill.

'Don't look at me!' he snapped, storming by her.

Agitated, she quickly turned back to Reece. 'Where's my—' She gasped, seeing the new scar on his face. 'What—what happened?' The barrage of questions began to fly, demanding answers.

Angry and frustrated, Gill walked away, his head pounding with concern for his abducted sister. He then stalled, reminded by something—something the creature had said. He turned his attention to the three Dhampir.

'What did she mean when she said Maw is "too old for certain needs?"'

'What direction did she go?' Reece enquired, avoiding the question.

Gill stared at him, mouth wide open, speechless.

'Where will *that* take us?' the Dhampir persisted, pointing in the Valkyrie's direction.

'North-west,' Rosalyn answered.

He turned to his daughter. 'Are you certain?'

'I assure you,' she replied, a little vexed, 'it is north-west. Why do you want to—'

'Is it possible?' Asai broke in.

Reece nodded.

'L'Ordana is arrogant enough.'

Gill joined them, suspicious. 'Are you suggesting …?'

'Perhaps,' said Reece. 'One thing *is* certain: we know the Sorceress sent the Valkyrie to track us.'

'Reece?' begged Rosalyn, looking for more understanding.

'Do you think they were right under our noses—all this time?' Gill surmised.

'We cannot assume this to be the case,' Reece retorted. 'Though … it *is* possible.'

Feeling detached by their assumptions, Rosalyn grew increasingly anxious and irritated; she desperately needed more answers. The strain of losing her daughter was now slowly being replaced by an unwavering strength. She felt the rise of anger, loathing the creature that had scorned them all. She stepped into the fold.

'How could they have possibly known where to find us?' she asked. 'Are we not secluded? You said it yourself, Reece—how well-hidden we are.'

Gill's mind raced as his mother's words resonated into more questions for the three Dhampir. Unable to think, he stepped away from the company, pondering over the Valkyrie's path, carefully analysing her last movements. Something in her conduct disturbed him—niggled on his instincts.

He looked back and stared at the others, now deep in discussion. Watching them, he noted something disreputable in the behaviour of one, in particular. As time took a breath, allowing him to relive the moment, it then dawned on him:

'That's it!' he blurted.

On hearing Gill, the agitated voices stopped and looked up.

'She *thanked* him!' Gill snapped, now convinced. Tilting his eyes, he met with another's and pointed— 'It was *you*!'

Chapter Forty-Three

Tam did not see it coming—Gill's blatant attack on him. However, it had come as no surprise to Reece and Asai, their shame displayed in the way they hung their heads.

Rosalyn paused, stunned and confused by her son's accusation. It was only then, by his immediate actions, her inner doubts were confirmed.

Still armed with his sister's dagger, Gill launched himself at Tam, pinning the Highlander to the nearest tree. The Dhampir jolted, taken aback by the young man's growing strength and speed. Despite it, he refused to defend himself; he would willingly take his punishment.

'Traitor!' Gill yelled in his face. 'I'll *kill* you for this!' As he drew back the blade—ready to thrust it deep into the Dhampir's heart—Reece and Asai rushed to protect their colleague, in the face of his naivety.

Rosalyn cried out to her son.

On hearing his mother's pleading voice, Gill turned swiftly, meeting Asai face-to-face.

Rosalyn screamed when the Samurai met with Eleanor's dagger—the full length of the lethal blade penetrating his heart, leaving only the hilt exposed.

At first, Asai felt nothing, then sensed the pressure of its presence lodged inside him.

Dropping to his knees, he grasped the protruding handle. Reece clutched his injured friend as he fell.

Rosalyn clapped her hand over her mouth, shaking her head, in utter disbelief. Her eyes then found the startled face of her son—Gill clearly distressed by his actions.

Gill stared down at his empty hand before meeting his mother's tearful face, silently appealing to her for help and forgiveness. In the distance, he could hear Rave's faint bark. The dog's sixth sense was at work. Gill then thought of his grandmother, praying she would not come. What would she say, knowing he had just killed someone? Regardless of his threats, it was never his intention to take the life of another.

Everything seemed to slow as he watched his mother go to the Samurai's aid. Gill moved to help, but something held him back. Turning his head, he was met by the look of remorse on Tam's face, and yet the Dhampir was keeping a firm grip on him.

Gill shrugged away from the Highlander's clutch as his grim reality came back to the fold. 'This cannot be happening!' he mumbled. 'I—I did not intend to—'

Reece raised his hand, prompting Gill to be quiet and remain still. The young man stepped back, distressed and shaking inside.

'This is all *your* doing,' Rosalyn growled at her father as he leaned over Asai. 'You brought him here, along with his betrayal. I shared my doubts with you yet you urged me to trust Tam.' Reece turned a deaf ear to his daughter's animosity. Offended by his dismissal of her, she glared at him with disgust.

But Reece, by now, had moved his attention to Tam whose eyes were shut tight, hiding his shame. '*Do* you know where she has taken her?' he asked—the calmness in his voice bringing with it an understanding and forgiveness for his colleagues' faults.

Tam looked down at him and shrugged. 'I cannot say, Reece,' he responded, his face solemn yet displaying an element of confusion, 'because … I don't know. My head is full of muddled thoughts and conversations. Somehow, I *know* I am guilty but … I can't remember why.'

'Then you had better try searching,' Reece warned him.

'How can you remain so … *composed,* when your friend is dying?' Rosalyn whispered, feeling helpless as she stared at the dirk still wedged into the Samurai.

Gill's heart sank as he looked away from Asai. *He's dying!* he told himself, knowing it was by his hand—the one that had held Eleanor's dagger. *She'll hate me for this!* The irony of it weighed heavier on his heart. He thought of running away—escaping—but to where? No, he would be caught, tried and punished for his crime, then tortured. Perhaps even … He froze when the Tolbooth in Eddin entered his mind—the infamous prison notorious for its horrendous penalties. He had heard about the dreadful things that went on there; Heckie had told him. He dragged his eyes back to where Asai lay on the ground. A rush of fear ran through him, seeing the Samurai's lifeless body. He swallowed then shook his head. *What am I going to do?*

His father entered his mind. Where was *he* when he needed him? His head ached, looking for solutions, when suddenly the Samurai's eyes flickered wide open.

Rosalyn fell back, stunned by his sudden reawakening.

Asai drew in a long, deep breath, glorifying in the cool night air.

Relieved, Tam released a long-winded sigh which was met by Rosalyn's steely glare of disapproval.

Placing a reassuring hand on Asai's shoulder, Reece smiled at his friend.

Gill's erratic thoughts ceased when the Samurai eased himself up. He then stared at his mother, sharing in her confusion, unprepared for what was yet to come.

'You are well, my friend?' Reece enquired, lowering his voice.

Asai lingered, glancing down at the blade still embedded inside him. 'I am … quite well,' he said, appearing unusually perplexed. He then turned his head slightly, eyes fixed, staring; he seemed distracted.

Reece narrowed his eyes. 'What is it?'

'I am unsure,' Asai replied, coming back to them.

While Tam kept his quiet distance, Rosalyn and Gill looked on, lost for words yet were relieved by the Samurai's apparent brush with death.

'Shall I?' Reece asked, offering the usual assistance to his fallen comrade.

Asai bowed, allowing him to proceed.

Reece leaned in. 'This will not hurt,' he whispered.

Aware of their audience, the Samurai tried, without success, not to respond to the personal aspect attached to his colleague's comment, then nodded at Reece.

Detecting their hint of humour, Rosalyn pursed her lips, trying to contain her anger. *How dare they!* she screamed inside.

But the faint smile was wiped from Asai's face when Reece gripped Eleanor's dagger, observing the initials of all its predecessors as the blade was gradually removed. Asai winced the instant it left the place where Gill had thrust it—into the centre of his heart.

Reece felt the long, drawn-out release of his friend's breath, as though it had been his last. Asai then shot a peculiar glance at him.

'I *feel* her—inside me!' he murmured.

'*Eleanor?*' Reece mouthed, aware his colleague wanted his discretion.

The Samurai slowly nodded. In a moment of doubt, they held each other's gaze, at a loss.

'Look at it!' Tam blurted, pointing to the dagger still in Reece's hand.

To their astonishment, the blade glowed crimson red—not of blood, but unknown energy from within its steel. Aware of the heat of its power, Reece looked at Asai, showing him the dagger. Feeling his strength return, the Samurai rose to inspect it closely. When he did, its glow intensified. Curious, Reece motioned him to move away; with each retreat, they watched it fade.

'There's no blood!' Gill remarked.

Asai paused, regarding the young man; Gill lowered his eyes, ashamed of his actions.

Rosalyn stared at the Samurai, in awe. 'How can he still be alive? Surely, not even someone of—'

'Our kind?' Reece cut in.

She nodded, without apology.

'Aye,' she said. 'Asai's heart took its full length. How can that be, if he is half-human? 'Tis unthinkable!'

'I have not seen this before,' said Reece, turning the dirk over, inspecting it.

Watched closely by everyone, he then approached Asai, intrigued. Rosalyn gasped when the blade glowed again. Reece held his friend's attention. Fascinated, he offered the dagger to the Samurai, but Asai hesitated, peering down at the weapon.

'Take it!' Reece urged him.

The moment it passed into his hand, the blade glowed with the intensity of a bright flame, dominating the hue of night. Raising the dirk—to the level of his eye—it illuminated his strong features. Asai felt its growing energy merge with him, joining them together until it glowed no more. Closing his eyes, he secretly searched for her. When nothing came, he scolded his imagination for playing tricks on him.

The Samurai then turned to Gill, his hand outstretched; the young man remained silent, uncertain of Asai's next move as he regarded the dagger in his hand. In their hesitation, Rosalyn quickly stepped forward, retrieving her daughter's heirloom. Gill caught her with a disheartened glance.

'Forgive me?' he begged, finding the courage to look Asai in the eye. 'I am ashamed to have even contemplated …' His words drifted on his guilt.

'No harm has been done,' Asai replied. 'Barely a mark,' he added, touching his breast.

'This time, perhaps,' said Gill, overcome by self-pity. 'How can I be the great ruler that is expected of me, if I'm unable to control my temper? It might have been someone else—someone who could not survive such impact.'

'There is no time for regrets, Gill,' said Reece, taking control of the situation. 'No life was lost ... thankfully. However—'

'I am to blame for Eleanor's abduction,' Tam interrupted, stepping into the thick of things.

The Highlander had taken no more than two paces, when he felt the sudden impact of being forced to the ground, followed by the unexpected sound of clashing steel. Tam found himself locked tightly between the crossed blades of the katana and the wakizashi.

Reece leapt forward, retrieving his broadsword from where he had offered his surrender to the Valkyrie, then stopped abruptly. Asai was leaning dangerously close, pausing within inches of his defenceless opponent's face. Leaning closer, he applied pressure to the weapons, until Tam felt their razor sharpness.

Things were now getting out of control.

'Stop him, Reece!' cried Rosalyn. 'No matter what Tam has done ...'

Bewildered by Asai's uncharacteristic behaviour, Reece now grew concerned for Tam's life. Then panic followed when the Samurai spoke in a menacing tone:

'Shall I tell you how to kill a Dhampir, Gill?' he snarled, adding pressure to the blades.

Asai's eyes burned into Tam's with the promise of death, telling his colleague he could no longer match his increasingly, overbearing strength.

Aware of his fate, Tam remained silent and still, knowing one flinch would ensure his demise.

'Leave him, Asai!' Reece commanded, with ill effect; he drew back, feeling powerless against his friend's unpredictable actions. Often, they had witnessed *death* together on the battlefield, with full recovery of their injuries, and yet he knew *this* was different. The Samurai was playing out his emotions for all to see—Eleanor's dagger being the instigator. Reece now feared his close friend was losing control of his calm and peaceful demeanour.

'If you truly wish him dead, Gill,' Asai persisted, in his deadly threat, 'it is important to complete the task, by removing his head after the stabbing. But be warned: should you fail, he will be blessed with added strength. However, unlike you, *I* do not intend to fail.'

Tam's eyes widened, feeling the sudden need to swallow, fighting against the urge to do so. He then became conscious of the importance of one of the most natural things required of the body—a requirement all living creatures took for granted—and one he could no longer resist; it was a necessity. As his throat tightened, he coughed, rising to meet the lethal blades.

Everyone rushed forward as Asai took a sharp breath, preparing to make his bold and lethal move.

'No, Asai!' came the soft voice of reasoning, from behind them.

The Samurai leapt to his feet, tearing himself away from Tam. He swiftly turned, having heard her voice.

'Eleanor?' he whispered to the lonely figure, standing at the edge of the clearing.

She smiled at him, in a familiar way—but it was not her; even though the resemblance in Onóir's smile and voice sang sweetly of youth. Accompanied by Kai, the old woman came forward.

'I had to intervene,' she revealed, approaching Asai, 'when it came to this.'

'You *saw* what happened?' Rosalyn asked her mother, throwing a scathing look at Reece.

'Most of it,' she replied.

'You should not have witnessed *any* of it, Maw.'

'Do not blame your father, Rosalyn. He made me aware of their traits, strengths and weaknesses. However, I believe'—Onóir looked up into the Samurai's lost eyes— 'you would not have killed Tam. It would reduce our chances of finding Eleanor, despite your feelings for him at this time. With great consideration, I know you will find her. And what is more, I do not fear for her life.'

'If only I could share in your sentiments,' Gill protested, turning away from them. Tired of their assumptions and speculations, he marched from their company towards the house. In the distance, he heard Rave's persistent howl, aware of her Master's return.

'Do *not* walk away, Gillis Shaw!' Rosalyn snapped, pursuing her son—the dirk still clenched in her left hand. Her voice continued to resonate as she followed him, hurling accusations of "denial" for refusing to accept their situation.

When Reece moved to follow, Onóir stopped him, quietly asking; 'Leave them be!'

Turning to his two colleagues, Reece regarded their state. Tam slowly found his feet, inspecting the scars that had now formed on his throat, knowing they would soon fade.

Hearing his movements, Asai spun, holding the katana at arm's length. Reaching for his claymore, Tam jumped back, now ready to defend himself.

'Please, Asai,' begged Onóir. 'Think of what I said.'

Lowering his head, he maintained a fixed and determined stare on the Highlander.

'Should any harm come to her … my *friend*,' he warned, 'I swear it, upon the souls of those gone before me, that *this*'—he tapped the point of the katana where Tam's heart was beating slowly— 'will *cease*. Then, I will cut it out and hand it back to the whore you betrayed us to before I kill her.'

No one was in more denial of Asai's vow than Reece. Despite being a man of honour, he knew the Samurai would carry out his threat, without fail. The friend, he thought he knew, had now taken on a new behaviour, bringing with it suspicion. But now another suspicion presented itself, when he sensed something hanging in the air—the lingering menace drawing his attention skywards.

'I think it wise to return to the house,' he stated, distracting the others. 'I do not wish the arrival of another unexpected guest while we are vulnerable.'

Asai reluctantly lowered his sword, his determined eyes still on Tam.

'It will achieve nothing, my friend,' Reece told him. 'We *need* him.'

'And answers?' Onóir insisted.

'Aye, and I'll do all I can to provide ye with them,' Tam promised. 'If only I could remember …' Despite his admission, the Highlander felt helpless. He did not doubt, for one instant, his life was at stake. But, if he were to die, he would rather it by the hand of one of his companions. Ashamed, he quietly cowered past Asai, diverting his eyes.

'He is telling the truth,' Kai stated, having observed the Dhampir.

Reece and Asai turned to acknowledge the Servitor, who had kept his silence throughout.

'And how would *you* know?' Reece snapped.

Onóir scowled at her husband for the scathing tone he continued to use towards her friend, prompting her to hit back.

'Did *you* know, Reece?' she challenged, stepping forward.

He drew his brows together, uncertain of her meaning.

'I saw the dishonourable look on your face when Gill made his discovery,' she persisted.

'I did not!' he retorted, aware he had just become Asai's new object of inquiry, feeling the Samurai's eyes on him. 'My only shame was for not realising it, sooner. It was then—when Gill made his assault—my fears were confirmed. But I am at a loss as to why Tam is unable to recall his obscure betrayal.' He scowled. 'I am ... *baffled* by it, even though he takes the blame.'

'Tam knows he has done wrong,' said Kai. 'I sense his torment. He battles between guilt and his loyalty towards you, now that he is aware of it. But, if you persist in forcing him, the outlook will prove unsuccessful.'

'Meaning?' Reece insisted.

'Be patient with him. Give him time to—'

'Be *patient*, you say?!' Asai interrupted. 'Time is something we do not have—or have you forgotten?' The Samurai's growing agitation was evident, in his reluctance to return his weapons to their resting place.

'I have not forgotten,' Kai replied, staying calm. 'But, if I am not mistaken, I believe I know the *motive* behind Tam's inability to recall what torments him.'

Onóir, Reece and Asai gave the Servitor their undivided attention, waiting for him to divulge his deliberations.

Kai hesitated, then looked in the direction the Valkyrie had taken Eleanor. For a moment he mused over his final thought, before making his deductions: 'I believe the Valkyrie *stole* his thoughts.'

Chapter Forty-four

'She stole my what?!'

Their faces continued to stare at Tam as if judging him.

'No!' he insisted, shaking his head, defiant. He paced the room, throwing his hands in the air, refusing to believe such nonsense. ''Tis impossible!'

Rosalyn threw him a glance as she occupied herself with their later-than-usual supper. Her head throbbed with harrowing thoughts of her daughter, and what she could be going through. She looked at the empty seat where Eleanor usually sat and stopped herself. *What am I doing? Why am I doing this?* she asked herself, then looked up. *And why are they not looking for her?* Her heart sank, recalling Reece's explanation. *He's right,* she realised. *The risk is far too great. No—I must keep busy.*

'Do you recall informing Kara of our planned escape?' Reece quizzed his friend.

'I told her nothing!' Tam retorted, taking offence.

'And yet, you willingly accept the blame,' Kai commented.

Dumfounded by the Servitor's statement, Tam slumped into the nearest chair by their dinner table, continuously scratching his deformed ear. 'I *feel* guilty,' he admitted, wholeheartedly. 'I *know* it was me but …' He groaned.

'But you struggle to understand *how*,' Kai said, 'when you have no recollection of it.'

'Aye, that's right!' said Tam, relieved to know at least *one* was on his side.

'And how do *you* assume to know?' Gill sneered, subconsciously stroking Rave, who was keeping a keen eye on Rosalyn's movements as the smell of food toyed with her senses.

'There is much you do not know about me, Gill,' Kai informed him. 'Although I am a servant to the Elliyan, I have been fortunate to be educated in the ways of this world. But, no matter how much I know, the learning process is endless. I am well acquainted with the myths and legends of many cultures—some of which remain a mystery. However, I *am* privy to the Valkyrie's "gifts".'

'Gifts?' Rosalyn echoed, shooing Rave's inquisitive nose from the table.

Kai paused, sharing a wary look with Tam; he would have to choose his words carefully, to spare the Highlander's embarrassment.

'The Valkyrie has ways of obtaining what she wants and *needs*,' he continued. 'She can *lure* her victims with one of her methods: a heavy, sweet scent that she carries. It is overpowering to males, though, some are immune. However, those who are unfortunate to be entrapped by it, lose all sense of purpose while she delves into their thoughts, stealing them for her means—with little or no recollection of it, later.'

Tam felt Rosalyn's look of contempt as he desperately tried to evade her gaze; it was clear she knew exactly what Kai had insinuated.

Gill smirked, shaking his head in disbelief.

'Do not judge his weakness!' Reece snapped, stepping in to defend his colleague. 'And do not condemn him for things you do not fully understand. Tam has not yet come into his own. He is not responsible for the way he is, and battles against the temptations linked to it. But he is learning fast. See how he sits with ease in your company now, when you consider his threat, on your first meeting.'

Tam looked up when Rosalyn stopped what she was doing, and smiled bravely at her, expecting nothing in return.

She forced a wry smile back at him, trying to understand.

'Tis a start, he thought.

'It seems plausible!' Onóir stated. 'I, for one, believe it.'

'As do I,' Reece added, waiting for a positive response from the others.

Rosalyn and Gill shared their thoughts with a single glance, before slowly nodding in agreement—as unbelievable as it seemed.

Reece then considered the silent individual hovering by the door. Asai appeared mislaid from their conversation. His deep eyes preyed on the dagger, which, to Rosalyn's annoyance, had found its way back into Gill's hand; the young man was reluctant to part with it, needing to feel close to his sibling.

Reece slowly approached Asai. The Samurai seemed unaware of his friend's presence until he spoke. 'What ails you, my friend?'

'I cannot be sure,' he replied, his frustration visible by the frown on his forehead. 'Say nothing—for now,' he added, in a whisper.

Tam regarded his colleague's private words with curiosity when Reece turned to address them.

'Then, we must assume,' he began, 'that Kara *did* steal his thoughts— to protect her Mistress.'

'Like a spy?' Gill surmised.

'Indeed. If there was a sinister threat made against the Sorceress, Kara would—in her own words— "dispatch" the traitor.'

'Such a callous word,' Onóir remarked.

'The Valkyrie has no regard for life or death,' said Tam. 'She believes she has the power to send her victims to *Valhalla*.'

'Where?' Rosalyn enquired.

'*Valhalla*,' Kai broke in. 'It is her *heaven*,' he explained, 'where—she believes—her victims wait for her when she dies in her final—and most glorious—battle.'

'Whereas *you*,' Gill insinuated, pointing his sister's dagger at Tam, 'were spared. Now why is that, I wonder?'

Tam slid his eyes towards his accuser. He was growing tired of Gill's tedious remarks. The young man sat up, turning the dagger over in his hand, and stared back, almost challenging the Highlander.

Sensing the tension, Reece moved to his colleague's side—this time with Gill's safety in mind.

418

Rosalyn sighed heavily, strained by the events of the evening. Her tired body screamed out for rest, but as long as her daughter was missing, sleep was out of the question. Inside, her patience was beginning to wear as she glared at the others. She wanted to yell—voice her frustrations—but refused to let it hamper what strength remained within. The pressure was mounting.

'There'll be no more ill-feeling in this house,' Onóir snapped at them. 'We have to find a way to get Eleanor back.' She turned to Tam, distracting him from Gill. 'You *must* try—try hard to recall what you told the Valkyrie.'

'I *am* trying, but all I see are conflicting words in my mind; they make no sense. My memory'—he scratched his head, trying to recall; it was clear he was struggling, though determined— 'tis vague and confusing but ...' He paused.

'What is it, Tam?' urged Kai, seeing a glint of recognition in the Highlander's eyes.

'Whatever I told the Valkyrie, I can only assume it was based on what *I* was told—' He stopped—the lines of concentration between his brow drawing tightly, willing the memory back. Suddenly his eyes shot up, then slowly moved across the room. 'Told ... by *you*!'

Everyone followed Tam's gaze.

'What?!' cried Gill, shifting uncomfortably in his seat.

Onóir shook her head and sighed. 'How could you?'

'But—I *lied* to him!'

In his admission, Reece turned to Tam, ready to justify his actions, but was met by a look of ignorance, tainted by betrayal.

'I don't understand,' Tam responded. 'Why would you do that? I thought you—'

'It was not my decision,' Reece cut in, plagued by the eyes of criticism staring up at him.

'Then *whose* was it?' begged the Highlander.

'Oran's.'

Rosalyn raised her brows at the mention of her husband's name.

'When Oran shared his intentions with me … he … forgive me, Tam, but he had his concerns, and strongly advised against sharing the *true* purpose of his plans with you—in case the Sorceress found out. It was his way of protecting us.'

'Am I to be trusted by no one?' Tam retorted, induced by almost everyone's bad opinion of him.

'I was reluctant,' said Reece. 'I assured him of your honesty. But, despite my objections, Oran was adamant, insisting on taking precautions—if he was to help us escape. I *had* to respect his wishes.'

'But if the Valkyrie *assumed* to know your plans,' said Gill, stepping in, 'why did she not "dispatch" Tam, then? Also, had she shared them with the Sorceress, why did they not intervene—prevent you from escaping?'

'Aye, he's right,' said Onóir.

Reece looked into the face of his innocent colleague, seeing nothing but truth and honesty, then sighed, having pieced it all together. 'And there lies the error … *my* error,' he stated.

'What exactly *did* you tell me?' Tam demanded.

'Does it matter now?' asked Reece.

'Aye! It does to me!' he argued back. 'I *need* to remember!'

Reece approached him, shaking his head. 'No, you do not. All you *need* to know is that you are blameless. It was *not* your fault, Tam. Do you understand?'

Tam looked away, in thought—the look of determination on his face telling them how much he was still trying to remember. He then looked sharp and stared at Reece. 'Auch! That's it!' he exclaimed. 'You gave me the *wrong* directions—on purpose!'

'It was a necessary precaution'—Reece reached out, trying to plead his case to the Highlander— 'you know what the Valkyrie is capable of, Tam.'

'Aye, I do,' he said. 'But it still begs the unanswered question: how in the world *did* they find us, if they had the wrong information, then?'

'L'Ordana must have suspected—sensed something,' Kai remarked, 'which is why …'

The Servitor's voice trailed as he toiled over his suspicions. His eyes met with Reece, for a brief moment.

'Kai?'

Distracted by Onóir's voice, the Servitor looked away from the Dhampir. 'There is only one source that may have influenced L'Ordana,' he stated.

'Surely, not the amulet!' said Gill. 'It can't possibly influence the Sorceress … Can it?'

'We do not know the extent of her power'—Kai stopped himself, then glanced at Reece, again, convinced by his deductions— 'Oran, it seems, *underestimated* her.'

All eyes turned on Reece, having observed the subtle exchange between him and the Servitor. The Dhampir lowered his gaze.

He now knew. They *both* knew.

Feeling contempt by their negligence—having failed to see it, *then*—Reece closed his eyes, reluctant to admit the error, as the silence surrounding him became unbearable. Despite his family's anxious wait, he remained quiet.

'She'—Kai hesitated, as they now turned their attention to him—'*let* them escape.'

The sudden revelation threw the small house into chaos. Jumping to his feet, Gill moved to challenge Reece, who was now glaring at the Servitor, enraged for speaking on his behalf.

'That Witch *let* you escape?!' Gill exclaimed. 'The stupidity of it. How could you be so—'

'Gill!' Onóir cried. 'There is nothing we can do to change it, now.'

'And what of Eleanor?' Rosalyn argued. 'Have you forgotten *her*?'

Their voices soared in continuous quarrel, spurring Rave to join in on the raucous. Tam slowly rose to intervene, only to be stopped by Rosalyn's verbal abuse. Outraged, she slammed her fist on the table, disturbing its contents—and alerting Rave to the possibility of another meal.

Soon, the noise of their scathing arguments became deafening. Caught up in the height of it, Reece began to feel the weight of his human emotions influence his reasoning. They were growing stronger, weakening his ability to retain his logic and control, driving him into a fury.

His eyes blazed.

Ignoring the raised voices around him, Reece continued to glare at Kai through the feud, and yet the Servitor remained composed as he looked on, antagonising him further—to the point where the Dhampir could no longer tolerate his presence. Nostrils flared, fists clenched, Reece prepared to leap at his wife's companion when something caught his eye, hindering his attack.

He looked sharp—towards the door.

Asai had left.

The heavy, blackened, oak door stared back at her, denying her the right to pass beyond the threshold where the Valkyrie had slammed it shut in her face. Her first instinct was to *get out!*

I must try, she thought, reaching for the round, iron handle, then changed her mind, wrenching her hand back as though it would bite. *It's useless!* she realised. There was no denying the grinding of the key that had been turned in its lock by the creature's coarse hand.

Eleanor cradled her aching body from the pain endured by Kara's firm hold, then felt the over-familiar sign of burning, rising from the pit of her stomach. She felt the faint tingling in her hands and feet, knowing they would numb if she did not act fast. Her vision began to blur, and she blinked continuously, fighting it off. Shortness of breath gripped her unexpectedly.

"Flight or fight!" was what Oran had always told her—should she find herself in "trying situations."

Flight or fight! she repeated in her mind, distracting herself from the onslaught of thoughts and dread, and self-doubt. Closing her eyes, she recalled the memory that would help chase it away.

Her mind took her back in time when she, as a child, would walk with Oran through the woodlands, surrounding their home. She imagined him taking her tiny hand into the protection of his, as he would show her the wild, pink rosebay and willowherb for the first time. She inhaled deeply, its subtle scent still residing in her memory, reviving her.

Released from her state, she felt a moment of peace, but it was quickly shattered; she jolted, thinking she had heard the Valkyrie's voice again. But it was there, only inside her head, reminding her of Kara's lurid insinuation, regarding Asai; despite it, she now believed she would never experience it. She felt a sudden closeness towards him, and yet she had no idea of her location, making her wonder how long she had been unconscious; it had seemed like an age.

Looking around she shivered, even though it was not cold. The surrounding walls—six in total—had retained the heat of the day, their warmth suggesting it was that of a solar room or chamber, and yet it felt detached from the rest of the building. She sensed a sadness seeping from its stones, reaching out, calling for her attention—its sorrow intrusive on her thoughts.

The softly lit chamber was angular in shape, giving her a sense of height. It was a small, private room of relative comfort, untouched for years.

She noted a small fireplace, where the embers had long burned out with time. Above the mantlepiece, panels of wood bore the arms of a family who once resided there. She did not recognise them. Beside the hearth, a fading tapestry hung lazily on the wall, as though it would slide from its perch at any given moment. She saw a decorative sideboard of dark wood—blackened by smoke—sitting opposite. Nearby, a small, plain oak table—scratched from years of use—stood beside two small decorative matching chairs. Above her, the ceiling rose high, crisscrossed with beams of red, painted wood. Patches of gold leaf glinted in the lamplight, as a reminder of its past glory. The suggestion that the chamber's former resident had, perhaps, been a woman, was evident in its décor.

But still, she could not shake off the residual sadness attached to it.

At the far end of the chamber, a single bed rested alone in its solitude. Eleanor stepped closer to inspect it, then noted a small shape at its side, lying quiet and undisturbed in its shadow. She felt a desolate chill brush over her as she approached the object, keeping her eyes fixed as it came into view.

A child's cot looked up at her from its hiding place, its ruffled blanket draped over the side, barely skimming the dusty floorboards. It was clear, by its faded colour, it, too, had remained untouched for years.

Eleanor stopped abruptly, reluctant to go any further when something suddenly registered—something Gill had told her: one of his stories.

Stepping away, she glanced back at the lancet window—cut high in one of the walls—and quickly ran to it. Looking up at the tall, narrow arch, she then stood on her toes, to peer out into the night. She strained to see, her vision hampered by the glare of the black, iron lantern hanging above. She blew out the flame, then anxiously waited for her eyes to adjust …

There, below in the distance, Eleanor imagined she saw a sight lost to her, forever. Feeling the threatening shortness of breath return, she pressed her hand on the cold window.

I have to know! she told herself, frantically wiping the dust away. To her horror, Eleanor now knew exactly where she was—the familiar outline of the landscape sweeping down to the loch, confirming her worst nightmare. She pressed her lips together, stopping them from quivering.

'No!' she whimpered. 'I can't be *here!*'

Shocked, she backed away from the window, shaking her head, then stopped, thinking she had heard footsteps. She held her breath, listening intently, then jolted, when her thoughts became a reality as the footsteps grew louder and heavier.

She's coming back!

Eleanor looked over her shoulder at the door, her breath now short. She wanted to scream—to let the world know where she was before *she* returned. But the tightness in her chest would not allow it.

"Fight it!" the voice, deep inside her mind, calmly told her. *"Fight it, Eleanor!"*

But it was not the voice of instinct helping her now; it was that of another—one she knew.

Eleanor threw herself at the window—

'Asai!'

To Be Continued ...

Now read on, for a sneak preview of the next instalment of
The Sixth Amulet series.

The
Moon
Chasers

M. A. MADDOCK

Coming Soon ...

Chapter One

The Realm of Meddian (middle Europe) – late Spring: 1630

'They have gone, my lady!'

L'Ordana spun on hearing the urgency in the voice, and yet the words had not registered.

'What?' she said, her brows knitting in a moment of confusion.

The small, agitated figure stood dwarfed in the great, oak doorway frame, staring at her Mistress, reluctant to enter.

'They—they have gone!' she repeated, her voice now low, and edged with fear.

L'Ordana moved towards Wareeshta—the look of confusion still etched on her face as she approached the Dhampir.

'They? Who?'

Wareeshta swallowed, took a deep breath then released it, along with their names; 'Reece, Asai—'

'What?!' she yelled. The mere mention of Reece's name was all it took for the Sorceress to grasp her servant's meaning. As the expression on her face gradually changed to one of realisation, her eyes widening, woken to it, she lifted her head. Wareeshta braced herself. She knew what to expect …

L'Ordana battled against her composure as Wareeshta's words now bellowed inside her mind. *"They have gone!"* The tension inside her mounted—ready to give way. Intoxicated by burning rage, she finally erupted, unleashing it on the nervous Dhampir.

'Gone?!' she echoed, her eyes now wild with anger.

Wareeshta jumped at the ferocity of her Mistress's voice, believing the whole citadel had also been subjected to it. Perhaps she could have worded it differently, broken the news to her in a gentler manner. Then again … What difference would it make? They had escaped …

'Impossible!' L'Ordana persisted.

'But—but, my lady, we have searched the grounds, and—'

'How could they possibly escape—when they are bonded to me?!' she roared.

Wareeshta flinched then, trying to hold her stance, replied; 'I assure you, my lady … they *are* gone.'

L'Ordana glowered at the Dhampir for her insolent tone, and yet seeing her look of determination—eyes set, lips pressed hard—it made her wonder … She lifted her head, eyes momentarily drifting from her servant, thinking …

'*If* what you say is true,' L'Ordana pressed further, now scowling at Wareeshta from across the chamber, 'then how did they go undetected?' When silence stared back at her, she snapped. 'Answer me!'

The Dhampir jolted from the outburst, shaking her head, unable to respond.

L'Ordana glared at Wareeshta—the turquoise in her eyes intensifying as they bored into her servant.

Tempted to run from her Mistress's fury, Wareeshta knew it was far better to face her wrath, rather than flee from it; to avoid any form of conflict was considered a sign of weakness.

The young Dhampir swallowed, desperately calling on her inner voice to justify the prisoners' disappearance. She also wondered *how* they broke free from their bonds; it had not been part of the plan. A thought struck her, but she was unwilling to speak it.

As Wareeshta contemplated her next move, her mind racing, searching for something to say—*perhaps I should tell her*—she flinched when the Sorceress turned her head sharply.

L'Ordana's eyes darted about the chamber, surveying its entire contents.

Something is not right, she thought.

Deciding to speak up, Wareeshta dared to step forward. 'My lady, there is—'

'Do - Not - Move!' the Sorceress growled, turning her attention back to the painting of the *Boy with the Flowers*. She was sure she had detected something in his stare before Wareeshta's untimely interruption. She approached it curiously, tilting her head until she came within inches of its canvas and stared up at him, hoping he would tell her something. But the boy, with the enigmatic eyes, persisted in his blank stare, reluctant to share what he *may* have seen. She stretched her neck and leaned closer, whispering, 'Traitor!'

Turning her back on the painting, she scrutinised her quarters, until her eyes fell on the heavy, burgundy drapes, drawn together. She rushed towards them, then stopped. She drew back.

'Someone has touched you!' she hissed, noting the slight ruffle in the material; she would always make sure they would hang perfectly straight—especially after each visit.

Wareeshta, wary of her Mistress's growing anger, kept her silence *and* her distance, just inside the doorway. Uneased, she looked over her shoulder, wondering where Kara was; she would not take the sole blame for the escape. No, the Valkyrie also had a part to play in their negligence; she, too, had been idle in keeping a watchful eye.

'What if it's gone?' L'Ordana muttered to herself, as her eyes ran over the drapes. She hesitated. 'No—impossible! They could not have'—she threw out her hand— 'part!' she commanded. The drapes drew back. 'Unlock!' she then ordered the ebony, panelled doors concealed behind them.

The doors swung open.

She stalled, holding her breath, fearing someone had entered her secret domain. Unsure, she barged into the sanctity of her hidden chamber.

L'Ordana froze on seeing the orb; although it remained on its red, lacquered perch, the light, however, that once glowed from its centre had now dimmed greatly, as if drained of its energy.

Eyes fixed, she slowly edged towards it, expecting to see Oran—the Warlock either bored in his luxurious prison or smiling to himself, as he often did, which irritated her. And yet, the closer she got, her heart pounded with unexpected dread.

She stopped, her eyes widening as she stared into the orb's void. She shook her head, her mouth opening and closing in silent fear. Then it came …

'No!'

Oran was gone.

So, Wareeshta was right about the others—and it was clear who had helped them escape. 'Damn you, Oran!' she seethed. Without thought—too caught up in her fury—she threw her hands forward. Before her eyes registered what her hands had done, the sound of glass shattering told the Sorceress all she needed to know.

L'Ordana stared down in disbelief, her mouth gaping at the remnants of the orb. The lengths she had gone to acquire it: the long and treacherous journey to the caves of Alucard, high in the red mountains, where the eccentric little old man had created it to her requirements. It had become her eyes, to spy on the Warlock. And now, the perfect sphere was reduced to nothing more than useless fragments of glass— gone beyond repair.

Outraged by her own carelessness, she turned to leave, pausing, when her eyes were immediately drawn to the strong, shard of light reaching out to her, between the two black wooden panels. 'It is still here!' she realised, sighing with some relief. She rushed towards them, then hesitated before opening the panels, her curiosity beckoning. 'But why did you not take it …?'

Pulling back the little doors, she drew a sharp breath as the intense light stretched out, dominating the chamber. It was evident, while the orb's light had shone, it had shrouded the item's true strength … until now.

The amulet, she had stolen from Magia Nera, had now lifted itself from the hook where she had left it. Now suspended in front of her startled eyes, its inner light radiated brighter than before; there was new energy surging inside the weight of its spectacular centred stone—the diamond, now a deep shade of yellow, resembling the lowering of a setting sun.

She reached out to touch it and recoiled from its penetrating heat.

'Is *that* the reason why Oran?' she muttered. She regarded the amulet with intrigue. Something had changed, driving her interest. She then gasped, suddenly aware of its force drawing her in. 'Can it be possible?' She considered its purpose, surmising it was now an object of greater importance; she could *feel* it. She leaned towards it. 'Can *you* show me the way?'

Spurred by the possibility, it could now lead her to the Shenn, she knew she would have to find a way to remove the amulet; she needed to have it with her when they left—sooner rather than later.

Encouraged by the prospect, she smirked to herself. 'You haven't won *yet*, Oran,' she said, turning on her heel. She then stopped, feeling the smugness being wrenched from her; while her thoughts had been dominated by the amulet and the Warlock, she had briefly forgotten …

Wareeshta remained rigid, inwardly cursing the Valkyrie as she waited with apprehension for her Mistress' return. The seconds passed in wary silence until she heard the muffled sound of L'Ordana's voice. *Whom is she talking to?* she wondered, wanting to look inside the hidden chamber, then thought better of it, on hearing the return of her hasty footsteps. Tempted to retreat, the Dhampir cautiously inched back towards the door, bracing herself when the Sorceress stormed back into her presence.

L'Ordana swiftly returned to the bedchamber and, ignoring the nervous individual lingering in the doorway, rushed to her most cherished item. Eyes narrowed, she looked over the large, circular bronze mirror with suspicion, carefully studying the precious antique; something was out of place. Raising her finger, she let it follow the faint outline of the long, hidden panel—on the mirror's reverse—until it found the tiny indent: the *secret* only *she* was privy to … or so she had thought. She let the tip of her finger hover over it. Holding her breath, she hesitated, her suspicions mounting, heightening her concern.

432

'What if—?!' she whispered.

She pressed the groove.

The long panel—no more than a foot in length, and the width of a slender hand—snatched itself away from her. Her mouth fell as she drew back, staring at the space where the weapon had rested in secret.

Her precious dagger was gone.

She then noticed the single, strand of black hair, caught in a crack below the groove. 'Oh, how careless!' she muttered, leaning closer to inspect it. She paused, noting something else that had not been there before. L'Ordana knew this was no error on their part; in the bottom, left-hand corner of the panel, she recognised the symbols where the perpetrator had purposely named himself:

浅井長政

'Asai!'

Inside, L'Ordana reeled from the theft of the dagger. In a moment of weakness, she lifted her hand to her face, letting her fingers touch her skin, guiding them over the contours of her features; it felt different. As fear seeped in, she promptly consulted the mirror, recoiling from her reflection, sensing the subtle change, it threatening to expose her vulnerability.

Her eyes flashed about the chamber, returning to the painting. The *Boy's* eyes continued to stare at her, but now in a different way, as though they were mocking her.

'Stop it!' she growled, confronting the canvas. 'Do not look at me like that!'

'My la—' Wareeshta stopped abruptly when L'Ordana spun round; she recoiled, seeing her maddening stare. Had her Mistress gone mad?

The Sorceress hesitated. Her eyes then slid to the little piece of furniture nestled beneath the window. She tilted her head, scrutinising it. Had that, also, been tampered with?

As panic took hold again, she shook her head, mumbling to herself; 'No. No, you wouldn't—you couldn't have—not *that*, too!'

Uncontrollable dread mounted inside her as she threw herself at the ebonised, wooden table. At first, it had appeared untouched, but as the dread persisted, spreading its shadow of doubt, she slowly lowered her eyes, seeing it—the small drag of dust on the floor; the inlaid, spindle legs, supporting the Moorish table, had *moved!* The same *thief* had neglected to check the small, ornate, piece of furniture before his hasty departure—the error heightening her fear.

She drew back, her chest heaving, afraid to look … And yet, she *had* to know.

'Open!'

Chapter Two

othing, but the space where she had left it, stared up at her now; the little table had been relieved of the sinister burden it had kept hidden, inside its sealed drawer.

'Damn you, Asai!' she whispered, trying to contain her anger. But her inner demon was battling against her composure. 'Damn *you*!' Her voice grew louder, unleashing her fury again. 'You will pay for this!' she yelled, wrenching the drawer from the table, before casting it away in disgust.

'What—what are you looking for?' Wareeshta nervously asked, having observed the frenzied attack on the invaluable piece of furniture.

Wrapped inside her frantic world of rage and uncertainty, L'Ordana failed to hear her servant. She had kept the other item hidden there since "unburdening" Magia Nera of its possession—before their untimely parting, in Triora—almost sixty years previously; it had felt, to L'Ordana, much longer. Yet, despite its constant presence, she had barely scratched the surface of its sinister knowledge—knowledge the dark Warlock had refused to share with her.

Only *she* had had the power to open the drawer, the panel on the back of the mirror and the drapes. *How could Asai have—* She stopped on her train of thought when it occurred to her: *Of course!* It was evident the Warlock had outsmarted her, by teaching the Samurai a *trick or two*, in exchange for getting him to do his dirty work. *And why not?* she surmised. Had he not taught *her* everything he knew? 'Not quite, Oran,' she uttered, through gritted teeth. *How could I have been so imprudent?* She reeled over her misjudgement, believing he had been unable to sever the bond that held her warriors. *More fool I*, she thought. Too self-indulged in her arrogance to notice his misconduct, she thought she had had the upper hand, assuming her plan to outsmart him had worked.

Having acquired the relevant information from the Valkyrie, with the help of the unsuspecting Tam—Kara's liaisons with him proving quite informative—she considered the situation … After countless bribes, to draw the secret of the Shenn amulet from him, she soon realised Oran would remain loyal to his Magus, by keeping his silence. Therefore, she made a point of taunting him, boasting that she still possessed Magia Nera's amulet—in the hope he would weaken—while making a point of revealing her "meetings" with the dark Warlock; she wanted Oran to believe Magia would side with her. She recalled the glint in his eye when she told him of their rendezvous.

Convinced she had won Oran's jealousy, she had then decided to take a risk: she would allow him, under pretence, to escape, by discreetly removing the invisible barrier from his *prison*. She was certain he would be tempted by its absence, regardless of any suspicions. He would then escape—alone—leaving behind his three conspirators; they would be unable to venture beyond the barrier of their bonds, causing her no concern. Then, she would secretly follow the Warlock, presuming he would lead her to the Shenn—*and* the Magus. However, after observing him for a while, through the orb, she grew frustrated and bored when he failed to "take the bait!" Certain he had not noticed the barriers' absence, she eventually restored it, discreetly, during one of her *visits*.

Yes, he *had* outsmarted her. *He knew all along*, she realised. He had been biding his time until it was safe to break the Dhampir's bonds, releasing them. He had played her, knowing too well she would tire of him and divert her attention to Magia, in a bid to prize the information she needed from *him*.

'What have I done?!' It had all been unexpected and swift—*not* what she had planned. And, to make matters worse, they had taken with them her precious items: the book and the dagger. The question now was who had them? The Warlock or his allies?

The dagger—once dominated by the *Order of the Dragon*—was recognisable by the unique symbols engraved below its black, onyx handle: an unorthodox, heretical cross; and along the centre of the blade, a winged dragon, displaying its malevolent strength, its tail touching the tip of the cross, uniting them in power. The long, steel dagger partnered with the book. Jointly, they were potent, giving her what she required: eternal youth and power. Together—and guided by the Shenn—she could reign supreme, possessing the ultimate dominance and revenge—everything she craved. But, with both items now missing, a sense of dread ripped through her; without the book, she would lose her power, and without the dagger—the weapon she had used on her victims—her beauty and youth would fade. Time was now her true enemy.

Her thoughts momentarily drifted back. She had forgotten all the other young women, except for one: her first; Oran never forgave her for the slaughter of their servant. The dagger had taken the girls' beauty and youth, as with the other victims. And, by giving it to her, she, herself, would never age. The thought of the weapons' absence horrified her, along with its missing accessory: the book.

The *book*, Magia had claimed from another—centuries before—had been the *Master* of all his teachings in the *Black Arts*, bestowing its unique powers on those who let it.

She had been ignorant of its knowledge when she first looked upon it, discovering later what it was truly capable of. Bound by the devil himself—according to myth—the hard, outer cover was made of thick, leather and dyed in oxblood. Shaped to fit its length perfectly, its spine was lined in black onyx, while its paged edges were, not of gold but, deep scarlet—said to be the blood of Vlad Tepés.

Seared into the hard-worn leather, the two symbols, matching those on the dagger, were vivid in detail, despite their age. The workmanship had been so precise, it was thought—if the eye beheld it for long enough—the dragon moved. She had tried staring at it once, but when Magia Nera mocked her, she quickly dismissed it as a *myth*, conjured up by those who had once briefly owned it, to send fear into the souls of anyone willing to challenge the evil of its pages. However, the malevolence attached to its antiquity was far from folklore. Having witnessed this, she had eventually persuaded the dark Warlock to share with her its "secrets"—some, at least. She recalled how he eventually bowed to her "persuasion", as long as she did not abuse its power. Naturally, she gave him her word. But, as time wore on, it soon corrupted her, its powers enticing her to steal it. How *could* she resist?

But what *she* had purloined had now been stolen from her. She might have laughed at the irony of it, had it not been for its necessity; without it—without both—she would fall victim to the plague of time. All her defences would gradually weaken, leaving her vulnerable to every source who would willingly prey on her. The Valkyrie came to mind; nothing would satisfy Kara more than to overthrow her Mistress. *Not if I can help it*, she thought, discarding all foreboding thoughts. *I must have them back!*

L'Ordana stalled, now sensing the other presence lingering at the chambers' entrance. She could feel their eyes burning into her, as the smell of their heady scent attacked her nostrils.

'I see Kara has not left you to deal with the consequences, this time, Wareeshta,' she stated, turning.

In the doorway, towering over the Dhampir, stood the Valkyrie, eyeing her Mistress, her manner smug and daring.

Inside, L'Ordana was seething. 'Where have you—'

'Searching for their trail,' Kara casually interrupted, adding fuel to L'Ordana's frustration.

'And did you find it?'

The Valkyrie sauntered over the threshold, followed by a nervous Wareeshta—who was prepared for the onslaught of abuse the Sorceress usually hurled at them when antagonised; to her surprise, it did not come.

Kara rolled her eyes. 'Of course,' she sneered, irked by the question. '*They* will be easy to track. However, I was unable to pursue the Warlock, after their footprints parted.'

L'Ordana cast a suspicious eye on her servants when Wareeshta's eyes darted towards Kara, throwing her a cautious glance. L'Ordana glared into the dubious face of the Dhampir.

'You *knew* the Warlock had escaped?!' she cried.

438

Wareeshta side-glanced Kara, who was smirking at her. L'Ordana then looked to the Valkyrie, who shrugged in return as if passing the blame to Wareeshta.

'Well?!'

'I tried to tell you, Sorceress,' the Dhampir pleaded, 'but ...' Her words drifted.

'The small detail you neglected to mention,' L'Ordana stated, casting her a scathing look before dragging her eyes back to Kara. Something then came to mind—something the Valkyrie had said. She recalled her words:

'Their footprints ... *parted?*' she said, turning to the Valkyrie with intent. 'What did you mean by it?'

'They had grouped,' said Kara. 'Before ...' She paused.

'Before what?'

'Before going their separate ways.'

L'Ordana drew her head back, frowning. 'Are you certain?'

'Almost.'

The Sorceress tilted her head forward. '*Think* before you speak again,' she warned. 'And, this time, I suggest you be more ... *specific.*'

Wareeshta looked at Kara, concerned; but the Valkyrie appeared unperturbed as she casually replied; 'We discovered *four* sets of footprints,' she continued, '... at first.'

'At first?' said L'Ordana, concealing her mounting fear. 'Do you mean ... *more* have escaped—to join them?'

Kara shook her head.

'Reece, Tam and the *Strange One* parted ways with the Warlock; *they* went north—not that they will make it far, by the time we—'

'North?' L'Ordana cut in, lifting a brow with interest. She paused, momentarily musing over it. Her eyes then slid towards Wareeshta, regarding her with another intimidating look.

The Dhampir, withering under L'Ordana's penetrating stare, slowly nodded, confirming Kara's words.

'What takes them north?'

'Tam did not say when I—'

439

'Then we must assume he did not know,' she surmised, aware that the Valkyrie's sordid, and regular, rendezvous with the Highlander was no secret, therefore, adding to her suspicions. 'I suspect Oran kept some vital information from Tam'—she glared at Kara— 'for *obvious* reasons. As for the others who escaped? Why separate, leaving my old adversary to his defences? How curious?' She then nodded. 'This may be to our advantage.'

'It is unlikely,' Wareeshta bravely joined in.

The Sorceress turned her attention to the Dhampir yet remained silent. Maintaining her stare, she waited for Wareeshta to proceed.

The Dhampir cleared her throat, then swallowed. 'Three sets of footsteps parted from the Warlock,' she went on. 'The fourth, however, was …'

'Well?'

'… *replaced*,' answered Kara, '…. by an animal.'

Turning away, L'Ordana resisted the urge to laugh. *Oh, how clever of you, Oran,* she thought, aware the Warlock had now reclaimed his powers. *So…you left this citadel as you entered it, allowing you to travel, undetected. But, of course! To travel on foot would only waste time,* she deduced, taking a turn about her chamber, paying no heed to the mirror or the little table; they were of no use to her, now. *A clever move, yet again, Oran. I almost admire you for it.* She paused by the window and looked out, staring at the wall of trees; lofty and vigilant, they stood like soldiers, masking what lay beyond their guard: the sheer drop to the rocks beneath the citadel— and *death* to the uninformed intruder.

'It appears we have *all* taken our eye off the mark,' she stated, turning to face her servants. 'Oran has … *fooled* us.'

Kara narrowed her pale eyes at her Mistress's hidden refusal to admit her own negligence—for letting the Warlock slip through her fingers. Still, she should have seen the signs herself: Reece's ability to distract her, by tempting her with Turloch—the new addition; he was, after all, a willing contender—too good to ignore. And Reece knew it. Then there was the *Strange One*—Asai; he had been more obliging in letting her occasionally train *his* warriors, knowing this little weakness of hers would distract her, while he discreetly slipped away. Yes, she could see it now. But *now* was too late. In a sense, she *was* partially to blame, for *letting* them indulge her ego, though she would never admit to the untimely *distraction*.

Kara glanced at Wareeshta with suspicion. *And where were you, all this time?* she wondered; she was sure the Dhampir was up to something. In the meantime—and as far as she was concerned—the blame would fall on their Mistress; after all, it had been *her* plan. *Some plan*, she thought; the Sorceress had completely underestimated the Warlock. It was clear he knew her better than she knew herself.

Turning to the Valkyrie, L'Ordana clasped her hands in front of her, in forced composure; Kara noticed the whites of her knuckles almost protruding as the skin stretched over the bone—a sure sign of her hidden aggravation. Nevertheless, the Sorceress would not give her servants the satisfaction of revealing her inner esteem for the Warlock— or her misjudgement of him.

'Two objects have been stolen from me ...' she blurted. 'A book and a dagger. I want them back. I can only assume Oran has them ...' She paused for thought. 'But there is only one way to find out ... and it is clear his journey is *urgent*—'

'But we cannot track the Warlock,' insisted Kara.

'We may not know what direction he has gone, as of yet,' said L'Ordana. 'But—'

'Yet?' Wareeshta interrupted, with new interest.

'I assure you ... we *will* find out,' she said. 'And I know *who* will tell us, 'she added, with certainty.

'His conspirators?' said Wareeshta.

L'Ordana's eyes met Kara's. The Valkyrie's mouth curled into a knowing grin.

'The Warlock may have released them from their bonds, but I have no doubt *you* will find them,' she said, confident of the Valkyrie's ability to track the absconders, while at the same time distracting her from her blunder. 'Use the wings you were given, Kara. Find them!'

Kara's eyes widened; the idea of having her way with Reece and his two companions stimulated her senses and stirred her blood.

'But do *not* intervene,' she then warned, stealing the Valkyrie from her merciless thoughts.

Kara's face dropped. 'But they must be stopped, and—'

'Do *not* destroy them,' L'Ordana persisted. 'Do you hear?'

Kara frowned. 'You mean—you would—'

'Why not?' she said, her tone mischievous. '*Let* them go! I want to know what brings them north. Find their trail, then return here,' she insisted. '*Then*, we will follow, see where their journey takes them, confront them—and find out where Oran has gone. *Then*, I will allow you to ... "dispatch" them.'

At first, Kara reeled from being denied her glory, then realised it had only been delayed. She sighed, nodding her agreement.

'I wonder why Reece and his colleagues have gone north ...' L'Ordana mused.

'Perhaps he—the Warlock—sent them?' Wareeshta suggested.

L'Ordana and Kara slowly turned to Wareeshta—who had been listening carefully. The Dhampir shrugged. 'Who knows?'

'Now there's a thought!' said L'Ordana, contemplating it. She looked sharp. 'Time to leave!' she blurted. Kara and Wareeshta glanced at one another. 'Aside from the fact that I cannot bear another day in this forsaken place,' she went on, 'we have outstayed our welcome here.' She looked at Kara. 'Yes, it is time to go.'

The Valkyrie displayed her approval with a sneering grin, and as it sprawled across her face, she said, 'North?'

'Of course,' she replied, with a wry smile. 'North to—'

"Urquille."

L'Ordana flinched, hearing the voice in her head, as the word unexpectedly slipped into her mind. What made her think it: *Urquille?* She lingered on the name, querying the familiarity it suggested when a murky image abruptly entered her head: her body was floating; she sensed its dead weight; the desperate urge to breathe; the struggle to escape from its suffocating effect. But the moment was short-lived, as

442

a sharp intake of breath filled her with life again, releasing her from its drowning influence.

'And the other one …?' Kara prompted, regarding her Mistress.

Ignoring the Valkyrie, the Sorceress hesitated, drawing on the unexpected images in her head, trying to make sense of them. *Urquille*, she thought, now conscious of its lure pulling her north.

Inside, Kara was seething, having been shunned by her Mistress. Mindful of the sword on her back, pressing against her silver bodice of armour, she fantasised about thrusting it through L'Ordana's heart. She then thought of her lance—the Obsidian—but had been forced to leave it outside the chamber.

"Never bring *that* into my presence!" the Sorceress had warned her before. She had witnessed the weapon's capability: driven effortlessly into its victim's torso, its silver tip would ignite in a spectacular display, lighting up the Obsidian's deep-emerald glass in all its glory, before consuming its victim in flames.

But it was nothing more than that: a *fantasy*. Despite L'Ordana's insistence, Kara knew she could no more inflict a scratch on her Mistress let alone kill her; although, perhaps, one day … It had been an alluring thought, nonetheless, but nothing more.

Still reeling from the sting of the insult, Kara boldly stepped forward. 'I said, what about the—'

'I heard you the first time!' L'Ordana snapped, dismissing the disturbing images from her mind. Settling into a poise of self-composure, she eventually turned to face her servants—Wareeshta, staring at her with her eager expression, while Kara remained frustrated by her Mistress's secretive behaviour.

L'Ordana paused, as though in a moment of reflection. Her eyes then glided to the oriental rug beneath their feet. 'I had almost forgotten *him*,' she replied, arching a brow. Lifting her head, she then regarded her servants' curious gaze and held it, keeping them in suspense.

Slowly, the vindictive smirk crawled across her face. 'Magia Nera will accompany us,' she announced. 'I should imagine *he* will be of great use to me, now.'

At the mention of the dark Warlock's name, Kara threw a sinister glance at Wareeshta. *I'm watching you*, she silently threatened, her deadpan look unnerving the Dhampir; Wareeshta promptly looked away.

The Sorceress swiftly turned to make her way back to her secret chamber, her mind on releasing the one object they had neglected to steal from her: Magia Nera's amulet, her only hope of finding the Shenn.

Before taking her leave, L'Ordana paused and glanced over her shoulder, her eyes resting on the mirror she had once held sacred; it appeared different, now that its beauty was *tainted*.

Unable to dismiss—or forgive—its new flaw, she turned to the Valkyrie.

'Destroy *that!*' she commanded, pointing to it, then turned away, leaving it for the last time. 'And when you are done, Kara, come with me.'

As the great, panelled doors closed behind her, they drowned out the sound of shattering glass ….

Photograph courtesy of Billy Aitken

Balloch Castle

Yes, it exists!

I've been frequently asked: "Why Scotland? And why Balloch?" Well, it was on my first trip there (2005)—while visiting good friends—when I fell in love with the place. Always the perfect hosts, whenever I visit, Billy, Ciara and Megan are lucky to live a stone's throw from Balloch Castle, on the stunning shores of Loch Lomond (definitely worth a visit if you happen to be passing through). It is truly a beautiful location. And when the sun shines … Glorious! So, naturally, I was inspired to use it as the backdrop for *The Sixth Amulet*. It simply felt right. And, who knows, maybe I'll retire there …

A wee bit of history

Balloch was once a property of the Lennox family from the 11th century, and it was in the 13th century when the earls of Lennox built the old castle. However, the old castle was demolished by John Buchanan of Ardoch, in the 19th century, and replaced by the present structure.

Balloch was then purchased in 1915 by Glasgow City Corporation. Since 1980, the estate was designated as a country park, and since 2002 has been part of Loch Lomond and The Trossachs National Park.

Balloch is a category A listed building.

You can learn more about this beautiful castle and its equally beautiful surroundings at:

https://www.visitscotland.com/info/see-d/balloch-castle-country-park-p252431

Acknowledgements

So much work goes into writing a novel—not to mention what goes on behind the scenes—as well as the help and support given along the way. I could not have done it alone. Therefore, I must thank the following people:

Cormac Fitzgerald, Claire Hennessy and John Kenny (The Big Smoke Factory). Nadine Ryan.

A massive thank you to Emma Moohan (a cool friend, talented writer and actor, and one of my harshest critics – and I mean that in the best possible way), whose help and advice mean so much.

Emma Ní Bhruachain, for her 'sprinkles' of advice and her help in editing the first two chapters of *The Moon Chasers – Book Two*.

Geraldine O'Malley: Illustrator, who provided me with some of her wonderful work for this novel.

Tegan Somers: who provided me with her illustration of the stag. Something to do with *The Moon Chasers*, perhaps? You'll have to wait and see.

Graeme Johncock (and the adorable Molly!) from Scotland's Stories (scotlands_stories) who so kindly provided the forward for this novel.

Lewis Hickson: I wanted an Olde Worlde map, and that's what he gave me. Here's to the next leg of the journey, Lewis!

Jake Warren Black: the 'wee master of my web' who did trojan work on creating it. Check it out and sign up to my newsletter for updates, including 'extras' - http://www.mamaddockauthor.ie

Grayson Garrett: Actor. For taking on the mammoth task of turning *The Sixth Amulet – Book One* into an audiobook.

Takashi Nara: a friend and Beta reader.

Niamh Foy: a friend and Beta reader - who read it twice (just to be sure), and who keeps asking; "What happens next?!" Patience is a virtue, Niamh.

I have to mention Ruth O'Shea - the best sis in the world, and my best friend! I would be lost without her. Thanks for being there for me (always!). Love ya, sis. X. I also have to give Ken, Naomi and Rachel a mention, too, for coming to my rescue—as well as helping out with those niggly, social media technical issues. X. And, of course, their three "fur babies" - Jake, Belle and Cooper - for being the perfect "tonic" during a time when I needed it.

A huge thanks to Adam O'Shea - my wonderfully talented Godchild - who slaved away on the trailer for *The Sixth Amulet - Book One (Revised Edition)* - in return for his favourite goody hamper. X

Conor Kostick from the IWU for his invaluable advice and help (hope you liked the vino, Conor!).

A special mention to Eileen Budd, Linda Ganzini, Julie Embleton and Sarah O'Neill: just some of the wonderful authors I know whose help, support and guidance have been invaluable. Sláinte!

Other special thanks to Billy, Ciara and Megan - great friends - who've always welcomed me into their home in Balloch, Scotland. Had it not been for my many visits there, I may have never found the inspiration to write this series or discovered my deep love for Scotland (as well as a good Scotch!). It's a Celtic thing! Also, Billy must be accredited for the photo of Balloch Castle.

Louise Fox – for her much-valued input in helping me understand what it's like to suffer from anxiety—a feisty girl who has come out the other side a survivor. Laura (Lucia) Power - for all her help.

Ursula Stapleton – a friend (and another of my harshest critics) who always came to my rescue when my laptop had other disruptive plans.

Chris, Mamie, Kate and Zara: remembering Jack and Raven. X.

And, of course, I must thank the other writers and authors I've made friends with on social media, for their ongoing support. You know who you are. Thanks, guys! Your support means the world to me. I also can't forget my close friends, Mary Byrne, Aileen Candon, Brenda Hassan and Mary Lyons who have also been supportive, especially through those tough times. Thank you, girls! X.

Diana of Triumph book covers, who excelled herself by going the extra mile on the new (ish!) cover for *The Sixth Amulet – Book One (Revised Edition)*; Linda Ganzini – for her additional input for the cover;

448

Becky and James Wright from Platform House Publishing - for bringing *The Sixth Amulet - Book One* - back to life! Thank you so much, guys! You've been a joy to work with—all of you. Here's to Part Two! I also can't forget the authors with whom I shared my misfortune, in 2021. You all know who you are. Together united!

For all my valued ARCs: Julia Blake, Sarah O'Neill, David Pelletier, Gavin Gardiner, Paul Frederick Waite, Stephen Mills, Anne-Marie Fitzgerald, Kevin and Fran. Thank you all so much for taking the time to read and review *The Sixth Amulet – Book One (Revised Edition)*. It's always a big ask - as it can be time-consuming. But know it's greatly appreciated.

As authors, we are all inspired by others. For me, one of my greatest inspirations is Diana Gabaldon. And though she may never read this, I'm thankful to her; her books, alone, are like a Master Class in writing.

Finally, I thank Mother Nature (where most of this series was written … in my head!) - for being able to take long walks through her domain (with my beloved Sherlock, who was my other inspiration), to figure out those nagging plot holes—or simply to allow me to free my mind to think, and let my imagination wander through the fantasy world I have created for you, the reader. Thank you. Enjoy. Sláinte, mó chairde! XX

If I've forgotten anyone, please forgive me, but know that I'm indebted to you, also.

"Sherlock"

Forever in my heart

06/08/'10 – 02/09/'22

About the Author

Asking an Irish person to write a 'few' words about themselves is, putting it mildly, almost impossible! But, here goes … My name is Miriam and I was born and raised in Dublin, Ireland.

Having dabbled in other 'interests' over the years (I won't bore you!), in the background, however, I was always an avid reader, with words constantly floating around in my mind yet doing nothing about them—in a literary sense. I used to always say, 'One day, I'll write that book!' But never seemed to get around to doing it. I think the mere thought of putting those words—along with my imagination—to literary use, was daunting, therefore, I was always putting it off. That is, until 2011 when I finally took the plunge and picked up that pen and notebook (still have them, too!). I began to string those words into sentences, then paragraphs, then pages, eventually joining them together to create my first novel—*The Sixth Amulet - Book One*. Then my imagination had other plans; it didn't want to stop at just one. Why would it? And so, one novel turned into two, then three, then … Who knows where it will end?

I believe everyone has a story to tell, a potential book tucked away inside them, just dying to get out. And all that's needed to create it is a simple recipe: a pen and a notebook. So, open your mind and let your imagination roam through the endless possibilities it has to offer … Then simply write!

An important note to you, the reader: Reviews are important to authors. Unfortunately, not many are aware of *how* important. They don't have to be long; a word, a sentence or a short paragraph is all we need—and it only takes a couple of minutes. Honestly! A simple acknowledgement means so much to us. So, please, make an author's day, and share your thoughts. Thank you so much. X

Feel free to check me out on the following:
http://www.mamaddockauthor.ie
Instagram: ma.maddock_author
Twitter: @mamaddock1_a
Facebook: M.A. Maddock @thesixthamuletseries

Printed in Great Britain
by Amazon